THE BEST OF INTENTIONS

REVIEWS

"Highly engaging, complex and well-plotted ... an intelligent and moving novel."
  KATE RYAN, Writers Victoria

"A moving work of literary fiction. Van Hoeydonck reins in maudlin sentimentality, letting the reader feel his story organically through a crisp narrative and effective pacing. He is expert at conveying mood and feeling through action: choice words create mood and atmosphere, while the action is gripping in its own right, making the story a feast for the senses. A vital and timely novel."
  SELF-PUBLISHING REVIEW

THE BEST OF INTENTIONS

GILBERT VAN HOEYDONCK

The Best of Intentions (edition: 1.1)
Published by Gilbert F. J. Van Hoeydonck, Melbourne, 2019
Contact: http://gilbertvanhoeydonck.com/gvhhome
Printed and distributed by IngramSpark
ISBN 978-0-6482586-0-5

Cover design by ebooklaunch.com

Disclaimer
This is a work of fiction. While this novel is set in Melbourne (Australia), it is in no way
intended to constitute a reflection upon specific aged care, education, child protection or
mental health services. Case scenarios and work practices in in those services are the
product of the author's imagination or used in a fictitious manner. All names are
fictitious and any resemblance to actual persons, living or dead, or actual institutions,
services or events, is purely coincidental. There are two exceptions to this: the story of
'Irene' and 'Leo' is loosely based on the last years of my parents; and the tale of 'Kylee'
and 'Jade' is inspired by a real event. However, I have made up the characters'
background and circumstances, as well as the unsupportive protective worker. My novel
does not purport to describe the care and intervention provided in the actual case.

This book contains adult themes, coarse language and some violence.

For Miriam, Astrid and Estelle.

CONTENTS

DECEMBER 2008

THROUGHPUT

"We need to shift stock," she said.

Kurt sat up with a jolt. "Excuse me?" he said, a slight quaver in his voice, "what did you just say?"

Fran faced him over the rim of her narrow glasses. "I said we need to shift more stock."

Kurt slapped his notebook shut. He had everyone's attention now. The normal meeting room murmuring had stopped. The fluorescent tubes overhead hummed, like lightsabers anticipating a mortal blow.

"These are vulnerable children you are talking about, kids who've been neglected and abused, who've been in and out of foster care placements, and you describe them as *stock*?"

Joe raised his eyebrows. One of the managers checked a page in her diary with great concentration.

Fran looked at him across the long table. Like a scene from *High Noon*, Kurt thought. Is she going to reach for that holster? Not now, Kurt. Stop the fantasy thinking. Too much at stake.

"I don't need a lecture about child protection from you," Fran began, "I've been in this game longer than you, so stop the bleeding heart stuff and let's be professional. At the end of the day we're accountable to the department and ultimately to the minister."

Debbie nodded in agreement with her boss.

"We're judged on outcomes," Fran continued. "That means children removed from dysfunctional families, young persons discharged from foster care. We can't just sit and gab about family dynamics—we need throughput."

Kurt leaned forward, a pudgy panther preparing to pounce. "Sure, we need to evaluate our practice in terms of outcomes, but it is important how we frame our thinking—"

She cut him off. Her face looked flushed now. "Look, this isn't second-year social work at uni. I'm not going to have this discussion. We have a long agenda to get through."

Kurt felt everyone's eyes on him. The telltale signs of anger he had so often explained to irate parents now raced through his body. Hot cheeks, tensed muscles, turmoil in your stomach. He looked down at the table. His eyes boiled. I should take a deep breath, he thought, but his heart was pounding.

"So, Petra, maybe you can walk us through the stats for the last quarter," suggested Fran. The tension in the room ebbed away.

The data projector added its hum as Petra showed her monthly slides. Number of notifications of abuse. Number of cases investigated. Number of home visits. Number of children placed in out-of-home care.

Kurt thought of the young family he had met that morning in Bayswater. The usual stuff. Two junkies too busy worrying about their next hit to give much thought to their baby, a pallid creature with dull eyes, weighed down by his soiled nappy like one of those dolls with a low centre of gravity that you can push without it ever toppling over. You could swan in and remove their child on the basis of neglect. Then what? There was no money to provide more state care and what care there was seemed so basic that its critics reckoned it was just another form of neglect. Planned sensory deprivation, one academic had called it. Or you could work with the parents, build on what strengths they had, teach them living skills and basic risk management strategies. Link them in with a detox service. That approach, of course, required a lot of time with the family. And in Fran's universe, time was not a gift between humans but something that ruined your throughput stats.

A commotion in the room brought Kurt back to the meeting.

"Her waters broke yesterday," he heard Fran say, "and she gave birth around 7:00 p.m. A healthy boy. Mother and child doing well. Husband slightly overwhelmed." Everyone laughed.

"We've sent flowers," said Debbie, "and I'm sending a card round the office. Please keep it moving."

"So, with one protective worker out of action in a maternity ward and two others still on stress leave, the Southern Outreach office have asked us to bring forward Jennifer's secondment," Fran continued. "I have authorised that, and Jen will take up her position as acting manager tomorrow."

"Tomorrow?" Joe raised his eyebrows.

"Yes," said Jennifer, "It's all rather sudden, but I've managed to catch most people about my current case load. It's just Kurt—"

Kurt looked up.

"You were out this morning and I need to brief you about one of my cases. It's a Srecko Bosovic—"

"How do you spell that?"

Jennifer spelled out the name. "The boy's sixteen. Serbian background I think, or Croatian, not sure. Always mix those up." She blushed. "Anyhow, kid grew up in the Latrobe Valley. Morwell. He was sexually abused in his early teens and has been in several foster placements since. He's now officially living with a foster parent in Silvan but he seems to spend most of his time in a squat somewhere in Heathmont."

"Is there a case plan?" asked Kurt.

"I'll give you my notes right after this meeting. It's straightforward, really."

"Well then, I shall tackle it with great efficiency," said Kurt. Nobody smiled, and he regretted the sulkiness of his sarcasm. The corner of Fran's mouth had twitched, almost imperceptibly. They were in opposing camps now, and he had blinked first.

As they milled out of the meeting room, Joe touched Kurt's elbow.

"Like your jacket. Real leather?"

"Yeah," said Kurt, "lamb."

"Looks great. I've always wanted one of those. I thought Buddhists weren't meant to wear leather though?"

"Oh," said Kurt, "Dunno. I suppose. Sometimes I think I'm not much of a Buddhist."

"Chin up, mate," said Joe, "we all have bad days."

THE WORST BUDDHIST

Shifting stock, for Christ's sake, Kurt thought as he drove home. Not our most vulnerable kids, no way! But Fran believed in managing upwards. That meant dazzling her superiors by claiming that she could do more with less. Inputs, outputs, throughput—it was all gobbledygook borrowed from industry. George Orwell would have been proud to come up with a self-congratulatory term like economic rationalism for a system so irrational in its blinkered view and so profoundly malicious when applied to welfare.

I am the world's worst Buddhist, Kurt thought. I should just notice these angry thoughts and let them go. Puff, gone, like a cartoony little cloud. That's what the books say. The mind a placid lake; thoughts no more than passing clouds. The lake briefly reflects those clouds, but is not altered by it. Good stuff, except at times his mind seemed more like a birdbath: small and confined, and a bathing finch was enough to whip up a storm. He had read heaps, oh yes, from the *Dhammapada* to the Dalai Lama. The quote that stuck in his mind was that, while even a three-year-old could understand Buddhism, a seventy-year-old would find it difficult to put into practice. *Touché*.

A butterfly wafted up from the kerb on the left, trying to gain height. The impact with Kurt's car reduced it to a greyish paste on the windscreen. He tried to squirt water, but the reservoir was dry and the wipers smeared the mess all over the glass. That's just great, he thought.

His whole day had been like this—a conference about Murphy's Law organised by gremlins. After his altercation with Fran, he had finalised two reports for the Children's Court. Then, as they were all updating their case notes, the useless database crashed again before he had saved his write-up of the Bayswater visit. He had logged off in frustration and gone home.

Kurt turned right into Waratah Drive. Their little weatherboard home was the third house past the strip of rundown shops that had seen their heyday in the sixties, before the supermarket giants had bled local traders dry. Emma, still pining for her parents, had turned the front garden into a memorial Latvian birch forest.

"Hey, Chuckles."

He couldn't help smiling when he saw Emma come down from the backyard. He took a deep breath.

"Are you okay? You're frowning."

"Just another run-in with Fran. How was your day?"

Emma kissed him on the cheek and stroked his hair. "Not bad. A bit crazy, of course, with the marking. The middle school kids are just hanging out for Christmas. I wanted to show a documentary on volcanoes to my Year 9s but it turned out Nola screened it last week."

"So what did you do?"

"I had to improvise. Divided the class in four groups and made them list all African countries they could think of. Ashleigh's group won, probably because they were sitting closest to the wall with the world map."

Kurt snorted.

"After that I got them to write on the blackboard what they knew about Africa. That started out with the wild animals of course, but then we moved on to poverty, education, AIDS. Colonialism and apartheid, even."

"Sounds like you did well."

"Thanks. Oh, and I almost forgot: there's a letter from your dad. They're in that respite place again for a fortnight."

"Oh, great! Dad really needed a break."

"And when they return home Corinne will increase her hours to three days per week."

"That's fabulous! He sounded so run-down last time we spoke. Dispirited. And no wonder—caring for someone with dementia when you're in your eighties yourself…"

"Yeah, it's a struggle. And he's done well." Emma looked at her watch. "Let's go in," she said, "then you can read his letter yourself. I'll make that pasta dish from last week and then I'd better get ready for Presentation Night."

"Oh, the graduation thing! I'd totally forgotten!"

"I thought it might be nice if you came along, seeing it's the last one at St Genevieve's." She tilted her head sideways—her *pretty please* expression.

"I'll be there," Kurt promised. "We'll mark the end of that era together. I might enjoy seeing happy, well-adjusted kids. You know, sheer novelty value."

Kurt went into the study and read the three sheets of blue airmail paper. His dad's scribbly handwriting conjured up the confined family room in Belgium. The heavily upholstered armchairs with lace doilies on the neck rests. The coal heater that sucked the air out of the room. He pictured the solid rectangular table at which he used to do his maths homework. In the 1970s Mum replaced it with a cheap wobbly round number. It had always been that way for him, in Belgium. Decline, decay, unravelling dreams. Like The-Secret-Place-Under-The-Poplars he would escape to when he was thirteen, instead of attending Mass. He would lie among the tall grasses and watch beetles clambering over barricades of bark. He would look up at the murky sky, an armada of clouds sailing in from the North Sea, trailing silver pieces-of-eight through the treetops. Then one day The-Secret-Place-Under-

The-Poplars was gone. Cranes had usurped the grasshoppers, yellow Caterpillar bulldozers pushed aside the beetles. Rugged men with hard hats and chunky watches had overrun his sanctum. A rectangular sign facing the wrong way announced, to no one in particular, that the extension of the A3 freeway would soon be constructed here. And Kurt had watched the devastation, from his bike, until one of the men waved at him. That's how it always went, back then. Pets would die, friends disappeared, girlfriends broke up with him. In the end he had bailed, to Australia, a cracked, stubborn land that had received him in its dry, bony embrace. And meanwhile, in Belgium, the wreckers had gone to work on his mother's brain.

This wasn't helpful thinking, though. Meditating would be wiser. Kurt glanced at his meditation cushion. It looked abandoned in that corner, out of place next to the pile of social work magazines, like a small wheel that had come off a fluffy car. No meditation today, Kurt decided. There were other ways to work the anger out of his system. He started up his computer and loaded *Trail of Heroes*.

Kurt liked these classic single-player games. It was just you versus the computer. No need to interact, no need to explain—an introvert's dream. His digital henchmen were waiting for him in the candle-lit tavern. He sold off the loot in their backpacks and bought three sheaves of acid arrows to use against trolls. As he clicked to leave The Wilting Widow for more mayhem in the wild, the voiceover announced *You are now entering a new area*. Kurt smiled. The game was formulaic only when it came to the stock phrases the characters or the narrator would utter. In all other respects it was fresh and engaging. *You have been ambushed*, announced the voiceover as Kurt's party entered the Trade District to question a corrupt customs officer. Kurt looked at the screen and smiled: the game always auto-paused when there was a hostile encounter, giving the player ample time to enter instructions for each character's response. If only the real world worked that way. The meeting with Fran would have frozen at the first sign of friction; he would have drunk a Potion of Poison Resistance and cast Damnation on her... Or Disintegrate...

He felt startled and guilty when Emma's voice called him to dinner. He had once told a woman in his Zen group about his predilection for

Dungeons and Dragons games and she had looked at him with sadness in her eyes and said: "What hope have we got?" It was just a game, he had felt like saying, but he understood what she meant. The pull of violence was so strong that even those who had chosen a path of peace were not immune to its attractions, however innocent the context.

LONGBOW OF PRECISION+3

Gecko clicked on the multiplayer icon in the top right corner of the screen: *Time waited 23:20 minutes*. He swore. Weekends were the pits. Everyone queueing for a raid. He clicked back on the main screen, but without enthusiasm—he had lost interest in the single-player game. Talk to some weird dude, get a quest. Mount your steed and gallop towards the Forest of Fear. Kill 10 Woodland Hunters and return to the dude, who gives you a bit of gold, some experience points. He sends you back to the Forest of Fear to kill 15 Accursed Shamans. More cash, more experience. Now he tells you that the real problem, the source of all evil, is the Pestilent She-Wolf who lives in a cave in the centre of the forest. As if he couldn't have told you that earlier—what a dope. So you gallop back, enter the cave and start harvesting wolves, who mysteriously drop potions of healing when you kill them, or maybe a Sapphire Longbow of Greater Precision +3.

Raids were a totally different matter. His favourite battleground was Dagger Dale. You got teleported to the Edge of Valour, where you had to wait on a rocky outcrop until the raiding party was complete. He liked the confusion, the colour, the flowing robes of the other mages. Some players would shout war cries, others swear words. The noobs would check your character's stats, place protective spells on you or talk strategy. Idiots. Then the portal would open with a flash of light and all thirty Council players would spout forth, mounted on dragons or polar bears, and rush down Gargoyle Gully towards the Acres of Pain. His favourite part, this. Better than the fighting that followed, in the bunkers, on the suspension bridges, in the Towers of Terror, coz the group was still together and unbeaten and he was part of it, his Poisoner leading the charge.

Voices outside, the front door creaked open.

"Hey, Gecko, do we still have grog?" Tags, with someone else.

Gecko swung round, nodded at the empty bottle on the coffee table. "Finished the vodka. Couple of beers in the fridge but."

"Cool. Hey, this is Shaun." An older guy, early twenties at least, came in.

"G'day."

Tags slouched off to the kitchen.

Shaun wandered over to the computer. "Oh, *Savage Glory*. What faction are you?" he asked.

Gecko felt irritation pool behind his forehead, above his left eye. Why couldn't this guy just piss off. He looked back over his shoulder at the screen. His avatar sat down in the snow. At least he was in a safe area. *You are now AFK*, said the message ribbon at the bottom of the screen. He was away from the keyboard anyway, might as well be chill in the real world, for Tags's sake. So he answered: "Arcane Council, what about you?"

"The Council sucks, mate! Bunch of bloody twelve-year-olds."

"I reckon they're cool."

"Yeah, right. That why they always lose? I used to play Steampunk Raiders but now I'm Nordic Legion."

Don't like them, Gecko thought, all their fighters look like rugby players.

Tags came back, handed Shaun a beer. "Did you get a raid?"

"Nah, waiting times are crap," said Gecko, logging out. "Can I have a beer too?"

"You finished off my vodka, you've done enough damage for today." He did the twitching thing with his eyes.

"You sound like my foster dad."

They sat round the battered coffee table on the floor, in front of the cracked vinyl couch, sharing a joint. Shaun's job at Heathmont Motors came up. His boss was okay, but one of the older guys was a total prick who would put sawdust in his lunchbox.

"We'll have to hit his car," Tags suggested. "Give it a nice spray job…"

They sniggered as they all came up with ideas. This Shaun guy wasn't so bad after all, Gecko decided. He told him about the wall Tags had done outside Laburnum station.

"You mean the dopey guy with orange eyes, that was you?"

Tags nodded.

"That's sick. I always notice him when I take a train into the city. And the cops've never nabbed ya?"

"Only once, halfway through a job. You know, in East Richmond, where it says *Legalise Mari*? Cops took my name and let me go. Had to go to court a couple of months later."

"Really?"

"Got ten hours of community work, cleaning up graffiti. They put me to work in Burnley, washing off tags by this Krill guy. His work sucks anyway."

"So it *was* community service," said Shaun. They laughed.

"Tell him about the train surfing," said Gecko.

"You done train surfing?"

Tags obliged. "Oh well, I had this dare with my mate Shiv—"

"Shiv's a mate of yours? That Collingwood bastard?"

Tags looked taken aback. "Yeah, bit of an idiot when he's doing ice. We go back a long time though."

Shaun frowned.

"So anyway," Tags continued, "Shiv reckoned I'd chicken out. We get on this train at Ringwood, right, and it's like 11:00 p.m. and going to the city, pretty empty. So I open the door between two carriages, step onto those little platforms and it's noisy as all hell and rattling like crazy."

Gecko raised his eyebrows, gave Shaun a *wait-for-this* smile.

"It seems like a really bad idea now," Tags went on, "but here's Shiv egging me on. Oh crap, I think, if they can do it in the movies then so can I. Had a couple of drinks, you know. Grab this handle and pull myself up. Before I know it my head's poking out over the roof. The wind's literally ripping my ears off and I'm facing the wrong way."

"Oh fuck, man." Shaun.

"I pull myself onto the roof and I go 'now what?' Here I am flat out, hugging this train roof with a gale blowing up my arse and not a clue about what to do next."

Shaun leaned forward. Gecko watching him, anticipating.

"So the train stops at Heatherdale and for starters I turn around so I'm now facing the right way. Before I can do anything else we're moving again and now my face gets sandblasted."

"Oh man," said Shaun, shaking his head.

"I'm holding on to the edge of the carriage. My fingers are icy, starting to cramp. I just want to get off but I think of Shiv. I have to stand up. We stop in Mitcham. Shiv pops onto that little platform and asks why I'm taking so long. I look down over the edge. I go: 'It's unreal, mate!' It comes out like 'sunneal' coz my lips are so cold."

Gecko puffed up his mouth and tried out the sound: "Sunneal. Sunneal mait."

"The train takes off again and I have to get up before I get shredded by the overpass at Box Hill."

"Happened to a guy few years back," said Shaun. "His head taken off by that low bridge."

Tags nodded. "Look," he said, "I'm beyond caring at this point, so I get up and I don't even have to stand. Just leaning into the wind. My eyes are watering and all I can see is the carriage roof and streaks of light. But I'm doing it."

Gecko looked at Shaun, triumphantly, scanning for his response.

"How did ya get off?" Shaun asked.

"Couldn't care less by this stage. Suppose I just expected to die. But the train slowed down, rolled into Nunawading. Then my legs turned to jelly. Started shaking all over. Somehow I managed to get off the roof and back into the carriage. Don't ask me how, don't remember."

"Aw man," said Shaun. "What did Shiv say?"

"Can't remember. He kept yapping on. I told him to shut it." Tags tilted his head. A knowing look in his eyes. "You don't tell Shiv to shut up… You don't wanna be on the wrong side of him. But I got away with it that time."

It sounded to Gecko as if Tags thought that was the bigger achievement.

They were silent for a moment.

"Train surfing, mate, I don't know," said Shaun. "Gotta be nuts to do that. Great way to make the front page though—splattered all over it… Would you ever do it again?"

"No way, mate, no way. Too frigging crazy." Tags stared at the carpet.

How come it had all become serious again, Gecko wondered. He broke the silence: "Another beer, anyone?"

Shaun looked at his watch. "Better not, long drive home. And work tomorrow. Better get going."

"Jeez," said Tags, "work's changed you, for sure. You always used to be up for a good time…"

Shaun shrugged and picked up his jacket. "Good luck fighting the Legion," he said to Gecko, "and don't dream of—who's that frost mage with the big tits—Lilith Cloudburst?"

"Piss off," said Gecko.

THE RIVE GAUCHE BOYS

Philip couldn't really get into it today. He rued the day that he had suggested condensing his doctoral thesis into an undergraduate course for honours students. Claire Forrester had been acting Department Head that semester and while the others had been ducking for cover when she invited innovative ideas for new courses, he had wanted to impress her with his responsiveness, with a nonchalance suggestive of a confident professional whose head was brimming with talent and ideas. She had taken him up on the course offer but turned him down later that night when he had suggested something altogether more intimate over dinner in Lygon Street. And now Claire had been back at Yale for six months but Philip still had to deliver on his generous offer, which had been duly recorded in the minutes of the Department of English and, worse, in the faculty course guides. Anyhow, there was still enough time to cobble together a respectable little course. Right now though, with all exams and term papers marked, Philip felt entitled to a little caffeinated treat. So he packed up his notes and shoved the whole bundle in his shoulder bag.

The sunlight hit him as soon as he stepped out of the Baillieu Library. Not too warm though, a perfect day. He started walking back to his office but slowed down as he spotted the two students ambling down the path ahead of him. The one on the left, a slight Asian girl, had the most perfectly shaped pert little bottom. He stretched his shoulders and groaned softly and—

"Philip!"

He spun round. "Di! You're back! Is that two years already?"

"Nothing's changed here, I see. Still checking out the local talent."

"I confess, your Honour. Though I will state, in my defence, that your absence has lowered my standards as well as increased my joy at coming upon you so unexpectedly."

"Ah, Philip, old bastard, it's great to see you," said Di, giving him a bear hug.

"You too, Fletchie," he said, holding on to her waist a tad too long, furtively smelling her long black hair. "So tell me all about Paris. Did you finally learn to cook something decent; and how's that book on Ionesco coming along?"

"I learned how to make escargots! I even bought the real saucers, with six little round dips for the shells and special spoons to pick up the snail shell. They're like curved clamps, you know, just the right size to hold a snail. It's really fascinating. You can catch snails just in your garden and put them in a cardboard box for a couple of days. You feed them nothing but lettuce so all impurities leave their system..."

"Which is a polite way of saying your dinner shits itself clean."

"If you must be explicit. Anyway, there's so much to say about preparing your own escargots. You should come over one day and I'll make you some."

"Any good news?"

"Don't be like that, Philip. I know you like experimenting," she said suggestively.

"Ah, about that," said Philip, "I have been experimenting with someone new."

"Anyone I know?"

"Don't think you'd know her. She studied at Monash. I bumped into her at Vic Market. She'd bought all these vegetables to make rata-touille and then her carry bag broke. Zucchini, eggplants, all at risk of being trampled by the hoi polloi. I had to intervene."

"Always the gentleman. Does she have a name, this harbinger of vegetarian cornucopia?"

"Her name is Caitlin." He was surprised to hear the tenderness in his voice. Di looked down for a second, as if to hide a tinge of sadness.

"She's a clinical psychologist. She works at Outer Metro Health, in Nunawading, in the mental health service there."

"I can't quite picture you on the Lilydale line train, Philip!"

"Oh no, she's an inner city girl. She's in Fenwick Street."

"Sounds like escargots for three, then."

"And what about you? You haven't met someone special in the City of Light?"

"Let's walk to Lygon Street and get a decent latte," Di said, grabbing him by the arm, "and I'll tell you all about my toy boys on the Rive Gauche."

She told him about Lucien as they crossed Swanston Street. "He always turned the footy on straight after sex," she exclaimed, shocking two high school girls who were demurely waiting for their tram. "And he had pimples all over his back." Guillaume had seemed charming and sensitive at first, adept at describing his emotions. He drove one of those sweet pale blue *Deux Chevaux* Citroen cars, the ones with the gear stick embedded in the dash board. The ugly duckling of the motoring world in the 1960s, now a prized possession. He even let her drive it once, in Paris traffic. As she got to know Guillaume better, she had been put off by the bleakness of his world view, his anxiety attacks, his increasing tendency to talk about his mother. Parting with the Citroen had been harder than saying goodbye to its boring owner.

"Two lattes," the waitress announced, plonking down the two saucers.

"Thanks," said Philip, smiling back at her freckly face.

Then there was Bernard, Di continued. He had been a bit of a hard man, living in the shady world of gambling and casinos. Sharp, nervous, unsettled and unsettling. He had been very insistent at first, whisking her away to a top hotel in Nice for a weekend of abandon. But he seemed to lose interest after his conquest, as he called it, while she grew wary of the thugs he hung out with, the likelihood that he was involved in something clandestine. By the time he ditched her for a hairdresser from Marseille she felt relief more than anything else. Being fed up with French guys for a while, she had agreed to pose for Stewart, an Australian painter who had just arrived in France and rented a garret in Montmartre.

Philip nodded appreciatively. "Bohemian street cred—very literary."

"Anyway, the posing led to a bit of hanky panky and I even moved in with him for a while. It was fun to see him explore his French fantasies—"

"What, like French maids?"

"No, shush. Nothing kinky about this guy. He was an innocent, a country boy from Kerang—"

"Ha, Kerang."

"—and he was so wrapped up in all these stereotypes about Paris. He would buy baguettes and bring them home in the pannier of his bike, sniff them and say, in broad Strine, 'amazing!' He would stare at the Sacré-Coeur Basilica, paint it over three days of total concentration, look at it again and say 'amazing!' He even bought a beret."

"Amazing!"

Di slapped his wrist. "He seemed funny at first. Then I realised that what I had taken for the gift of childlike, wide-eyed wonderment turned out to be the curse of limited vocabulary. We ran out of things to say."

"Not that there was much to begin with."

"You're such a cynic, Philip. I'm surprised you've found someone nice."

"When did I say she was nice?"

A TRIP TO SILVAN

Kurt revved up the under-powered office car and willed it up the hill. He passed the Twisted Vine Winery on the left. Good, that was a landmark he recognised. He had been there once with Emma. He was still on the right track. On many occasions he had resolved to prepare his field visits by looking up the route before getting into the car. The road to hell and all that, hey. So here he was again, trying to find blooming Wirruna Drive in Silvan. First left past the nursery, Jennifer had said. Ah, here we go. Number 16 was a rambling property whose sole charm was that it was framed by stands of tall gum trees. Overgrown grass, several clapped-out cars in the yard, straggly geraniums planted in discarded tyres. Mr Morrison is not houseproud, Kurt thought, as he walked up the rickety wooden steps to the porch. What a middle class notion for a social worker to trot out, his mind annotated.

As he was looking for a bell, a voice boomed: "Come in, door's open."

Kurt opened the flyscreen door and stood facing a giant man clad in a singlet and blue shorts.

"You're here about young Gecko," he said, "I spotted the red plates on your car. Thought here's another lass from welfare. Except you're not a lass."

Before Kurt could introduce himself, the man continued: "I'm Bob, anyway, come through."

With surprising agility for a man his size he opened the frosted glass double doors to off the hallway and pointed at two brown couches.

"Have a seat. You want a drink?"

"No thanks," said Kurt, as he sat down in the seat that gave him the best view of the lounge room, "I'm Kurt Edel—"

"Merchant navy," said Bob.

"Pardon?"

"Was in the merchant navy," explained Bob. "In case you was wondering about all the ship pictures and stuff."

Kurt looked at the walls: framed sepia photos of steam ships and tug boats, a painting of a sailing ship in a storm, a poster of a lighthouse lapped by gigantic waves. A copper diving bell sat on a chipped wooden dresser.

"Of course the place was much nicer when the missus was still alive."

"When did she pass away?"

"Two years ago."

"I'm sorry to hear that."

"So, tell me about Gecko—what's he done now?"

"I have the name down as 'Srecko'—"

"Yes, and that rolls off the tongue so beautifully that all his mates call him Gecko."

"Fair enough. I—"

"So what's he done?"

"Well nothing, I'm his new case worker and—"

"You sure you don't want a drink?"

"I'm right, thanks. As I said I'm his new case worker—"

"How long have you had your GP?"

"Pardon?"

"How long have you been to the same doctor?"

"Well, I don't see what that—"

"Just answer that question please."

"Well, about eight years I suppose."

"Exactly. You get to see the same doctor for your aches and colds or when you have a pimple on your bum. And here's this boy who's been fucked around in more ways than one and everyone plays pass-the-parcel with him. It's not fair."

"I hear what you're saying, Bob—"

"Oh please, cut the social work crap. Talk straight."

"Well, his previous case worker's gone on a secondment—"

"I understand people move around, mate. That Jennifer lass tried. Chances are you will try. You'll try to talk to Gecko but he'll pull up the gangplank. If you're any good, you'll continue trying. You may get through to him. And just as he lets you in a little, you'll break a leg, get a divorce or set up a landscaping business and you'll be out of his life from one day to the next. And he'll be back where he started, except a bit more hurt, a bit more lonely, more suspicious."

"But—"

"I'm not saying it's your fault; it's the system. If we worked like that in the navy we'd never get a ship out of the harbour. Who's your captain? Is there anyone in charge?"

Kurt looked down, swallowed and tapped the ends of two biros on the coffee table until they were perfectly aligned.

"Okay," he said, looking up, "I'll be straight with you." He sat back in his chair, ran his hand through his hair. "You're quite right, there can, at times, be significant discontinuity in care arrangements—"

Bob raised his left hand. "Plain English please."

"Sorry. I suppose what I meant to say was, yes, staff come and go. And yes, that's not ideal for the kids."

"Not ideal," Bob sneered.

"Far from ideal," Kurt conceded.

"It's bloody irresponsible."

"It is," said Kurt, "but I can assure you no one wants things to turn out this way." Fran Esposito flashed through his mind and he wondered whether he was technically fibbing. "We've got young social workers coming in, fresh from uni. All starry-eyed, wanting to change the world. They could work wonders with a family. Problem is, they carry a case load of twenty-five, thirty families. Five days in a working week—you do the maths. Team meetings, home visits, court reports, entering data…"

Bob shifted on his seat, raised a hand. Round this off, Kurt thought, don't make it into a lecture.

"Before you know it," he went on, "our young idealists morph into expert gatekeepers. They learn to balance risk against workload. They cut corners. They may accept a nurse's assurance, over the phone, that an infant is doing well, when in fact they should go out again and check in person. But, you know, that means maybe two hours in the car and writing yet another report."

"You're saying I should feel lucky to see you here at all?"

"No, but—"

"Look, I appreciate you being frank and all, but you're rabbiting on about infants and nurses and I've got a sixteen-year-old on my hands. That is, when I get to see him."

"I'm sorry," said Kurt, "I got sidetracked. Let's talk about Srecko. Gecko. So, when I joined the Eastern Outreach team and became Srecko's new case manager—"

"One of your thirty cases."

Kurt let it go. "And in order—"

"Actually, how come you're such an old bloke? For a case worker I mean; no offence."

"I've done other stuff," Kurt said, "I retrained as a social worker and joined protective services. Worked for Western Outreach and for Northern. Would you like to see some references?" That was uncalled for, he thought, that bitchiness; the guy just wants to get my measure.

Bob leaned back into his cushion and cracked the faintest of smiles. It seemed wise and sarcastic at the same time, Kurt thought. As if those steely eyes were saying "I've seen all sorts of people in the navy and I know your type."

"Don't get me wrong," Bob said, "I don't mind you being older. Seen a bit of life. Better than being straight out of school and telling people what to do. So, back to Gecko. Where do you want me to start?"

SLEUTHING

I am such an arsehole, Kurt thought as he drove back. I can't help lecturing a foster parent on the workload of protective workers. As if he cares. At least we get a proper salary. This Bob guy could have thrown in the towel when his wife died, but he stuck with Srecko. I could have encouraged him, shown a bit of appreciation. But no, I have to get all defensive and ask whether he wants to see my references. Where did that come from? Not professional, not at all. Not having a great day, Kurt. Let's hope you do a better job engaging Srecko. Finding him, for starters.

It was hot already, over 30, and only just past 11a.m. He turned on the radio. The mellifluous tones of the Artisans' *Heading Down the Runway*. Last time I heard that song was in Brussels airport. About to fly out to Australia. Leaving it all behind, my parents, the Renata saga. He turned the radio off and opened the windows on the passenger side. The wind was picking up.

As he drove through Bayswater, Kurt ran over Srecko's case history again. The son of Bosnian Serbs, who had migrated to Australia in 1998. Srecko was five at the time. He grew up in the Latrobe Valley, where his father worked as a security guard. If he remembered correctly, the first protective notification dated from 2000, when Srecko was seven, and related to possible neglect. A neighbour had reported that Srecko's mother was sick and unable to look after her son, and that the father was drinking heavily. The file showed no follow-up action after the initial home visit. The second notification, about a year later, related to suspected sexual abuse. Because of understaffing in the Gippsland office it was not investigated until a third notification, also alleging sexual abuse, was received. With Srecko's mother dying from leukaemia by now and his father out of the picture, an uncle had assumed responsibility for day-to-day care of the boy. While there was no proof that the uncle had abused Srecko, the Children's Court had accepted child protection's recommendation that the boy be placed in out-of-home care after his mother's death. Srecko started in foster care with a family in Dandenong some time in 2003. Things did not work out, though, and Srecko went through four or five foster care placements in under three years before settling down with Bob and Edna Morrison in Silvan.

These were the facts as recorded on the file. Chronological. Clinical. Cryptic. Kurt suspected the usual chasm between the bare-bone entries on the client record and the messy chaos of the boy's life.

He had set out for what he thought would be a routine visit. A stable placement, a quick check-in with the foster parent, talk to the boy if he's around. Write up notes back in the office and keep the case on the backburner until the boy turns eighteen and can be discharged from foster care. Focus on urgent cases. But a couple of things Bob had said had set off alarm bells. Srecko had got on well with Edna, Bob said, and had become withdrawn and gloomy after her death. The loss of another mother figure, Kurt had suggested. Bob had just stared at him and continued. Srecko's school attendance was erratic. He'd been in fights and was now hanging out with older guys in a share house somewhere in Heathmont. Bob had picked him up from there one night when the boy had got himself drunk. Inverloch Road, just off the Mountain Highway. Number 12 or 14? Bob couldn't remember.

Inverloch Road turned out to be a short street between the highway and a railway line. Dilapidated weatherboard bungalows on quarter-acre blocks. Kurt parked and a white van pulled in behind him. Okay, Sherlock, he thought, which one will it be? A low wire fence had once tried to contain the overgrown garden of number 12. A rusty white metal letterbox next to the gate. Junk mail strewn across the concrete path. At number 14, the lawn was well-trimmed. A birdbath. Rose bushes. Elementary, my dear Watson. He strode towards number 12 and pressed the doorbell.

It didn't work. He tried again. Nothing. He banged on the flaky white paint of the door and waited. He had a vision of sweaty bodies in sleeping bags lying around a bong in a smoky room. It would take a moment to crawl out of that primordial fog. He banged the door again. No response. His mind reeled off his SAS fantasy: Okay Major, we're going in. Major Tom smashed the front door with a sledgehammer and his platoon rushed in. Stun grenades, flash bang confusion. Kurt realised this was a repugnant fantasy. Stun grenades are a big no-no for a social worker. A big no-no for a Buddhist. Tell that to his unruly mind. Kurt's Involuntary Cinematic Productions operated as a pop-up corporation with a weak CEO and a feral board unhindered by either logic or inhibition.

As he turned round, he tripped over a paver and propelled himself towards the nature strip.

"Are you right, there?" A repairman peered out of the sliding door of a telephone company van.

"Yeah, I'm fine." Kurt blushed. "Wrong house. I need *that* house," he mumbled, pointing next door. Why am I explaining myself, he thought? And what do you say to a man who's just witnessed my impromptu attempt to attain the speed of light? He felt the eyes of the technician on his back as he walked towards the door of number 14.

A small elderly man opened the door. His beady eyes a penetrating blue. Beige hearing aid curled over the rim of his right ear. A faint smell of soup wafted out.

"Good morning, sir," said Kurt.

"Not bad, yourself?"

Kurt explained he was a social worker. Needed to talk to Srecko Bosovic, who probably lived next door.

"What sort of name is that?" the old man asked. "Must be foreign. Anyway, I see these boys here, coming and going, all hours of the day and night."

Kurt nodded.

"And then that awful music, if you can call it music… So loud, I've rung the police once or twice. Three times, actually, yes, three, but they can't come every day. It's the missus I worry about. She's very poorly, she is. Needs to rest. And now I ask you, Mr…"

"Kurt," he prompted.

"Now I ask you, Mr Curd, would you be able to rest after an operation, you know, with all hell breaking loose next door? It isn't right, you know. And wheelie bins full of bottles and cans. Smoking drugs too, most likely."

"I understand things must be difficult for you, Mr…"

"Harris. Howard Harris. Know what, Mr Curd, maybe you and I, maybe we can go over there together and set these young blokes straight."

"I don't think we can do that, Mr Harris. But it was nice talking to you and I hope your wife gets better."

"That would be grand, Mr Curd, that would be just grand." His eyes looked as if he'd stopped believing things could go his way.

Kurt walked back to his car and looked at his watch. He could grab a bite to eat and swing past again to see whether anyone had turned up at number 12. Not the best use of time but he had to eat anyway—and he needn't tell Fran his every move.

He picked up a burger in a drive-through and pulled into a service lane. As he turned his burger around, nibbling the shreds of iceberg lettuce, he watched the heat shimmering over the Dandenong Ranges, colouring the mountains blue. He contemplated the troubles Mr Harris was facing. An elderly caregiver, just like his own dad. The eruption of modern life, right on your doorstep. Noise, confusion, alcohol and drugs. A threat perceived where none was intended.

He finished his burger, took two paper napkins off the passenger seat and wiped the grease off his fingers. He took his black notebook out of his backpack, pulled the elastic back and folded the book open. He'd numbered all pages in his spidery scrawl. This was page 46. *Howard Harris,* he wrote, *14 Inverloch Rd Heathmont—aged care assessment re in-home support? Ring Fiona.*

DOING DANIKA PROUD

This time Kurt was in luck. Just as he pulled up again in front of number 12, the door opened and a pale creature came out. It squinted into the harsh light, squatted on the porch and rummaged through a backpack. Kurt recognised the boy's pallid face and sharp features from his profile picture on the Childproof database.

"You must be Gecko," he said, blocking the boy's path at the letterbox.

"What's it to you?"

"I'm Kurt Edelman. Your new case manager. I've taken over from Jennifer. She—"

"I've got to go to school." Gecko tried to shuffle past Kurt, but he insisted.

"Listen, at this time of day it'll take you another hour to get there by public transport. If you're lucky. And I need to talk to you." Kurt nodded at the house. "Let's get out of this heat first. A quick chat and I'll drive you to school. I'm headed that way myself."

"How do I know you're not some sort of perv?"

"I was in Silvan this morning, spoke to your foster dad. Ring him on my phone if you like, or I can show you my ID."

"Never mind." Gecko sighed, turned round and went inside.

He flung his backpack down, plopped on the couch, looked away from Kurt with an expression of endless boredom. Kurt knew how much depended on the next step. Ask an inane question, like *how is school* and the walls would go up even higher. *Engage the young person,* they had taught him in his social work courses, *and the rest will follow.* He wanted an opening line that would show his perceptiveness, establish his street cred and wash away Srecko's resistance. Gecko's resistance. All at once. He wished Danika, silver-haired senior lecturer and font of all wisdom, was here right now to suggest prompts for such a winning opener. Kurt felt tense, his temperature had gone up a few degrees and he was uncomfortably aware of his shirt label chafing his neck every time he moved. And then he said it.

"So do you come here often?"

The oldest pickup line in the book—he cringed as soon as he'd said it. Idiot.

Gecko stared at him now, in baffled disgust. At least I have managed to make eye contact, Kurt thought. And, liberated by the realisation things could not get any worse, he continued.

"Whose place is this, actually?"

"Tags." The boy's disdain was palpable.

"Tags?"

"Mate of mine." Gecko pulled at a loose piece of vinyl on the armrest.

"And he rents this place?"

"Look, why does this matter?"

"I'll be straight with you, Gecko. You're sixteen and meant to be living in foster care. You're meant to be attending school. Every day. Now, I understand that you want to make some of your own choices, but for that to happen I need to know a bit more about you and your friends."

"I've told that woman."

"And Jennifer's briefed me, and I've read your file—"

"What file?"

"Well, back at work, the history of your involvement with protective services since you lived in the Latrobe Valley—"

"What, and you've read all of that? You're a fucking stranger and you come here knowing all about my past? Are you a weirdo or something?"

"Gecko, as your case worker I need to understand what's happened to you. I'm here to help you."

The boy snorted.

"Fuck, mate, I mean it." Kurt regretted swearing but at least he had Gecko's attention now. "I'm in this job because I want to make a difference. I've seen too many good kids blow all their chances, run head-first into a wall. It pisses me right off—it's such a waste. If you let me help you, I'll be there for you. Trust me—I'm on your side. Together we can work through your issues."

"What issues?"

Easy now, Kurt thought, let's not rush things. "Well, for starters, why don't you tell me about how you've ended up living here."

Gecko hesitated, then seemed to relent. "Dunno, I was at this party, right, getting pissed… Tags was there and he was okay and said I could sleep it off here…"

"So that's how you met?"

"Sort of hung out, the next day, got along fine and he got a bunch of mates over for a LAN, if you know what that is—"

"Yeah, a Local Area Network party. I'm a gamer myself."

"Oh yeah?" Disbelief in his eyes. Then the gleam of a challenge: "What do you play then?"

Kurt pointed at the *Savage Glory* game manual on the table. "*Dungeons and Dragons* stuff, like you." Just fancy, Kurt thought, all those hours of slaying orcs and goblins coming in handy after all.

"You're just making that up. Cause of this book."

"No, seriously."

"What faction are you then? What class? What level?" Gecko asked, his chin moving upwards with every question.

"Arcane Council. My warlock got to level 81. But I'm playing *Trail of Heroes* now. What about you?"

Gecko told Kurt about his avatar, about where he was in the game. How he'd saved various combinations of spells into deadly combos bound to hotkeys on his keyboard. Kurt didn't know how to do that. Gecko explained it.

Kurt steered the conversation back: "So after that LAN party you ended up staying here?"

"Yeah, well, on and off. This other guy had moved out. Tags said I could have his room for a while if I wanted."

"What, just for free?"

"Yeah, he was cool with it."

"So Tags didn't need the money? What does he do?"

"Nothing really. Hangs around here, goes to Melbourne couple of times a week."

"He doesn't have a job?"

"No, not really—look, I don't know what he does."

"Okay. What about the guy who moved out?"

"Shiv?"

"What does he do? Does he hang out here too?"

"He's a mate of Tags. Haven't met him."

"So tell me a bit more about this… Tags."

"But why? What's he got to do with anything?"

Kurt decided not to push his luck. If Tags was using drugs or dealing, or somehow taking advantage of the boy, Gecko was unlikely to dob in his housemate in this first conversation.

"Fair enough. So how do you get along with your foster dad?"

"Well, you know, you've met him… He's always on my case, telling me to clean up my room, hassling me about school stuff."

Gecko expanded on that theme and Kurt listened closely. Given Gecko's history, Kurt had his antennas out for any suggestion of impropriety or worse, but Gecko seemed to have a grudging admiration for Bob Morrison. It was also clear that the boy shuttled between Heathmont and Silvan. He would leave Tags's place whenever the food or the booze ran out or the distance from school became too onerous, and bolt from his foster care home whenever he felt bullied at school or upset after a clash with his foster dad. Gecko had developed a routine of sorts, Kurt decided, and he'd seen many young people do worse. But he had to find out more about this Tags and his entourage before he could undertake a comprehensive risk assessment.

Kurt saw Gecko looking at the clock on the wall.

"Hey, do you still want a ride to school? Probably last period by the time you get there…"

"Yeah. I'd better. Also have a stupid detention."

"Okay," said Kurt, "we can talk more in the car."

Danika would be proud after all, he thought.

CARLTON BLUES

Caitlin looked at her watch and pedalled harder. The lecture at RMIT had started late and gone over time. But Frank Catchpoole was such an engaging presenter that Caitlin had lost all sense of time. He had high-lighted the need to intervene early when young people experience a psychotic episode for the first time and had torn strips off the govern-ment for underfunding youth mental health services. Classic Catch-poole stuff. She had hung around after the lecture hoping to get hold of Dr Jeanne Dubois, the eating disorders specialist, but the rising star, on loan from the Sorbonne for a six-month stint, had been engaged in a lively conversation with the executive director of Western Plains Health, a hard man in a sharp suit, whom Caitlin suspected of regarding mental health as a career path rather than a vocation.

Alarm bells had gone off in Caitlin's head when she noticed Professor Jeremy Ambrose navigate towards her, all raised eyebrows, goofy smile and lecherous intent. Not again.

"Caitlin," he oozed, "how nice to see you!"

"Hi, Jeremy."

"Caitlin, if I remember correctly, you are a psychologist by training, are you not?"

"I am." She scanned the room for escape routes.

"I was wondering whether you could entertain me"—and here he paused suggestively—"about the psychometric properties of the *Life Skills Profile*. We've been thinking of introducing the questionnaire in our long-stay unit." She averted her gaze from his purple velvet bow tie. The backside of a passing drinks waiter reminded her of—oh my god, Philip!

"I'm sorry, Jeremy," she said, now genuinely panicked, "sorry to do this to you, but I just realise that my boyfriend, my partner, is waiting for me. He's helping me pack for my move. Must run. Bye!"

"Where are you moving to?" attempted her faithful conference stalker as Caitlin headed for the exit.

"Far away," she yelled. "Western Australia. The Sorbonne. Anywhere. Must run!"

Jeremy Ambrose frowned.

Frank Catchpoole walked over and handed him a glass of red: "Here mate, have a drink."

By the time she crossed Grattan Street, Caitlin had relaxed. A strong tailwind propelled her through the streets of Carlton as she weaved in and out of the pre-Christmas traffic chaos. Elgin Street was clogged as usual but Caitlin smiled as she saw the daylight fade into a glorious pink sunset in the distance. Unbelievable colours, really. She loved Melbourne, with its ugly shop fronts and its beautiful parks, its teeming markets and its sociable, tolerant people. Caitlin felt at peace with the world. Things were falling into place. She loved her job. Philip had agreed to buy a house with her, to move in together. He had certainly taken his time to make a commitment... Anyway, that was all in the past. She felt her chest expand with joy. I could design a T-shirt or a bumper sticker, she fantasised: *Happiness is cycling up Rathdowne Street on a summer night*. Not quite catchy, but it was heartfelt. If only this moment could last.

The sense of yearning reminded her of *Faust*. It was years since she'd read Goethe's play at night in her cramped little flat in Berlin, where she was studying Cognitive Behavioural Therapy under Weissmuller. She had been struck by Mephistopheles' demand that Faust never savour or attempt to prolong the present moment. Under the terms of his pact with the devil, Faust was to keep on striving, never settling down—the original rolling stone. Goethe had contrived an apt curse. Diabolical indeed. Western culture was focused so much on goal attainment, on living in a virtual future rather than enjoying a tangible, messy present. A world of compulsive choreographers. Philip always teased her when she brought this up and called her his hippy chick. He could be so irritatingly flippant at times.

A sense of foreboding washed over her. What had happened to her endorphins, and why was German literature raining on her parade?

She wheeled her bike up to the tiny porch of her terrace house and locked it. No sign of Philip. Had he waited for her and stomped off in frustration? Not likely. Philip was no drama queen—though he would make sure to signal his irritation in different ways. She rang his mobile.

"Hey, baby, it's me. I was late, I hope you haven't been waiting."

"No, I'm late myself." He paused. "I caught up with Di Fletcher at Brunetti's and we had a drink."

"Oh, is she back?" Caitlin tore a stalk off the jasmine creeper, crushed the flower.

"Yes, she is. Anyway, I'm almost at your place. I'll see you soon."

"Okay. Love ya."

"See ya."

"I brought your mail in," said Philip, as he closed the front door behind him.

"Oh, thanks!" said Caitlin, "just put it on the little stand there, next to the vase. It's a shambles inside."

"You've started already?"

"Yes, there's just so much. And that's only my stuff. Then we still have to pack everything at your place too. So good that Kevin and Ramon dropped off all those packing boxes."

"Hey, how was Catchpoole?" asked Philip, throwing his linen jacket on the couch.

"The usual, both riveting and predictable."

"Is he turning into a one-trick pony?"

"Well, his message is compelling. The bulk of mental health funding goes into services for adults. Mental health services for young people and for the elderly are underfunded. And Catchpoole's point is that by intervening early—early in life and early in the course of the illness—you can prevent a lot of problems down the track."

"Placing guardrails on top of the cliff or an ambulance at the bottom, hey," Philip crowed, showing off a well-remembered classic metaphor for dilemmas in public health.

"Precisely," said Caitlin, pleased that Philip was showing an interest in her work. She gave him a peck on the cheek. "Kiss from the teacher and a gold star."

"Does this teacher have any other goodies?"

"Maybe later… Jeanne Dubois was there too. From the Sorbonne—do you remember me telling you about her?"

Philip's eyes had glazed over, but he managed a neutral "Ah, yes."

"I wanted to get hold of her," Caitlin went on, "because we could learn so much at Outer Metro from her work on eating disorders and—"

"Ah, that reminds me, Di wants to feed you snails."

"That sounds rather hostile."

"Escargots, she calls them. Does that make it better?"

"When did she get back?"

"Oh, last week. I bumped into her outside the Baillieu Library."

"And you didn't tell me?"

"Must have escaped my mind."

"You didn't think I'd be interested?"

"Let it go, Caitlin. All that is in the past. It meant nothing."

"But you decided to have coffee with her all the same."

"We're colleagues, Caitlin. I can't avoid her. We just had coffee. Twice. Espressos. One sugar. Each. She told me about this string of lovers she's had in Paris."

"Why does that not reassure me?"

"Look Caitlin, if we're moving in together—"

"If?"

He trotted out his pedantic voice: "Oh, Excuse Me... Now that we are moving in together I want you to trust me, okay? You're The Only One, *capiche*? You are the Juliet to my Romeo, the Heloise to my Abelard—"

"Don't be flippant, Philip. You want me to share my life with you. I have a right to know what I'm in for."

"A wild ride, darling, a fantastic fandango around the stars and associated heavenly bodies."

"You can't help yourself, can you?"

Caitlin put on a bandana. "Like a real fifties housewife," was Philip's take.

They started packing in different rooms. Caitlin went through her utensils in the kitchen, Philip through the bookshelves in Caitlin's small study that looked out on the herb garden.

"Surely you're not taking this," said Philip, walking into the kitchen holding up a well-read copy of *The Sage*. Caitlin looked up from the undies she was stuffing into the salad spinner.

"What's that—oh yeah, I want to keep that."

"But my dear, it is sentimental drivel. Full of inane philosophy. Prescribed reading for civil celebrants in the seventies. Listen to this." He read her some lines and snorted. "That's just mawkish."

Caitlin tapped the open flap of the cardboard box. "Are you done? I read it when I was in my teens and I loved it."

"Is it something you could read to your patients maybe, to restore their hope in humanity?"

"God, Philip, you can be such a patronising bastard."

Philip grinned. Caitlin pushed her bandana back. It slipped off her right ear and a long curl of brown hair escaped. She tucked it in and walked into the bathroom.

She brushed her teeth. Furiously. She was used to Philip ribbing her about all sorts of things. He was like a fencer, he had to test his agility and intellectual versatility in daily combat; and she had been a willing sparring partner. She was not competitive herself and that made it easier to accept his thrusting and parrying without feeling threatened. She felt no need to outdo him, to meet each witticism with a cutting repartee. In fact, she considered his habit a form of immaturity, all this

needing to dazzle and shine. Maybe that was her way of being conde-
scending. She had a feeling of unease, however, that the teasing had
recently acquired a nastier edge. That had started, if she remembered
correctly, shortly after they had bought the house in Creswick Street. It
was as if he wanted to stress test their relationship before moving in
together. Was this your everyday male anxiety to commit, or a more
morbid desire to pluck defeat from the jaws of victory? And now there
was the reappearance of Di Fletcher, floozy supreme.

Maybe she was over-analysing his behaviour. She wouldn't have
been the first psychologist to bring her work home.

"What are you doing there, my love? Not sulking, I hope."

"No," she lied, "just sorting out the sun screen." Sun Protection
Factor 50 my arse, she thought. She tossed the sticky plastic bottle into
the metal bin with a loud bang.

After an hour or so Caitlin, still annoyed, steamed a cup of basmati rice
and heated a bowl of leftover dhal. She also found a half bottle of
cabernet sauvignon and some brie.

"Do you want a bite to eat?" She tried to sound conciliatory.

"That would be great!" Philip gave her a friendly smile and she felt
her tension ebb.

"Look," he said as he sat down next to her on a blue sequinned
cushion, among the cardboard boxes, "I'm sorry about earlier. Of
course you can take the books you want. I was just teasing."

"Thanks. And I don't want to be stupid, it's just…"

"Yes?"

"Sometimes I think we're rushing into things. I mean, we're so
different. And we've only lived together on holidays."

He leant over, looked into her brown eyes and gently kissed her on
the lips.

"The French got it right," he said. "*Vive la différence*. We'll be fine,
my love. And those holidays were pretty incredible, weren't they?"

She nodded.

"Remember what we did in our hotel room in Phuket?"

Caitlin felt herself blush. He moved closer to her.

"Hey," she exclaimed, "there goes my bond money!"

He looked at the wine he had spilled.

"I should get some salt."

"Leave it," he said, "it's only money. Forget about the bond."

He kissed her and expertly unbuttoned her blouse with his right hand.

Caitlin listened to the regular sound of Philip's breath. He looked so boyish as he slept. An innocent expression and none of the arrogance. She felt happy that he had apologised. That was unusual—he didn't often climb down. He'd also been extra attentive during sex. She smiled and stretched. Maybe it would all work out. Sure, Philip was highly strung and competitive, but wasn't that because he aimed for excellence? He wanted to push boundaries, in love and in life. Take the way he was examining narrative structures—that sounded impressive. Innovative, and totally different from the vacuous, wishy-washy discussions about books that she was used to. And he had an instinct for seeking out interesting people, like that South African playwright, or the journalist who'd been jailed in Russia. He was good at drawing people out, making them reveal their dreams and aspirations. Not that he was a good listener—rather a ruthless one, fascinated by stories and determined to extract their details at any cost. Never mind discretion, sensitivities, good taste or trauma. The exact opposite of therapeutic interviewing, come to think of it. He could be demanding that way, overbearing perhaps, insufferable at times—but never boring.

The soft breeze coming through the open window made the curtains shiver like angel wings. Caitlin smiled and drifted off to sleep.

CHRISTMAS SHOPPING

The man with the goatee blocked her path as she walked out of the Megasavers supermarket. She tried to walk around him but he moved with her.

"Just a minute there."

"Get out of my way, creep," Kylee snarled.

He flashed an ID card. "Store security. I must ask you to sit on this bench for a minute."

"Fuck off mate. I done nothing."

"Well, there won't be a problem then, will there, but I need you to sit down here."

"Let go of me, this is a public place." She felt the eyes of shoppers on her.

"And we will want to have a look at that," he said, pointing at her navy sports bag.

'What's it to you, dickhead?'

Two school boys sniggered, ran off laughing as she gave them the evil eye.

Should I do a runner, Kylee thought? Scanned her surroundings. Hemmed in on her left: a woman with a pram, two Greek women gesticulating. On her right a Megasavers guy pushing a line of nested trolleys. All routes blocked. She felt paralysed.

"Don't even think about it," said the security guy.

Bloody mind reader, was he? Snarky dick.

And he's got reinforcements. A chunky woman in black was working her way through the aisles towards them, holding her walkie talkie ahead of her.

The sound system piping *'Tis the season to be jolly*. Yeah, right.

"Head of store security," the woman in black introduced herself. Pointed at a laminated photo on her chest. Same wart next to her nose.

"We have reason to believe that you've taken a bottle of liquor from the store without paying."

We have reason to believe, Kylee echoed in her head. Why did they always sound so up themselves. *I have reason to spit in your face.*

"Fuck youse. Just bought some snags and tomato sauce is all." She lifted her bag. "I need to get going."

They stopped her.

The woman began again. Broken record: "We suspect there's a bottle of liquor in that bag. Can you open it for us please."

Can't believe this is happening again, Kylee thought. Was just gonna duck out. Be ten minutes, twenty max. Jade would be okay.

"I'm not opening my fucking bag for youse. None of your business."

"In that case we'll have to involve the police. Please come into the store with us."

They gave her no choice, really, marched her through the aisles, like sheepdogs at her heels, through that gate with the big folding plastic flaps near the veggie section, past a cool store, into a corner office with a photocopied sign on the door: *Store Security*.

Why did I have to be so stupid, Kylee thought as she sat on the plastic chair in front of the woman's desk. Cameras everywhere... It's bloody Christmas that does it. Such a big deal, all needs to be special. You get caught up in it, then you get caught. Again. While I'm still on parole. Fuck fuck fuck. What's gonna happen now? Don't wanna go back inside. Jade, baby, why am I such a rotten mum? And when are the cops gonna turn up, I need to go home. And these two idiots yabbering about cricket teams.

The door behind her creaked open. She turned sideways. Two coppers: young guy looking bored, woman chubby, friendly face.

"Who did we catch this week?" the young cop asked.

"We caught this woman shoplifting. Spotted her on CCTV, slipping a bottle of cream liqueur in this sports bag. Left the store without paying for the grog. Doesn't want to open her bag."

The cop turned to Kylee. "Alright, here's the deal: I'm going to ask you once to open your bag. I suggest you cooperate."

Young or not, Kylee could tell this one wasn't going to accept any bullshit. Game over. She opened her bag. A bottle of ketchup, a black tray with a dozen pale sausages. A bottle of liqueur.

"I suppose this bottle's not on your receipt?"

"Have a heart. It's Chrissie coming up. I wanna celebrate too."

"I need to see that docket."

She handed him the scrunched receipt.

He nodded. "Okay, I'm gonna need your details."

"Oh, come on."

"Name and address?"

She sighed. "Kylee Watson, Carlton."

"Whereabouts in Carlton?"

She told him.

"Oh, the commission flats." A note of confirmation in his tone. "This your first offence, Kylee?"

"Can we get on with this, me daughter's at home."

"How old's your daughter?" the other cop asked.

"Six."

"And who's with her now?"

"No one."

"She's at home without supervision?"

"Yeah well, if youse let me go I can be with her."

"Well, you're gonna have to come to the station with us."

"You can't lock me up. What about me girl? If that bitch from community services finds out, they'll take her off me."

"So what you're saying is, protective services have been notified about your daughter, right? What's her name?"

"Jade."

"Well, Kylee, we won't lock you up," she said. "We can drop you off back home so you can look after your little girl. But we're going to check your record at the station and we also need to discuss this incident with child protection. And Megasavers may want us to press charges..."

Shit, Kylee thought, they don't know the half of it. Her life was a house of cards and she'd just pulled one out from its base. She slumped down, deflated, shook her head.

"Do you understand all of that, Kylee?" the male officer asked.

"Please don't ring community services! Can't you leave them out of this? What if they take me daughter away? Please, I just wanted a little treat."

"If I want a little treat, I have to pay for it," snapped the Megasavers security guard.

The young police officer looked at him askance. "You've made a bit of a mess of things here, Kylee," he said. "Shoplifting is an offence. And the child protection people need to know about this too, like your daughter, left without supervision..."

Kylee snorted. "Well thanks for nothing, Mr Smooth Talk cop. I've been doing the hard yards, you know, trying to look after me girl. And now you're going to dob me in with that bitch. All coz of one lousy bottle. Merry fucking Christmas."

ENOUGH

Kylee had fried up the sausages, folded them inside a slice of white bread and squirted sauce over them.

"We're having a hot dog party," she said.

Jade took up the chant: "We're having a hot dog party, we're having a hot dog party." She jumped up and down on the couch. Kylee didn't tell her off. What was the point now? "Farty farty party. Farty farty party."

Kylee smiled. They sat at the square picnic table she had shoved next to the window. She rubbed her thumb over its metal edges. Grime. Everywhere.

"What's wrong, Mummy?"

"Nothing, sweetheart."

"You were at the shops soooo long, Mummy. I was soooo hungry."

"Sorry, baby."

"Can we look at the animals again?"

"What animals?"

"In the shops. The goat and the piggy and the sheep and the ninny pig. On the straw."

"They're all gone, back to the farm."

"Why?"

"They visited the city just for one day."

"I liked them."

"Well, they're gone. Eat your sausage."

"Yummy."

Jade knocked papers off the table. Kylee picked them up. The electricity bill and that other stuff. She looked through the gauze curtains over the Carlton Baths, the blue haze of the Dandenong Ranges in the distance. A cop car crawled towards the Eastern Freeway. Then the boomerang of the morning's events came swishing back, hit her right in the head. They'd enjoyed a couple of sausages, so what, they were on borrowed time.

The cops would find out she was still on parole for that burglary in Fenwick Street. They'd tell her parole officer about Megasavers. She could see them piece it all together, like dominoes. Caught shoplifting at the petrol station. Getting the sack from the cleaning job at the evening school. For pilfering, the guy called it.

No way was she going back to prison. She shuddered.

Then the cops would tell community services and the hoity toity bitch would come back with her purple eye shadow and her clipboard.

That just isn't acceptable parenting, Kylee.

She could hear it already, that clipped, whiny voice. How could she ever hope to wow someone like that, get her off her case?

Kylee felt the fear stir. A wet dead hand that sprang from her stomach and grabbed her by the throat. She trembled, stood up, walked to the laundry and fished up a ziplock bag from the bottom of the laundry basket. Back in the kitchen, she sat down at the table again and rolled herself a joint. She inhaled deeply, reassured briefly by the deep musky scent. But smoke would not dispel the fear. What was that again about smoke and mirrors? She hated mirrors, the harried ruined face that stared back at her in the morning these days.

She was trying though, she'd gone off ice, but everyone slips up and she always got caught. Like when she left Jade locked in Dave's car and everyone screaming neglect, neglect. You're doing it tough, single mum on the dole, you want a break now and then. But no deal, says that bitch from welfare, messing with her life, calling the shots.

She'd come across some tough numbers but this harpy rattled her, made her freeze up. How could she ever be on her best behaviour, how could she ever expect this Rottweiler to see her smiles for Jade, the little jokes, the cuddles at night? That Kurt had been better, more relaxed, a guy who would listen. But he'd moved on of course. They always did, the guys. Boyfriends or case workers, they never stayed. Took what they wanted and left. And this piece of work had a done a degree in misery, Kylee reckoned. The bitch had a special kinda radar, for stains in the kitchen, mouldy cheese, unpaid bills, forgotten appointments, missed vaccinations. She made Kylee so tense that she snapped at Jade over the slightest thing. Not good. None of it was any good.

We have serious concerns about your parenting, Kylee.

Serious concerns. That meant she stank as a mum. And if the bitch ever needed an excuse to take Jade away, well, Kylee had just delivered her one on a platter. Klepto mum. A crim as well as a pothead. That would go down well in the Children's Court. A free pass to take Jade away while she rotted in jail. We have to escape, she thought, fly away while we still can.

The Thought had been with her for a while now, worming inside her head. It had scared the shit out of her at first and she couldn't tell anyone. Not ever. But what lay ahead of her, and what hope did Jade have? Fuck all. That's why The Thought kept coming back, looking more familiar with each visit, wearing down her resistance, insistent as a young guy with a hard-on who kept bothering you until he got his way.

"Let's get dressed up, Jade, we're gonna have a roof party," she said. "I want you to look really pretty," she added, with a lump in her throat.

She drank the last stubby in the fridge as she helped Jade into her fairy dress. It was a bit tight, but it was the best she could do. Finding something for herself was harder. She rummaged through the cupboard and settled on the burgundy jumper that mum had given her in Year 8 after she'd taken part in school athletics. She hadn't won anything but her mum had been proud regardless when she showed her the green *Participant* ribbon. Mum was already sick then. Kylee had loved that jumper. It made her look like a girl from some fancy private school, so she never wore it in public. She put it on at night though, to do her homework.

Tears welled up in her eyes as she remembered those quiet nights in the weatherboard house in Nunawading. Sunk in the orange bean-bag, watching telly in her pyjamas. Before the leukaemia got mum. Before foster care. Before Dave. Before it all went off the rails. Still, no good crying about it now.

She found Jade's magic wand under the couch and they snuck out the door. "You have to be very quiet," she said, "this is our own, super secret roof party."

"Yay!" cheered Jade.

"Shush!"

"Sorry Mummy, I forgot." That glint of fear flashed across Jade's eyes, as if she expected a slap.

"That's okay, baby."

She opened the fire door and they snuck up the concrete stairs to the roof. The roof access should have been blocked, but never was, and Kylee had often come here at night for a smoke, looking at the lights of Melbourne, watching the toy cars below trickle through Rathdowne Street to the CBD, wondering where so many people might be going.

"It's windy!" said Jade, "I don't like it."

"You'll see lots of houses if I hold you up," said Kylee.

She took Jade in her arms and walked to the edge of the building. Kylee could smell soy sauce. The afternoon light was fading and the pinkish glow in the high clouds meant tomorrow would be warm and sunny. No deal. Three crows wheeled over the Carlton Baths. In the distance a plane was slowly climbing, a steel bird with too much to carry.

"I don't like it here," said Jade, "I'm scared. I wanna go back in."

"Mummy loves ya, you know that, don't you?" Kylee asked, clamping Jade against her chest. The course fabric of a fairy wing scratched her cheek.

"Yes, Mummy. Can we go now? I'm cold."

Kylee opened her mouth to say something else, something that would make things better, but she could only taste her tears.

So she jumped.

THE EVENING NEWS

Kurt pulled up the stiff rubber spout of the cask, pouring himself a glass of cabernet sauvignon.

"Hmm, Château de la Casque 2008—not bad," he muttered, taking advantage of Emma's absence to trot out his much-used line once again without attracting scorn.

He turned on the international news on SBS. Another suicide bombing in Helmand province in Afghanistan. Ten dead. In the US, President-elect Barack Obama had announced the composition of his administration. Funny how the Yanks have such a long lead time for all these political processes. The four-yearly ritual of the primaries. The mumbo-jumbo of the party conventions. The long wait until the president-elect finally takes office. Here in Australia you just vote and by the time of the late night news you know who's won. That person is sworn in the following working day and gets on with the job.

He switched to the ABC news. Court cases followed by sports news. Then an item that made him sit up straight: a woman in her early twenties had jumped off the roof of a housing commission flat in Carlton. Footage of the familiar grey high rise, the wheelie bins at its base, police tape along the crumbly concrete path.

"In a tragic twist," said the newsreader, "the woman took her six-year-old daughter with her."

"Oh my god, no," Kurt said, "surely not!" He felt nauseous. Hold on, he thought, there's other mums in that building and Jade's not the only six-year-old. He tried to regulate his breathing as he flicked across the other channels. Caught the end of the same footage on Channel Seven—nothing else.

He thought of his last visit in that grimy flat on the sixteenth floor. Kylee had been down, but no more than usual. He pictured the yellow speckled picnic table with the unopened mail shoved underneath the jar of instant coffee. Bills, reminders, letters from the Parole Board. The weekly ritual of opening these messengers from a hostile world, one by one, as Kylee watched, rubbing her fingers. She was off ice by that stage, but fragile, very anxious. Still, he could not imagine her jumping to her death, let alone taking Jade with her. Had to be someone else.

He went into the study and checked the news online. Found a short article on the ABC website. The incident had happened last night, it said.

This story will be updated as further information comes to hand.

He hit the refresh button, just in case.

Kurt felt confused, keen to find out whether this was a tragedy that had befallen strangers or whether—inconceivably—Kylee and Jade were no more. Kylee had no evil in her, but could he vouch for her despair? Had she changed since that last visit? And Jade—oh god…

He had told Kylee, on that rainy morning, that he was changing jobs, transferring to Eastern Outreach. Her blue eyes made him look down, as if he had just admitted to something base. He had expected Kylee to arc up, but she remained impassive, expressionless, which unsettled him more than an outburst would have. As he explained that a new case worker would be allocated, Jade had pushed in with a sheet of paper: "I drawn a fairy. It's for you."

He swallowed. He had to know. Grabbed his mobile and rang his former supervisor at Northern Outreach.

~

That hollow feeling, sickening emptiness. It made Kurt think of that other phone call, last year. Emma's dad had been admitted for minor surgery. They were due to pick him up the same afternoon. But at 2:00 p.m. the nurse rang, all polite and circumspect. Emma's dad had suffered a cardiac arrest. Just one phone call, one sentence, that changes lives, irrevocably. What if you put the receiver down, Kurt had thought, what if you ran away, pretended the call never happened? He felt the same impulse now. Still sat on the couch when Emma returned from her shopping trip.

"The last of the Chrissie presents," she called, holding up two shopping bags. "Yay! Go me!"

He stared at her. The smile disappeared off her face.

"Kurt, what's happened?" She put her shopping bags down on the hallway tiles.

He gestured at his mobile on the coffee table.

"What's wrong Kurt? Are your parents okay?"

"Oh Em—" His voice quavered. "Kylee and Jade are dead. It was on the news…"

"Kylee and Jade?"

"The single mum in Carlton. The daughter who draws all those fairies, remember? The mum had been on ice…"

"Oh Kurt, no! That's awful. What happened?"

"She jumped off the top of the building. Took Jade with her."

"Oh Kurt," Emma gasped, "how could she do that? That's dreadful." She covered her mouth with her hand. Started crying.

Kurt walked over and hugged her.

"I can't believe she could do this," he said, "I feel all empty inside."

"Oh honey. I remember your stories now… But are you sure it's them?"

"I rang Mick. He confirmed it all… Kylee had gone into a tailspin again after she lost her job."

"I didn't know she worked."

"Part-time apparently, as a cleaner. Got sacked for pilfering, Mick said, but he also mentioned something about shoplifting. Sounded like something recent; it was a bit confusing. Mick figured Kylee was convinced she was headed for jail again."

Emma shook her head. "At least they'd still be alive. I can't understand how a woman could kill her own child, how..." Her voice trailed off.

"I know... You just feel gutted." Kurt's eyes welled up again. "Poor Kylee, poor poor Jade. Six years old. Holy fuck."

"I don't know how you can say *poor Kylee*. She killed her kid... I have no sympathy for her."

"But you didn't know her, Em. What she's done is horrendous, beyond comprehension, but she was not a bad person. One day I'll probably curse her for what's she's done to Jade..."

"One day?"

"Right now I don't feel anger... maybe because it doesn't feel real yet, that Jade's gone, forever... I feel dazed... crushed, immensely saddened that people in our midst can be driven to such despair."

"This isn't about sociology or demographics, Kurt. There's many poor people. Single mums without support. Quite a few of them will feel cornered, desperate. Doesn't turn them into murderers. Child killers..."

That wasn't like Emma, Kurt thought. When we experience brutality, we often allow our language to harden in response. That's how violence can feed off itself. He decided to let it go.

He looked at Emma without really seeing her. "I should have stayed at Northern Outreach. I sometimes got through to Kylee; she'd started trusting me. I might have been able to settle her, shown her a way out. A different way out..."

"Oh Kurt, I understand how you must feel. But don't blame yourself... This is so terribly sad. Come here."

They hugged in front of the television. Over Emma's shoulder, Kurt half registered an ad for a furniture store. Mum, dad and two kids ensconced on a generous leather couch. *Togetherness*, the voiceover said, *the spirit of Christmas*. He shut his eyes.

FULL MOON, CHEAP WINE

They had talked until two o'clock and gone to bed exhausted. Emma had dozed off quickly. The light of the full moon filtered through the venetian blinds and Kurt could discern the outline of all objects in the bedroom. Emma's metallic bedside light held hostage a shard of moonlight. This cask wine was making him poetic. The slats of the blinds looked like a gigantic xylophone. In the top right corner of the window he saw the familiar soft orange glow—a lozenge of streetlight crowned with liquidambar leaves.

His eyelids: lumpy slabs, yet he could not fall asleep. Fall. Jesus. His gaze shifted to Emma sleeping next to him. Gratitude welled up in his heart, gratitude for being alive. Sentimental fool. He could see her form through the thin sheet. If he was a character in a novel, he could wake her up now and they could have consolation sex. *Their hot bodies locked together in a passionate embrace.* Stuff like that. But he was a social worker in the suburbs and he had just lost two people. And all he could think of was sex. Surely this was some sort of moral deficiency.

He rolled over and stared at the wall. The rectangular reflection of Marcel Duchamp's *Nude Descending a Staircase*—a cheap print picked up at St. Kilda Market. Right now, he felt like the figure in that painting: fragmented, a clatter of shadows. Sure, he loved order and structure and neatness and all that. But deep down he also knew it was only a game, a set of preferences, his weirdo default setting—not an organising principle for the world at large. Hmm, getting all philosophical now. He burped.

Buddhism understood chaos, Kurt decided. Everything interrelated, everything transient. Things certainly felt interrelated right now, not to say jumbled. And transient, ah well... He got out of bed and walked to the ensuite. He lifted the toilet seat and emptied his bladder. Washed his hands, carefully dried them.

Maybe I should meditate, he thought. But first another drink. The kitchen light seemed inordinately bright. All the glasses were in the dishwasher so he took a mug and held it under the spout of the cask. A purply spurt washed up against its sides. There would be an investigation and he would probably be called upon to testify. A coronial inquiry, for sure, as these were reportable deaths. A child death inquiry commissioned by the department, maybe. Possibly a police investigation. And, if they were unlucky, a full-blown Royal Commission. He could see it already—a neatly bound white paper. *Report of the Royal Commission of Inquiry into the Deaths of K.W. and J.W.; Victorian Government Printing Service, Melbourne, 2012* or thereabouts. And it would say what these investigations always say: improve service training, document case planning decisions, improve communication and coordination between providers. Top bureaucrats would insert a generic statement about how the government of the day was committed to *strengthening service provision,* carefully worded to ensure it could not be mistaken for an enforceable recommendation with funding implications. The report would make news headlines on the day of its release and maybe Mick's boss would end up on *The 7:30 Report.* And then the whole sorry thing would subside and the report would sit on a shelf, gather dust, fade and be ditched in the next office move. But Kylee and Jade would still be dead.

He opened the fridge and took out a block of cheddar. Where was the cheese slicer—oh, here. He sliced off crumbly little rectangles and placed them on crackers. A midnight feast, except it was way later. He rinsed his mouth with more wine. He would fight back, he decided.

Things would be different. He'd fight for this Gecko kid. Engage him. Support him. Keep him on the straight and narrow.

Kurt went to the lounge room, sat down on the couch and switched on the reading lamp. He picked up yesterday's paper and saw that Emma had gotten stuck in her sudoku puzzle. He leafed through the paper. A journalist in Baghdad had thrown his shoe at President Bush and called him a dog. The Yanks had thrown worse at the Iraqis... A United Nations court had convicted some Rwandan colonel, a Hutu, for his complicity in the 1994 massacre of 800,000 Tutsis. Kurt marvelled at that number. Eight-hundred-thousand deaths. A number so enormous as to be almost meaningless. Or not meaningless—beyond comprehension. Like killing everyone in Bendigo eight times over. He could not get his head around 800,000 deaths. He couldn't get his head around two. Kurt flung the paper on the coffee table, switched the lamp off and sat in the dark for a while. So the Rwandans had nabbed their colonel, he thought—who do you bring to justice when a woman jumps off a block of flats with her kid? And Kylee herself, he thought: a murderer now. A label both undeniable and inadequate. But anger was creeping in now, at how Kylee's decision had robbed Jade of her choices, her future, her life.

He got up, bumped his shin against the edge of the coffee table, swore under his breath. Felt his way to the bedroom and lay down, hoping to sink in a deep sleep. His eyes so heavy, his head a blur now. His brain a no-go zone. He pictured it draped in plastic garlands: *police line—do not cross*. The sheets felt clammy. There would have to be autopsies, of course. Don't go there.

He fell into a fitful sleep. In his dream he was back in Belgium. He had just separated from Renata but was reminded of her on every street corner by a billboard advertising *Renata Shoes,* her boutique having inexplicably grown into a business empire. His own father had somehow bought 800,000 pairs of shoes and proceeded to throw those at Kurt. They whizzed around his head in all shapes and sizes. "Soft Italian shoes," his dad said, reading the label before flinging the footwear at his only son. "Trekking shoes," he said. "You dog, you had to migrate. Left us behind." Then his mother appeared from behind a stack of shoeboxes. The vivacious, elegant woman he had known suddenly morphed into the one gutted by dementia, her hollow eyes staring in different directions. "Mum," he wanted to shout, overcome by terror, love and grief; but somehow he could not utter a sound. "Weren't you looking after a little girl?" she mused. "Yes he was, wasn't he, Leo? But he threw her off the roof." Kurt twisted and turned, wanted to defend himself but his mouth was sealed with police tape.

He woke up drenched in sweat. A demolition crew was hammering on the inside of his forehead. His mouth a brackish lagoon at low tide. Emma was now facing him, still fast asleep. White flag, Kurt thought. It's just too much. Kylee. Jade. Mum. Belgium. Fran Esposito. White flag. Outside magpies were warbling about the new dawn. A truck started up somewhere. And the universe, selective in its mercy, allowed Kurt to slide into slumber.

JANUARY 2009

RED ROCKS BEACH

Libby headed straight for the furthest part of the beach: past the families, past the Lebanese boys playing cricket, past the smooching couple, not stopping until she reached the rust-coloured outcrop that had given Red Rocks Beach its name. She felt grateful for the sudden shelter. The hot wind had sandblasted her face and twirled her skirt around her spindly legs but she had marched on, determined to be out of public view. Her beach towel had sand on it as soon as she put it down. She secured a corner of it with her beach bag and brushed the sand off the light blue cotton fish that eyed her from below. It was no use. The wind was howling, a high-pitched banshee wail that drowned out even the surf. It reminded her of the cheap round vacuum cleaner at home when she was little. She would sit on the floral rug in front of the fireplace while her mum stabbed at the skirting boards. The noise was threatening—the roar of an ancient dragon. It was also strangely reassuring, in a suffocating kind of way, preventing you from thinking, just like raindrops running down the windowpanes on a wintry afternoon, drawing a veil over the outside world. Hey, she was getting all poetic again. Better save all that for her English lit essays. Wonder who the new teacher would be? Stupid Mr Kerslow, leaving them all in the lurch. Taking a year off to travel. Something you did after high school, not in your forties. Hadn't he had a gap year? He was the one always going on about continuity and now he'd just shot through, abandoning them at the start of their final year to a teacher new to the school. Libby pursed her mouth and flicked a March fly off her ankle.

The plastic of her beach bag had already gone soft in the heat. She took out a tube of sunscreen, factor 30 plus. She pulled up her skirt and squeezed a fat white squirt of cream out of the tube. It lay there glistening on her freckled thigh, looking out of place, self-assured and unspeakable, a maggot maybe. With a shudder she squashed the blob, rubbed it down to her knee, over the bony bits, down to her ankles. Then repeated the process for her other leg. Next she took off her sunnies, gathered her thick blond hair into a ponytail and slid a hairband around it. She applied the cream to her face, massaging it into her forehead much longer than was necessary. Libby loved the soothing effect of repetitive movement. In bed she would often massage her left wrist between the thumb and index finger of her right hand, in soft circular motion until she felt drowsy, ready to slide into oblivion. If she had a boyfriend, she would like him to just stroke her back, over and over again. Right, as if that would ever happen. Maybe she should morph into a cat, like in an *anime* movie. Then she would sit on her owner's lap and purr as she was patted.

As a cat, of course, she would have to eat cat food, and that thought made her retch. Oh no, not here... She looked around, but apart from a one-legged beady-eyed seagull no one was paying her any attention. In spite of the heat she kept her top on: exposure was to be avoided at all costs. She had invented countless excuses over the years to avoid the swimming carnival at school and other events involving change rooms and states of undress. She had invoked headaches, period pains and scores of distant relatives dying interstate. After so much effort, she was not going to disrobe, not even in front of a seagull.

She squeezed the tube again and with an obscene sound it spat another blob of white on her hand. She particularly hated applying cream to her feet. No matter how careful you were, they would invariably already be covered in sand. Spreading the cream just created a gritty mess, like coating yourself with sandpaper. Gross. Libby also hated her feet when her weight was down. Dark blue arteries would show as the flesh retreated into narrow valleys between the bones of her feet. They made her think of bat wings: all gossamer mystery and tiny folds of purplish flesh. So unlike the smooth Barbie dolls she played with as a child, the rainbow ponies and the twinkling fairies. The world was all new and shiny then; Mum was at home, Dad was still there and she had disappointed no one yet.

I'd better read, she thought, 'cause I'm drifting away from my happy place here. She pulled a copy of *The Great Gatsby* out of her beach bag and looked at the cover. It featured a photo from the movie made in the seventies, with—was that Robert Redford? Mia something? Anyhow, she looked all swish and classy with her Charleston hat. Libby sighed and looked at the seagull that was still perched on its one dark pink leg.

"Hey buddy, want some chips?"

The bird blinked and moved its beak as she pulled a shiny yellow pack of chips out of her bag. Mum had put those in. Always trying to feed her. It was puffed up like an over-inflated rubber cushion and the foil crackled in the wind as she opened it. The bird hopped closer, using his wings for balance.

"You can be in my club, The Rejects."

She tossed it a potato chip, which was blown away by the wind, cartwheeling over the sand. Stumpfoot attempted to chase it, but gave up when a flock of gulls lifted off from the waterline and descended upon the chip. Libby threw more chips into the wind and was soon surrounded by a group of squawking gulls, with Stumpfoot standing back, at the periphery. She felt like crying.

"Yoohoo."

Libby looked at the approaching figure. A girl, waving. That hair— Monique! Libby waved back. How did Monique know she was here?

"Hey girl!"

"Hey Monique."

"Oh my god, Libby, I'm totally exhausted. You couldn't go any further?"

"Sorry."

"You're, like, almost in New Zealand. And me slogging through this hot sand."

"It's easier if you walk on the hard wet sand."

"I suppose… I'd just done my feet, kept looking down. Aren't they pretty?"

Libby looked at Monique's toenails. They were lacquered kingfisher blue, matching Monique's bikini and offsetting her black hair. Raven black hair, Libby thought, like Snow White. Monique flicked open her beach towel next to Libby's and sat down.

"You're nice and brown already," Libby said, looking sideways. And my legs are pale, she thought, like those sickly shoots that sometimes spring up under that sheet of plastic near the compost bin.

"Thanks. I bought this tanning cream last week, it's called Golden Bodies or something. Got it at that Nature Enhanced shop. You know, the one in Eastland? Near Myers? Tracey put me onto that, her cousin works there. She can give you a discount."

"Hey, how did you know I was here?"

"Well, you remember Jason?"

"The guy from Brent's party who—"

"Yeah, him! He's a hoot! Well anyway, long story short, his dad had the lawnmower for their holiday house repaired in Melbourne and asked Jason, could he, like, take it back to Philip Island in his ute. So Jason goes, do I wanna come down for the day and I go: sure!"

"So where's Jason?"

"He had to go see a mate of his in Ventnor, so I said, can he drop me off at your mum's holiday house. He's picking me up after lunch and then we're back to his place for a bit of you know what."

"Ugh," said Libby, "I don't want to know."

"Oh don't be such a killjoy." Monique frowned. "Anyway, I thought you'd like to see me. Your mum said you might be here. Reading most likely." She pointed at Libby's novel. "So what are you reading?"

Libby held up the book with the defeated air of someone caught red-handed.

"*The Great Gatsby!*" Monique exclaimed. "You're reading a school book! On the beach! Are you for real? Girl, we seriously need to get you a life. If I tell Nikki this—"

"Please don't."

"Okay, but seriously, I've got to say, this is pretty weird!"

Libby started packing her belongings.

"Hey," said Monique, "don't be like that. I'm sorry. I just got here. I want us to have a good time. Let's go for a swim."

What about your nails, Libby wanted to ask. She thought better of it.

They waded in together, holding hands, jumping through the breakers and laughing. When they were deep enough, they swam parallel to the beach for a while, their young bodies lifted by the ancient green waves of the heaving sea.

Back on her towel Libby could taste the salt drops on her lips. Seawater had pooled in her left ear. She turned her head sideways and a warm jet flowed out. She put her sunnies on and settled into her own imprint in the sand underneath her, caressed by the warmth of the sun above her. Things may work out after all, she thought.

"I'm bored," said Monique, "let's head back."

Libby nodded. They packed up their gear.

"I really like your mum. She seems nice."

"Hmm," said Libby.

They strolled back along the water's edge. The wind had subsided.

As Monique described her cousin's engagement outfit, Libby waded through the shifting boundaries between land and sea. The deep brown sand opening its pores to the light only to be overrun by the next silver blue wave, its memories of a brilliant sun fractured, the steps of a random girl erased right after creation.

MIDNIGHT CONVERSATION

Our stories are so different, Emma ruminated as she drove along Harris Gully Road. Operatic lives for some, bonsai lives for others. Hers was definitely among the latter. The irony of having taught English literature for all those years, helping kids understand all these strong emotions, grand visions and impossible dreams. The blind leading the blind. Maybe it would be good to be a careers adviser. Still help kids while allowing yourself to sink into obscurity.

Her parents had seen plenty of drama. As teenagers they'd lived through the Second World War in Latvia. In the second year of the war her dad had seen a Jewish classmate shot before his eyes by a fascist militia unit. In the last year Red Army soldiers had requisitioned her mum's house. That's all they ever let on... After the war, as a young married couple, they somehow ended up in a displaced persons camp run by the Red Cross in Cremona, in Northern Italy. For almost two years they lived in a dilapidated classroom that they shared with a perpetually drunk Polish refugee... With their vocabulary enriched by Italian cooking terms and Polish curses, they accepted an offer for resettlement in Australia, even though it meant Mum had to put up with being seasick for six weeks.

And Kurt too had lived his life on a broad canvas. The abrupt course corrections after a protected, uneventful youth in Belgium: a divorce, a migration, numerous career changes. And his job, of course, steeped in turmoil, controversy—tragedy, of late.

But Midnight took the crown. Nothing about that woman was straightforward. She'd been born in Vietnam but was ethnically Chinese. Spoke five languages, including French and Danish. Had gone from asylum seeker to fashion photographer and shop owner. A vegetarian who would go on a burger binge a couple of times a year. Emma smiled. She couldn't wait to see her friend.

She passed Gold Memorial Road. Warrandyte was an old gold mining town that had grown on the southern bank of the Yarra river. The village centre was like a heart. Three main roads led into it like arteries. Its chambers, to the south, consisted of weatherboard dwellings hidden in dense bush. And alongside the arteries, each period of its history had left a cluster of deposits. First a pub, bakery and post office. Then the Mechanics' Institute. In the seventies a bus stop and a library. In the eighties a tennis court and a real estate office. Finally, when Warrandyte was rediscovered in the nineties as a favoured Sunday outing destination for Melburnians, a sprinkling of coffee shops and a cluster of art, antique and souvenir shops, where you could buy anything from an art nouveau mirror to a colonial rocking chair or a Sioux dreamcatcher. And Midnight had bought one of these little shops, the weatherboard one with the purple shutters near the bridge. She'd named it *Oriental Vibes*. It was crammed to the ceiling with Afghan rugs and Nepalese silk, Buddha statues, jewellery and incense sticks.

"Why is she called Midnight?" Kurt had asked when Emma mentioned her on their first date. Emma had her story down pat. She had explained on numerous occasions that she and Midnight had done Year 12 French together, and the French teacher had corrected a boy who mispronounced Midnight's surname.

"'Nguyen' is one of the ten most common surnames in Victoria," Madame Leclerc had said, "so you may as well learn how to pronounce it." She wrote the name on the blackboard: "'Minh Nguyen' is pronounced *minwin*, almost like *minuit* in French, which, as you Einsteins all know, means midnight."

The class had laughed, as they'd all poked fun at Minh's habit of going to bed around 8:00 p.m. so she would feel fresh the following day. Calling her Midnight was like calling a ginger cat Bluey or a bald man Curly. So of course the nickname had stuck.

Midnight had told her story to Emma way back in Year 10 when they were sharing a tent on a school camp at Wilson's Prom. She had come out as a refugee in 1979, on her family's second attempt. The first time round, the smugglers had pocketed the money and abandoned twenty bedraggled families on the beach, where they were picked up by Vietnamese police. It meant two years in a re-education camp. Minh's father taught her French there, at night, when it was too dark to sew hessian bags. When Minh was fifteen, the family tried again. One hundred and eight people crammed into a rickety fishing boat that in its past had been crewed by five fishermen. She remembered the puttering engine, the competing smells of the diesel fuel and the latrine, the rusted crab pots, the faded blue and white paint along the sides of the cabin, the old men spitting on the deck when they could have aimed their stringy mucus at the yellow waters of the South China Sea. She told Emma about the hunger and the sweat and the copper sun overhead. The starry nights and the fear of pirates. They did not encounter any storms, just one night of heavy swells which made almost everyone on board vomit. One night, sleeping on the spongy deck planks, she woke up when someone bumped her toes. In the moonlight she could make out the old man with the wispy beard and the yellow headband. He stared right past her, with lifeless eyes, she said, and then he stepped over the side, just like that. By the time she'd woken her parents, the sea was a dark blue mirror again, its waves lapping the sides of the boat. Nothing to substantiate her story —the old man had probably just gone down into the hold, her father said. Hunger could make you imagine things. But Midnight knew better.

They had both cried, that night in the tent, and sworn to be best friends for life.

Emma pulled up just past the bus shelter, in the shadow of a majestic gum tree. Such luxury visiting Midnight on a weekday. Finding a parking space along the bank of the Yarra or in the narrow main street was nigh impossible when the day trippers were out in force. She crossed the road. Kookaburras called out from across the river.

She pushed the door of the stone cottage open. A string of bells chimed.

"Hey," Midnight called out as Emma entered, "Happy new year!"

"A happy new year to you too," Emma said. They hugged.

"It's not Chinese new year yet, but anyway…" said Emma.

"Oh sweetness, I'll use any excuse to party! And anyway, my mother reckons I'm becoming a banana!"

"A banana?"

"Yes, yellow on the outside and white on the inside!" She laughed heartily.

"Why would she say that?"

"Lots of stuff. Me belting out Cindy Lauper songs instead of devoutly sitting in front of her little Buddhist shrine. Preferring burgers over her turgid dumplings. Not to mention the elephant in the room of course—Gordon."

"How's things with Gordon?"

"We're fine, getting along really well. Mum's deadset against him, though. She wants me to find a nice Vietnamese Buddhist boy."

"A boy—hasn't she figured out yet we're in our forties now?"

"I'm still her baby, Em. It's not funny. Tran and Hung moved out years ago even though they're younger than I am."

"I normally have these sorts of conversations with sixteen-year-olds. Mum doesn't like my boyfriend, what do I do?"

"I know, Em. It sounds ridiculous. But I respect mum and I don't want to hurt her feelings—"

"At the expense of putting your life on hold. And you used to be such a rebel."

"What can I say, Em. I don't know what to do."

"How's Gordon with all this?"

"He's pretty good actually. Another guy would have walked. He's very patient."

"Well, you're lucky there."

"And how have you been? It's been ages!"

"Guess what—I have a new job! Careers teacher and counsellor. And guess where."

"Surprise me!"

"Banksia High!"

"Oooh, fabulous! We'll be able to have lunch together!"

"Well, maybe not lunch, with yard duty and all that, but we should at least be able to see each other more often."

"That's great, Em. The counselling too—you'll be able to use your second degree! And careers, you said, so no more English literature?"

"That's right. I needed a change. I'm a bit over teaching literature to the pubescent ones. They're impervious to all notions of literary technique, you know. Every discussion, every essay ends up in value judgements about character and morality."

"Ah, young people these days," Midnight grumbled, "at least we had some nihilism."

Emma smiled. "Maybe it was me. Maybe I just wasn't any good at inspiring them."

"It's not you," Midnight said emphatically, looking Emma in the eyes. "It's never you. You're such a talented woman. Get that social worker hubby of yours to teach you about positive self-talk. How is he, by the way?"

"He's going through a rough patch. Did you hear about that woman jumping off a building in Carlton last month? With her child?"

"Oh, that's terrible. I must have missed that."

"We were so upset. How could you do such a thing? To your own child? Kurt had worked with that family before he transferred. He knew them both quite well."

"How awful for him."

"Yeah, he was devastated. Thinks it might have played out differently if he'd stayed at Northern…"

Midnight sighed. "I get that. If you know the person you start thinking could I have done something? But he mustn't blame himself."

"That's what I keep saying… Easier said than done though. And it's not as if he's enjoying his new job either. He hates his boss."

"Oh dear."

"And then there's his parents. Kurt's dad is just exhausted from caring for his wife, as you can imagine. He rang us again last week. Said he'd had to stop on his walk to the supermarket. He had vomited, from fatigue and exhaustion. But he'd pushed on, he said, and done the shopping—all of this with Irene in tow, you realise, because he can't leave her alone."

"Poor things. Can't they get any help, or have their shopping home delivered?"

"A council worker's helping them out three days a week now. Kurt arranged all of that online. And his mum's in respite care one morning a week. But that's not enough. Still leaves them without support for half the time. And they just won't have shopping home delivered. That inconveniences others… Taking a cab's not on either; that costs money."

Midnight rolled her eyes.

"Kurt actually got angry with Leo on the phone, when he told him about the vomiting. 'You're well beyond the point where you can still manage things, Dad,' I overheard him say, 'the time's come to sell your place and move into care, so you can both be supported.'"

"What did his dad say?"

Emma paused. "Leo started crying… Awkward. Awful. It must have felt like a capitulation. But it also meant relief, the thought that he could hand over the reins, that more help was on its way."

"Emma, how difficult for you guys, and from such a distance too."

"Yeah, and Kurt promised to help his dad, so he's flying to Belgium next week to help Leo and Irene move into a nursing home and to place their house on the market. It's full of stuff, so Kurt will have to go through all their belongings and sort something out. He's taken three weeks' leave."

"Can they get into a nursing home just like that?"

"They were already on several waiting lists but they'd declined every offer that came along. Corinne, the council worker, reckons she can swing something for them."

"She sounds like good value."

"She is. She's a godsend, especially with Kurt being an only child. He'd have to sort it all out by himself otherwise. And Belgium is like a foreign country to him. He left in his early twenties, so he hasn't got the foggiest about health insurance or aged care in Belgium, let alone pensions or real estate."

"What a mess."

Emma nodded. "Anyhow, I have been staring at those silk scarves behind you. Do you want to show me what you've got?"

"I'd love to," Midnight replied.

SHAUN IN CHARGE

"Did you replace the fan belt on that Holden?" asked Bruce, his face all sweaty.

"Yeah, I'm all done," said Shaun.

"Okey-dokey, see you tomorrow then."

Shaun strolled down the concrete driveway to his car. A 1970s Ford Falcon GT Coupe Classic, lovingly restored. Midnight blue, mag wheels. No air conditioning though. He always parked it next to the rubbish skip. Bruce often teased him that it was hard to tell the two apart. Shaun chucked his tool bag on the back seat and got behind the steering wheel. He looked at his watch. Still early, enough time to drop in and see Tags, have a beer.

He loved driving this old beast. It was generous and forgiving. It swayed like a schooner on corners and burned like a rocket on the open road. His left hand found every button without looking, his ears understood every noise, his eyes directed the wheels. Like an extension of himself. And if something went wrong, he could fix it at home—no on-board computers to deal with, just pure mechanics.

He pulled up in front of Tags's wheelie bin on the nature strip. A foraging magpie looked up, flapped away through the afternoon heat.

Loud music—somebody was home. Tags hopefully. With a bit of luck he could get his fifty bucks back.

Shaun opened the door and went in. All curtains were drawn and the room smelled of beer. Gecko turned round and looked at him. The boy looked wan in the blue glow of Tags's computer.

"You're sitting here in the dark, mate. It's beautiful out there."

"It's too hot."

"Tags not around?"

"Nah, he got a call about his mum. He's gone to the hospital."

"His mum's in hospital?"

"Yeah, but nothing serious I think. He said something about insulin and stuff. His mum's got diabetes. She drinks way too much."

"That's no good, poor thing. Although, speaking of drink, I'm pretty thirsty meself."

"Tags bought a slab of beer yesterday. Actually."

"I'll help meself then." Shaun grinned. "The bugger still owes me fifty bucks anyway. Let's sit outside on the porch and enjoy the sun. Like this track, by the way. Who is it?"

"Jackhammer Groove. I'll turn it up a bit."

They sat on the concrete slab of the porch, the music pumping from behind. Shaun stretched out his legs, enjoying the heat on his crotch. Gecko, bent forward on his rickety kitchen chair, hoodie down against the glare, clutching a lukewarm beer can with both hands, looked utterly miserable.

"That your car?" he asked, nodding in the direction of the Falcon.

"Yeah man, that's me Blue Lady." He yawned broadly. "Always faithful."

"I drove a Falcon once."

"Did ya? How old are you?"

"Sixteen, but this was a couple of years ago. Off-road, you know, at someone's place in the bush."

"Whose place?"

"Uh, an uncle. Doesn't matter."

"Tags said you had no family in Australia."

"You talk to Tags about me?" Gecko sounded peeved.

Before Shaun could answer, a commotion of limbs attracted their attention. A little old man stood on the nature strip, gesticulating wildly, mouthing an impotent tirade.

"Ugh, not that old fart again," moaned Gecko.

"You know him?"

"Lives next door. Forever complaining about the music... God, such a pain, I could belt him."

"Cool it, man, he's just an old bloke. Go inside and turn the music off."

"But—"

"Just do it," Shaun stated, calmly.

Gecko went inside, swearing and mumbling under his breath, and turned the music down. The heat, the nagging old bugger, thinking about his uncle. It was all wrong. The blood was spurting through his veins, a red mist hung over his brain. He felt like that time he had punched through the plaster wall. Tags hadn't liked that, not at all. He'd come this close to kicking him out on the street. Better cool down a bit. Gecko took a deep breath and sat down on the couch. He looked at the pale green walls, the rusty gas heater in the pretend fireplace. He sighed, stood up and got himself another beer.

Shaun came in again.

"I had a little chat with your neighbour," he announced, "Mr Harris. His wife's had a cataract—I think he means a heart attack—and needs to rest. That's why he's all worked up about the music. I talked him down a bit, said you'd keep the noise down. He'll tell 'the welfare man' if you don't."

"The welfare man?"

"He spoke to someone last week. A guy with a red plates, a government car."

"Shit. Why does he talk to the neighbours?"

"Who?"

"My new case manager," Gecko fumed. "Thought it was all meant to be confidential. 'Trust me,' he says."

Shaun raised his eyebrows and disappeared into the kitchen.

Gecko thought of his awkward meeting with that new case worker. Nervous little guy with a notebook. He snorted. Soon the holidays would be over and the whole circus would all start all over again: adults telling you what you could or couldn't do. Making promises they never kept.

Shaun came back in carrying a badly scorched chopping board with some cheese and crackers on it. He put it on the coffee table.

"Here mate, have a bite to eat."

Shaun sat down opposite Gecko. He leaned forward and took a cracker too. Rubbed some cheese crumbs from the corners of his mouth. Seemed to be building up to something.

"Hey, remember what we talked about the other day? About you dropping out?"

Great, Gecko thought, another Deep Conversation…

"What about it?"

"I reckon you should go back to school when the year starts."

"School sucks."

"I know. It can be a pain in the butt, but you can't keep living like this."

"Why not?" He'd only seen Shaun a couple of times and here he was, telling him what to do. He already had a foster dad, teachers, a case worker. He wanted a friend.

"Cause this is no life. A couple of days at school. Then someone pisses you off and you run away and hide here. You play *Savage Glory*, get pissed, have a joint with Tags. And when the food runs out you head back to your foster dad."

"I thought we were mates."

"We are, you idiot. That's why I'm telling you to pull your finger out."

Gecko stared at his runners.

"You can't let others call the shots," Shaun continued.

"What do you mean?" Gecko asked sullenly.

Shaun had to think for a moment. Gecko, begrudgingly, liked this about Shaun, how he didn't have all his words lined up, ready to bombard you. Gecko got that: finding the right words was hard, crafting a sentence a challenge.

"Okay," Shaun said finally, "this may sound lame, but hear me out."

Gecko shrugged.

"Think about the Steel Cathedrals raid in *Savage Glory*," Shaun began.

"What about it?"

"What happens if everyone hangs back, waiting for the Steampunk Raiders to attack?"

"You get wiped."

"Exactly. And what do you do to win the game?"

"You rush them, you capture their energy nodes and stuff—you know the game, I don't know why you're asking me this crap."

"Because life can be like that, mate. If you hang back, you just cop everybody else's shit. You have to fight for what you want because nobody is going to give it to you, you know. You may not get it, but at least you tried."

Gecko mulled this over. "What if you don't know what you want?"

"Give it time," Shaun said, "I can't just pull me spuds out of the soil back in Kinglake. They have to grow, that takes time."

Gecko marvelled at the image of Shaun pulling potatoes out of the soil. It seemed odd that Shaun the grease monkey, with his grubby hands and his clothes smelling of oil, also farmed veggies up on the mountain. He sighed, felt his muscles relax.

"What if you never figure out what you want to be?"

"I reckon make yourself stronger while you wait. Talk to people. Learn a trade. Take in everything that may come in handy one day." Shaun took the last cheese cracker. "You know, when I was little me dad once gave me a turtle."

"A turtle?"

"Yep, a turtle. I called him Jimmy. Fed him every morning and waited for him to grow. It seemed as if he never would. Except in the family photos, over the years, Jimmy got bigger and bigger, his shell got stronger. I loved how he used to peek out from that hole in his shell —looked a bit like that ET movie, you know."

"Do you still have him?"

"Nah." A gloomy expression fell over Shaun's face.

"What happened?"

"It wasn't good."

Gecko insisted. "What happened?"

"Shiv and his mates turned up one day…"

"And?"

"They played frisbee with Jimmy."

"Bastards."

They pondered Jimmy's fate in silence for what seemed like a minute. Gecko didn't think it was an inspiring end to Shaun's pep talk. He got up and made some more crackers.

LIBBY, DRAWING

Libby loved being home by herself. Mum was at work and Nathan had been picked up by Josh's mum; he was going to the cricket or something. She could play songs on repeat for as long as she liked. Or sit and watch, taking in the scenery. Never mind that the scenery was the family home where they had lived since she was born. If you wanted to do things properly, thoroughly, there was always something to discover. There were the baby skinks, for example, heaps of them this season. They were only three centimetres long, but they liked sunbathing on the ledge of the kitchen window. And she had seen the adults fight, three of them locked together in frozen combat, on the vertical side of a redgum sleeper, each holding the neck or the tail of the other in their tiny jaw, as if acting out a secret Hindu symbol, a reptilian swastika. So weird. And the orchids had flowered again, for the first time in three years. Deep purple flowers with a lacy edge and a secret yellow column, just visible above the lip of the flower, like the fangs of a crumbly golden spider. Bet Mum or Nathan hadn't noticed any of that. Always running somewhere, always busy, always stuffing their faces with vile stuff. Meat pies, pork chops, all kinds of fatty fare. And Mum was packing on the weight. Her arms and legs looked puffy in her dark power suits, almost cylindrical. It felt oppressive to even look at her. Fancy having to carry all that weight around. Libby thought it was a special kind of arrogance, letting your cells go rampant, taking up so much space—an imposition on the universe. And to think Mum had been slim in her youth…

Libby fetched a block of drawing paper from her bedroom. Last week she had drawn the kitchen, with its multi-coloured splash-back tiles and the wood-framed seascapes that her dad had put up. This week she decided to draw the lounge room again. Every rendition was different, like her mood. Every attempt made her look at the familiar with new eyes. She lined up her graphite pencils. The lounge room, with its many textures, presented a particular challenge. There was the dark veneer of the Tasmanian oak coffee table, the stone wall around the fireplace, the rendered mudbrick of the side walls, the hand-woven straw padding between the ceiling beams, the coarse linen throws covering the couch and chairs. The stripped wooden door with its stained glass side panels, which Dad had bought when a library was being demolished, was especially difficult. So hard to capture the dappled light that fell in through the gum leaves. She could still remember the Saturday afternoon Dad had brought the door home, fastened to the back of his ute with inner tubes of old bicycles. His torn blue T-shirt was covered in dust and he was grinning like a schoolboy who had just been given his first bike. "Isn't this fantastic," he kept saying as he stepped round the ute to inspect his find from all angles. Mum had said little and gone inside to cut veggies.

This was still so much Dad's room, Libby thought, as she fleshed out her sketch in soft grey tones. Natural materials, earthy colours. Mum's real estate business had kept her so busy over the years that she'd been unable to redecorate her own home, much to her chagrin.

Libby heard the soft whirr of her mum's car coming up the drive. Here we go, she thought.

Her mum swanned in, all bangles and shopping bags. "Hi, darling. Nathan not back yet?"

"No. How was your day?" Libby followed her to the kitchen.

"Surprisingly busy for this time of year. As if everyone's stayed in Melbourne instead of heading off to the beach."

"How come we're not going back to the holiday house?"

"We've just been, darl. Remember?" her mum said, putting milk cartons in the fridge.

"Sure, only a couple of days though. I don't have to go back to school until the end of the month."

"Well, some of us have to work. And there's big changes ahead. I've been having lots of meetings with the guys at work. They agree that it'd be a good idea to establish a Comaro office in the CBD."

"In Melbourne?"

"That's where the CBD is, yes." Her mum plonked the cat food on the kitchen bench.

"Why?"

"We've pretty much saturated our coverage in the Warrandyte–Eltham corridor. Our clients like our business model and we could leverage our brand recognition to enter a new market."

Libby scrunched up her nose. "What does that even mean?"

Her mum tried to push the frozen peas into the freezer compartment. "We want to set up a branch in Melbourne and sell office space." A packet of frozen falafels fell on the floor.

"Who's going to do that?"

"You're looking at the new branch manager!" She slammed the freezer door shut with a triumphant flick. "Can't wait to tell Nathan. He'll be so thrilled."

"I'm proud of you too, Mum, well done. But you'll have a long drive in peak hour every day."

"Not quite actually. That's the other bit of my news: we'll be moving."

"Moving? Where? When?"

"To Melbourne. When things are settled. August maybe. September? We'll see."

"But Mum!"

"What?"

"Hello—Earth to Mum—I'll be doing Year 12 this year, remember? You know, final exams and all that? University entrance score—rings a bell? And you want us to move now?"

"Don't get your knickers in a knot, sweet thing. I'll get you into the best local high school. I hear those inner city schools are really good. You'll be fine; I'll work something out for you."

"Don't patronise me. How dare you make me change schools in my final year? Take me away from my friends too!"

"Oh come on Libby, what friends? Don't make this bigger than it is. You only see that Monique, don't you? She wouldn't be a great loss."

"Why, what's wrong with Monique?"

"Well, I don't know—she's not classy, is she?"

"Classy?"

"I've always thought..."

"What?"

"Well, she's a bit—you know—slutty, I reckon. The way she dresses and all."

"Slutty?"

"Always popping out of those tiny tops. The skimpy skirts... I wouldn't want my daughter to look like a streetwalker."

"Oh," snapped Libby, with intense irritation, "you can be such a bitch."

Her mum looked bewildered for a moment, then surged forward and slapped Libby.

"Don't ever talk to your mother like that again!" She rubbed the palm of her right hand. Looked confused, as if she didn't know what to do next. "You should respect your parents," she added, as an afterthought.

"What, like you respect Dad?" Libby fired back, holding her left cheek.

"That's different. He's made his bed and can lie in it. With that Karla he was so besotted with. He can have her and smoke all the weed he wants in that beloved Byron Bay of his. So pure and simple. So back to nature. His true nature, sure. Walking out on his wife, leaving behind his young son..."

"And daughter."

"Yes yes, you too. But it was especially hard for Nathan, being at such a young age."

"It's always about Nathan, isn't it? Nathan this and Nathan that. I might as well be invisible."

"Oh god, enter the drama queen! Quick, throw in some violins. What a sob story! It's not always about you, you know—"

"It's never about me." Libby trembled. "I hate you!"

Her mum sighed and put the celery in the crisper. She sat down at the kitchen table and shook her head.

"If you knew what I've been through as a single parent…" she began. Her mobile rang. She switched effortlessly back into work mode. "Comaro real estate, Melanie speaking…" she said cheerfully.

Libby swallowed. Her heart was still hammering; her cheek felt hot. She sat down at the table.

"Yes, it is…" her mum went on. "Correct… Yes… Yes, that property is still on the market… I'd be delighted to show it to you… Okay, see you in ten."

"We'll talk later," she said, shooting Libby a meaningful glance. She grabbed her keys and clipboard and marched out. The door fell shut.

Libby buried her head in her hands and closed her eyes. Mum had never slapped Nathan. She knew where she stood now. She didn't feel surprised, really, and that saddened her. But the move, the school stuff —that was new. Unsettling. She couldn't think properly, it was too much to take in—so she just listened to the sound of her breath.

After some time she got up and collected her drawing materials from the lounge room. She flicked through her work. Where was the girl who had drawn these textures and fabrics? And how had she found joy in scratching on a piece of paper? It felt like a different era. A poisonous yellow light slanted through the kitchen window, sullied the scenes she had drawn.

YELLOW STICKY

"Damn," said Kurt, staring at the peeling door paint of number 12 again, "dammit." Why did he have to score the only kid in Melbourne without a mobile phone? He rang once more and waited while he ran through the options in his mind. He had to see Gecko before flying to Europe. You just could not promise support and then shoot through. That would merely confirm what Bob Morrison had thought all along. Worse, it would undo whatever progress he'd made with Gecko during that first visit. He had to see the boy before he flew out. That meant today.

He rang Bob Morrison but got no answer. Gecko might still be in Silvan, though. Kurt took a deep breath. One thing at a time. He had to visit the Robinsons and then, back in the office, write up the McCafferty case and bring his Childproof entries up to date. He decided to pop in at Bob's place after he'd seen the Robinsons. That wouldn't be too much of a detour and it was his only chance of seeing Gecko.

"The Robinsons, James, and don't spare the horses," Kurt instructed his imaginary chauffeur. Great to have staff, even if you had to invent them. Emma and he often fantasised about tasks they would delegate to Boris and Natasha, two imaginary refugees from Russia who were happy to attend to household and gardening chores in exchange for board and lodging. Emma was such a good sport that you could tell her stupid stuff like that and be confident that she wouldn't blab. It would not be a good career move if he became known in the sector as the social worker whose feudal fantasies involved taking advantage of refugees. God, there was so much drivel in his head—where did it all come from? His thoughts were not just solitary clouds above a placid lake, more like a contrail of brain farts.

Still, he reflected, thoughts could lead you down far darker alleys. He'd been doing child protection work for, what, eight years now, and it had remained as confronting as on day one. Cases of emotional abuse or of neglect could be heart-rending, but Kurt secretly wished that there was a special hell for people who physically or sexually abused kids. He could never say that publicly; and he also realised that his private views were not wholly fair, for some perpetrators were repeating abuse that they had been subjected to themselves. But that was rational thinking, the part of his brain that had shut down instantly when he visited the Robinsons that time and saw Lucy's crayon drawing of a small girl, no more than a red circle really, sheltering in a blue house edged on the bottom left of the page. And all around the blue house she had drawn, in angular black stripes, stick figures with penises. He had been thankful that Marianne's partner had not been there on that occasion, for Kurt had found it difficult to mask his rising anger.

Marianne Robinson looked much happier when he arrived at her unit. Kurt realised he'd never seen her smile. She'd finally broken up with her partner, who was now living interstate. She had also found a part-time job, doing data entry for an accounting firm. It didn't pay much, but she could work from home. Lucy and her sister were playing in a wading pool in the backyard, supervised by Marianne's mum, who visited twice a week to help out around the house. Great to see things fall into place once in a while.

Kurt drove on to Silvan. He loved this country. The scarred, parched landscape. The straggly shrubs. The absence of anything that was quaint or symmetrical. It was a landscape for people tempered by fire and raised on its ashes. A landscape that sang to you raucously from its iron throat, all rasping power and dissonance.

The paddocks were already shimmering with heat and when the road climbed into the Dandenong Ranges, the smell of eucalyptus wafted into the car. An old white Commodore turned into Wirruna Drive just ahead of him and swung into Bob's driveway. Kurt pulled up behind him.

"Gecko's not here," said Bob as soon as Kurt stepped out of the car.

"He's not in Heathmont either, so I rang you but—"

"Yeah, left my mobile at home, I'm sorry. Dashed out to get some pellets for the chooks. You've done well though."

"What do you mean?" asked Kurt, bracing himself for sarcasm.

"He was here yesterday. Seemed pretty happy. More relaxed than I've seen him in yonks. You must have done something right."

"But I hardly—"

"Let's go in though. Today's gonna be another stinker," said Bob, opening the front door. "Come in," he said in the hallway, "you know the drill."

Kurt sat down on the couch and took out his notebook. "So where's Gecko now?"

"Dunno. He said something about hanging out with a new mate of his. Shane, Shaun, something like that. He kept banging on about the guy—seems to think he's a top bloke. They play computer games. Waste of time if you ask me, but better than stealing cars I suppose."

Kurt lifted his biro. "Has Gecko ever done that?"

"No, no, but I'm talking from experience, if you get my drift. I was pretty wild before I joined the navy. But the service straightens you out, no worries."

"Do you happen to know whether this Shaun works?"

"He's a mechanic or something. There's that repair yard, near the station, you know—Heathmont Motors, I think. He must be one of their apprentices."

"I actually wanted to catch Gecko urgently—"

"Why, what's wrong?"

"Nothing, except that I am flying to Europe tomorrow—"

"Fair dinkum? Why?"

"My parents are elderly and in poor health. I'm helping them move into a nursing home," said Kurt, bracing himself for Bob's wrath.

"That's a tough gig. How long will you be away for?"

"Three weeks," said Kurt, relieved.

"Oh well, I suppose we can keep young Gecko on the straight and narrow for a couple of weeks. And you've done a sterling job with the boy so far. As I said—"

"I've only seen him on—" Kurt tried.

"As I said," Bob recapped, "he was pretty relaxed yesterday. He even fed the chooks."

"This is my manager," said Kurt, handing Fran's business card over to Bob, "you can ring her if anything crops up while I'm overseas. And please tell Gecko I'm sorry I couldn't spend more time with him. I'll look him up as soon as I'm back in the country. He's a good kid and I'm keen to help him."

"Righto," said Bob, standing up, "I'd better go and check on the chooks now. Make sure they have enough water in this heat. And good luck with your oldies, mate."

Kurt pulled into the petrol station at the foot of the mountain. He filled up his tank and bought two limp sandwiches in a square plastic box. As he opened the container, he cut his thumb and a drop of blood fell on his trousers. All this crappy food, he thought; why is it so hard to get a decent meal around here? He drove back to the office, that soulless building, all steel and glass, bent around a corner of the highway and supported by pillars that always looked too narrow.

"Fran in?" he asked her secretary as he whirled past the reception counter.

"She's at head office for the regional managers meeting," answered Debbie, "back around five."

"Thanks." He popped into the restroom, then collected the coffee plunger from his desk and walked to the kitchenette.

"That smells nice," said Joe, raising his bushy eyebrows. "That'll keep you awake during the presentation."

"What presentation?"

"Protective work with Indigenous families. You know, the consultants from Wirralong Partnerships or whatever they call themselves these days."

Kurt knew, as did everyone in the office, that Wirralong Partnerships was just about as Indigenous as a wine bar on Southbank. Its principals, Eileen and Damian, had held the Indigenous policy portfolio in the department for several years before realising that they could charge four times as much for their advice by leaving the department, making up an Indigenous sounding business name and setting themselves up as expert consultants. Damian was Fran's brother-in-law, which smoothed the procurement process. As a finishing touch, they had employed an Indigenous receptionist, who featured prominently on all their promotional material.

Kurt rolled his eyes. "Oh shit. Totally forgot. I've got so much on this afternoon…"

"Yeah, but you can't skip this one, mate," cautioned Joe. "You have to be seen there."

Kurt sighed and took his coffee into the meeting room.

Eileen started by acknowledging the Wurundjeri tribe of the Kulin nation as the traditional owners of the land. She then launched her PowerPoint presentation. The first slides showed the distribution of the Indigenous population across the Eastern Outreach catchment area. The charts looked familiar, probably because Eileen had created them when she was still working for the department and had shown them at a staff meeting. Damian's slides showed the number of child abuse notifications pertaining to Indigenous families, by suburb and compared to the overall population. If these charts looked familiar to Kurt, it was because he had prepared them six weeks ago, shortly after he had started at Eastern, when his case load was still low. Kurt remembered the definition of a consultant he had once read: someone who borrows your watch to tell you the time.

After Eileen had talked about building cultural competence among child protection workers, Damian described family case conferencing approaches that had been developed with Indigenous families in New South Wales. The heat of twenty bodies in a confined space made the room feel uncomfortable. Kurt's attention began to drift. Removing a child from their family was always a last resort, and even more vexed with Indigenous families, where the traumas and the injustice of the Stolen Generation remained open wounds. But keeping any child safe within a dysfunctional and often poverty-stricken family required a massive amount of work, a lot of time. And time was what Fran Esposito doled out so grudgingly. Sure, you were allowed to attend presentations, such as this one. You were entitled to enrol in training sessions, obliged to attend staff and team meetings, expected to rock up for conferences, Melbourne Cup and Christmas parties and encouraged to read theoretical frameworks developed by softly spoken sages, preferably bearded Brits. But spending too much time with a client family was seen as an extravagant indulgence. Who were you to think that your intervention would succeed where others had failed? It made you look like a prima donna, a spoiler, a one-man-band. You were trying too hard, making your team's activity stats look bad.

Child protection work, Kurt thought, was like playing Russian roulette with five bullets in the chamber. Remove a child too soon and you rip a family apart, causing lifelong trauma for all concerned. Keep the child at home for too long and the abuse or the neglect continues. And if the parent gets too desperate, they may decide to jump off a building, he thought. Jade's image hung over his life every day now, like a shadow, and he didn't want other kids to follow her.

Faint applause brought him back from his musings. "Thank you, Eileen. Thank you, Damian," Petra said, "for an excellent presentation that's given us food for thought. We look forward to your paper on cultural competence."

Debbie called Kurt back as he came out of the meeting room. "Phone message from Caitlin Murphy from the psych team at Outer Metro Health," she said, waving a yellow sticky note in his direction. "She rang twice actually—said it was urgent."

"Thanks Deb," said Kurt, picking up the yellow square, "I'll give her a bell." Along with everything else, he thought.

He stuck the note on his desk and decided to write up his case notes from the Robinson visit while it was all still fresh in his head. He was halfway through his report when he remembered he was meant to be chairing a case conference about the eleven-year-old from Doncaster next Wednesday. Christina had a mild intellectual disability and she'd been beaten by her father on a number of occasions. As her mother's attempts to rein in her husband had proved ineffective, more intensive intervention was necessary. Kurt had organised the case conference in a last-ditch effort to keep the family together. It had taken him ages to line up the Domestic Violence Alliance, Disability Services, Greek Welfare Eastern Suburbs, local police and one of the child's teachers; and now he might have to cancel the whole thing as he would be in Belgium next week, attending to an entirely different set of problems. How could he have missed this? See, the insomnia was getting to him, no wonder. He was tripping up.

Kurt felt panicky. He fumbled as he picked up his phone. He tried Joe first, but he was flying to Sydney for his brother's wedding. Isabelle was attending a case conference herself in Lilydale about a kid who had been chroming and Petra was chairing an interview panel. No luck, so Kurt had no choice but to make another five phone calls. He couldn't get hold of the teacher but left a message for her. "I'll ask Debbie to come up with another time in February," he told the others, but nobody had seemed too impressed by that vague promise.

Just as Kurt returned to the Childproof database to complete the reports from his home visits, Fran walked past his desk.

"How did you go with the Robinsons?" she asked, on the fly.

"All good," he replied, "all protective concerns have been addressed and—"

"Great. Keep up the good work."

He called her back. "Fran!"

"What?" she said, reluctantly turning back.

"Fran, I tried to visit Srecko Bosovic today, you know, the sixteen-year-old who—"

"Yes, yes, I know who he is. Go on."

"I didn't get hold of him and it would be great if you could send someone out while I'm away to follow up—"

"He's your case, Kurt. I can't backfill you while you're away. Your cases will just have to wait unless there's an emergency."

"It's just that I feel that, with a bit of in-home support, we can stabilise this boy. He's a good kid, he's got a number of strengths. He's been wagging school a fair bit, but he hasn't totally disengaged from education as we often see with kids like him—"

"But it's school holidays, Kurt. Does not sound like an emergency."

"No, but there's some risk factors. He's hanging out with guys who may be using drugs."

"So, is Bosovic doing drugs?"

"No—I don't think so. But he might."

"No, yes, maybe. Look Kurt, sounds like you haven't done your homework on this one and I haven't got the resources to send out somebody else to mop up after you."

"What about David?"

"I'm sure he'd like a little outing but I need him to double-check our second quarter performance stats before he retires. Look, there's nothing to suggest that this case will blow up. You may have some concerns but, hey, comes with the territory. We're not his parents and we can't hold his hand. So why don't you just fly to Holland—"

"Belgium."

"Yeah yeah. And get your folks sorted out and then you can follow up Bosovic when you're back. But scale back intervention to just quarterly foster care check-up visits until he turns eighteen. One for the rearview mirror."

"But—"

"Look, Kurt, we've got child abuse notifications coming out of our ears. We need to get those investigated and logged pronto or we'll look as bad as the Leichardt office. We can't provide one-on-one care for all of these kids. This is the real world, and it's a bitch. What I need you to do now though, before you go, is to lodge those investigation reports, what were they—Robinson and…"

"McCafferty."

"Right. Get those into Childproof and then why don't you take the rest of the day off."

"Okay. Thanks," said Kurt. Thanks for nothing, he thought. It was a quarter past six, anyway.

"My pleasure," Fran said. "Have a good time in Holland! Bring us some clogs!"

WITH A LITTLE HELP

Caitlin pulled the door shut behind her, picked up the junk mail from the doormat and edged past the last removal boxes in the hallway.

"Are you there?" she called.

"Ta–da!" Philip came out of the kitchen holding a silver serving tray with two champagne glasses.

"Oh, Philip, what's this for?" She smiled.

"Just thought we'd celebrate your first day coming back from work to our new home."

"That's lovely, Philip. I could do with a drink."

They sat down in the lounge room. Caitlin loved this room, with its soft grey walls and the yellow and black expressionist prints she had bought in Berlin. But tonight it felt as if something had shifted, disturbed the balance of the room. Philip had pulled down the blinds against the fierce heat. It made the fireplace look redundant, like a freezer at the South Pole.

"Do polar bears live in the Arctic or the Antarctic? I always mix those up."

"The Arctic," replied Philip, slightly bewildered. "Why?"

"Never mind."

"So, how was your day?"

Caitlin sipped some bubbly. "Pretty awful. We had a situation in the car park."

"A situation. In the car park," Philip echoed.

"There's this nine-year-old boy who's been suicidal for a number of weeks. His mum keeps bringing him to our intake team, but triage refuses to admit him because he hasn't made an actual suicide attempt."

"That's outrageous."

"Well yes, but the service is under a lot of pressure. We have heaps of clinicians on leave, so triage has to do some gatekeeping."

"Sounds like *Catch–22*. We won't admit you just for feeling suicidal, you have to actually top yourself, after which admission becomes a moot point. Is this how mental health services operate in Victoria in the twenty-first century?"

"It sounds crass when you put it like that."

"How could it sound any better?"

"I know, Philip, I hate it too, but that's the system I have to work in. I can't overrule triage. And the service *will* see the boy, just not admit him outright. But there's a three-week waiting period for all new client assessments. Far from ideal. Anyway, so this mum is at the end of her tether and turns up in the car park with her son. She sounds the car horn until the reception staff come out to investigate and she announces they'll stay put until the boy is admitted."

"So what happened?"

"They eventually declared a Code Grey—"

"What's Code Grey again?"

"An aggressive person without a weapon."

Philip nodded.

"They called the police," Caitlin went on, "but the cops didn't want to intervene because the woman was just sitting in a car… The DCS—"

"DCS?"

"Director of Clinical Services. The guy I told you about, Dr Ratnawarpal—"

"The Rat."

"Yeah, him. So, the Rat had to get advice from legal about how to proceed. It all took a while. In the meantime I found out that the boy has been seen by child protection. I wanted to get more information about their investigation but Eastern Outreach protective services weren't returning my calls—"

"Couldn't you look the case up on your database?"

"No. All the psych data are on SWIFT. Child protection uses Child-proof. The two are not connected."

"Your database is called SWIFT?"

"Yes. It's an acronym—"

"A rather unfortunate one."

"Anyhow, I walked into the Rat's office. Said we should maybe fast track seeing the boy, given his young age and the persistence of his ideation. He sent me away. Talk to your supervisor, he said, you're disrupting my train of thought. A dreadful day Philip. And then I get stuck on the freeway on the way home."

"What happened to the boy and his mum?"

"In the end the police did turn up. They asked them to leave and they did. They must have got hungry. But I'm sure we haven't seen the last of them…"

"Sounds like a tough day. Enjoy your bubbly, darling."

She smiled at him. It felt good to have someone to come home to. Someone to share your day with.

"Hey, I'm feeling peckish," he said. "What are we going to do for dinner?"

"But Philip, you were going to cook, remember?"

"Hmm, I sort of forgot."

Caitlin recognised his schoolboy act: trying to look contrite in the hope of being forgiven. She felt a tinge of irritation.

"Let's eat out then. I'm not going to cook… What have you been up to all day?" She tried not to make it sound challenging.

"Thought you'd never ask. Come and see." He took her by the hand and led her to the study. The shelves were up and nearly full. All Philip's boxes had been unpacked.

"Wow, Philip, that looks great."

"Yeah well, it took us ages."

"Us?"

"Yeah, Di helped a bit."

"You set up this room with Di Fletcher?"

"Well, I drove to the university, you see, and boxed most of the books in my office too."

"You brought those home? All of them?"

"I thought it would be nice to have them all together, the entire collection. Di gave me a hand carrying boxes to my car."

"How noble. Why did she have to come here with you though?"

"I invited her over, for a coffee. We looked through the boxes and thought it would be fun to put up some shelves, to surprise you."

"You know what would be fun, Philip?" she snapped, "If *we* in this house meant you and me, not you and that hussy."

"Oh come on, she's not a hussy. Don't get narky, Caitlin. We did it for you."

She snorted. "So what about my books? Where will they fit?"

"We didn't touch those. Your boxes are in the spare room."

"In the spare room." Caitlin felt livid now. "I thought we were going to have a shared study."

"I know that's what we said, Caitlin, but it just doesn't all fit. Circumstances change and one has to adapt."

"Well, *one* is feeling pissed off right now."

"I thought it made sense to have all my books together in the one place, that's all. It's my job after all, and for you…" His voice trailed off when he saw the fiery look in Caitlin's eyes.

"And for me… yes, say it," she prompted.

He hesitated. "Well, it's more of a peripheral interest, isn't it?"

"A peripheral interest? Like psychology? Like mental health?"

"That's not what I mean. You work with people, I thought, books are secondary—"

"For heaven's sake, Philip!" Caitlin stomped out of the study.

"What about eating out?" he called out behind her.

"Ask Di," she said.

TRANSIT

Kurt hated flying, especially the long haul from Melbourne to London. The first leg had been pleasant enough. He had talked to a nice Indonesian woman on her way to Singapore, where she was catching up with relatives. He tried to engage her in a discussion about Buddhism but she said that she came from a Catholic family and was an atheist herself. Kurt deemed Buddhism perfectly reconcilable with atheism, but by that stage of the flight they were zoning out, beaten down by the lack of fresh air and the oppressive drone of the four Rolls Royce engines. An intelligent conversation about spiritual subtleties seemed no longer feasible or desirable.

He had enjoyed stretching his legs during the stopover at Changi airport. He'd looked at all the shops in the transit hall three times, inspecting, initially with interest, then with weary recognition and finally with boundless boredom, the orchids, scorpions and gigantic spiders set in glass, the *free duty* whisky, as one shop called it, and the electronics accessories.

Boarding the flight to London had given him a brief rush of energy. The new cabin crew looked fresh and cheerful. Kurt picked up a copy of *The Strait Times* and shuffled towards row 23. Seat 23B was now occupied by a massive middle-aged man in a beige suit. He looked Middle Eastern, Lebanese maybe, Kurt speculated.

"Excuse me sir, could I squeeze past, please?" Kurt asked. "I'm in the window seat," he added, in a somewhat redundant territorial claim. As if the fellow would think he was heading for the wing.

The man made no effort to get up but shifted two massive knees slightly to the right in a token display of courtesy. Kurt started edging past this extraordinary human, his bottom burnishing the seat behind him. I could use a Sherpa, he thought. He moved right into the scent cloud of his neighbour: strong coffee, hazelnut, aftershave and a hint of halitosis. This moment too will pass. Just then, a large Fijian passenger in 22B reclined his seat, catapulting Kurt onto the man he had so studiously avoided. Two black hairs protruded from the man's left ear. "So sorry," said Kurt, "the guy behind…" Beige Man did not say a word but just sat there, like a malignant mushroom, his dark brown eyes following Kurt as he scaled his girth. Finally Kurt reached the relative comfort of what remained of his seat. Then the Fijian's partner reclined hers, boxing Kurt in from the front. Oh well, he thought, there's worse things in life. I'll just have to Zen it. Reading a book was nigh impossible, so Kurt turned on the flight tracker after take off. *Flight time remaining: 13 hours 9 minutes*, it said. Kurt groaned.

He looked out the window. A series of ponds—a fish farm possibly —cut out in the dense jungle. A chain of small islands. A flotilla of freighters heading towards Singapore. The clouds reflected in the jade green sea below.

Kurt pictured Jade drawing her fairies on that rickety table high up in their Rathdowne Street apartment. His plane was already higher now, and climbing. He imagined the terror Jade must have felt in her last moments and cursed Kylee for acting on her despair, crystallising it into something irreparable, an act of evil. The memories of his last visit so vivid, the sense of loss still an abstraction. The dissonance between what he knew and his persistent sense of disbelief. As if he could rock up at the apartment and they would all have a good laugh about how he'd fallen for the story.

The plane vibrated as it climbed through the clouds. His delusion was like an image in a kaleidoscope: it would fall apart as soon as you shook it. No matter how often he replayed that last visit in his head, racked his mind for more supportive, validating statements he might have offered, Kylee and Jade were gone forever. All he could do was honour her memory by fighting for every kid he encountered from now on, making sure they got the best possible outcome.

He smiled wryly as he reflected how often he had already fallen short of that objective in just a few weeks. He'd only managed to see Gecko once. He had totally forgotten about the Doncaster case conference. Suddenly he also remembered the yellow sticky message from the psych service at Outer Metro Health. Urgent, it said, and the woman had rung twice. Kurt's heart was racing and his temperature shot up. Sure, he could blame the insomnia that had plagued him since —well… But it wasn't like him. Not at all.

He looked between the seats in front of him. The Fijian guy was watching an inflight movie. Spiderman jumped from one skyscraper to the next, rescuing women in distress and keeping New York safe. If only it were that simple. It was hard, keeping kids safe in a world without heroes. He closed his eyes and tried to sleep.

When the cabin crew woke him for breakfast they were already flying over Belarus. This is the closest I've ever been to Latvia, Kurt thought. Must tell Emma.

As the plane flew further into Europe, Kurt's thoughts turned to what he would find in Belgium. He had looked forward to visiting his parents but had also feared seeing his mother in her new, reduced state. Would she recognise him? Had she retained any of her old spark or had the wrecking ball of dementia demolished all the chambers of her complex, loving, playful brain?

And Joris, with his nervous mannerisms and his laconic sense of humour. Kurt's friendship with Joris had only truly blossomed after they had left high school. Joris used to live only a few streets away from his parents and often bumped into them at the weekly market in the town square. As Kurt's parents had aged and become more frail, Joris had visited them more frequently, especially after his own parents had passed away, and had often alerted Kurt to emerging issues. Invaluable, if you were an only child and living on the other side of the world. Loyal and unassuming, Joris was a great mate and Kurt always felt indebted to him.

~

The shock of arriving in winter. Wet runways. Melting snow. Cotton wool behind his forehead. Immense fatigue. Orange flashing lights, forklifts. "Please leave your seat belts on until the aircraft has come to a complete halt." Farewell, Beige Man.

Security again. "Remove your shoes please, sir. And your belt, please." Yet another boarding pass. British Airways. "Yes sir, your luggage is going straight to Brussels." Gate 11. Last boarding call.

The short flight to Brussels felt different. The international travellers had been replaced by a contingent of business folk hopping across the Channel for a day's work. Kurt sat next to two software developers who were reviewing a printout of their presentation. "Make sure you mention agile systems," the elder one said, "that's what they want to hear." Kurt looked out the window. There, below him, was the silver snake of the Thames again. It seemed so wasteful to fly east again, over ground he'd covered less than two hours ago. It was pretty special, though, to see England covered in snow. They crossed the Channel and Kurt saw his native country come alive in the morning light. The quilts of Flanders fields, where his grandfather had fought. Strings of red brick houses alongside the highways. The urban sprawl of Brussels, zipped together by converging train lines.

~

Kurt felt grateful when things went unexpectedly smoothly at Brussels airport. He cleared security and customs. It felt weird that he could not use the fast-track queue for European citizens. He was a foreigner now, like the African woman ahead of him with her purple dress and yellow headband. Less colourful though. How long had he been away? He couldn't think straight. Twenty, no, twenty-two years since he migrated; and he'd only been back once, in 1995, to introduce his new bride to the relatives. He smiled at the thought of Emma. She would still be asleep. He pushed his luggage trolley forward, careful not to hit the African woman's ankles again. He didn't want to feature in her travel story as Trolley Man.

"*Heb je een goeie vlucht gehad?*"

Kurt turned around. Joris, in the same blue jacket he used to wear all year round. A bit of grey in his hair. Kurt confirmed that, yes, he'd had a good flight.

"Great to see you mate!" He gave his friend a bear hug. "Sorry if I'm a bit on the nose."

"You can have a shower at my place. And you have that sing-song English accent in your Dutch—that's quite funny."

They chatted as they ambled to the car park. Kurt zipped up his coat. He felt zonked in the warm car and tuned out as Joris told him about the Belgian elections, the complex negotiations to form a new coalition government. Kurt admired Joris's new car, a Subaru. He had received a good trade-in price for his old Golf. Joris fed his ticket into the yellow slot of the machine. The boom gate went up.

"As I said on the phone, I visited your parents last week," said Joris as they drove down the freeway.

Kurt looked at the industrial zones interspersed by snow-covered fields. He'd forgotten how flat everything was.

"They've now been admitted to hospital, to the geriatric ward," Joris continued. "It's a temporary solution until you can help them move into the nursing home. The only way to provide full-time care, and that's what they need these days."

"That's great, to have that continuity of care. I doubt that would happen in Australia. Not without an acute health problem." And then the question he'd been busting to ask. "How was my mum?"

"She's fine physically, but she didn't recognise me. She's still lucid on occasions though. When I was there last week, she asked your dad about you."

Kurt felt tears well up.

"We could go there now," Joris suggested, "it's not visiting hours yet, but I'm sure they'll let you in."

"No," Kurt said, "I want to do this properly."

"Your call," said Joris, shooting him a sideways glance.

Kurt unpacked his suitcase in Joris's spare room. This was base camp. He would stay here for just a few days, while he helped his parents move from the hospital into the nursing home. He would then move into their house, clear out their remaining possessions and place it on the market. But right now he needed to Skype Emma, then get some rest.

REUNION

Kurt looked through the gauze curtains at the strip of gunmetal grey sky above the apartment building on the other side of the street. When he lowered his gaze, he saw that all the residents had opened their curtains to make the most of the morning light, each revealing their compartmentalised universe to the world. On the tenth floor, a woman rummaging in her kitchen. On the seventh floor an elderly man in a wheelchair, staring at the absence of traffic below. It struck Kurt how alike these doll's house cubicles were—off-white or beige wallpaper, solid wooden furniture, the sword-like leaves of sansevierias on the window sill. And not a child in sight. It seemed as if Belgium was a country of old people, stacked up in death's waiting room. Shallow, unfair and stupid as that notion was, Kurt thought, right now it matched what he saw around him, in the bleakness of the skies, in the pallor of the people, in the stillness of the day. An appropriate overture to what he had to do today.

Joris was off to work already. Kurt helped himself to two slices of bread, flopped a thick slice of Gouda cheese in between, and figured out how to use Joris's espresso machine. He planned out his day as he ate his breakfast. First he would buy a SIM card, then go to St. Jozef's Hospital

The bus to Mortsel, his parents' suburb, followed a circuitous route. Kurt recognised the bicycle repair shop that his father had taken him to after he had crashed his Raleigh into a snowman and bent the front wheel. The mental health facility that had inspired standing jokes at school. 'He's ready for St Amadeus,' his mates would say about anyone saying or doing something deemed outrageous by the group. Kurt got off the bus near the church where during Sunday school he had paid more attention to Annemarie's ponytail than to the parish priest's pious ramblings.

He went into one of the cafes dotted around the church and ordered a coffee. Am I a cold fish, he wondered. Here's me delaying my first visit to my parents in over a decade when I could storm into the hospital right now and make the most of every moment. He spooned the foam off his cappuccino. He keenly anticipated the reunion with his parents, but his excitement was tinged with dread.

He pondered the development of his mother's dementia. At first Irene had repeated herself during their weekly phone calls, but that could easily be ascribed to normal ageing. Then she started misusing words, often replacing one word by another one from the same category. "I was eating my soup with my knife," she would say, or "it's busy when the kids are let out of the office." He had laughed at first, until it became apparent that these were not just innocent mistakes, but rather the harbingers of something sinister, a cognitive takeover that was changing the locks on the world she had inhabited. Leo had covered up for her initially, blaming fatigue, insomnia and ageing. He wanted to protect Irene's dignity, but he also needed to vent, so he had started writing more frequently to Kurt and Emma, gradually letting on what was happening to his wife. Irene herself became quite adept at masking her illness too, in those early stages. Her answers became evasive, and she became agitated if questions required a clear yes or no, or any sort of specific answer. "That's hard to say," became one of her stock phrases. Nuance covering for confusion. She became crabby and defensive if you referred to her difficulties. And all along Leo had stood by her, as Irene peeled potatoes, not remembering that they had just had dinner. As Irene set fire to the kitchen. As Irene ran into the street, telling the neighbours Leo had locked her up. Then Irene began staring at *the other people* in the room, visible only to her. She became terrified when she had to leave the house. Finally, she became incontinent.

Time to go, Kurt resolved. He popped into a florist and bought a bunch of roses. In the bakery he ordered three chocolate éclairs, his mum's favourite.

He opened the door of room 11B onto a little tableau: his parents, facing each other like bookends across a square little table pushed against the hospital wall. They looked up from their stewed apples. Leo got up first, a broad smile on his face. Then, as he hugged Kurt, he started sobbing.

"It's all right, Dad," Kurt said, as he watched his mum get off her chair, gingerly, and move towards him in slow motion, her arms wide open in a silent welcome.

"Well, well, look who's here," she said slowly.

Kurt gently let go of his dad and said "Hi, Mum," looking at a figure so familiar and yet so strange, one eye expressionless, the other shiny with muted joy. He embraced her. She recognised me, he thought, and started crying.

Kurt stayed in the hospital all afternoon. He answered Irene's questions over and over again. He listened to Leo's detailed account of an administrative problem with their health insurance. He told them about Emma's new job. Leo introduced him to the nurses as *our son from Australia.*

"Yes," said Irene, "we only had the one and he went away."

"Well, I'm here now Mum." He had learned, over the years, to sidestep the feelings of guilt. He had made his own life, though he understood how his absence had weighed on his parents. You had to migrate while you were young, before you could think through all the implications.

"I used to listen for the *postbode* every morning. To see whether he had a letter from Australia."

Kurt knew this story, braced himself.

"And sometimes it would go *plof* in the letterbox and I knew there was a letter from you. And I would jump up and run to the letterbox and call out 'Leo, a letter from Kurt!'"

And after a few years, Kurt thought...

"And after a few years the mailman knew about this and he would ring the doorbell. 'A letter from Australia,' he would say."

"And now I'm here again," Kurt said airily, "and we can catch up, talk for hours."

Irene, her face suddenly worried, looked up at the clock.

"We must make sure we're not late for the train," she said.

Kurt recognised that phrase too. The weekly rejoinder from his childhood, as the three of them set out on Sunday mornings to visit Irene's mum. Kurt let it go. Didn't have the heart to remind Irene that her mum had passed away in the mid-nineties. Hugged her instead.

Leo handed Kurt a scrap of paper with the mobile number of Corinne, their support worker, and asked about the move to the nursing home. In a few days, Kurt said, when he'd had a chance to set up their room. And what was to happen to all their belongings? Leo was particularly concerned about the garden furniture. That was teak, from Indonesia, and it was brand new. And all along Irene held Kurt's hand and stroked his forearm, unable to take her eyes off him.

"My baby," she said.

BAG OF BAGS

Kurt had treated Corinne to lunch in The Golden Finch. In a moment of Dickensian fantasy, he had expected a rotund woman in her forties with a ruddy complexion, smelling of fresh bread and apple crumble. Instead, the woman who kissed him on the cheek before sitting down on the plush bench opposite him was a tired blonde approaching fifty, thin as a rake and smelling of ashtrays. They soon hit it off though. Corinne was a straight talker who obviously felt a genuine affection for his parents and had, in return, gained their trust over the past three years. It was unsettling how much she knew about Emma and him. She had seen their letters and photos, had heard embarrassing tales about his youth and knew about his first marriage. But Kurt brushed his unease aside as he felt immensely grateful towards Corinne. She had been there when he had not; and if you were vulnerable and needed support, as his parents did, help mattered more than privacy.

After lunch they visited the nursing home that Corinne had organised. Residentie Vitalis Bosch was a grey monolith overlooking the railway yard, but the staff seemed friendly enough. The room allocated to his parents, at the back of the building, was clean and freshly painted but looked down on a dispiriting street of drab little houses. There was no way their massive Flemish oak dining table would fit, so

Corinne drove him to a furniture store, where Kurt bought two chairs, a small kitchen table and two comfortable armchairs; and had it all delivered to the nursing home. On the way back, Kurt asked Corinne to drop him off in Mortsel, as he wanted to inspect his parents' home.

The iron lacework grille of the front door looked familiar in the dusk. He recognised the distinctive click of the lock—a sound he hadn't heard in fourteen years. The hallway of the unheated house, with its chequered marble tiles, felt like a vault. Kurt opened the doors to the lounge room and saw the heavy curtains, the velvety couches, the marble topped coffee table with its ornate legs, the piano that was never used. "Little Versailles," he had always called his mother's lounge room, and her taste clearly hadn't changed. He went upstairs. His parents' bedroom smelled musty, and the bedsheets had been stripped back. The doors of the linen cupboard were open and its shelves bare except for one of his dad's fedoras.

He went into his old bedroom. His posters of Roxy Music, Lou Reed and David Bowie had long been removed. The striped wallpaper he had helped pick in the early seventies had been replaced by a more heraldic pattern: *fleur-de-lys* against a Prussian blue background. The bed had been pulled apart and the room was full of cardboard boxes. Some, marked *Clothes* or *Admin*, were clearly meant to go to the nursing home. Lord knows what was in the others. Leo and Corinne had sorted and culled more than Kurt had realised and it was clear he would not be able to stay in the house as he had intended. There was no linen, and most of the crockery and cutlery had gone too. He'd have to ask Joris whether he could stay there longer.

The following day passed in a whirlwind of activity. Kurt hired a small truck and moved all the labelled boxes and two favourite paintings to the nursing home. Corinne helped him set up his parents' room. Above the table she mounted a corkboard with a photo montage of Irene and Leo's lives. She'd made it at home, she said, by cutting out photos that she had selected with his mother. There were shots of Kurt's grandparents, of his parents grinning broadly from a white

Cadillac on their wedding day, of his eight-year-old self in a cowboy outfit, of Emma on the beach. Corinne is incredible, Kurt thought. Okay, she'd struck a few false notes: there was a photo of a brother Irene had fallen out with, and one of a stranger, whom Corinne must have thought significant. Still, this went well beyond the call of duty. For a moment he fantasised about making photo boards for the kids he was working with. He'd struggle to put together much about Gecko. He'd do better with others. Like Jade… He dismissed the idea. This was not a good time to let his imagination run rampant. Not a good time to focus on loss.

That afternoon Kurt returned to his parents' house and met a real estate agent Joris had recommended. He signed a listing agreement and rushed to the hospital to see his parents again. Irene seemed to think he was a doctor this time.

Kurt felt ragged the next morning. He had stayed up too late, Skyping Emma, then chatting with Joris about nursing homes, about their old teachers and classmates, and trying out new craft beers. When he turned up to help his parents move, Corinne was already there. Leo kept looking out of the window, as if expecting somebody else. Irene was unsettled and kept checking the contents of her handbag: a smaller handbag.

Kurt remembered how Irene always used to keep her valuables in a black leather handbag, which she never let out of sight. Now, that sense of preciousness had attached itself to bags per se, and she had stuffed several smaller handbags into a large one. A bag of bags. Like those nested Russian dolls. The bags themselves had become an object worth safeguarding, never mind that they were empty. It was just form, a meaningless ritual—all content was gone. An apt metaphor for her illness.

Kurt and Corinne loaded the suitcases into the boot of Corinne's old sedan, then walked back across the hospital carpark to collect their human load. Kurt held Leo's arm and Corinne helped Irene as she shuffled across the carpark, her icy breath hanging above her like a question mark.

It was only a short drive to the nursing home. No one spoke in the car. Irene smiled as she walked into her new room and recognised the two Chinese vases on the window sill.

"I know these," she said, tracing the intricate floral designs with her finger. Then she walked over to Corinne's corkboard and pointed. "There's Mum. We haven't seen her in a long time, Leo. We should go and see her."

Leo had the look of a shipwreck survivor who, having fought his way through the surf, collapses on the beach.

"This is our new home, Irene," he explained in a weary voice, "our new home." He slid his hand over a box marked *Files*. "All our stuff is here. And look at the new chairs Corinne bought—they look really comfortable."

Corinne smiled, Kurt noticed, happy to take the credit. What did it matter?

"This is not our home," said Irene, "I want to go to the other place."

Kurt caught a tram back to Mortsel and walked to his parents' house. Cold as a crypt, full as an egg. He started going through the unlabelled cardboard boxes on the first floor. Emotional minesweeping. Trivia and non sequiturs, then something that blows up in your face.

He had rifled through a box full of old recipes, dusty doilies and warranties for whitegoods purchased in the 1960s, all jumbled together. And just as he was about to ditch the whole box, he had come across a letter from Axel, his uncle, who had died in 1952, when his Spitfire crashed into a forest near Brussels. Axel had been the golden boy of the family, self-assured and handsome, with his dimpled chin. Irene's favourite brother. Kurt had no idea how the pale blue aerogramme had ended up here, in his parents' place. He felt he had no right to read it but there was no way he would throw it out. He dug deeper and found a cigar box with Axel's empty wallet in it, a drive-in ticket and a stubby pencil. This was family archaeology: digging up the long-buried shards of disintegrated lives. Every find threw up new questions.

Who would have gone through Kylee's apartment, he wondered? Maybe Amanda, who'd taken over the case from him? Would Kylee's sister have flown down from Mackay? Would anyone have bothered to keep any mementoes? Or would Jade's little diary have ended up in a bin?

Next he found a photocopy of a letter from Irene's grandfather to his brother. It was dated 12 October 1889. *My beloved brother*, it began, *finally the fate of my beloved wife has been decided. Finally the sad tunes of the church bells have announced to the villagers that another mortal has vanished from this earth.* The two-page letter still conveyed the raw sense of loss from more than a century ago. Kurt felt strangely moved.

A white fog hung in the garden and the sky looked oppressive. So many ghosts, he thought. So many lives lived and lost. So many dreams crushed in bitter ashes. He felt cold and lonelier than he had ever been. Emma, he thought, if only you could be here now, I need to feel the warmth of your body, I could really do with a cuddle.

At night he discussed his options with Joris. Kurt's cousin in Limburg had already made it clear that she was not interested in any of his parents' belongings. He could try to sell the lot, but that would take time. Joris agreed that it made sense to keep Leo out of the decision-making, as he was stressed as it was, and a micromanager at the best of times. There was a charity, Joris said, that employed recent refugees from Eastern Europe. They collected estates for a nominal fee and sold the goods at op shops. This option appealed to Kurt, and he booked the folk at *Renewal Inc* for the day before his return flight.

Over the following days Kurt cancelled his parents' telephone account and newspaper subscriptions, and helped them transfer their bank account. He made phone calls to insurance companies and met with a solicitor to make arrangements for the sale of the house. At Leo's request he wrote and posted more than a hundred change of address notification postcards, most of them to distant relatives he'd never heard of. It gave him a glimpse of what might have been if he'd stayed in Belgium: a gigantic network of family connections. He also photocopied Leo's address list—one day he would need it for sending out funeral notices. His contingency planning habit had never felt so macabre.

Sometimes he worked all day from Joris's flat, where he had internet access, and then rushed to the nursing home to spend a couple of hours with his parents. Leo seemed quite happy in his new environment but Irene kept talking about going home.

Other days he went back to his parents' house to keep sorting their belongings. He made a selection from what his parents had left behind: a pile of photo albums, a mediocre but atmospheric painting of a country lane, some Delft Blue porcelain, and had the consignment shipped to Australia.

One night, as Kurt looked for his parents in the nursing home dining room, they were nowhere to be seen. The woman at the counter recognised him, saw his bewildered expression.

"Your parents now have their meals on the second floor," she said.

Kurt thanked her and headed for the elevator. The second floor dining room was exclusively for high-dependency dementia patients. What had happened?

"They asked us to move," explained Leo. "When Irene wanted some milk at dinner she drank it straight from the jug. She put the butter knife in the jam jar… It wasn't hygienic."

Irene was wearing a coffee-stained apron over her top. "I wanted milk in my coffee," she said, "I find this all very difficult. Those people are mean."

"It's not your fault, darling," Leo assured her. "But there were complaints," he told Kurt.

"Complaints? About me?" Irene looked alarmed.

Kurt patted her forearm. "It's okay, Mum, you've done nothing wrong."

"I don't want to do the wrong thing." She became agitated. "What can I do? Someone has to help me."

Irene started crying. It took Leo and Kurt quite a while to console her, reassure her; and even after the sobbing had stopped her eyes remained dull. Dejected. Irene's emotions were more persistent these days than her memories, Kurt had noticed.

He looked across the other tables. There were three, four residents seated around most of them but there was hardly any conversation. Everyone a captive in their own universe. One man was kneading his sandwich. His companion drooled into his soup. Kurt felt grateful that Irene's illness had at least blunted her perception, blinded her to the full horror of her new life. On Corinne's photo board she failed to recognise herself in the smiling, impeccably dressed and groomed woman holding a sunlit parasol. But Leo, who had been a senior executive in government, had gone into voluntary exile in a dementia ward so he could be with his wife, look after her. Kurt scanned the room again, felt a confusing mix of compassion and despair. He wanted to rail and rage against our malfunctioning genes, against ageing and decline. Right now, the tenets of Buddhism felt like a rationalisation. You were expected to accept the moment as it presented itself, without preference or aversion. By that standard, by calling this hell home, Leo surely was an enlightened being. My father the *Bodhisattva*, Kurt thought, tears rolling down his cheeks.

SHOSTAKOVICH

On the penultimate day of Kurt's stay a truck from *Renewal Inc* pulled up outside his parents' place. A stocky man in burgundy overalls and a black beanie rang the doorbell.

"You order Renewal?" the stubbly man asked in broken Dutch.

"I sure did," answered Kurt. He was intrigued by the accent. "Where are you guys from?"

"Renewal."

"Yes, but where did you come from? I'm from Australia."

"Grozny."

"Ah, Chechnya. How did you end up in Belgium?"

"Grozny. Germania. Belgium."

"And now you work for a charity?"

"Renewal. We work one year. We learn language. We go."

"I see," Kurt nodded.

"We start now. One truck? Two truck?"

"Hmm… I don't know…"

"No problem. We see." And with that he nodded at his three compatriots. They jumped off the truck bed and swarmed over the house. Wasn't it ironic, Kurt thought. Ever since the collapse of the Soviet Union, Irene had feared that refugees from across the Iron

Curtain would flock to affluent Belgium and loot her house. Her xeno-phobia probably sprang from her increasing anxiety—a harbinger of dementia? Kurt didn't know. But her fears were coming true now, he thought, except that the Grozny raiders were acting on his behalf, in a twist Irene could never have foreseen. Irrespective of how irrational her views were, throwing the doors of her house open felt like a betrayal.

Kurt had improvised a workstation of sorts by placing a kitchen chair in the corner of the lounge room, next to a power point. A neigh-bour had given Kurt his wifi password, and coverage extended just into his parents' lounge room. From this improvised vantage point Kurt confirmed his flight reservation and signed off on changes to his parents' health insurance policy, while around him the Grozny gang gutted Irene's interior. The television went, then the television table. The pink armchairs and the couch. Mum never just called them pink, Kurt recalled, as if that colour was too ordinary. She called them *vieux rose*.

"You don't want this?" the crew leader asked, pointing at the coffee table. "Is marble. Is very good. Expensive. Not broken."

"No," Kurt replied, surprised by the stream of words. "It can all go." He realised how bizarre it would seem for refugees trying to eke out a living, him throwing out all this good stuff. They would see his actions as wanton waste. Think that he was filthy rich or totally unhinged, probably the latter. And so the cull continued. The Flemish oak dining room table went, as did the Afghan carpet underneath. The carved wooden dresser, the lampshade on top of it, the rustic milk jugs, the painting of the shepherd girl with the lamb. In some tradi-tions, Kurt remembered reading, Buddhist monks were only allowed to possess seven items, including their robes, and one of those had to be a tea strainer, so they could rescue insects that fell into their drinking bowl.

"You can't take it with you," his grandmother used to say, and today her dictum had come true. You can't even take it to a nursing home. Maybe holidays weren't about going to a different place, Kurt thought. Maybe they were a training exercise in coping without all your stuff. He sniggered as he thought of all those hordes of tourists going off on annual Zen boot camp without realising. From the corner of his eye he noticed the crew leader look at him with some concern.

Kurt had not seen the lounge room this empty since the day they moved in. He was six then, and he had been allowed to draw on the bare plaster walls before the wallpaper went on. But the emptiness back then belonged to the imagination. It was the emptiness of the blank page, of potential and promise yet unfulfilled. The emptiness now belonged to memory. The dusty rectangular shapes on the carpet spoke of absence, of objects dispersed, a vision unravelled.

The removalists nudged Leo's bookcase out the front door and placed it on the pavement. A light snow had started to fall now and soft flakes settled on the shelves of the bookcase. At least Mum doesn't have to witness this, Kurt thought, she would be beside herself. He walked to the front door and saw that the men had placed the piano in the front garden, over a bunch of azalea shrubs. The piano stool stood in front of it, as if, out of some sort of piety, the men had tried to keep together what belonged together.

The stubbly man saw Kurt look at the piano. "Too big," he yelled, "truck two."

Kurt nodded. There was also all the stuff in the attic. The shortest man closed the latch over the truck gate and climbed in the cabin. He handed his mates a heavy canvas shoulder bag. They shouted him some sentences and the truck took off in a belching cloud.

"Drink coffee in house? Okay?" the leader asked, pointing at a thermos flask that he pulled from the bag. Kurt saw his gruff features from up close now. A swarthy man, who could have passed for an escaped convict.

"Yes, in house okay," answered Kurt, feeling instantly sheepish that he had dumbed down his own syntax. He felt like saying "take a seat," then realised that would be pointless, so he went for "that coffee smells nice."

"You want some?" offered the Chechen.

"No, no," declined Kurt, "but it smells good."

"Yes. Smells good," confirmed the man. His mates had started playing cards while they were waiting for the second truck to arrive. Kurt wandered back to his laptop and jiggled the connecting cables a bit. Why did he find it so hard to talk to macho men? It was the same back home. "Who do you barrack for?" was their standard opener. "I'm not really into football" was not a great rejoinder. He had tried "I'm a football agnostic" once, but that fell flat too. Many men would give up on you there and then. The ones who persisted would try "so what do you like?" "I'm into Buddhism," he might respond, or "I like classical music," or "I play fantasy role-playing games," none of which would make the conversation any easier. As Kurt was musing about his social ineptitude, he heard a familiar sound. It sounded like... No, couldn't be... And then he recognised the tune for sure. Shostakovich. *Piano concerto no. 2 in F Major*, a rare harmonious piece by a composer generally known for the dissonance of his work; and one of the most touching melodies Kurt knew. He walked through the hallway and opened the front door. On the velvet piano stool, amid some dead azaleas, sat the swarthy man from Grozny, working the piano keys like the gentlest of lovers, a soft cloak of snow falling around his burgundy overalls.

FEBRUARY 2009

BANKSIA HIGH

"Focus. Persistence. Excellence," said the sign. The large orange metal board with its blue and white lettering clashed with the muted colours of the surrounding bush. Emma walked along a broad path heavily planted with native grasses and shrubs and found herself in a throng of teachers waiting outside the auditorium.

"Where's Henry James?" asked a bearded man, looking back over his shoulder.

"Long dead," quipped one of the English teachers. They laughed.

"I wish," muttered the science teacher. Emma had forgotten his name.

"Oooh," said a stout woman in a flowing blue dress, "is that still bad blood from last term?"

"Never mind that," grumbled the science teacher, "I wish he'd hurry up."

A balding little man came rushing down the path. "Morning folks. Sorry Keith, can I just wiggle past."

"Wiggle all you like, Henry, just let us in so we can get started."

The caretaker unlocked the double metal doors and the mob of teachers pressed forward, loud and unruly, like their charges on a normal school day.

The vice principal took the microphone. He was the only one wearing a suit. "You realise of course," he said, "that all you guys in the back row have just volunteered for a month of yard duty."

Laughter, shouted banter. Emma felt like a Year 7 kid again, surrounded by strangers.

The vice principal waited for a moment, scanned the auditorium.

He enjoyed being on a podium, Emma thought. One of those people with an indisputable presence, supreme self-confidence. It helped to be young and good looking.

"You know he separated from his wife, don't you?" the woman in front of Emma whispered in her neighbour's ear.

"Really? No, I didn't know that. Well, that was on the cards anyway, wasn't it?"

"Come on guys," the vice principal urged, "just move down a couple of rows. The principal will be here soon."

Emma recognised Roslyn McArthur from her interview. A tall, dignified woman in her fifties. She looked like a female incarnation of Abraham Lincoln, Emma thought. Her opening speech, however, was significantly longer than the Gettysburg Address and less memorable. She introduced Emma when she touched upon pastoral care arrangements for the new school year. Emma stood up and grinned sheepishly into the spotlights. The bearded man whispered something to the sports teacher and they both laughed.

The heads of science and humanities delivered their overhead presentations. Emma kept looking at the purple pashmina of the woman in front of her. The fabric conjured up images of the Silk Road, Afghan traders, fresh dates and strong black coffee. Instead there were updates on discipline, communication with parents and insurance cover for school excursions. Emma found it both familiar and bewildering. She resisted the urge to brush the dog hairs off her neighbour's pashmina.

"Okay," concluded the vice principal, "time now for subject teachers to break up in year level groups. Year 12 teachers in the Yarra

Room. Other year levels please check the notice next to the door on your way out. And please, form teachers, don't forget to pick up the box of combination locks for the new lockers and the code sheet for your form."

Emma's new colleagues filed through the door. Nerissa, the librarian, spotting her hesitation, came over to her.

"We can go now," she said, "we're no longer needed."

Emma found her way to the careers centre, a grand name for a rectangular room at the far end of the library. It smelled musty and the olive wall-to-wall carpet was threadbare. Her desk was on the right, backed by a mudbrick wall, with two lime green chairs stood in front of it. On the left, floor-to-ceiling windows looked out on the library. Not great for privacy, she thought. At least there were venetian blinds. The other two walls were covered in shelves. In the centre of the room three brown beanbags. This was her domain now.

She felt weary. Not surprising, given Kurt's late arrival from the airport. It had been good to catch up, but she was paying the price now. At least she could coast today… there were no kids yet. She started up the computer. It hummed and beeped itself out of digital hibernation and asked her for a user name and password. Fair questions, she thought—here was something to follow up. She walked to the school office, past the classrooms where her colleagues were engaged in lively discussions. There were diagrams on whiteboards, bullet points on butcher's paper. And she, by her own volition, was not part of this planning frenzy. No longer in the vanguard of education now, but part of the support crew. Had she made the right choice?

Just as she was about to head home, Emma noticed the head of the English department coming her way, zigzagging between book trolleys. She had met Raeleen Osmond at interview and disliked her brusque manner.

"Emma, welcome to Banksia High," Raeleen declared. She added a pleasantry about becoming part of the school community before firing off pointed comments about how the kids at Banksia High came from a range of backgrounds and how a role as a careers teacher was *an adjustment* for a former teacher of English. A step down, she meant.

"I hope you'll find here whatever you were looking for," she concluded.

Emma smiled broadly.

"And there was something else," said Raeleen.

Emma raised her eyebrows in anticipation.

"My Year 10s will be doing work experience placements in March and I'd like to offer them a number of choices early in term. It would be great if you could compile a list of available placements, say by week two?"

"Week two?"

"Yes, that's when Rosemary used to give me her options."

"Oh my god, that soon? I'll have to check what, if anything, Rosemary has left behind." Emma's brain was racing. "I may need to develop new arrangements with local employers—"

"I don't need to hear all the details," Raeleen said. "I'm sure that, with your background, you'll do a splendid job." She sailed out of the careers centre, leaving Emma bug-eyed in her wake.

DOWN BY THE RIVER

Mark held the faded grey rope back so the tyre was near the bank. Jake ran at full speed, jumped and grabbed the rope. The tyre swung across the surface of the water and, at its furthest point, accompanied by the screeching of the girls, Jake splashed into the Yarra. Mark whooped. The girls cheered. Jake swam back to the riverbank and climbed out. His hair hung down in spikes, like a character in a manga cartoon. He spat in the grass. The tyre drew a decreasing pendulum underneath the gum tree. The ripples subsided. Jake lay down next to Libby again.

"Have we got any cans left?"

Monique rummaged through her shoulder bag. "Yeah, two bourbon and coke, we'll have to share." She threw a can at Jake and opened the other one herself.

"Hey," shouted Mark, "leave some for me."

"Come and get some," smirked Monique. She took a big mouthful and didn't swallow.

Mark brought his mouth to Monique's. They spilled.

"Look what you've done, you moron, I've got it all over my bra."

Jake leered at her.

"Take it off then," said Mark.

"You wish." She looked annoyed. "Mum will smell the alcohol. Great."

"Why don't you wash it in the Yarra," Mark tried again.

"No way. You're in my bad books now."

"Ouch," said Mark, "what if I act real cute?" He rolled on his back and batted his eyelids.

"Oh, you idiot." Monique smiled. They kissed.

"Have some more," said Jake, offering his can to Libby. She had a sip. He looked at the river.

"Why don't you take your top off too," he tried, "like Monique." He licked his lips.

"Cause I don't want to."

"You'd still have your bra on, and your shorts."

"No."

"Go on, I'd like to see you."

"I said no."

Jake swallowed and said nothing for a while. A wattle bird flew over with an angry cackle. He nodded at Monique and Mark. "They're having a good time."

"So am I."

Suddenly she felt his hand on her thigh. She slapped it away.

"Aw, crazy bitch, that hurt."

Monique and Mark sat up.

"I told you not to touch me."

"Why did you have to hit me?"

"Why did you have to touch me?"

"They're doing it," Jake said, "everyone does. It's fun. It's normal."

"It's not fun if I don't want it."

"Oh, Libby, chill out," said Monique.

"I said I wanted to come to the river. I didn't say I wanted to be groped by this moron here."

"Whoa, nasty," Mark weighed in.

"Well, stuff you all," said Libby. She grabbed her bag.

"Libby, wait, how will you get home?" said Monique.

"I'll walk," she said, stomping off along the clay path.

Now what, she thought. She'd have to walk home through this heat. She had taken big strides at first, replaying the scene in her mind, but now fatigue set in and she slowed her pace. She reached the picnic area car park. Jake's prized Camry was the only car there. For a moment she fantasised about dragging her house keys along its length, but that would just be mean. She followed the long track towards the main road. She felt calmer now, sadness seeping in where her anger had been. Why couldn't you just be friends with boys? Why did they have to fondle and grab? She had enjoyed lying in the shade of that huge gum tree, watching dragonflies dart over the river. She'd laughed at Jake's stories about his crippled dog. And now it had all ended up in anger.

Bull ants were swarming all over the track. One of them dragged an emerald beetle twice its size into a hole. The path looked grainy here, as if clay, glass and pebbles had all been ground together and spread in a line through the bush. The scent of eucalypt oil and formic acid made her feel drowsy.

Libby finally reached the main road. Now what? So stupid she'd left her phone on the charger. She decided to hitchhike. First time for everything. What could go wrong in a five-minute ride?

She started walking. The tarmac felt soft under her sandals. Not much traffic on the road. Most cars were going in the wrong direction. What if the next car was a red Camry?

A big blue Falcon pulled up next to her. One of those old seventies cars. She felt the ground vibrate as the engine idled. Was this wise? But so much throbbing power, come to a standstill because of her—too late to bail out now.

"Where you going?" asked the driver, a guy in greasy overalls. Early twenties maybe. Looked friendly, not creepy. You never know of course. She'd thought Jake was okay.

"North Warrandyte."

There was a boy her age or younger in the passenger seat. Pale. Silver stud in his earlobe.

"I can drop you off at the bridge."

She climbed into the back seat and looked through the rear window. No red cars in sight. The Falcon took off in a cloud of dust. The driver turned on the radio. Convex Laughter. Libby recognised the song. *Love is a Hoax*. In her head she sang along with the lyrics. No one spoke and that was just fine. She relaxed. It would have taken her at least an hour to walk. So funny, she thought, how I feel safe with these strangers. And harassed by people I thought were my friends.

They dropped her off at the bridge roundabout, right across from that funny little shop with the purple shutters, and drove on into the melting afternoon heat.

ROSLYN'S PARTY

"Yes, it's all gone," said Kurt, "except for the garden furniture."

"Oh? Why's that?" asked Emma.

"Dad kept going on and on about it. Teak. From Indonesia. Brand new. I didn't have the heart to have it removed too."

"So what will happen to it now?"

"Goodness," snapped Kurt, "don't you start about the stupid furniture too."

Emma looked at him. "You're still tired, aren't you?"

"Sorry. I didn't mean to be crabby."

"Do you think the house will sell?"

"That's hard to say, with the crisis. But the real estate agent seems competent. And the house is in a sought-after location. It's not ideal though, trying to sell an empty house in winter…"

"I reckon you've done a fantastic job! You've achieved so much in a couple of weeks…"

"It was so hard, Em, that last visit…"

I'm sure I've already told her this, Kurt thought, but he had to tell her again, not to make sure she understood, but to clad the raw upset of those moments in words. Neutral words, that could be repeated, that might demarcate the boundaries of pain.

"We hugged, the three of us... Dad was crying... Walking away from them, leaving them behind, so helpless and confused—that's the hardest thing I've ever done. I'm abandoning my parents, I thought, so I can fly halfway around the world to go back to helping strangers." His eyes welled up again.

"Oh, Kurt." Emma hugged him and they sat like that for a while.

"Maybe we can Skype them soon," she said. "Maybe Corinne can take her laptop in. Maybe that'll help, if you can see them happy and settled in."

"Maybe."

They got dressed for the party. It was the principal's habit, the librarian had explained to Emma, to invite school staff and their partners to a social *do* at the start of the school year. "They're well off," Nerissa had commented, "her husband's a pilot with Qantas."

The McArthurs were indeed well off, Kurt thought. Their mansion sat on a heavily treed lot at the end of a long driveway. It was built in a U-shape around a paved courtyard. The entire property was brightly lit, like a landing strip in the dense bush.

Henry, the school caretaker, had taken it upon himself to welcome guests as they arrived, and to act as an impromptu tour guide for some of them. The central section, he explained to Emma and Kurt, consisted of the kitchen and an entertaining area. The bedrooms were in the west wing. The east wing required no explanation: the blue water of a vast indoor swimming pool was there for all to see.

"What a funny little man," Kurt said after Henry had finally wandered off. "How he latched on to us. I think he likes you."

"Oh, I don't know," said Emma, "I noticed he got ribbed by some of the teachers the other day. Maybe he tries to engage with new staff before they are absorbed by one of the cliques."

"I had to smile about his diatribe against tourism. No need to travel —you can watch it all at home on YouTube, for free."

"I like him, though," said Emma, "I think he's a lonely soul."

"You're such a softie."

They walked over large slate pavers to where most people were congregating. A tall handsome man in his fifties holding a glass of champagne blocked their path. He looked like Cary Grant, Kurt thought. Square jawed, dimpled chin, broad shoulders. Like a fitness ad from the sixties. Use Steel-O-Bar and you'll look like Iron Man.

"So, what do you teach?" asked Kurt, pushing his reveries aside.

"I don't teach," the man said, "I'm a pilot."

What's with pilots and dimpled chins, Kurt thought. "Oh, so you're the principal's husband?"

"Heavens no, I mean, no disrespect to Mrs McArthur, but no, I'm Gareth, a colleague of her husband's."

Kurt fell silent after his faux pas.

"I'm staying here as their guest," Gareth went on. "I used to fly for British Airways until recently. Then Qantas made me an offer I could not refuse…"

"Good for you," said Emma.

"That's how I found myself based here, in the antipodes," Gareth continued. "I must say, it does take some adjusting. For example, when I first met Paul—that's Roslyn's husband," he added for Kurt's benefit, "he told me that they had a garden full of natives. I rather imagined an unruly band of semi-naked warriors with spears. It turned out that the so-called natives were in fact indigenous shrubs." He roared with laughter.

"Nice to talk to you," said Emma, "but I just need to catch one of my colleagues."

"Cheers cobber," said Kurt, giving the pilot a thumbs-up sign. He hastened to follow Emma.

"What's with you, Kurt?" Emma asked. "Stop the *Crocodile Dundee* act. You can't even get the accent right."

"He deserved it," said Kurt. From the corner of his eye he saw Henry move in Gareth's direction. Yep, he thought, instant karma.

They helped themselves to kebabs while having a painfully polite conversation with Raeleen Osmond. The blistering heat all week provided a safe topic. Emma grabbed a gourmet sausage encased in a roll of Turkish bread and Kurt flopped some slices of mango and watermelon on a plate and they sought refuge at the other end of the courtyard. They walked over to a small group that had gathered in the light of an ornate lantern. A cloud of lacewings and fat moths kept punctuating the glow. The lacewings were like flying hyphens, Kurt thought, little green tubes with wings. The moths red-eyed cardinals cloaked in dust. Boy, he needed sleep.

A young woman said something and the group opened up to let them in. They introduced themselves, for Kurt's sake. Betty Randolph, English. Pam Chesterfield, history and geography, and Darren, her husband. Liz Anderson, science. John Carver, PE.

What had Emma thought of the staff in-service day, Liz wanted to know. Betty asked her about St Genevieve's. Pam asked Kurt what line of work he was in. He told them.

"So..." Betty said, "if I have a child in my class who I think is being abused or neglected I could ring child protection?"

"You have to, actually," said Kurt, "it's a legal requirement. We have mandatory reporting in this state."

"Oh, I didn't know," said Darren, "Did you, Pam?"

"Yes, we received a flyer from the Education Department... And it's covered in our in-service training every year... But if we have concerns we generally discuss them with the year level coordinator. Sometimes Roslyn gets involved. We've rung the police once or twice."

"Well," said Liz, "our new careers teacher will certainly be supremely informed about child protection protocols." They smiled at Emma. Darren raised his glass.

"How common is child abuse these days?" John asked.

"We receive about 38,000 notifications of abuse and neglect a year," said Kurt. Betty gasped.

"Is that across Australia?" asked John.

"No, that's just Victoria."

They were silent as they let the number sink in. Aren't I always a wet blanket, Kurt thought. I'd be the one citing divorce stats at a wedding.

"How do you cope with that," asked Darren, "dealing with such depressing work day after day, year in year out?"

"Well, before I joined child protection I used to get depressed too. All those stories in the media. They seemed like pointless eruptions of pure evil. Another child bullied. Abused. Neglected... Mind you, I still get upset now, but I also see the fantastic commitment of protective workers, and the successes, where a parent learns to take time out, gets a job or goes into detox. Cases where the abuse stops or a family is helped to stay together." He thought of Kylee and Jade; and it felt as if he had just trotted out a sanitised media release, a gigantic falsehood.

"That's so nice," said Betty.

"But you'll never get on top of it, though," said John.

"The way I think about it..." said Kurt. Oh no, not the bus drivers, Emma's eyes seemed to say. "Is that we are like bus drivers. We drive at night, along a narrow rocky road and it's raining." He noticed Liz frowning. "So you need to turn on the windscreen wipers. Those wipers go like crazy, but they can never clear the rain away. But if you turn them off, the bus crashes." Or people fall off buildings. He licked his lips and looked down. He had dropped a sliver of mango on his shoe.

"So, protective workers are like windscreen wipers," said Liz. Darren looked puzzled. John was looking sideways, no doubt hoping to defect to a more congenial congregation.

"I like it," said Betty, "that's a nice image. It's about persistence. Not giving up hope." She gave Kurt an encouraging smile.

"Yeah," said Kurt, "exactly." Note to self, he thought: drop the bus drivers simile.

"Come on, guys," the vice principal called out into the courtyard, "all come to the kitchen please. It's Keith's birthday. Roslyn might say a few words. And we've got cake!"

BRUMBY'S WARNING

"I've just had it with this heat," moaned Emma as she ambled into the lounge room, wearing a pair of Kurt's boxer shorts and a T-shirt. All the windows were open but there was no breeze, and the house felt suffocating after the stifling heat all week. Three days in a row over 43 degrees. Clothes felt hot as you took them out of the drawer. Fruit went off in a day. They had two fans whirring in the lounge room, stirring the heat, not making a difference.

"I want an air conditioning unit for my next birthday," she announced as she plopped down on the couch in front of the television. "Why don't we go and buy a unit tomorrow?"

"Listen to this," Kurt said, "this is unreal."

Emma looked at the image of John Brumby on the screen with a vague sense of dismay. She wanted Kurt to focus on hardware shops, not on some political drivel. The Premier of Victoria was announcing a state-wide total fire ban for tomorrow. What did he think he was doing —moonlighting as a weatherman?

Then it dawned on her that he was emphasising the severity of the fire danger: "It's just as bad a day as you can imagine and on top of that the state is tinder dry. People need to exercise real common sense tomorrow. If you do not need to go out, stay at home." They looked at each other in disbelief. Then came Brumby's closing sentence: "Tomorrow is expected to be the worst day in the history of the state."

"Wow, that's unprecedented," said Emma.

"It is," Kurt agreed. "Do you think he's just trying to cover his butt though? By issuing some sort of disclaimer?"

"I don't think so. Politicians are not generally held accountable for the vagaries of the weather. And it's been such a diabolical week already."

"What's the forecast for tomorrow?"

"Forty-five, and a strong northerly wind." She hated those northerlies, straight from the desert—like blasting your eyes with a hairdryer.

Kurt whistled through his teeth. "Good thing we don't have to go out tomorrow."

"Yeah, the weekend helps us, but I worry about the kids. Most of them live in Warrandyte or Eltham. They're such high fire risk areas."

"Yeah," said Kurt, "it's a real problem, those built-up semi-urban areas. So many people packed so close together on what are effectively bush blocks. Being surrounded by other houses gives them a false sense of security, so they have shrubs growing right up to their doorstep. If a big fire got in there, it would be a deathtrap. Further out —St Andrews, Kinglake—people understand fire better. They clear their land more and they have pumps and stuff."

"Pumps and stuff, hey?" laughed Emma. "My little migrant understands the bush, does he? He's getting all technical now."

"Oh, piss off," said Kurt.

Emma picked up the soft toy kangaroo next to her: "Did you hear that, Mr Kanga? Daddy used a rude word."

Kurt laughed and got up. "Okay," he said, "I'll get us some beer and chips."

"I'll just ring Midnight. In case she didn't hear the warning."

"Good idea. Tell her she can stay at our place if she's worried."

"I will. She may not want to swelter here, though. She's got air conditioning, like most civilised people."

"I can hear so much pain in what you are saying," said Kurt.

Emma threw a pair of socks at his head.

BLACK SATURDAY

They looked at the skyline. A column of grey smoke was visible in the northwest. "I wouldn't trust it mate," said Bruce, "you can stay at my place tonight if you like."

"Nah," said Shaun, "I have to get back. Me mum's up the mountain. And the animals. Anyway, the fire's at Kilmore. That's what they said, on the radio. That's, what? Forty, maybe fifty clicks away?"

"If you say so," said Bruce. "These things can change quickly though, with a strong northerly like this. Why don't you take the rest of the afternoon off and drive back now. Things are pretty quiet round here, anyway."

"Thanks boss, that's great," said Shaun. He got his gear together.

"Hey, boss," yelled Brendan, who had overheard the conversation, "can I go home too? The missus is on fire." Ralph and Barry laughed. Brendan thrust his pelvis back and forth. "Ooh," he said, "so hot, gotta see mummy." Shaun gave Brendan the finger and walked off.

High winds buffeted the Falcon as Shaun drove through the patches of open grassland at Kangaroo Ground. This was not your regular northerly, he thought, these were gale-force winds. A massive column of smoke rose to the north. He turned on the car radio but he couldn't make sense of all the gibberish. The fire had started northwest of Kinglake, one bloke said. A guy on another station kept rabbiting on about a large fire at Murrindindi. Now, last time he looked, Murrindindi was to the northeast of Kinglake. These city journos couldn't tell their bum from a pumpkin if they used both hands. Or were there two separate fires? Kinglake West was under threat, some joker had said. Shaun could not see how a fire could have moved from Kilmore to Kinglake, all across the mountain ridges of the national park, in so short a time. Anyhow, this fire was a real bitch, and it was coming their way.

He had tried ringing his mum at home but there had been no answer. Maybe she was having a lie-down again. She wasn't good in this heat.

He drove past the St Andrews pub. Normally the road would have been swarming here on a Saturday, on account of the market. Old hippies selling their crap, bikies stopping off for a beer, rich folk from Melbourne with nothing better to do than to drive for an hour so they could buy stone-baked bread. Tell you what, he thought, chuck a lump of dough on any stone today and it'll bake.

Just outside St Andrews, at Wild Dog Creek, he pulled over to let four fire trucks pass. He got out of the car to take a leak. The hot wind slammed in his face. Like having your eyes soldered. A crumpled cockatoo sat on a fence post, a couple of metres from him, its beak open. The bird made no attempt to fly away. Shaun rang his mum again. Same deal—no answer. He looked at the column of smoke. The fire was coming this way for sure. He hopped back into the car. You wouldn't want to be stranded in this heat, he thought. Felt like way over 40.

The road started its long winding climb up the mountain, hemmed in by its stone flank on the right and the steep drop on the left. On a good day, Shaun loved this part of the drive. You had to handle your car just right, revving her up and easing her back. Every bend revealed another stand of peppermint gum or mountain ash, as far as the eye could see. But today was different. The sky had turned a gunmetal grey, with a pinkish glow in places, and he could smell the smoke of the approaching fire. He'd never known a fire to move this fast. Visibility was getting worse, so he slowed down. The wind hurled embers through the forest, coughed up burning leaves and ribbons of bark. Shit, he thought, that's going to start spot fires all over the place.

Then a bikie burst out of the smoke ahead. He rode fast, in the middle of the road. Shaun pulled off to the left and flattened a road marker. The rider flashed past. Shaun yanked the steering wheel hard right, got his wheels back on the bitumen but scraped the rock wall on the other side. Pulled left to take the next bend. Fuck. That would be a nasty scratch on the paintwork. His fingers were white from clutching the steering wheel and a vein in his temple was throbbing. Where did that guy even come from? The rider had a forked beard, like Shiv. Or had he imagined that? Maybe it was just the wind blowing it that way. What really creeped Shaun out was that the bikie had been smiling.

It was hard to make out the road now because of the smoke. Shaun drove up Smithy's Track. He avoided the familiar potholes and swung up Mum's driveway. The weatherboard house looked neat in the pink glow. He reversed the Falcon so they could take off straightaway because the fire now seemed to be raging all over the mountain. How will we ever get out, Shaun thought? He ran into the house. The door clanged shut behind him.

"Mum," he yelled, "are you there?"

He spotted a note on the kitchen table, recognised the scrawls: *Shaun. Phones out. Dougie picking me up to CFA. Let the chooks out.*

Shaun could only hope that Mum had made it out in time. That Dougie for once hadn't taken a wrong turn. And did she mean that she had let the chooks out, or that he should? And what about the goats? He ran out the back door, towards the shed. The door of the chook house was slamming in the wind but all the chooks had chosen to stay put. Well, there was nothing he could do about that now. Then he heard an almighty roar, like a thousand V8 engines revving up all at once. He turned round. The two large gums at the front of the property erupted in flames. White swirls of gas escaped like solar flares. The oxygen was being sucked into the fire. The goats, he thought, with difficulty. Have to keep thinking. Keep moving. He opened the goat shed. Bessie jumped out, ran away before he could get hold of her. Leah sat on the straw, cowering.

"Come here, girl."

Leah bleated softly. He grabbed her in his arms and ran out of the shed just in time to see his Falcon turn into a fireball. Hell no, he thought, and tears came to his eyes. Then the house burst into flame. He dashed down the hill, towards the dam. The old bathtub near its edge. From when they still had the horse. Get shelter from that radiant heat. Burned his fingers on the tub. Turned it over anyway, slid underneath. Rust and gum leaves on his hair and neck, spiders and millipedes scurried off. He pulled Leah under with him. A shell, just like Jimmy. Leah's fur prickly and hot. Eyes wide with fear. His throat bone dry. And then the firestorm swept over the dam.

AFTERMATH

The smoke hung everywhere, that grainy, throaty smoke that made breathing difficult and coloured the daylight pink and the sunsets a glorious orange. Refracted by the afterglow of thousands of living beings. Massive stands of mountain ash had been atomised on Black Saturday. Koalas incinerated high up in their trees. Soft-bellied echidnas, their defensive spikes rendered useless. Mobs of frantic kangaroos, unable to outrun the firestorm. Scores of people huddled together in their bathrooms after the fire cut their exit roads, melted their hoses, pumps and generators and made their windows explode.

There was a sense of disbelief at first, at the scale of the disaster. Sadness hovered at the back of your throat all day long. Commuters wept openly on the train as they read their morning paper. The pictures showed some of the horror: a farmer in tears shoots his dying sheep; an injured koala sips from a firefighter's water bottle. Bloated cattle carcasses clumped together in a scorched meadow. A jumble of burnt out cars, at odd angles on the edge of the road. The five devastated towns: studies in grey and black, with rusty brown highlights. Aerial photos showed where the houses had been—grey patches on a brown quilt.

Forensic teams in white protective suits scoured Marysville, until a couple of days ago a leafy holiday village. Yellow flags amid the ruins marked where the bodies lay. And the nightmare was not over yet. Twenty-five fires still burned across the state. Where the fires had been, the soil was scorched. Leaves, grass and fences—it was all gone. No sign of birds or insects; an eerie silence reigned.

Then, like a nation at war, Victoria pulled together in those first days after the fires. People seemed kinder, more patient, for a couple of days at least, as if they were valuing more what they had. Philip and Caitlin stopped quarrelling. Kurt ran up the stairs from the car park and came upon Fran Esposito in tears in the stairwell. Her sister had been missing since the fires. He felt awkward as he gave her a hug.

Libby watched a video clip of a burnt down home. The camera panned from the collapsed walls to the children's swing, miraculously untouched in the backyard, with a toy giraffe lying underneath. She cried a little, up in her room, and wrote a poem. Her mum was busy at work. Two houses had burnt down hours after the contract of sale had been signed and the new owners were asking questions about insurance cover. She would also have to revise all portfolio valuations for fire-prone areas.

Caitlin put together a mental health support guide for community agencies. It suggested strategies for dealing with stress and bereavement and for discussing the fires with young children. She emailed flyers to local schools and kindergartens. Attended community meetings in churches, scouts halls, RSL clubs. She barely saw Philip.

Emma spent a lot of time with a Year 9 student. Nathalie had felt unwell on Black Saturday, so her mum had left her at home in Warrandyte when she drove to Strathewen to pick up Nathalie's younger sister, who had spent the afternoon on a friend's alpaca farm. They never came back.

∼

Fran Esposito ordered a stocktake of all child protection clients. The department needed to know whether any of them had been affected by the fires. There were potential liability issues, she explained. Kurt rang Bob Morrison first.

"No, there's been no fires out this way," Bob said.

"And when did you last see Gecko?" asked Kurt.

"Friday. The lad had been doing really well, going to school—most days anyway—and coming home to Silvan."

"And you haven't heard from him since?"

"No. I think he must be in Heathmont, but I can't be sure. I drove up there on Sunday morning but the place was closed. I rang the cops. Take a number, they basically said. They'd had calls about hundreds of missing persons…"

"But you have no reason to believe Gecko would've been anywhere near the fires?"

"Not normally. Thing is, though, he's been hanging out with that Shaun bloke. He lives out Kinglake way."

"Oh no." The news footage of towering flames flashed through Kurt's mind. Don't tell me I've lost another child, he thought.

"Yes, you can see why I'm worried," said Bob. "I rang Heathmont Motors on Monday, and they hadn't heard from Shaun since the fires. He left mid-afternoon on Saturday, his boss said."

"And he was by himself?"

"Yes."

"It's unlikely that this Shaun would have picked up Gecko as he was driving into a bushfire area."

"It is, but you never know. The male brain's a funny thing until it turns 25 or so."

"Hmm, you've got a point… I'll try to get out to Heathmont myself and I'll give you a bell if I find Gecko."

On the Thursday Kurt finally managed to extract himself from the myriad crisis response tasks in the office and drive to Heathmont. A Blunta motorbike was parked on the nature strip. Joe had one of those. Imported from Bulgaria and supposedly more powerful—and definitely louder—than American touring bikes. Its paintwork was all blistered, as if someone had applied a blowtorch to it. What sort of idiot heats up a fuel tank? A weedy guy in his early twenties opened the door. This might be Tags. The musky smell of marijuana drifted out of the house. Over the guy's shoulder, in the darkness at the far end of the room, Kurt could make out a stout figure in leathers. His head was covered in tattoos and he had a forked beard. A pair of hard eyes took him in briefly and Kurt felt fear slide up his midriff like an icy blade. Then the bikie walked into another room.

"Hi, I'm Kurt. I'm looking for Gecko."

"Are you a copper?" the weedy guy asked. His eyes twitched, as if his brain had just short-circuited.

"No. I'm his social worker. I've been here before."

"Ah yeah," he drawled, "he's mentioned you."

Kurt waited. "And? Is he here?"

"No… there's no one here… Just me."

Why would he lie about the bikie, Kurt wondered.

"And are you Tags?"

"What's it to you?" He rubbed his left arm as if he had accidentally put it in a wasp nest.

"Well, when did you last see Gecko?" Kurt asked.

"Oh, man, you're stressing me out, man…" He shifted his weight from his left leg to his right and back again.

"Take it easy. I just want to make sure Gecko's safe. That he wasn't in the fires."

"Oh yeah, those fires. That's bad shit, man."

"When did you last see Gecko?"

"Don't know man, last week. I have to go now. Sorry." He squinted into the sunlight, shut the door in Kurt's face.

Kurt had another look at the motorbike. One of the rear indicator lights had melted. Something made him turn round and look back at the house. A curtain fell back into place.

～

The mechanic pointed Kurt to the office, a weatherboard shed that sat on concrete posts above a nest of rusty oil drums. Like a dishevelled cormorant incubating its oily brood, Kurt thought. He climbed the pine stairs and, pleased with his simile, slipped on the last step and bumped his head on the low door.

"That would've hurt." A paunchy man in his thirties, a clipboard on his lap, reclined in a swivel chair in front of a fan. A faded beige computer sat on his desk, its screen covered with yellow sticky notes.

"It did," said Kurt, frowning, rubbing his forehead.

"What can I do you for?"

"I'm looking for Shaun."

"You family or something?"

"No, social worker."

The man nodded. "Don't know, mate," he said, "don't know if Shauney's still with us. I got real worried when he didn't turn up for work on Monday. That wasn't like him—he would have rung, for sure."

"And you still haven't heard from him?"

"Nah. Kept trying his mobile. No answer. Drove to Kinglake after work on Monday but the roads were blocked. Still human remains in the area, the cops said. Can't get through."

"That's pretty awful."

"Sure is. All I know is he wanted to get his mum off the mountain. That's what I told the others."

"The others?"

"An older bloke rang on Monday. Next day a young fellow turns up in the yard—did I know where Shaun was?"

Kurt felt a wave of relief wash over him. "Did the boy say his name?"

"Nah. Just a kid—fifteen, sixteen maybe. Do you know him?"

"Does the name Gecko mean anything to you?"

"What, like a lizard?"

"Yeah. That's the boy I'm looking for.

"Never heard that name. Weird." The man's expression seemed to hover between suspicion and concern, not sure where to land.

"I'm his social worker. I just want to know he's safe."

"He's safe alright. Wish I could say the same about Shaun." The man chucked his clipboard on the desk and got up. "Watch your head," he said.

But Kurt was already running down those stairs. For once he was looking forward to ringing Bob.

STICKS AND STONES

Libby sat on her bed, the ceiling fan going overhead. *Hope you're having a fantastic time*, the card said, *Happy Birthday from Dad and Karla*. Well, I'm not having a fantastic time, Libby thought. And thanks for the card, Dad, even though it was a week late. Dad: always so cool, self-contained. It made him seem cold, detached. She had a mother who didn't want her and a father who didn't need her. Libby's eyes skimmed the heavy, home-made paper, the uneven, fibrous edges, the blurry watercolour flowers painted by Karla, who considered herself quite the artist. And then she tore the card up in a sudden spurt of anger that surprised her. She regretted it as soon as she had done it. She looked at the creamy pieces of paper in her lap, soft as oatmeal, and cried.

God, she hated this year. First there had been her mum's shock announcement. Moving to the city. In the middle of Year 12. Thanks for thinking of me, Mum. Then it turned out the hot new teacher wouldn't be taking Year 12 after all. No, Mrs Osmond had taken the class instead. Literature, as taught by a Neanderthal. Rumour had it Mrs Osmond was Head of English only because she had nabbed that role from the start. She had something to do with setting up the school or something. She was like Mum, actually, a woman on a mission, full of energy, always dreaming up new schemes.

Teaching literature, Libby imagined, required a love of words. The new careers teacher had written a clever article in the school magazine about how a writer, using just twenty-six letters and some white spaces in between, could conjure up the past as if she'd been there, or invent a whole new universe where a person could be invisible, morph into a beetle or meet an Elven queen. You had to consider not only the lines on the page, she wrote, you also had to figure out why the author had chosen those words rather than others. You probably needed to learn, Libby thought, how, every word carries its own baggage, just like people. If you read carefully, you could sometimes tell where an author had overworked a passage. It was like getting a portrait drawing almost right, and then spoiling it at the last minute by that extra shadow under an eyelid, by a line that was not true. And then there's Mrs Osmond, describing *The Great Gatsby* as "a bit slow".

Then there had been that dreadful afternoon on the banks of the Yarra. Back at school, Jake and Mark had given her the cold shoulder. Shortly after, the sniggering had started. She was called into the vice principal's office. Did she know, Mr Wilkins had asked, why someone might have written this text on one of the doors in the boys' toilet block. *Ring a root*, it said on the photo he showed her, and then *Libby*, followed by her phone number. She had been speechless, mortified. Trembled with anger and embarrassment. "That's okay," Mr Wilkins had said, "sorry to bother you with this," but he had looked at her in a weird way, as if he deemed her slutty by association. Then he had changed tack, as if he suddenly remembered the school's policy on bullying. "This is of course unaccept-able behaviour," he'd said, "very upsetting for you. The school will look into this. You may want to talk to the Year 12 coordinator or the school counsellor if you need more support." But she could not forget how he'd looked in that first moment. There was a word for this, she'd thought that night, going over the encounter again and again: victim blaming.

A couple of days later the chalk messages appeared. *Libby is fridgid*, the first one said, in the middle school breezeway. Somehow the bad spelling made it more irritating. *Libby the ice queen*, claimed another.

Two cheeky Year 8 boys came up to her, asking "are you Libby?" She gave them the finger and they ran off sniggering. It continued, with *Libby the lezzo* and *Libby has no tits*. That last one was on the blackboard in C-12 as they filed in for maths. Libby dashed out of the classroom as soon as she saw it. Monique had come running after her and had held Libby while she sat crying. But Monique was Monique—she kept reassuring Libby about the size of her breasts and, as such, had missed the whole point. And anyway, she was still seeing Mark, which meant Libby couldn't trust her anymore.

So she had stayed at home, for a week now. Mrs Osmond had rung her once, as had Monique. No one knew who *knightw@tchr91* was, who had been posting poisonous messages. Libby's mum, making a rare foray into parenting, had rung Jake's parents. Jake had denied having anything to do with the bullying.

Libby had watched the bushfires coverage on her laptop, up in her room. She had seen the ferocity of the fires, the destruction, the endless interviews with distraught survivors and it had fed the bleakness in her heart. It wasn't her suffering, but it had become part of her pain. Like a piece of paper towel touching a used teabag, she had soaked up all its darkness, made it her own.

She stared at her body with dismay. I live in my head so much, she thought. There was so much to read, so much to draw, so much to learn. But she was stuck with this needy body. It required feeding, three times a day. Dollops of fat, fibrous roots of plants, gross bits of dead animals. Every month it racked her with pain, for days on end. The blood would flow and she'd have to eat more. Retain her strength, the doctor said. And the boys only ever noticed the bits that stuck out, the wobbly bits. Weren't boys like mindless puppies, play fighting, running in a pack, pushing each other aside, sniffing out the female. Except these puppies uploaded their snarls in chatrooms. Nothing cute about that. It was all unbelievably trite though. Was this all there was? Libby looked at her hips. Her pelvic bones stood out, like parentheses. That's how she wanted that area—in brackets. One day those bones would still be there, but all the muckiness in between would have melted away.

She grabbed her toiletries bag. The shower razor slid out, and she picked it up by its short ribbed handle. She twirled it around. The familiar feel of the soft stubby plastic. I can cope with pain, Libby thought. What causes pain, after all? Those same twenty-six letters that could create so much beauty. Or cuts to the flesh, like the ones we inflict upon sheep and chooks and cows. She looked at the razor blade, moved it to right in front of her iris. No. Then she looked at her upper arm, that pale bulging area covered in freckles. Would it hurt? She drew the razor over her flesh. Nothing at first, then a sharp searing pain of flesh rent asunder. A drop of blood appeared. Anger welled up now, with the pain. Anger at the hurt, anger at this body, anger at the shadows in her head. She cut her arm again. And again.

EPIC FAIL

Kurt was grumpy. He had reacted rather irritably when Emma had asked him to hang out the washing before leaving for work. And why? He tried to reconstruct what he'd been doing. That's right—an article in *The Age* had caught his attention. Gunmen had attacked the visiting Sri Lankan national cricket team in Lahore. He could have put that article aside; it was just that he had started reading it and had become immersed in the story. Emma's request had disrupted his Quality Time with the Morning Paper ritual—big deal. It showed, he ruminated, how easily the rhythm of others can create tension. And he had fallen for it, like Pavlov's dog. A small, unwelcome stimulus had been greeted with aversion. Good old amygdalae, that pair of walnut-shaped thingies in his brain, placing emotions on autopilot, channelling them through the well-worn tracks of the ego. That's why mindfulness was such an important tool in Buddhism. It helped you to notice these patterns as they occurred, instead of retrospectively, when the damage had been done. Anyway, this one had gone through to the keeper. And he hadn't learned from it. He had felt frustrated again when, on the way to work, his car had been held up, first behind a garbage truck, then a learner driver.

Fran summonsed him into her office before he'd had his first coffee and told him to group the data for his monthly statistical report differently. He had been surly and recalcitrant throughout the brief meeting and that had been poor form. Fran did have a point this time. His view of her was so clouded that he found it difficult to see value in anything she proposed. It was unprofessional. Flint-hearted people could have productive ideas, just like well-meaning folk were not immune to the occasional stuff-up. That was the glorious curse of teamwork.

Kurt hated conflict. Its creepers poisoned your body with their vile green sap. Its stiffness lurked in your neck, in your arms, for hours afterwards. It bleached the memories of joy with its noxious breath. He still felt disgruntled when he got out of the car. Somewhat indifferent even, at the prospect of seeing Gecko, and that surprised him. I need to stay open, he recited inwardly, like a mantra. Stay receptive and vulnerable and lay it all on the line, or I'll be a hindrance, not a helper.

Gecko opened the door this time. It felt incongruous to see him in school uniform.

"Oh, you," the boy mumbled, "come in."

Kurt apologised for his absence and explained why he'd gone to Belgium. Gecko listened impassively, his ankles crossed, his arms clasped across his chest so far back that it seemed as if his hands were bound behind his back in some invisible straitjacket. His head lolled from left to right as Kurt completed his tale.

"And I may have some bad news for you," said Kurt.

Gecko looked at him now.

"Your friend Shaun," he started. Gecko sat up, alert.

"I spoke to his boss… He was afraid Shaun got caught in the bushfires." Kurt deployed the look of devout empathy reserved for these occasions.

"Bullshit," thundered Gecko.

Kurt was taken aback. "What do you mean?"

"I rang his boss yesterday. Shaun's alive."

"Oh, that's good news then…" Kurt swallowed. "I'd spoken to his boss earlier and—"

"Shaun's alive but got burned. Real bad, he may not make it. His mum found him near the dam. That's how much you know—fuck all."

Kurt let Gecko's anger wash over him. Serves me right, he thought.

"I'm sorry," he finally said, "really sorry. Shaun obviously means a lot to you and I shouldn't have spoken without knowing all the facts. I was wrong."

Gecko stared at the carpet.

"Do you know what hospital Shaun's in?"

"No."

Kurt thought. "Maybe that's something I could do, find out where Shaun's being treated and let you know." He let his words sink in. "Would you like me to do that?"

"Suppose."

"Okay," Kurt said, "I'll try to find that out for you and I'll let you know."

No point in asking my other questions now, he thought. Anything I ask—about Tags or school or drugs—he's just going to stonewall.

"I'll see myself out," he said, "take care."

Two days later Tags handed Gecko a note he had found under the door. *Shaun Metcalfe*, it said, *The Carnegie Trauma Centre, Burns Unit, room 12.* It also listed the address and phone number.

MARCH 2009

COUNSELLING

Emma walked across the car park. She felt subdued. Kurt was easy to get along with, mostly. Sometimes though, he could get crabby and lash out at her. A sarcastic aside or a harsh reply—unremarkable in itself and noticeable only because of the rarity of such exchanges. It was work, probably, that preyed on his mind. But she felt as if these skirmishes blemished their relationship, like scratches on precious mahogany.

What Kurt had with his habit of lining up objects, straightening the world around him, trying to impose pattern, routine and order, she had that with relationships. They had to be clear and consistent and protected from change. That was nonsense, of course, but it was her deepest wish. And like Kurt had his work cut out keeping his order fetish alive amid the turmoil of his work, Emma was confronted, every day now, with people whose lives had changed irrevocably. They weren't talking about scratches on wood—the whole forest was gone.

She made her way through the library. Only Johnno was there, as usual. His father, a plumber, always dropped him off first thing, sometimes before the school was open. Emma walked into her office, plonked her bag down and went back out to the kitchen. The librarian had plastic containers all over the workbench.

"Pardon my mess," Nerissa said.

"Looks like a healthy breakfast."

"It is," she said. "Gluten-free muesli. Rice bran." She held up the containers in succession. "Dried apricots. Rolled oats. Sunflower seeds. Keeps me regular."

Ew—too much information, Emma thought.

"How's that poor girl who lost her family?" asked Nerissa. "I keep thinking about her."

"She's moved in with her aunt. It's all still very raw of course. It'll take time."

"You sure have been busy. I haven't spoken to you in ages."

"Well, talk about being thrown in at the deep end. Things should settle down now that the group counselling sessions have finished."

Nerissa poked her head outside the kitchen and scanned the library. She turned back to Emma. "And what about our friend Raeleen," she whispered, "and that unreasonable deadline?"

"Oh, the principal decided to defer all work experience placements because of the fires. Local businesses are scrambling to get back to normal. So that buys me more time." Emma stirred her tea. "But it looks like if I've got a customer, Nerissa. Better go." Her spoon clattered in the sink.

She smiled at the gangly blond girl loitering outside her door.

"Hi there," Emma said, "did you want to see me?"

The girl smiled back. "If you have time. I can come back too…"

"No, now's fine. You're in Year 12, aren't you?"

"Sorry. I'm Libby. Libby Rogers. And yes, Year 12." She blushed.

Emma ushered Libby in and gestured at the chairs in front of her desk. Libby sat down and put her hands in her lap.

"So are you the sister of Nathan in Year 9?"

"Yes."

"He's a nice boy."

Libby smiled.

"How can I help you?" God, she's thin, Emma thought.

"Well, I thought—my mum wants to move, to the city, and I'm doing Year 12, so, you know, with assessment and stuff..." The girl couldn't get the words out fast enough.

"Slow down, Libby, slow down. Are you saying your family's planning to move this year?

"My mum, yes. My dad lives in New South Wales."

"And how do you feel about that? About moving?"

Libby swallowed. "Well... pretty upset, actually. I mean, how's that going to work, with assignments and exams and new teachers and a new school?" Her eyes welled up.

"I can see you'd be worried about your studies being disrupted. Have you asked your mum to reconsider? Postpone the move?"

"She doesn't listen to me. The move's crucial for her business, she says."

"What does she do?"

"She manages Comaro."

"Comaro?"

"Her real estate company. Congreve, Mac somebody and Rogers. She wants to set up shop in Melbourne."

The name rang a bell now. Emma could picture the laminated black flyers in her letterbox.

"Could you still attend school here? Commute from Melbourne?"

"Not by public transport. Not in peak hour. Would take me almost two hours to get here from the city. And I can't drive."

"And has your mum already looked at schools in Melbourne, made any arrangements?"

"She says that she can get me into an inner city school. That it doesn't matter where I do Year 12. The curriculum's the same across the state. That I don't have friends anyway."

The things some parents say, Emma thought.

"It might be a good idea if I have a chat with your mum, would that be okay? It'd be good to get more clarity from her about timelines, so we can see how that would work with the assessment calendar. Would you mind if I rang her, and then you and I could meet again in a week or so? Would you be fine with that?"

"Do you have to ring her?"

She's afraid of her mum, Emma thought. And she's just escalated the situation by coming to see me.

"I think it's the best course of action, Libby. Otherwise we'd have to deal with so many different scenarios, most of which might never come to pass. If your mum can be more specific about her plans, we can see what your options are, take it from there."

"I suppose." Libby sounded deflated. "Thank you, Mrs Roo—sorry, how do I say your name?"

Mrs Roo, is that what they call me, Emma thought? Kurt will crack up when I tell him. Will probably wave Mr Kanga at me all night.

"Call me Emma."

"Thank you… Emma."

"And how are you feeling generally?" Emma probed. "Is there anything else you wanted to talk about?"

"No, I'm fine," Libby said, flashing a brilliant smile. "Thanks for your time."

HOUSEWARMING

"Why is it that we've invited all of your friends and I'm doing the cooking?" asked Caitlin.

"Why is it that all your friends have moved to Sydney?" Philip retorted. "What does that say about you?"

Caitlin gave him a death stare.

"Just joking."

"One more joke like that and you're doing your own cooking."

The doorbell rang.

"I'll get that," said Philip.

It was Kevin, clad in lycra and all sweaty, standing next to his bike.

"Don't tell me you cycled all the way from home?"

"I did. You wouldn't believe that traffic. Hi, Caitlin!"

"Hi, Kev. Where's Ramon?"

"He had a sore throat, so he got all wimpy and decided to drive, in that beastly four-wheel-drive of his. He was watching the footy when I left. A penalty shoot-out or something. A horrid thing, that sporting stuff."

"Well you're safe here. And you haven't seen our new place, have you?" asked Caitlin.

"No, I haven't. Looks great. Can I have a shower though? I might be a bit on the nose. Thought I'd scrub up before we meet the legendary Bas."

"Sure," said Philip, "up the stairs, first door on your left."

Kevin placed his bike in the hallway and headed for the bathroom, clutching a change of clothes. Caitlin looked at Philip.

"What?"

"He didn't seem too interested in the house."

"He just got off his bike. Let him catch his breath."

Ramon arrived together with Anaïs and Bas. Anaïs was wearing a long white dress. Under her arm she carried a rectangular package wrapped in brown paper. Bas wore a purple polo top that accentuated his dark skin, his brooding intensity.

"I made something for your new place," said Anaïs. She handed the parcel to Philip and kissed Caitlin.

"For you," said Bas, handing a wine bottle to Caitlin.

"Oh, wow, look at this," said Philip, "Anaïs, this is your masterpiece."

Caitlin looked at the painting. Sunset colours and a nude man wading into the ocean at some tropical beach.

"I painted this at White Beach," Anaïs said, "about two weeks after we met." She smiled at Bas. "Wasn't that a magical afternoon?"

Bas nodded.

Ramon came over to look at the painting. He whistled between his teeth. "Nice butt."

"Let's have a look at the house," Caitlin suggested.

"Yes, always revelating to see what people do with their interiors," said Bas. He followed his host up the stairs, Ramon and Anaïs behind him.

"We love this parquet flooring on the landing." Caitlin pointed at the gleaming oak mosaic.

"I don't like it," Bas said cheerfully. "It is, how you say, old fashion?"

Ramon, looking perplexed, raised his eyebrows, looked at Anaïs.

"Some people might think so," Caitlin said calmly. "I suppose fashions come and go. We like it."

Bluntness, she knew, did not necessarily equate with boorishness. Not if the speaker was struggling for expression in an unfamiliar language. She had dropped enough clangers during her stay in Berlin…

The bathroom door flew open and Kevin burst out. He'd swapped the lycra for a more urbane outfit but his glasses were still fogged up. "You must be Bas. So nice to meet you. I'm Kevin." Then, in mock tour guide mode: "This is the bathroom. Note the quality furnishings. Note also that it is sopping wet."

"He makes a mess at home, too," said Ramon.

And why does he always have to be flippant, Caitlin thought. She showed them the rest of the house and when they were all done Di Fletcher turned up.

"You missed the guided tour," Ramon said.

"I've seen the house," said Di. She looked at Caitlin and flashed a pained, mechanical smile.

"Well, we can start dinner then," said Caitlin.

For entrée she served avocado mashed with feta cheese, on toast, with a poached egg on top and a sprinkling of dill.

The wine seemed to make Bas relax. "It's such a funny thought," he said, "a house warming party. When Anaïs told me about it, I first thought she means it literally. I thought we are going to light a fire or something…" His voice trailed off.

"Where did you say you were from again?" asked Kevin.

"Suriname."

"And the capital is called Paramaribo," said Anaïs, "Paramaribo, now isn't that beautiful?" She smiled at Bas, as if he had merit in the matter.

"Suriname is between Guyana and French Guiana, isn't it?" asked Kevin.

"That's right," said Bas. "And Brazil to the south."

"Ah," said Kevin, "then you're neighbours with Ramon—he was born in Rio."

"São Paulo."

Kevin disregarded the correction. "But *Bas* doesn't sound like a South American name."

"It's Dutch, short for Bastiaan." He explained how Dutch was still the official language of Suriname. Gave a potted history of Suriname's colonial past. Anaïs hung on his every word.

Ramon was cleaning up the leftover Tzatziki dip. Di whispered something that made Philip laugh.

It was strange, Caitlin thought, how no one mentioned Black Saturday. The chaos, the suffering that had kept her preoccupied at work for the past six weeks. She found it hard to engage with the dinner party banter, the vapid conversations—her head was still in a different space. She served the main course, masking her sense of alienation behind a benevolent grin.

"*What* is your cat called?" asked Anaïs as she forked through the mushroom risotto.

"Zebulon Pinkerton," announced Kevin, looking pleased that someone had taken the bait.

Di raised her eyebrows. "What sort of name is that for a cat?"

Ramon rolled his eyes, but Kevin reeled in his catch.

"Zebulon Pike was an American explorer. Allan Pinkerton was a private investigator who provided security for Lincoln in the American Civil War—"

"He slipped up big time," said Philip. Di giggled.

"Kim Beazley was a real Civil War buff," Anaïs threw in.

Kevin persisted. "Pinkerton died after biting his tongue—"

"Oh please, don't mention Beazley in this house," said Philip. "Remember the Tampa? Beazley had an opportunity to take a stand on refugee policy when John Howard sent in the bronzed boys of the SAS against a few dozen miserable refugees on a rickety boat. And what does Labor do? Instead of being an opposition party worthy of that name they come out channelling Howard on border protection. They've been trying to outdo the conservatives in callousness and disregard for our international obligations ever since."

"Hear, hear," Di and Anaïs chimed in, smugly smiling at each other.

Kevin pursed his lips and lined up his dessert spoon with his napkin.

"And it's a real dilemma for Labor," Philip continued. "They'll never outflank the conservatives in callousness—"

"Hope not," said Di.

"And at the same time they're losing support in their heartland, haemorrhaging members by the dozen… What do you make of it all, Ramon?"

"I wouldn't mind some of those bronzed boys of the SAS."

"You're a slut Ramon," said Philip.

They all laughed.

"So, how long have you guys been here now?" asked Anaïs.

"Two months," said Caitlin.

"Wow, you've done a lot in that time. You've made it look like a real home. I love what you've done with your study."

"Oh, that's Philip's," Caitlin said airily. "Di helped him set it up."

Philip blushed. Di knocked over her wine glass.

"Oh," Di said, looking at Caitlin, as the red stain spread through the white linen in front of her, "that was clumsy, ungracious even."

"You must put salt on it," said Bas, "that will suck up the wine." Ramon looked at Kevin.

"How's your book coming along?" Kevin asked Philip.

Caitlin let herself fall backwards onto the bed. She had been chef, head waiter and kitchen hand. She had been a gracious host, even to that sniping bitch, but she was determined not to let those brief exchanges with Di sour the evening. She felt resentful, but she did not want a tiff with Di to riddle her body with anger and to cloud her relationship with Philip yet again. It made her seem territorial, possessive, slightly desperate perhaps. Philip should come to her because he thought she was fabulous—not because she harangued him into stopping seeing someone else. But fatigue and simmering resentment conspired to drain what remained of her energy. They slid past all vestiges of reasoning, sucked the joy out of the air and left her spoiling for a fight.

Philip walked into the bedroom and took his shirt off. He reeked of cognac.

"That was a good night, wasn't it?"

"Dunno, Philip. I'm glad if you liked it. I've had it."

"I had a really good chat about my book with Kevin and Di... She made some good points... What did you talk about?"

"Nothing much. Ramon and Bas kept banging on about match fixing. They're both into football, big time. Ramon asked Anaïs about her painting... I asked Bas about his work."

"What does he do?"

"He's a painter's apprentice. A housepainter..."

"Oh, sweet irony..."

"Philip, why does nobody ever ask me about my work?"

He lay down beside her and stroked her neck.

"Maybe... because it's rather depressing?"

"Oh. I see."

"Don't be upset. Come here, my tigress."

"I don't like it when you're drunk, Philip," she snapped. "You get all gropey."

She turned off the light.

THE BURNS UNIT

Room 12, it said on the ochre yellow door. Gecko pushed the metal handle and poked his head in. A human shape covered in thick square dressings, like a cross between a mummy and an all-white Rubik's Cube, sat propped up against puffy pillows. Its head was encased in some sort of balaclava. What if this is a stranger, Gecko thought. Panic flapped through his chest. Then he noticed the clipboard at the foot end of the bed. *Shaun Metcalfe*, it said above the tables and graphs. Something stirred and Gecko looked up.

"Hi…" said the shape, slowly. It was more like a sigh. The voice did not sound like Shaun.

"Shaun? I'm sorry—were you sleeping?"

"That's okay… I sleep a lot…"

Shaun was wearing a black elastic mask that covered his entire head and went down to his neck. Big round holes had been cut out for his eyes. The hole for his nose seemed way too small and sat too low. Shaun's ears, which had always been hidden by thick mops of hair, stuck out from vertical slits. The overall effect was sinister, especially that severe black rectangular slot through which protruded two ridges of hard, wild flesh, in the place where Shaun's lips had been.

"Why are you wearing a mask?"

"It compresses the burns, the doctor said."

"It's good to see you, man," said Gecko.

Shaun stuck out his arm. Gecko grabbed hold of the bandaged lump at the end of it and held it. He thought he could see moisture in Shaun's eyes. He stood like that for a while, bent awkwardly, as if holding the handle of a defunct hand pump.

"Sit down," Shaun whispered.

Gecko pulled up a chair. He tried not to look at the angry patches of red and black flesh in between Shaun's dressings. It took him back to that nightmare day in Bosnia, when the neighbours placed what remained of Stevan on a tarpaulin. His mother and grandmother wailing, his father cursing the heavens, no one to take him away from that carnage. He swallowed. Shaun, think of Shaun.

"What was it like?" he asked after some time.

"Frigging hot, mate. And then I blacked out... Mum found me... I was unconscious. Dying, basically... Mum freaked out, she said, but Dougie spotted a fire crew nearby. They radioed for help... A chopper came. That's what they told me anyway, I've got no memory of no frigging chopper."

Shaun fell silent for a while. His breathing sounded laboured.

Gecko shifted on his chair. "Maybe I should go," he said.

But Shaun continued his story.

"First thing I remember is someone sticking a tube down me throat... It felt all raw, like a bull ant sting. Could barely breathe, and there's this bozo poking around, stuffing drain pipes in me face... Then I had the wildest dreams. Purple flames everywhere, and the devil on a motorbike, riding through it. Probably the morphine..."

Shaun paused again. Gecko looked at the tangle of tubes going in and out of Shaun. Like the alchemist's laboratory in *Savage Glory*.

"A couple of days later I felt a bit better. Spoke me first words. They told me a bit more... I had burns to thirty-two per cent of me body, they said. A wonder I was alive. I was fused—that's the word the doctor used—fused to a dead goat. Leah... They had to prise me loose... They patched me up with some newfangled stuff, synthetic skin... Don't know what it looks like... I guess I'll find out at some stage. For all I know I may still have goat's hair on me chest."

Gecko smiled. That joke, that was the old Shaun shining through. His friend would make it.

"Did they, you know, tell you how long you have to be here?"

"Not sure, mate. Months, they said."

"Wow."

"There's gonna be more surgery. And when that's all done, rehab. I'll be here for a while yet."

"Have you had other visitors?"

"Mum's been, with Dougie... How's Tags?"

"Same old. Haven't seen much of him. He's been sleeping most days, off to the city at night."

Shaun looked as if he could drift off to sleep again.

"I'd better go now. Let you rest some more."

"Gecko."

"Yes?"

"Come again. If you can."

PRINCES BRIDGE

The steady rhythm of the train made Libby sleepy. She didn't want to go out at all. But this was Monique's eighteenth. She'd been seeing more of her after she broke up with Mark, so she couldn't really skip her party. But why the hell had she put on her blue jumper with the bright yellow stars? This wasn't a kids' party. They weren't going to play pass-the-parcel. Oh well, Libby thought, it's not like I need to impress anyone.

She got out at Flinders Street Station, crossed Swanston Street and ducked into the narrow streets behind St. Paul's Cathedral. It was easy enough to find The Iron Dove, an industrial warehouse that Monique's uncle had converted into a function centre. Libby felt out of place as soon as she entered the long rectangular hall. The throbbing beat of the music bounced off the concrete floor, hot and thick, filling the space. Spotlights mounted on rails carved up the hall in wedges of blue and red.

Monique looked fantastic. She was wearing a low-cut slinky pink dress and her make-up was done to perfection. They hugged, exchanged some cheery sentences about how great the venue was and then Libby felt herself pushed into the background by a new tide of guests.

She sipped an orange juice, had a shouted conversation with Monique's mum and tried to avoid girls from school. I should so not have worn this jumper, she thought. I can't even take it off and it's boiling hot in here.

Libby was considering feigning a sore tummy and leaving early, when the music stopped and Mr Prescott took the floor. Monique stood right beside him.

"I know that a good speech is a short speech," he said, raising Libby's hopes. After that he did his utmost to deliver a bad one. He opened with an ancient episode of the Prescott family at the beach. A one-legged man had come out of the surf and Monique had exclaimed "hop, hop, kangaroo." Next came the story of young Monique setting fire to the Christmas tree...

Libby noticed a boy standing opposite the Prescotts. He was holding a plate of food and looking as if he wished he could blend into the wall. A phalanx of what must have been rugby players stood behind him, highlighting his puny physique, a marsupial mouse surrounded by a line-up of lumbering wombats. He looked cute, though, with his grey hoodie and cargo pants and his bulky sneakers. He also seemed vaguely familiar...

Mr Prescott had now reached Monique's adolescent years and was trying hard to embarrass his daughter.

"And these boys would do anything to attract her attention," he said, raising a finger for dramatic effect.

At that moment Grey Boy must have lost concentration, tipped his plate a bit too much... An olive fell off, hit the concrete and rolled in a greasy track towards Monique, coming to a halt between her feet.

Mr Prescott capitalised on the moment: "As I said, absolutely anything to attract her attention—even baiting her with olives in the middle of a speech." Everyone laughed, except for Grey Boy, who seemed to wish he was in a different solar system. Libby felt sorry for him. And with his face now turned sideways, she noticed the silver stud in his left ear and remembered where she'd seen him.

After the speeches several guests went out to have a smoke in the laneway. Libby snuck out on their tails. She hesitated—should she thank the Prescotts first? As she turned around she saw Grey Boy come out, hands dug in his pockets, looking determined to leave. She smiled when he looked her way.

"Hi," she said, "weren't you in that car that gave me a lift?"

"What?" Grey Boy frowned.

"Last month, in Warrandyte. Your mate was driving and you guys dropped me off at the bridge."

"Oh yeah."

"Anyway," she said awkwardly, "I'm Libby."

"I'm Srecko."

"Srecko?"

"Yeah."

"That's kind of unusual."

"Maybe I am unusual."

Putting up his shield, Libby thought. But she persisted: "Where's it from?"

Srecko sighed. "It's a Serbian name. But my friends call me Gecko."

"Gecko?"

"Yeah."

"As in a lizard?"

"Yeah."

"That's so cute. I love lizards." That's a bit forward, she thought. "We've got skinks at home. In the garden."

Gecko looked at the cobblestones of the laneway. Tried to dislodge some dried-up chewing gum with his boot.

"So... how do you know Monique?"

"I don't. I came with my mate. He knows Steve."

"Monique's new boyfriend?"

"Yeah."

"And your mate, is that the guy with the car?"

"Nah, that was Shaun. He was in the bushfires."

"Oh no!"

"Yeah, he got burned real bad..."

"Oh my god, that's so bad. Is he going to be okay?"

Gecko told Libby about his visit to the hospital. She liked how he spoke about his friend with so much care. Somehow the conversation turned to Libby's parents, and she told him about her mum. About having to move in the middle of Year 12. About her brother Nathan never putting a foot wrong with mum. She was surprised at how freely she told this strange boy about her life. There was something disarming about him. She'd never trusted anyone so readily, so soon.

"And what about your parents?" she asked.

"Let's walk a bit," suggested Gecko.

Libby looked at him. There was a dreaminess in his eyes, nothing scary.

"Okay."

They walked to the banks of the Yarra and sat on the granite blocks of the quay, overlooking the river. Gecko told Libby his mum had died when he was nine and that his dad had gone off to work on an oil rig in Bass Strait. He was always getting drunk and after a while he stopped coming home. He was last seen in a pub in Lakes Entrance, but that was years ago. Gecko's older brother had died back in Europe, in the Balkan wars, when a soldier threw a grenade in the well where Stevan was hiding.

Libby felt moved by Gecko's story, and embarrassed that she'd talked about herself in such detail. What a tough life—her own problems paled into insignificance. But as she ruminated on his story she realised the dots didn't quite connect. Who had looked after Gecko while his dad was working stints on the oil rig?

The river flowed past, flat and black, fast and silent. There was a soft murmur of voices from the opposite bank where a group of people was sitting underneath a gum. Every so often the red glow of someone's cigarette—a short-lived star. Did he have any other relatives, Libby wanted to know. Yes, no, Gecko answered, as if he was confused by the question or unwilling to answer it. He'd been in a gazillion foster homes since he was twelve or thirteen, he wasn't sure. His current foster dad lived in Silvan but he spent most of his time at a mate's place in Heathmont.

"With Tags," he said, "the guy I came in with. Did you see him?"

"No. His name is Tags?"

"Yeah, he's awesome, lets me stay at his place. He does a lot of graffiti. And tats. Wants to be a tattoo artist…"

He sounds like Nathan now, Libby thought. Super excited about his latest thing.

"Tags says one of his mates, Shiv, is covered in tats. His whole head. I haven't met him yet. He rides this heavy bike, a Blunta G-40."

She shuddered. "He sounds creepy, that guy. Let's walk to the bridge."

They talked about music and about where they went to school. Libby sensed Gecko was normally quiet, not a show-off. She felt lucky he'd opened up, she sensed a kindness in him that could easily have been squashed by all the troubles life had thrown at him. What a remarkable boy, she'd never met anyone quite like him.

It was only last month that that stupid episode happened with Jake, she thought as they walked towards Princes Bridge. And here she was at the Yarra again. The same river. Hemmed in here, by stone quays and high rises, but freer in different ways. And once again she stood on one of its banks with a boy, but this boy was just talking. Talking and listening.

"Are you okay? Why are you crying?" asked Gecko.

"It's nothing," said Libby, "I'm okay."

"Did I say something wrong?" He looked confused.

"No, Gecko," she said, "I'm kinda happy, and I'm just not used to that anymore."

He looked her in the eyes and gently drew her towards him. They hugged. She felt the softness of his hoodie. His neck smelled of macadamia nuts.

APRIL 2009

MONKEY MIND

"Look," said Kurt, "this is what she gives me!" He fished a yellow sticky note out of his backpack and gave it to Emma.

She looked at the crumpled note. It said: *KE RSVP CWAV AGM ASAP FE.*

"Oh-kay," she said, "so... it's from Fran to you... and she wants you to RSVP about the Annual General Meeting of whatever the CWAV is. As soon as possible. Is that it?"

"Well done," Kurt said. "The CWAV is the Children's Welfare Association of Victoria. But who communicates like that? Who does she think she is? Alan Turing?" He put the lunch plates in the dishwasher.

"Who's Alan Turing?"

"The decryption whiz who cracked the Enigma code in World War Two."

"And you know such things because...?"

"Oh, I used to read a lot of military history—"

"As behoves a good Buddhist."

"Behoves, hey? Have you been talking to that stuffy librarian again?" He tickled Emma. She pulled away, laughing.

"Oh, Nerissa's okay. She's just lonely."

Kurt started the dishwasher. "Speaking of Buddhism," he said, "I might go down to the Zendo tonight. A bit of meditation might do me good."

"Aren't you meant to meditate with no ulterior motive?"

"Ooh," said Kurt, "I'm impressed! Full marks for listening."

"It's probably a good idea," said Emma. She opened the stove top percolator and scraped out the coffee grounds into the compost bin. "You've been a little tense, haven't you, the past few weeks? That ambulance bill mix-up didn't help."

"Yeah, that really rattled me. I thought I had the Belgian stuff all bedded down and then something like that happens." Kurt took the gas bill off the edge of the kitchen bench, folded it and placed it on top of yesterday's paper. He lined up the notepad and a biro alongside.

"Have you told your parents?"

"No, I just paid the damn thing. No point telling them. Mum wouldn't get it and Dad would get distraught about the whole affair. He's such a control freak."

"He is, isn't he?" Emma smiled.

"What?"

"I know someone else who finds it hard to let go."

"Meaning what?"

"Well, this boy you've been telling me about…"

"Gecko."

"Yes. You seem so… focused on that one case."

"I want to make a difference, Em. I want to keep that boy safe. I've seen too many kids slide."

"But Fran's told you to ease off."

"And I think that's morally wrong. We remove kids like Gecko from their family because of protective concerns and just park them somewhere. But we don't do anything to help them, to teach them life skills, to make them more resilient. Instead of being neglected by their parents, they're being neglected by the state. Way too many of our kids end up homeless, in juvenile justice or overdosing."

"I know, Kurt, we've talked about this so often and I think what you do is wonderful. But how can you, Kurt Edelman, turn that tide? And how can you keep seeing Gecko if your manager doesn't want you to? You can't freelance, without a legal mandate. Not in your field."

"He's still a foster care client, I can check on him every once in a while. Fran doesn't need to know."

"But what good will checking do? You won't have the time to do what you said earlier, teach him life skills."

"Well, I've not been lucky so far, with the trip to Belgium and all that. But I know I can get through to that boy."

"But why him, Kurt? Without Fran's support your hands are tied. Maybe you should let this one—"

"Let him go? Like I let go of Kylee and Jade? No Em, I want to win this one."

"I think you're playing with fire," Emma said.

Kurt felt like an impostor, walking into the Zendo. All these serene, smiling faces. The black robes, the shaved heads. These people had it together. He felt like a fraud, an interloper, smuggling in vats of turmoil, grudge and upset. But when had he not felt like an outsider? At his grandparents' place maybe, in his childhood. That crumbling house with its outbuildings and rambling garden. The dark stubble of his grandfather's beard, his grandmother's even temper, that had been Eden. Ever since then he had felt at odds with his environment.

"Hi, Kurt," said Yasmine, "we haven't seen you for a while. How's your practice been?"

Kurt looked at her, lost for words. He sighed.

"That bad, hey," said Yasmine, "I'll let you go to your zafu." She flashed her trademark smile.

Kurt took in the room, picked a mat facing the window and placed his meditation cushion on it. It was cheating, he knew, picking a window mat. A good Buddhist had no preferences, no aversions. But facing inwards, to the line of mats in the centre, brought its own distractions. Yasmine, for example, but also Howard's flatulence, or the thick pearly sweat that would build up and run down Malcolm's neck. No, better then to watch evening fall, through the wire mesh covering the windows. He'd still have to face inwards, but only for the chanting at the start.

The large copper bell sounded three times and each time the achingly beautiful sound reverberated through the Zendo. There was the usual final bit of shuffling and coughing and then the Ino led the *Heart Sutra* chant. It was in Japanese, this week. Kurt had never managed to learn the sutra by heart, so he followed it from the sheet. It was more melodic than the cumbersome English translation and reciting it in group filled him with joy. It was brisk and choppy and full of vowels and he could surrender himself to its rhythmic beat. The English version always got him thinking. In essence the Heart Sutra was an affirmation of emptiness. The void was the nature of all being, it said, and understanding that fully would relieve all suffering. Just like that—all problems gone. Its reasoning seemed profound but felt as bankrupt to Kurt as Fran's talk about moving stock. Sorry, Jade, the Heart Sutra might say, form is emptiness and emptiness is form, so you're not really gone, for you were never really there.

"We sit facing out," the Ino repeated. There was a terse note to his voice.

"Shit," said Kurt. Yasmine giggled. Everybody else had already stowed away their sutra booklet and completed the 180–degree turn on their zafu. Kurt followed suit and assumed the lotus position. His heart was beating fast and his palms felt sweaty.

Oh well, he thought, someone had to be the worst meditator. Just like the weekly schoolyard pick: they would sooner have picked a one-legged boy than have him on their football team. And with good reason. Kurt Klutz, they called him. Where would they all be now, the boys in his class? Thomas, with his curly hair and deadpan face? Or Andre, his teeth brown from smoking too much, just to rile his parents? At least he knew what Joris was doing.

Kurt cursed himself. He had not driven all the way into the inner city to sit uncomfortably on a cushion and reminisce. Let's take it back to the breathing, he resolved. What had Akura-Osho said again? Inhaling reminds us that we cannot exist without the world. Exhaling reminds us that we have to surrender everything again. Breathing therefore reflects and transcends that dualism. In and out. Slow and deep. Take and give back. World and self. Breathing makes us whole.

Okay, he thought, at least I am now thinking about breathing, but I am still thinking rather than just breathing. Time to take it back to the basics. He breathed in—one. Breathed out—two. He counted to ten and started again. There were a couple of false starts, where he inadvertently counted up to eighteen before he realised, but after a while he captured the rhythm and the counting dropped off. He felt the air flow in through his nostrils. Noticed how his ribcage expanded. His lungs were full. He let go and followed the breath out. His shoulders lowered and his midriff sank back into place. His body settled down, the tension ebbed away. This is going pretty well, the tiny voice said, somewhere in his head. He visualised himself in a black robe, serenely seated on his zafu. His head was clean shaven and his eyes radiated loving kindness. That is Kurt–Sensei, he heard someone whisper, he has attained deep realisation. Families made up long-standing feuds, violent husbands dissolved into tears and apologised to their wives, Fran Esposito resigned—

A short angry slap of Akura–Osho's stick against his shoulder blades made Kurt sit upright again. That really hurt! He couldn't believe he had dozed off—that had never happened. Maybe it was all that squinting into the setting sun. Or that cloying smell of incense, body heat and wet wool. He blinked and focused his eyes on the white painted bricks in front of him, underneath the window ledge. Wonder what this place used to be, he thought. Some sort of machinery workshop, maybe. Here I go again, he thought. Monkey mind. Thoughts hopping all over the place. He felt tired and slightly desperate.

The Ino sounded the bell. "We sit facing inwards," he said.

Kurt turned around. Yasmine looked at him with concern. He smiled weakly. Halfway, he thought.

THE BREAK ROOM

Caitlin needed a coffee. Even instant would do.

"There's a girl on a mission," said Jackie. "Are you okay? You look desperate." She held the olive green door of the staff room open for Caitlin. The occupational therapist had an uncanny ability to pick up on people's moods, Caitlin had noticed that before. And she loved Jackie's Irish accent.

"I'm fine," Caitlin lied, "thanks Jackie!"

"Well, enjoy your break. I'll see you tomorrow!"

Much as she liked Jackie, Caitlin felt relieved to have the staff room to herself, for a moment at least. She took a grey mug and walked over to the coffee jar. Fumbling, she dropped the lid. It clanged onto the floor and came to rest after a weird elliptical wobble. Did you see that, Dr Ratnawarpal, she thought, yet more confirmation of my incompetence.

"Do you mind if I join you for a cuppa?"

"Oh, hi, Suresh, I hadn't heard you come in, I was just making coffee."

"Of course, that's what this room is for." He smiled.

She grinned sheepishly at her supervisor, unsure of what to say next.

"How are you, Caitlin?"

"I'm well, thank you."

"How are you really?" His big brown eyes seemed to look straight through her.

She plopped down on the old green leather couch, forgetting that the cushion on this side still had some springs. Enough to give her a ridiculous little bounce.

"Aw, shit!"

"Oh dear, now you've spilt. Have you burnt yourself?" Suresh pointed at the expanding pale brown stain on Caitlin's thigh. He pulled up a kitchen chair and sat down opposite her.

"No no, it was lukewarm anyway. I'm okay."

Then she started crying.

"I'm sorry," she said, "this is so unprofessional. I'm the clinical psychologist, for heaven's sake, and I start sobbing in the staff room. You must think I'm an idiot."

"I think nothing of the sort, Caitlin. You are such a strong contributor to the team. You always have the best interests of the patients and their carers in mind. Your work is perceptive, timely and accurate."

God, she thought, this guy never drops the ball. You could type up what he just said, verbatim, and you'd have a pretty good job reference...

"Thanks, Suresh. I really appreciate that... but not all clinical leaders would agree with you."

"If I am not mistaken, I think you may be referring to Dr Ratnawarpal."

He seemed to hesitate.

"I do not normally discuss the Director of Clinical Services with my staff, but I have noticed that there has been some tension between the two of you recently and I have, I suppose, been waiting for an opportunity to talk about that with you."

Caitlin paused for a moment, decided to accept the opening.

"It's just that I don't feel valued by him. He seems to be dismissive of everything I do. I will write a detailed assessment and he'll totally disregard it when we review the patient in the team meeting. Last week I spent hours with the carer of a patient with a severe intellectual disability to document ways of communicating directly with the patient. I wanted to empower her, give her a voice in her own treatment. Ratnawarpal deemed it 'nice to have—but not essential' and totally disregarded my recommendations."

"Yes, I remember that discussion. I don't think it is personal though."

"It may well not be personal. Actually, Jackie feels pretty much the same. She's such a talented OT and the Rat, sorry, Dr Ratnawarpal treats her like a basket weaving hippy chick."

Suresh smiled.

"She's looking for an opening in Southern Corridor Health or Western Plains now," Caitlin continued. "Sorry, I shouldn't have let that slip. Gee, I'm doing well with boundaries today…"

She looked sideways, only to be met by the irony of a *Mental Health in the Workplace* poster.

"It may not be personal, Suresh, but it certainly feels crushing and demotivating. And why would you want to be in charge of a multi-disciplinary team, with psychiatrists, nurses, social workers, an occupational therapist and a teary psychologist if all you're going to deliver is a one-dimensional medical treatment model?"

"Dr Ratnawarpal means well. We also have to understand where he comes from. Starting out in Horsham in the early eighties would not have been easy. You come up against a lot of racism in the country, even as a professional, and to this day, so Dr Ratnawarpal may still feel a need to protect his authority…"

"But Suresh, you've pretty much had the same career path, haven't you, except in India? And you had to work as a council clerk before your psychiatry credentials were recognised here. That can't have been easy. How come you've emerged from your experience as a reasonable human being and not a grumpy ogre who feels threatened by a free exchange of ideas?"

"That is maybe a bit harsh."

"Well, I'm sorry about the ogre bit, but I'll ask you this: just try to notice, in our next staff meeting, who the DCS makes eye contact with. My prediction is it will be the medicos. They're the only ones who register on his radar. The rest of us might as well not be there."

"Well, I'm pleased we've started addressing this topic. You have certainly given me food for thought, Caitlin, and let's just keep this exchange between ourselves for now."

Caitlin felt a bit bewildered at Suresh shutting down the conversation. Had she been too strident? Should she have suggested a way forward? Had she compromised Suresh by canning his boss? Had she just pulled the plug on her career?

It seemed as if Suresh picked up on her confusion. He smiled reassuringly.

"You've made me think of back home," he said.

"Is that a good thing?"

"It is a distant thing. An unexpected journey, from northern India to here."

Nunawading didn't seem such a great outcome to Caitlin.

"Do you have any regrets?"

"Only that I've not been able to do more in return for my family."

He paused for a moment, as if weighing whether to elaborate.

"I grew up in Lakhimpur Keri, a small village right up in the north of Uttar Pradesh, close to the Nepalese border. I was lucky: my parents allowed me to go to school. A two-hour hike each way. When I set out early in the morning, the path would still be covered in mist. I would walk quietly, hoping to spot deer in the tall grass. Once I came across a dancing peacock. Its feathers made an arc of colour that spanned the width of the path… In the morning I would go over the previous day's lessons in my head. That was my study time. At dusk I would pray to the Buddha to keep the tigers off my path. When I got home I ate my dhal, sat by the fire a little and went to bed, too tired to help in the household. Nobody ever commented on that, no one begrudged me my learning. 'It is a gift,' my father used to say."

Suresh looked out over the staff car park. "I wanted to repay my family, make it worth their while."

"Well, they must be proud of you."

"My father died not long after my graduation," Suresh continued. "He'd worn himself out. Two years later, my mother followed him to the grave. My teenage brother and sister were placed with an aunt. I have always contributed to their care but at the same time always found an excuse to keep working in the West. I suppose I still feel uncomfortable, some might call it guilty, that I've given back so little to Lakhimpur Keri, which has given me so much."

"You're a nice man, Suresh."

"If you say so."

The awkward silence of an unexpected friendship hung between them for a moment. Then the door flew open and three nurses barged in, hyped up and raucous after their shift.

PUBLIC LECTURE

The weather had turned. There had been a chill in the air for a couple of nights now and the concrete path was strewn with russet leaves.

"You'll do well," Di said, "I'm sure you'll shine."

"Thanks, Fletchie," said Philip. "I wonder whether any of the old guard will turn up."

"Terrence Winterbottom said he was coming—"

"That old fart." They walked up the sandstone steps and entered the Old Arts Building.

"He mentioned your talk to a visiting academic, from Canada. I forget his name, but he seemed interested too. He looked like Hemingway."

"Hmm. The more the merrier. But Terrence would love to see me stumble."

"After you shot him down in flames in Adelaide…"

"Exactly."

"Look," said Di, "your groupies are there."

A young woman in a gypsy dress stepped out of the shadows. Laura Banks. Of course.

"Hi, Dr Wheelwright. I'm so looking forward to your talk. It'll be brilliant!"

"Thanks, Laura." Philip and Di entered the auditorium. Philip put his papers on the lectern and tapped the microphone. Di whispered something in his ear then sat down in the front row.

Philip took in the audience. His honours students were there, his postgraduate students and some first years, including Nicole. So hot, that girl. Who else? Laura, Judith and Cinnamon, looking at him with great expectations. A couple of his colleagues. And there, appropriately on the far right, Dr Terrence Winterbottom, engaged in an animated discussion with a grey-bearded gent.

After the Dean, Dr Barbara Jovic, introduced him, Philip launched into his lecture. He explained how Vladimir Propp had studied Russian folk tales and discerned several underlying narrative patterns. Philip noticed Laura smile at Judith with an expression of we-learned-this-in-class. Di winked at him.

In the 1970s, he continued, Valérie Humboldt had used Propp's concepts to develop her own *Taxonomy of Narrative Semiology*. Humboldt's work, Philip explained, was like a grammar for story-telling. Cinnamon nodded with great conviction.

In his latest work, Philip said, he had been applying Humboldt's classification to Australian indigenous stories. And while Russian fairy tales inevitably ended with a wedding—he paused for the anticipated sniggers from the audience—indigenous stories often culminated in transformation. A man changed into a rock, a snake into a river, five sisters fleeing a rapist into stars in the night sky.

Philip was on a roll now. He cited leading theorists, spun an enthralling aside on Humboldt's concept of discursive platforms, then brought all the strands together in his closing remarks. Voilà, he thought. He smiled at Di. Applause.

The Dean thanked Philip and turned towards the audience. Were there any questions?

"If I may," said Terrence Winterbottom, "I would first like to thank our colleague for his... interesting presentation. It is always refreshing to hear about research that departs from well-established paths. I do wonder, though, whether this type of... formulaic analysis can do justice to the subtlety of great literature?"

"Dr Wheelwright, would you care to answer that?" said the Dean.

"I have some difficulty with your concept of 'great literature,'" said Philip, "some of us might see that as a rather elitist notion. Leaving that aside, I think it is important to understand patterns and techniques that underpin all writing—"

"I am more interested in studying Tolstoy's unique gift," proclaimed Dr Winterbottom, "than in finding out what he might have in common with modern bestsellers or some sort of ... detective story." His disdain was palpable. Some of Philip's colleagues nodded in agreement.

Dr Jovic took the next question to the Hemingway lookalike sitting next to Terrence.

"Dumortier. Pascal Dumortier," he introduced himself, in a strong French accent. "I lecture in literary theory at the University of Ottawa. When I was based in Paris, I collaborated with Valérie Humboldt."

"You worked with Valérie Humboldt?" The name of Philip's idol had just acquired a real-life dimension.

"I did. At the Sorbonne. And I can tell you that your analysis grossly distorts some of Humboldt's key concepts. The way you describe discursive platforms, for example, or how you redefine her tipping points concept. I regret to say, but I find your approach both shallow and misleading." A murmur rippled through the auditorium.

Philip defended his approach but Dumortier countered by citing arcane sources that Philip had never heard of. The exchange became technical and heated. Di's smile had vanished and the groupies looked alarmed. Terrence had a smirk on his face.

Dr Jovic cut the discussion short. "Well, that was a vigorous and stimulating debate. I'll allow one more question from the audience. Something of a less technical nature, maybe. Yes, the gentleman in the blue shirt."

Philip hadn't spotted the Koori man in the audience before. Warrin, from the library.

"I want to know," he began, "how you have the nerve to talk about stories from my culture. You chop them up into little bits, you compare them to this Russian shit. I mean, what gives you the right? Have you spoken to any Elders? Have you ever visited an Indigenous community?"

The audience was stirring now. Di was making a chopping motion with her hands. The Dean looked at Philip and tapped her watch.

Philip just stood there, frozen behind his lectern. He could think of nothing to say.

THE NEPALESE CABINET

"You're kidding me," said Midnight.

"No," said Emma, "I've never been here."

The Yarra seemed to come from two directions. A slow, steady flow on the right coming from Pound Bend, and a torrent of water from the left, from a tunnel that had been carved through the bedrock.

"They dug it in the days of the Gold Rush, this tunnel," Midnight said. "The idea was to change the course of the Yarra so they could mine the old river bed."

"Did it work?" People with big lives again, thought Emma. Fancy changing the course of a river to suit your plans…

"I don't know. It's all on the historical marker back there. I only read the first paragraph. Then I lost interest. You know me, I wasn't paying attention when they handed out focus and concentration…"

Emma laughed. "I'll have to check it on the way out," she said. There was something strange about Midnight's behaviour this afternoon but she couldn't place her finger on it. She seemed preoccupied.

"I often come here," said Midnight. "It's a good place to think. It's as if the flow of water makes my thoughts flow too. Except sometimes it makes me rush to the loo."

"That's a bit of a drawback."

"Oh well, it's not as if I sit here for ages, anyway."

"Kurt sits for two hours when he meditates with his Zen group."

"I couldn't do that. I'd go bonkers if I couldn't move for that long. But tell me, how did he go with his trip to Belgium?"

"It was tough, emotionally, but he got heaps done." Emma listed Kurt's achievements.

"He's done well," said Midnight.

"Yeah, but it never ends. The other day he got a phone call from the real estate agent, saying his parents' front garden had been plundered."

"Plundered?"

"Someone dug up all the shrubs overnight. Who would do such a thing? The agent said it looked like a building site. Not a good look for potential buyers…"

"How did Kurt's parents react?"

"He hasn't told them. It would only rattle them. The real estate agent placed a tarp over the holes. Not ideal, but what can you do? Kurt was upset by it all. It's the distance too, you can't just hop over and sort it out yourself."

"Oh wow, that really is upsetting, isn't it…" She looked at Emma. Her eyes seemed dull. "I've been burgled too."

"What, recently?" So that's what it is, thought Emma.

"Yes, just last week."

"Oh, Midnight—what happened?"

"Well, I opened up on Monday morning and I could sense that something was not right. The shop smelled weird, like rancid sweat."

Emma shuddered.

"It's a funny thing to say, but it terrified me, that odour. Then I noticed the till was open. I'd emptied it out on Friday night, so all he would have found was some coins. I took another step and saw a bundle of fabric on the floor. My scarves. Sixty of them. All torn. That's Kashmiri silk—all wasted. I checked the rest of the stock. Jumpers, shoulder bags, rugs—every item had been cut. He would have needed a hunting knife—some of that fabric is incredibly tough."

"Midnight—that's dreadful."

"And that's not the worst of it. You should see what he left behind."

"What do you mean?"

"It's too awful to say. Let's pop in at the shop on the way back and I'll show you."

Midnight's battered delivery van started with a sickly rattle and laboured its way up the ridge. She asked Emma some questions about Banksia High, but her heart wasn't in it. You can always tell when a friend is just being polite.

"We're off to Tassie," Emma said. "Next week. Just six nights, but Kurt can do with a bit of a break. We're staying in a renovated loft on a winery, near Kettering."

"That sounds lovely," said Midnight. She sounded distracted.

"And is your mum warming to Gordon yet?" Emma tried.

"Yeah, Dad's computer broke down and Gordon ended up fixing it. He's in Dad's good books now, and Mum ended up inviting him over for dinner. He's meeting the whole family next week."

"Well, that's a breakthrough!"

"It is. We're both dreading it, though. Gordon hates dumplings and I fear that's the least of his worries."

Midnight braked and sounded her horn at a golden retriever who was taking his time crossing the road. That wasn't like her, Emma thought, being so on edge. A sense of foreboding hung in the car. Broaching a new topic seemed inappropriate. Like checking the weather forecast at a funeral.

"You're still thinking about this burglary, aren't you?"

"I am," said Midnight. "It was so... invasive, so vile. A robbery I could have lived with. A junkie in need of cash, I would have thought. But this... The wanton, systematic destruction. And then, the other thing—you'll see."

"Did anyone notice anything?"

"The plumber two houses down the road told the police a loud motorbike woke him up around 3:00 a.m. It sounded like a Blunta, he reckoned—that sputtering sound—but he hadn't seen anyone."

∿

Emma pointed at the hand written sign on the door. *Closed until further notice.*

"So you haven't reopened yet?"

"To be perfectly honest," said Midnight, "I want to be here as little as possible. I've been here to let the cops in and the guy from the insurance company. And Gordon helped me put all the wrecked stuff in boxes and take it to the tip. But I feel like closing the shop."

"But Midnight, I get that you're upset, but you can't let these people win—"

"What if he comes back, though? When I'm here… You haven't seen everything yet. Come through, to the back room."

Emma followed her. She remembered to duck below the low lintel which had claimed her scalp before. Midnight walked to the far end of the room and opened the doors of a large, intricately decorated Nepalese cabinet. On its back panel someone had carved a message with a knife. Emma read the words and looked at Midnight, aghast.

"That's just sick. Did you tell the police about this?"

"No," said Midnight, "I only found it after they'd gone."

"I think you should ring them. A guy who writes that needs to be caught and locked up. Before he acts on it."

COMMUNITY MARKET

Libby thought the vendors all looked smiley and chatty. The weather had turned, after a week of pelting rain, and while the grass was still brown from the scorching summer, the clay paths between the market stalls glistened in the mid-morning light. It was a day of grace, a perfect Saturday. Thin grey smoke rose against the ironbark gums and the smell of Johnno's gourmet sausages set dogs straining at their leash. Two kookaburras sat on a high branch, waiting for an opportunity to swoop down on Johnno's grill.

This was the first time they had gone out together to a place where they might bump into people she knew. What if a kid from school spotted her, Libby thought, or a teacher? She felt guilty, as if there was something bad about her walking alongside this boy on a sunny morning in April. Someone might come up to her and expose her delusions. Look at this bag of bones, they would say. Posing as a girlfriend, pretending to lead a normal life. What gives her the right? What was she thinking? She frowned.

"Are you okay?" asked Gecko.

That striped shirt looked like something a gnarled old aunty in Sarajevo might have bought, except he had no relatives there anymore.

The cheery stripes made him look younger, less streetwise. A kid coming over to play video games with Nathan.

"I was thinking we might buy you a cool shirt. I know just the place, at the other end of the market."

"I can't buy a shirt. I've only got enough money for lunch."

"That's fine, I can get it for you."

"I don't want you to buy clothes for me though."

"Like, a present, just for fun."

"But I can't buy you anything."

"Doesn't matter."

Gecko looked at his runners. They were scuffed and dirty.

"Sometimes I think, why do you… hang out with me?"

"Because I really like you." She smiled at him and he couldn't help smiling back. Libby took his hand. It felt warm and soft.

They stepped aside to make room for a pregnant woman pushing a double-seater pram with twins in it.

They looked at each other. Gecko raised his eyebrows.

"Better luck next time lady," whispered Libby.

A young goat was tethered next to a bale of hay. Libby patted it.

"I love animals," she said, looking up at Gecko. "Do you?"

"Yes."

"What's your favourite animal?"

"Dunno. I've never thought of that."

"What if you think about it now?"

Gecko sighed. "That's hard. I like all animals I guess. Except for spiders and stuff."

"Do you like geckos?"

A bashful smile. "I suppose."

"Show me your hands."

"What for?"

She took his right hand. "I just want to see whether your fingers have ribbed pads, for climbing up walls."

"Sure," he said, "and I eat flies too."

She smiled. "Now you're playing along. Hey, did you know that geckos can't blink? They lick their eyes to keep them moist."

"I'm not even going to try that."

Libby stopped at the next stall to look at the jewellery. She tried on a couple of rings but Gecko seemed a bit restless, so she moved on.

"Well, you keep an eye on him then," shouted a chubby woman in a tracksuit to a man in the throng behind her. "He's your frigging kid too."

"Fresh apples, fresh apples," yelled a vendor. "They were still hanging on the tree at Shepparton this morning. Nice and tart, just like the wife. Whoops, she heard that—I'm dead now!"

Gecko stopped in front of a Turkish stall. "Let's have one of these," he said, pointing at three puffy envelopes of dough on a hotplate.

"What are they?"

"They're like pizza wraps. I've had them before. They were really nice… I think they're called golem or something."

The young woman in the white headscarf looked up at Gecko. "Gözleme," she said. Gecko blushed. The woman smiled, turned around, scooped some feta cheese from a plastic container behind her and spread it over a fresh sheet of dough. From another container she grabbed a handful of shredded spinach.

"Will I get one?"

"Not sure…" said Libby. Was it hygienic, she wondered. All this food, just in the open. What if there were flies?

"Come on, let's just share one. Do you want meat or veggies?"

Share one, she thought. She'd never done that. The woman threw diced pumpkin on the dough and rolled it all up into a soft, bulging cylinder, which she handed to an older woman, who slid it on the hotplate and brushed olive oil on it. The wrap sizzled and the woman turned it over with swift, well-practised movements. The wobbly cylinder had burn marks now, like spots on a Dalmatian.

"Okay then. Veggies please—I don't eat meat."

Gecko ordered a gözleme and scraped together enough coins to pay. They walked down the bank, towards the river. They sat on a log and looked at the Yarra. Gecko peeled back the greaseproof paper and offered Libby the first bite. The heavy smell of hot oil escaped from the wrap. A sharp smell too—lemon or lime.

"That's nice," Libby said.

"How come you don't eat meat?"

"I don't like the taste much. And I always think about the animal. I don't want things to die for me." That sounded a bit dramatic.

"I love meat."

They sat in silence. A freckled duck waddled through the onion grass towards the water. Her brood—eight ducklings—clambered behind her, each twig, each blade of grass an almost insurmountable obstacle.

"So yeah, tell me about your friends…" Gecko said. He offered her another bite.

"No, thanks, I've had enough."

"You don't eat much."

Here we go, she thought. But he changed the subject.

"So about your friends…"

"I don't have any, really."

"What about Monique?"

"Oh, we've just been in the same class forever, but we're not close."

"Anyone else at school?"

"You know, school just sucks this year." She was taken aback by the vehemence of her own words.

She told Gecko about the bullying and how she'd stayed away from school. He asked her questions, of course, and she had to provide more detail. It was like telling a story back to front. If, at any moment, Gecko had sneered or joked or probed too much, she would have walked away for good. But he just sat and listened. So she told him about that afternoon by the river. She hated these words and sentences; it was like smearing spider webs over your face. The more you talked, the more the sticky threads went everywhere, until your head was encased in a putrid cocoon.

Gecko held her hands when she was finished.

"I've been bullied too," he said.

He told her about his placements. Different foster parents every year. Some wanted you as a stand-in for the kid they never had. Others had so many kids around the place that they barely remembered your name. One foster mum took ice, was off her face half the time. Different bedrooms, different house rules. And always a new school.

Always the outsider with the weird name and the complicated story. And the others all ganging up on you because you were different.

Libby had understood Gecko's silence after she had told her story. It was not the silence that came with embarrassment or indifference. It was the silence of understanding, respect and empathy, woven together into a strong bond. So she remained silent too. She thought, hoped, he would understand. Libby did something else, too. She leaned her head on Gecko's shoulder and they looked at the endless play of wind on water.

"Let's get you that shirt," she finally said.

As they approached the furthest part of the market, they heard someone playing guitar. But there was an open space where Libby had expected the stall of the *Oriental Vibes* lady with her colourful scarves and clothes. She'd closed shop, another vendor said. After a robbery. So they walked on to check out the busker. He was twenty maybe, with a tentative beard and a knitted vest that seemed too hot for the weather. He thanked a man who threw some coins in his guitar case and started a new song.

"*Three Things About You*," said Gecko. "I love this song."

"Who sings it?"

"The Purple Gargoyles, a Melbourne band."

The busker sang, in his grainy voice, and the rueful lyrics resonated with Libby. She looked sideways at Gecko. His intense concentration showed a depth of feeling that she had not expected—she couldn't really explain what was happening. She loved the song too, she decided. It more than made up for the stripey shirt.

MAY 2009

SLIP SLIDING AWAY

The guy in the bomber jacket looked as if he was barely fifteen. He pulled two yellow straps to fasten the harness. Kurt hoped the boy knew what he was doing, or Emma would go home alone. What had been billed as a flying fox ride through the treetops was in fact a zipline ride under a hang glider. Its sail was a large canvas triangle, maybe four metres wide at its base, and painted in garish red and brown.

"You'll feel a thud when you hit the lock on the other side," said the boy. "Just give me the thumbs-up when you're ready and I'll release the catch."

"Okay," said Kurt. His fingers felt cold. He grinned at Emma. She looked cute, all rugged up, as she waved and mouthed "good luck." She'd had those red woollen mittens since they started dating…

"Here we go," said the guy, "have fun!" He flicked a switch and an engine sputtered to life. The glider moved backwards, with Kurt hanging underneath. The zipline rose steeply, over the river and into the treetops and Kurt felt like he was being carried off by a giant eagle. Emma and the operator had become tiny figurines on the edge of a rectangular gash in the bush. Below him the Huon River boiled in brown torrents. The colour of the Yarra, but furious, turbulent. Maybe dying would be like this, Kurt thought. The ultimate zooming out. Then the back of the harness banged into a metal contraption behind him and a shot of pain arced through his lower back. He felt hot and nauseous, but that dissipated soon. On the other bank a figure raised its arm. Kurt responded with a thumbs-up sign and a latch clicked open behind him.

The noise of the descent surprised him. The wind whipped around his ears and twanged in the metal cables. His eyes felt the size of pancakes as he flashed through the treetops. He screamed in terrified delight as he swooped over the river, bent forward in his buckled seat, his shriek taken up by startled black cockatoos as he sped down towards the bank. He came to a halt on the dusty rubber mats he had started from. Emma cheered. It was all over way too soon.

They walked back through the forest. Up here in the national parks, the Apple Isle was much the way Abel Tasman would have found it in 1642. The Huon pines were its cathedrals, rising twenty, thirty metres into the air. Up high, their stems glistened silver. Down below, their dark brown bark bled into centuries of topsoil.

"Look how beautiful this is," said Kurt, pointing at a pod of ferns growing from a tangle of dead branches.

"It's a big mess," said Emma. "How come you like this? You're normally the neat one."

Kurt considered that for a moment.

"Come to think of it," he said, "I only line up man-made stuff… In nature, I love what is wild, asymmetrical." He grinned. "Shows you what a deep and complex bloke I am." He brushed a leaf off his sleeve.

Emma snorted.

Kurt laughed. "I remember when Mum first came out to Australia. She had no concept of how we use layers of mulch to protect our native gardens. She'd been raking furiously and proudly showed me a large pile of leaves and twigs."

"Poor Irene."

"It often takes us Europeans a while to understand this country. It's so different from what we're used to. The explorers saw a savage land, a way station where they could stock up on water and wood, a strategic base to keep the French at bay… You've seen those early drawings, haven't you, where the trees had upright crowns and the kangaroos looked like mutant dogs."

"And how come you're so cluey then, Mr Migrant? Your mum sweeps up some gum leaves and you start pontificating about Captain Cook. What makes you think you understand Australia?"

"I don't know, Em. I've always felt an affinity with this place, from the start. It seemed an honest place, without pretence. Nature always in your face, with heat waves and bushfires and gale force winds—"

"A fun place."

"I suppose I liked its intensity. You had to be resilient. Belgium was so… balanced. Wishy-washy. Everything based on sensitivities and compromise. And you've seen where I used to live. All bricks and stone and high-rise buildings."

"We'd better get back to Kettering or you might have to spend a night in your beloved bush, with a dozen leeches up your pants. That would test your resilience."

Back in the loft Emma lit a fire in the wood stove while Kurt made a pasta puttanesca. A light rain had started to fall. They looked out over the vineyard until it was dark. They read and talked. Had some wine. Kurt handed his iPod to Emma to let her listen to a song he'd bought online, a seventies classic. They did the cryptic crossword together. It was blowing a gale now.

Then—it must have been after ten—a loud knock at the door startled them. Kurt's first thought was of an intruder and he scanned the room for a possible weapon. The caveman reflex, it made him feel slightly ridiculous. But who could it be, at this time of night, in the middle of nowhere, in a storm? He opened the door and recognised Anne, the landlady, in an oilskin greatcoat.

"Come in," he said, "you're dripping wet."

But she shook her head. "You should come to the house," she said, "I've had a phone call from Belgium."

Kurt's heart sank. He had emailed their accommodation details to the nursing home, just in case.

"It was a Peter. From..." She looked at the streaked note in her left hand. "Reez dancy fit Alice boss. That's what it sounded like."

"Residentie Vitalis Bosch," Kurt said, automatically.

"They said it was urgent. You can ring from my place."

Kurt felt panicky. This meant a major crisis. Maybe a death. Mum? Dad? He scrambled for his phone even though he knew there was no coverage, grabbed a notebook and a pen, a coat. Decided, for some obscure reason, that Emma would stay behind to mind the fire. Dashed down the steps of the loft and followed Anne to her car. It was only a two-minute drive to the house.

He got out of the car and was beset by a yelping ball of fur.

"Toby," yelled Anne, "quiet! Go inside."

Kurt's fingers were shaking as he dialled the number. He got through on the third try.

"Residentie Vitalis Bosch. Emma speaking."

Emma, he thought—what are the odds? He explained who he was and the voice on the other end became extra gentle, extra courteous, extra helpful. This did not bode well. The poodle, delighted at the arrival of a nocturnal visitor, jumped up against Kurt's legs as the receptionist put the call through to the nursing home manager. Anne lifted Toby up and held him in her arms.

Peter stated the obvious. "You know I wouldn't ring you out of bed for a trifle." Leo had died half an hour earlier, he explained. From a high fever. Arrangements would have to be made. Kurt listened, answered. Polite, mechanical exchanges, but something bigger was building in his heart. Don't go there, keep it under control. No good rattling Toby. He thanked Anne, offered to pay for the call. She declined. Drove him back to the loft. Emma was sitting in front of the fire. He told her.

They talked and talked. One of those nights outside time, on the edge of darkness, where sadness is blunted by memories, gratitude lacerated by loss, pain cauterised by sharing. Eventually they went to bed. Kurt slept, but not well, and only for two hours. He dreamed of Leo, in pale blue pyjamas, strapped underneath a giant angel, flying backwards, receding into the distance. "Wear something warmer," Irene called out. Kurt woke up and the world felt terribly awry. Someone had pickled his eyes in rock salt and screwed them in again. He stared through the window at the rows of vines in the pale moonlight. Then, hesitantly, the sun rose, and the window framed a world of golden light on moist gum leaves. It was beautiful; and nothing had ever seemed so inappropriate.

FICTION, FRICTION

Caitlin felt she deserved a treat. Ratnawarpal had been a real prick all week, making work extra difficult. Anyway, she didn't want to think about the new client record system anymore. She nestled down on the couch in the front room next to the fireplace and began rereading *The Corsican's Challenge*, the first volume in Adrian Tetchley's *Nelson's Armada* novels. She had discovered the series in her first year at uni when Adrian Beecher lent her a copy of *A Swamp in the Quiberon*. It had seemed a strange suggestion at first, a novel about naval warfare in Napoleonic times. To her own surprise, she loved the book so much that she worked her way through all twenty volumes in under two years. The novels provided her with an antidote to the staleness of the statistics and mathematics lectures of her psychology course. She had two Adrians in her life in those days, statistical Adrian and nautical Adrian, both of whom she took to bed on occasions, though never at the same time. Nautical Adrian had easily outlasted his statistical counterpart.

This time she was going to read the series in the right order. She had even bought the Boccherini quartet that featured in the opening chapter of *The Corsican's Challenge*, and uploaded it to her iPod. She pushed play and started reading. It was important to get rituals right.

Philip came into the room wearing a faded red windcheater and his oldest jeans. His handyman clothes. She gave him a smile.

"How'd you go with that shelf?"

"Yeah, good. I used a larger drill bit and put in a toggle bolt. It's sturdy now." He sniffed the collar of his T-shirt, frowned. "What are you doing?"

She held up her novel.

"Don't tell me you're starting on that again," he said wearily.

Caitlin put her book down, turned towards Philip and took her earbuds out with the inevitability of a sailor opening a gunport.

"What's wrong with Adrian Tetchley novels then?"

"Well, 'wrong' is not apposite here. 'Wrong' is not an analytical term. It seems to suggest a moral category—"

"Philip!"

"What?"

"You're pontificating again. Spouting bullshit."

"Well…" He sat down on the edge of the green chair.

"Tell me, in plain English, why you don't think much of his novels."

Philip pursed his lips. "I see no reason to get all worked up about this."

"Philip, tell me right now. Why you don't like Tetchley's work."

"Well, they're pseudo-historical novels. You know, swashbuckling heroes, adventure on the high seas."

"How many Adrian Tetchley novels have you read?"

"Oh, I can't recall." He swallowed.

"That means none, doesn't it?"

"Not necessarily." He pulled his sleeve down, shifted in his seat.

"Be honest, Philip."

"Okay, I haven't read any."

"So how can you say they're no good?" She felt so irritated that she didn't even allow herself a triumphant look.

Philip looked at the reclining Buddha on the dresser, as if help might be forthcoming from there.

"Well, sometimes you just know whether a work has literary quality."

"How interesting. That sounds pretty intuitive. Can you tell me more about how that process works?"

She sensed she was trespassing on his domain, lashing out at his core. A tiny voice in her head yapped frenzied warnings. Do you really want to argue about this? Do you want him offside about a bunch of novels you happen to like? Do you realise ridicule is love's kryptonite? She dismissed the voice.

"Well?"

He took a deep breath. There was a chill in the room now.

"If you insist. Some novels are just longish stories. The plot is pretty basic and predictable. The characters are one-dimensional. When you read a lot, you learn to spot such novels. They may not be altogether without merit" (Caitlin blanched at the condescension) "but they're not what we call literature. A literary work requires, how shall I put it, a more modern sensibility."

"Ah, a modern sensibility."

"Yes."

"Would you say Salvador Dali has a modern sensibility?"

"That's a rather arbitrary choice—"

"Yes or no?"

"Well, yes naturally but—"

"What about Marcel Duchamp?"

"Yes, but I don't understand where this is going."

"I'll tell you, Philip. Adrian Tetchley translated Marcel Duchamp's memoirs from French. He wrote a biography of Salvador Dali. Can you explain how an author with those credentials manages to shed his modern sensibility as soon as he sets out to write a novel himself?"

Philip frowned.

"Well, I haven't read his work—"

"And your intuition let you down too." I rest my case, said another little voice in her head, a meany one, with a lawyer's wig.

"Why are you all narky about this?"

"Because it irks me that you reject stuff out of hand. Generally stuff I like. It's elitist."

"Elitist?" Philip echoed, but with alarm in his voice.

"Yes. Parochial."

"Parochial?" he repeated, startled now.

"Yes. You only like what is familiar. Some names are in, some names are out. You don't even have to read it. You just know."

"Goodness," he muttered, "where did all this come from?"

Caitlin felt spent. If this was a victory, it was a Pyrrhic one. So costly it felt like defeat. She picked up her book again and turned it over. The grinning photo of Adrian Tetchley on the back cover seemed to say "now you've done it." She walked over to the window. The terrace house opposite looked unchanged. A hidden world behind the iron lacework. The blistery grey paint. The sky dull today. A chance of rain? A sourness at the back of her throat pulled her back inside the room though she kept staring out. Anger, irritation—it was all so banal. A sense of grief too; that was new.

SCAR TISSUE

Gecko walked up to the mudbrick house. He had borrowed Tags's mobile and rung the night before. Libby's mum was in Adelaide at a conference. Her little brother was staying with a friend in Hurstbridge. Did he feel like coming over? You bet!

The door needed a coat of paint. A brass bell hung on the left. Looked like something for a Swiss cow—surely you weren't meant to ring that? He knocked instead. A shape approached from the other side of the stained glass. Libby opened the door.

"Hey!" she said. She was wearing a grey T-shirt and grey cotton pants. Her hair looked so blond, her eyes so shiny. He still couldn't believe he had a girlfriend now!

"Hey!" It always felt awkward when he hadn't seen her for a couple of days. Like they were strangers again. Like they had to start all over again.

"Come in," she said.

Gecko felt overwhelmed by the light that flooded from the kitchen, by the wood panels, the special rugs, the paintings. This was a house of colours. It smelled of toast and hot milk. He turned back towards Libby and smiled.

"Nice place."

He opened his arms and they hugged. She smelled of shampoo and freshly washed clothes. He could feel her shoulder blades, bony angel wings.

"I brought you something," he said. He took a CD case out of his backpack and handed it to her.

"Oh, wow, you've copied The Purple Gargoyles for me! That's so nice." She kissed him.

"Well," she said, "this is the kitchen." She giggled. "Like, you'd never have guessed!"

They sat down. Libby moved a pile of brochures and fridge magnets out of the way and poured him some lemonade. He'd seen beer in the fridge but didn't want to ask. What an unusual kitchen. Tiles in all different colours. So quiet. She told him about the paintings on the wall. Her dad had done them, years ago. There was one of her family on a bay beach, one of Libby and her brother. The others were landscapes. Pretty good stuff.

"And your mum kept them even though your dad did them?"

"I know, weird. Mum hates his guts, but she's kept all his stuff and the house is like the day he walked out... He could, like, walk in and everything would feel familiar."

"Would you want him to come back?"

Libby snorted. "They wouldn't last two minutes. They're so different. He's so laid back and all into his painting and organic farming. Mum's the total opposite. She's all about selling property and making money."

We're different too, Gecko thought. He didn't know what to make of that. An unspoken idea that hung between them. He smiled at Libby.

She blushed.

"Do you want to come up to my room and I'll show you some photos?"

Gecko followed her up the stairs. His heart was beating fast. He'd never been in a girl's bedroom. The walls were pink. A make-up mirror stood on a dresser surrounded by lots of bottles and tubes—girl stuff.

Another wall had a bookcase crammed with novels about magic and girls in pony clubs.

"Yeah, sorry," said Libby. "I don't read that stuff anymore. I also hate the colours in this room. All the vomity pink. We just haven't changed anything in the house since Dad left."

"Do you like cooking?" Gecko pointed at a vegetarian cookbook on Libby's desk.

"No, I never cook, but sometimes I look at photos of fruit. I like the colours and shapes. Look at this avocado, that's my favourite. I was going to draw it." She showed him a glossy photo of an avocado, sliced in two, resting on a thick purple serviette. "Look at that pip," she said, "it's like a secret egg in a nest of yellow… Avocados are never like that when Mum buys them. They've all been patted and bruised. When Mum peels them you can see someone's thumbprints. Yuck!"

Gecko didn't know what to say. He'd never had an avocado. He didn't know what they were meant to look or taste like. They just looked weird, like an ostrich egg made of plant stuff.

Libby took a pale blue cardboard box from the shelf and sat down on the bed. He sat down next to her.

"This is my dad," she said, "Murray." She handed him a photo of a tall, tanned man. He had wavy blond hair and was wearing a loose white shirt over board shorts.

"He looks nice" said Gecko. Nice enough, he thought, but one of those people who walk past him in the street without ever noticing him. Like a racehorse pays no attention to a grasshopper on the side of the track.

"That was years ago," Libby said. "This is a more recent one. And that's Karla."

Her dad looked older in this shot. The wavy hair now had grey streaks. The woman next to him looked weird, with her braided hair and bangles. She was lean and tanned. Kind of young and energetic even though she had grey hair and deep grooves on her face.

Libby showed him more photos, of her as a baby (unrecognisable), as a toddler (cute) and a primary school kid (silly). Libby with buck teeth before she had braces. Libby on a pony. Libby holding up a swimming carnival trophy. Libby at the Year 9 dress-up party.

"Have you got any photos of your mum?"

"No."

"How come?"

"I tore them up."

"Oh." He often didn't know what to say when things turned tricky. How to deal with the deeper stuff. Never found the words. Like looking through frosted glass. You could make out shapes but they remained blurry. That was him when it came to talking about feelings and stuff.

"What about you?" asked Libby. "Do you have any photos of your parents?"

"I had one of my mum, but I lost that a couple of years ago... My foster parents split up and it was chaos at their place. The guy had been caught cheating and his wife was throwing plates. Mega tantrums. Someone called community services and I had to pack real fast."

"Wow, that sucks. Do you remember what your mum was like?"

"Yeah, of course. But they're all memories from when we lived in Morwell. I don't remember anything from Bosnia... except for one dream."

"What's the dream?"

Gecko blushed. "It's nothing, really. There's not much to tell..."

"Please tell me," asked Libby. She stroked his arm.

"It's kind of a memory dream... Nothing happens. There's lots of people in a garden with trees. It smells like apples."

Libby smiled, as if to encourage him.

"There's loud voices, lots of laughter... I'm sitting on Mum's lap. In front of us there's like this white table cloth that seems to go on forever. There's a bump under the cloth where two tables have been pushed together..." Gecko paused. "This is dumb."

"No! Please keep going!"

"I touch the fabric. It feels kind of stiff and it's warm from the sun. I try to smooth over the bump but it won't go away. I know my mum smiles at me, even though I can't see her... That's all. It's a bit weird."

"No it's not, it's such a nice memory, Gecko... Thanks so much for telling me."

She leaned in and kissed him. They kissed for a bit and then they fell back on the bed and cuddled up.

"This is so nice," Libby whispered in his ear. "Do you like it too, like this?"

"I do," he answered. He felt the possibility of happiness, but it was contaminated with sadness. Telling her the dream had stirred up the past again, and talking about Bosnia always brought up memories of that room at Morwell, at Uncle Milosh's, and then he felt like a heavy toad was crapping on his heart.

"What's wrong?" asked Libby.

"Nothing."

"What are you thinking?"

He looked at her. Her T-shirt sleeve had slid upwards to reveal deep dark lines gouged in her upper arm.

Gecko sat up. "Who did that to you?"

Libby pulled her sleeve down and her eyes went dull. "I did."

"Why?"

She told him, as the room grew darker, about the bullying again. About how it made her depressed. Desperate at first; angry later. Gecko listened to every detail. When she was done, he didn't say a word. Just kissed her on the forehead, once. Then they cuddled, fell asleep for a while.

It was dark when Gecko woke up. His mind was racing. He looked at Libby next to him. He sensed that she did not want the other thing, or not yet, and that was fine by him. The other thing, for him was all tied up with Uncle Milosh. He wondered whether he would ever be able to see past that. Libby deserved someone better, someone who was not damaged goods, someone who could give her the real deal. Not a dopey loser who would just infect her with his sadness. And so then why hang out together? Why pretend that this could lead somewhere? It would just make things harder. But part of him did not want to give up, not just yet. He had this weird feeling that he would have to choose, soon. He could just walk away; that was the road he knew. He would smoke a joint, drink himself into oblivion and throw up in an alleyway somewhere. Or he could stay—and do what? That felt like a journey into the unknown, without a map. No one had ever shown him how to make things work. It was all so complicated, he was getting a headache.

ASHES TO ASHES

Kurt hadn't expected to be back in Belgium so soon. He stood on the church steps and looked at the houses across the street. The one on the left, with its dark brown clinker bricks, might have been built in the eighteenth century. It had iron grilles in front of its windows and a side door entrance under an arched gateway—for servants? The constant drizzle, like clouds being sifted, made its slate roof shine. The one on the right, built of small bricks, red and white intermingled, was of a more recent vintage. It looked tidy, with its white shutters, almost edible—a gingerbread house in a fairy tale. Or was that because he had skipped breakfast?

"There's people coming," Joris said.

It was hard to make out the faces underneath the umbrellas. Kurt recognised Aunty Lisette and Uncle Albert. Behind them Edgar, who had been his parents' handyman. He walked with a limp now. A hearse pulled up in front of the church and something fluttered in Kurt's chest. That was his dad in there, in that simple coffin. It did not bear thinking about. The undertaker's assistant motioned Kurt to take up position in the church entrance. Aunty Lisette and Uncle Albert lined up next to him.

"Irene not here?" whispered Lisette.

"No, she's unsettled. She wouldn't be able to sit through the service. And the incontinence…"

His aunt stared at him with disapproval.

"What about Emma?" she snapped.

"She's just started a new job—"

"I see." She pursed her lips.

The undertakers carried the coffin past. Kurt swallowed. He pictured how his father had taught him to read. Every night after work, Leo sat on the couch next to Kurt, pointing out words in a comic strip about *Johan the Red Knight*. Kurt could still see his father's slender finger with the red-gold wedding band. Unspeakable loss. The congregation filed in. Everyone greeted Kurt, whispered their condolences, shook hands with Lisette and Albert and found a seat. There were school friends of Leo's. Colleagues, cousins twice removed, neighbours and the greengrocer. It was unsettling to see these once-familiar faces after a twenty-year absence. Children Kurt had seen playing hide-and-seek were in their twenties now; their parents middle-aged, faces sagging with excess or leathery in gaunt austerity. *The body tells where you have been*, a Buddhist saying went, *the mind where you are going.*

After the service they walked behind the hearse on its short trip to the cemetery. The prayer, the incense, the stacked flowers—nothing could mask the brutality of that hole in the ground, with its sheer sides dug out in the clay. Tears streamed down Kurt's face as Leo's coffin was lowered. He wept for Leo, for the full life that had come to an end. A part of him died with his father; a part of his father lived on in him. That's how we are intermingled, he thought, we who have families. Far lonelier even for those who fall into that darkness unremembered, and sometimes way too soon.

Joris drove him back to the apartment and they changed out of their suits. Joris was wearing the jumper with the hole again. They had multigrain rolls with young gouda and Dijon mustard in the galley kitchen. Kurt looked at the gleaming linseeds falling on his plate, kept his thoughts at bay.

"That was a good eulogy."

"Thanks. It was hard but I wanted to get it right, for him—though that doesn't make much sense."

"I know what you mean." Joris had lost his mother two years before.

"It's weird, though," Kurt said, "with my mum's dementia... I don't think she understands he's gone."

"Do you want to visit her later this afternoon? I can give you a lift."

"That would be great. Thanks." Can't get through this day without involving Irene, Kurt thought. It wouldn't feel right.

Joris turned the radio on. Wagner? An aria from *Tristan und Isolde*, maybe. The sort of swelling music that could fill the room and drain all energy from it. Kurt thought of Leo as he rinsed the dishes in Joris's tiny sink. Every Sunday afternoon his dad would listen to an opera program on the radio. The saturating effect of the lilting choruses and an epic lunch used to leave Kurt feeling inert and despondent well into the afternoon. He looked across the street. The pavement had been dug up and blue pipes lay everywhere. In the seventh floor apartment the old man was still sitting in his wheelchair. Waiting.

Joris dropped Kurt off at the nursing home. The lift was lined with mirrors. He looked pale and podgy, sleep-deprived. As he stepped out a startled face looked sideways, then shot past him. Mr Strider, he had dubbed him. He had noticed the man on his first visits, in January. He had to be in his seventies but still seemed lean and fit. The most noticeable symptom of his dementia was his agitation. Kurt had never seen him at rest. Mr Strider paced the U-shaped corridor of the nursing home, back and forth, all day, every day. He kept up a brisk pace and shot an angry glance at anyone who crossed his path. A scarecrow on speed.

Kurt walked to the end of the corridor. A nurse came out of his parents' room. His mum's room.

"Irene's not here. She's in the day room."

"Oh, okay. Thanks!"

"Oh, and, Mr Edelman, the manager's asked, could you please look through your father's belongings and, you know, make arrangements."

Kurt looked at her, not understanding.

"It's just that we'll need to free up the bed… for another resident."

Of course, Kurt thought. Life would go on, and change would muscle in the way it always did. He was behind the times, still focused on his dad's absence, not even beginning to engage with what might fill that void. Irene would have to get a companion in her room. If he was struggling with change, what would that mean to someone with dementia?

He walked to the day room—a fancy name someone had conjured up for the eating area outside meal times. It suggested the nursing home had dedicated functional areas when in fact there was only the one shared space. Eight elderly women sat around one of the large tables. "I have a bra," one of them chanted, like a mantra. The other women paid no attention to her. And there was Irene, her once luxuriant black hair now a wiry grey, staring out of the window at a strip of red tiled rooftops. He walked up to the group.

"Hi Mum."

"That's her son," a woman in a brown cardigan said to her neighbour. "He's from Austria."

Irene slowly turned around. When she noticed Kurt, recognition lit up her eyes. She smiled and stood up. Happiness rushed through Kurt's heart.

"Oh," she said, "you're here."

"Yes, Mum. Come here." They hugged.

After a couple of seconds, Irene wriggled free.

"There's something I have to tell you."

"What's that?"

She looked around. "We can't talk here. Let's go to my room."

"Okay." Kurt offered his arm and Irene shuffled away.

"Don't go now," the woman in the brown cardigan shouted, "they're going to bring food. You'll miss out!"

"Don't listen to her," Irene whispered, "she's quite mad, that one. We've just had lunch."

"Oh, what did you have?"

She looked puzzled. "Oh, the usual. Food and stuff."

"There was something you wanted to tell me?"

"That's right. Something serious."

Mr Strider hurled past them, casting furious looks.

"I don't like that man," said Irene, "he's always angry." Kurt noticed she had ulcers in the corners of her mouth. Her skin looked dry and blotchy. He should get her some moisturiser.

Kurt opened the door for Irene and she stepped inside. His dad's bed had been stripped bare. The room smelled of ammonia.

"I have to sit down now," Irene said.

She lowered herself into her armchair. It was covered in stains. Kurt poured Irene a glass of water and sat down next to her.

"So what did you want to tell me, Mum? There was something serious?"

"Ah yes," she said, dribbling water onto her blouse. "Leo's run off with another woman. I haven't seen him for days."

Kurt stared at his feet. This would be hard again.

"No, he hasn't Mum."

"Well, where is he then?"

"But Mum, remember, Dad died."

"Died?"

Kurt nodded.

"Why hasn't anyone told me? Are you sure?"

"Yes, Mum."

Irene's eyes welled up. "What will happen to me then? I have no one now." One of her eyes looked panicky; the other stared at Leo's chair in dull acceptance.

THE OTHER WOMAN

When Kurt came back the next day Irene wasn't in her room, but a strange woman was fast asleep in Leo's bed. Kurt felt on the back foot. He had intended to prepare Irene for the arrival of a room mate, sort out Leo's belongings, make space for her new companion. An orderly transition. Instead, he found a hotchpotch of carry bags at the foot of the bed, spilling over onto Leo's filing boxes. He felt he was intruding into a stranger's bedroom. A hot flush raced through his chest. Kurt collared Peter at the reception desk. But the manager towered above him, a lighthouse, unmoved, the angry foam of Kurt's reproaches washing up around him.

"Look," Peter said, "I run a business. We waited a week so you could come over from Australia. We waited until after the funeral. I have to fill this bed now or we lose money. That's just the way it is."

Turnover, Kurt thought. Occupancy rates. Shifting stock, as Fran would put it.

"Where is Mum anyway?" he asked.

She was having her hair cut, the nurse explained, he'd just missed her.

Kurt beat a retreat to Irene's room. He knocked, but there was no response, so he went in. The strange woman was still asleep, but she had rolled over and Kurt could see her face now; it looked pallid.

He opened one of Leo's boxes and flicked through the files. There were draft job applications and reports from the 1960s, written in blue biro. A dossier about building repairs to Leo's parents' house after it had been damaged by a V-1 bomb in 1944. What the hell was he to do with all this? Kurt felt overwhelmed and shut the box. He asked the nurse for plastic bags and went through Leo's cupboard, throwing his father's suits and ties into them. All clothes would go to communities in Africa, Peter had assured him. How could you ever check? Maybe one day, on the evening news, Kurt would spot a goatherd in Malawi wearing a familiar tweed jacket. Everything was connected.

Kurt had just placed the last of four green bags outside the room when Irene returned.

"What do you think of my hair?" she asked, turning her head.

"You look like a queen."

Irene beamed. Kurt remembered how she'd always cared so much about her appearance. Long white gloves just to drop him off at primary school.

"And what do you think about the lady there?" he asked, pointing at Leo's bed.

"Oh," Irene said offhand, "she lives here now. You know, Leo's gone. He's shacked up with another woman. Don't tell anyone though, people will gossip."

Kurt shook his head. Should he spare Irene's feelings or defend Leo's honour? And did any of it matter?

"Let's go down to the cafeteria," he suggested, "and have a beer."

"Ooh, I love beer!"

She followed him to the lift but when the doors opened she hesitated.

"Come on, get in," said Kurt.

"Don't be rude," she said, "we should let those people get out first."

"Which people?" The lift was empty.

Irene pointed at their reflections in the mirror.

"I'm sure we'll all fit," said Kurt. He gently nudged his mother into the lift.

The beer put Irene in a right royal mood. She was going to take the tram into Antwerp and buy a new dress, she declared. A white one. With a veil. For her First Holy Communion.

The tables had been turned now. While his dad was still alive, Kurt had missed his mum. The witty, charming, elegant woman of his youth, who had cared for him so well. When the dementia took hold he could only see the destruction, the reduced persona, the wrecking ball that smashed the walls of her brain. Leo's death, though, had introduced the ultimate absence—and Kurt now appreciated more what he still had in Irene. His mother recognised him on most days and at times that old spark was still visible in her good eye.

He visited her every day. He got used to Paula being in the same room. She was bed-ridden, hardly spoke and never had any visitors. On her bedside table stood a statuette of cherubs holding up a large white heart covered in roses. She stared at it all day.

Kurt culled Leo's files. At night he Skyped Emma and cooked for Joris when he came back from work. One day he told Irene he was in his fifties now. She hooted with incredulous laughter.

"Oh, my precious baby," she exclaimed, "in his fifties!"

Irene could not remember facts, but Kurt had noticed that she remembered emotions. If he left the nursing home on a sour note, she would still be grumpy the next day. So he learned to listen for the underlying emotions in what she said, and practised that new language. When Irene announced her plan to visit her parents, he did not point out that they had been dead for twenty years. Instead, he responded with "yes, you must miss them so much." He told Irene stories from her youth that she had told him when he was a child. How she had cut off her long black hair and hidden it underneath a cupboard, thinking her mother wouldn't notice.

"Yes, I was naughty, wasn't I!" Irene said cheerfully.

She had given him so much time and attention, and now he was returning the favour. He racked his mind for anecdotes that his mum would recognise. His brain had become her life's back-up database, incomplete and unpredictable, but it could delight her by serving up long-forgotten phrases that her parents had used. He sang nursery rhymes for her. Irene did not remember any of the lines, but she could sing a verse right after Kurt had sung it. They were getting along famously, but Kurt dreaded his approaching return date. He would be taking all this away from her. One day Irene mistook him for her favourite brother and called him Axel. Kurt took it as a compliment. Irene seemed more lively, though there were also days when Kurt returned to Joris's place after an hour or so, as Irene was unresponsive, sunk in deep torpor.

It was on one of those stolid afternoons that they were shuffling through the corridors. From one end of the nursing home to the other and back again. Irene did not utter a word. Mr Strider passed them three or four times for each lap they completed. Kurt thought of the walking meditation he had practised once or twice, back in Melbourne. It was called *Kinhin*. You just walked, mindfully. You noticed the sights and smells, and the feel of your feet on the ground. Okay, he thought, yellow painted walls, nursing station, duty rosters, toilets, ammonia, squishy rubber carpet. It was as if, by listing these objects, he had set them free. This is all I do in this moment, he thought. I am walking. With my mum. And look, there comes Mr Strider again. He is stronger than Mum, but he has to walk alone…

They walked to Irene's room, turned around and walked back again. And then, inexplicably, Irene, who had not said a word all day, stopped in the middle of the corridor and looked Kurt in the eyes.

"Don't worry about me," she said, "I want you to be happy in Australia."

JUNE 2009

THE LETTER

Gecko willed the school bell to ring. He looked forward to the relative safety of the classroom. Safety was a big word. Low level bullying, more like. Behind the teacher's back. Whispers, sneers, notes and gestures. He could just tune out. The schoolyard was different. At times it resembled the Acres of Pain battlefield in *Savage Glory*. Free for all, no quarter given.

No luck today: Matt had spotted him. He lumbered towards Gecko with a malicious grin, his lieutenants in tow.

"Hey, Gecko, where have you been, you slacker?"

Gecko didn't answer, looked around him for escape routes. Too late. Matt stood right in front of him now. His breath smelled of tuna. "Those shoes of yours look like shit, mate. Doesn't your mummy clean them?"

"His mum's dead," said Bevan.

"Yeah," Adam weighed in, "probably topped herself when she first saw you."

"Yeah," smirked Matt, "because she'd given birth to a piece of shit."

They sniggered. Gecko's temples throbbed.

"And what happened to this?" Matt asked, pulling up Gecko's jacket by the collar. "Looks like something from an op shop." Gecko brushed his hand aside.

"Ooh, getting upset, are we?" said Matt. His sidekicks grabbed Gecko by the arms.

"Let go of me you dickheads."

"Now you're being rude, Gecko," said Matt, "the teachers won't like that. And they already don't like you much, do they?"

"Let go of me." Gecko struggled.

"And how could they like you, if you look like this?" Matt continued, "you look like you've tried to fuck a garbage truck."

"Fuck a garbage truck," snickered Bevan, with incredulous mirth. Other kids were gathering.

"Just bash the weirdo," said Simone, licking her lip stud in anticipation.

Gecko moved his right hand to his pocket.

"Oh, what have you got there? Something interesting? Hold him guys, we'll have a look." Matt fished a piece of paper out of Gecko's pocket. Unfolded it.

"Give it back, you moron. It's mine."

"Here we go," said Matt, disregarding Gecko's protestations, "a letter. A love letter."

"Oooh," went the onlookers.

"It says 'Dear Gecko. Thank you for last night.'" The crowd hooted.

"Loser here found a girlfriend! As if. She must be blind! And a retard." Laughter.

"Give that back, you fuckwit."

"I will, I will. We're just gonna read it first. 'Thank you for being so gentle.' Huh, when a chick says that, it means the guy couldn't keep it up."

Raucous laughter. Then Adam released his grip on Gecko's right arm to adjust his glasses and Gecko's fist shot out, hitting Matt in the face.

"Fight, fight, fight, fight," the crowd chanted.

"My nose! The arsehole broke my nose!" Matt shouted, blood running down his shirt.

Gecko broke free, grabbed his letter and ran away.

"Bosovic, come back," Mr Alexander called, but Gecko was already headed for freedom. Clutching the blood spattered letter, he jumped over a row of schoolbags, bolted between two portable classrooms, spun around the wheelie bins and vaulted over the fence.

SUBURBAN VALKYRIES

Gecko had hung around in a shopping centre for a couple of hours, and decided to make tracks when the security guards started to notice him. When he arrived at Tags's place, the red mist was still inside him. In his fury he didn't register the heavy motorbike parked on the nature strip. He stormed inside and let the door clang shut.

The curtains were drawn, and the room smelled of weed. Tags was on the couch, looking pale. There were a couple of baggies on the coffee table. To his right, deep in the shadows, lurked a massive presence clad in leather. Gecko found it hard to make out his face. A forked black beard. As he stepped closer, he noticed tattoos all over the man's head and face, like the photo of a Maori warrior he'd once seen. Every square inch of skin had been inked. Gecko felt faint. He could make out skulls, a large spider, and one of those occult symbols, a pentagram or something? He didn't want to stare, but felt unable to look away. There seemed to be swirls and curls on the man's forehead, and lightning arrows on his eyelids. It was hard to see the details, with the drawings so dense and dark, a blue black sheen that merged into a sinister mask.

A gravelly voice spoke. "This the boy?"

"Yeah," said Tags, "this is Gecko." Tags looked miserable.

Gecko stood there, not knowing what to do. He felt as if he had burst in on a crime scene or interrupted some ancient ritual.

"Oh, and this is Shiv," said Tags, like an afterthought.

"Hi." Gecko lowered his eyes. I should've gone to Bob's, he thought.

"You've got blood on your shirt," Shiv observed.

"What happened?" asked Tags.

Gecko told them about the school fight. Didn't mention the letter though.

"So you broke his nose," said Tags.

"Think so." Gecko swallowed.

Shiv looked at Gecko. His eyes were cold and hard. "He's got more balls than you," he said to Tags.

Tags frowned, looked as if he was about to say something but decided against it. He took three, four baggies off the table and put them in his backpack.

"I'll see you on Thursday then." He sauntered off.

Shiv did not respond but kept staring at Gecko.

"Ever been on a Blunta G-40?" he asked.

"Who, me?"

"Who else is there?"

Gecko felt uncomfortable with Shiv's gaze upon him. He wished, vaguely, that he could turn the clock back, that he had somehow not entered this house on this afternoon, so that this monstrous man would not have been aware of his existence. Too late for that.

"Let's go," said Shiv.

Gecko followed him out of the house. *Mutineers* emblazoned across the shoulders of Shiv's jacket. Underneath the silver lettering the picture of a grinning skull.

"Don't I need a helmet or something?" Gecko tried.

Shiv opened a leather bag, chucked him one.

"Tell me where that sucker lives, who's such a hero when he's got his mates with him."

Gecko was confused. It was all happening too fast. To say *no* to Shiv seemed physically impossible. Gecko needed to think but Shiv was a step ahead of him, throwing him off balance. He gave him Matt's suburb and said he didn't know the address. But those penetrating eyes made him blush and look away.

"He's on my bus," he mumbled, "I know where he gets off. Opposite a park."

He didn't want Matt to be hurt, he added. Shiv told him not to worry.

Shiv started the bike and the whole street echoed with its rolling thunder. Gecko couldn't help smiling. This was power, raw power. The wind whooshed round his helmet. Pedestrians looked up and motorists moved over. He was invincible. How cool was this.

He also felt torn. Part of him hoped they wouldn't find Matt. That would keep things simple—just a ride on a motorbike. Another part of him wanted to taunt his tormentor, show him he had some serious backup. But what would Shiv do?

Shiv only slowed down when they reached the crescent that wound around the park. The bike now chugged along like a steampunk contraption from *Savage Glory*, Gecko thought. Tugboat of Doom. Shiv could pass for a barbarian fighter, all bullish muscle and strength.

Gecko spotted four kids in his school's uniform up ahead. When the roar of the bike made them turn around, he recognised Matt, a bandage across his nose. With him were Adam, Bevan and Simone. He hesitated, then tapped Shiv on the shoulder and pointed at the foursome. They had seen him too, and understood the danger. They ran across the street and up a driveway as Shiv accelerated towards them.

Shiv pulled up in front of the house just as Matt opened the door and hurried in his friends. A terrier ran towards them, barking. Shiv revved the Blunta, and the dog ran off into the backyard, yelping. Someone pulled a curtain aside—Matt. Shiv gave him the finger with his massive, gloved hand and the curtain fell back.

Shiv revved his bike again and again, sending shockwaves and tremors up the drive, through the street. Finally he wheeled the Blunta around. On the nature strip he gouged dark channels in the fat green grass and kicked over two wheelie bins, sending bottles crashing into the street. Old newspapers blew away.

They made off in a low rumble. Gecko smiled as he replayed the scene in his head on the way back to Heathmont. Matt, with that dumb bandage, looking stunned. The fear on Simone's face, Bevan falling into a bush while Matt was fumbling with his key. And that stupid little dog who was braver than the lot of them. Wait until he told Tags. This was better than a raid in *Savage Glory*. He'd totally owned them.

As the sun sank behind the trees, he shivered. His joy was disappearing faster than the light. He knew it was fanciful to think of Shiv as his backup. All Gecko had done was hold on to a bike. This hadn't been a raid in a game; he knew there would be consequences. I've made enemies now, he thought. I can't ever go back to school.

SYDNEY HARBOUR

Philip sat on the bed in his hotel room. He sloshed the whisky around in his glass, pouted his lips and sighed.

"Maybe we should have gone with the others," said Di. She swivelled in her armchair.

"What, and listen to that interminable bore?"

"I know, but this attracts attention. They'll be gossiping."

"And do you mind that?"

"We have our careers to think of, Philip."

He snorted.

"Winterbottom's clique has grown stronger over the past year," she continued. "We can't just disregard them. We've lost Forrester, Dunham and Pilcrow."

"Pilcrow—what a name. I miss the bastard. If I ever buy a pub, I want to call it The Prefatory Pilcrow."

"You're being flippant, Philip."

"You sound like Caitlin now."

"That's grim. What I mean is that we have to take into account the other blocs in Faculty. Our power is waning."

"You make them sound like Afghan warlords."

"Less firepower, I suppose, but bigger egos."

"Who's flippant now?"

Di got up and walked towards the window.

"Look at that skyline," she said. From this angle the Opera House looked like alien shoulder pads hunched up against the night sky. The neon signs on the skyscrapers behind it threw a band of electric blue light across the harbour.

Philip got off the bed, but walked towards the fridge instead. He took another tiny bottle from the mini bar.

"I can't even tempt you with the Sydney skyline?" asked Di. The light under the pelmets cast a greenish tinge on her face. She looked lined and tired.

"I'm hard to tempt these days Fletchie." He sat down against his stacked pillows again.

"When did we get so jaded?" She pulled the curtain shut. "Sometimes it all seems so trite. The name dropping. The vacuous journal articles. The bovine expression of first-year students... This conference for that matter. *Proust to Beckett: Early Modernism and the Construct of Identity.* 'Sounds like a bunch of wankers,' my cabbie said."

"Ah, the cab driver. That oracle of the modern world." Philip sipped his whisky. "I know what you mean, though. But what else is there? Doing good? Like Caitlin, rescuing those less fortunate? There's a lot of crap going on at her work, too. People jockeying for position, protecting their reputation, stealing each other's ideas."

"Sometimes I think of my school days—"

"I can quite imagine you in a school uniform—"

"Aw, shut up, you perv. What I mean is, I loved literature in those days. Every book was an adventure before it became my job. I was a country girl from Ballarat. Entertainment meant playing hockey, and a dance in the church hall on Saturday night. I can still picture all those girls with bruised legs waiting for a dance."

"Oh, the humanity!"

"Going to the library kept me sane. I started by reading Graham Greene. His prose was a bit too—brittle—for my taste. Then I discovered the French classics."

"Did you read them in French?"

"Get real, Philip, I was seventeen. My French was of the *Monsieur*

Dupont fume une pipe variety, not quite up to Balzac or Proust. I discovered Zola and worked my way through the Rougon–Macquart series."

"All twenty novels?"

"Yes. It was such an education. Reading about painters and harlots, washerwomen and train drivers."

"And Ballarat was never the same…"

"Exactly!"

Philip's mobile rang. He looked at the screen and frowned. "Caitlin," he mouthed at Di. He put his index finger over his lips.

"Hi, darling." He sounded self-conscious.

"Oh, disappointing actually. Winterbottom excelled at mediocrity again." He raised his eyebrows at Di.

"Yes, at Palatino's. A rather unadventurous lamb roast. With lots of garlic and dill."

Di had swung her legs over the armrest of her chair. She was rubbing her underlip. Slowly, as if lost in thought. Philip knew she was listening to every word.

"I'm back in my room." He rolled his eyes at the ceiling.

"I felt tired. Didn't want to hang around with Terrence et al."

"Yes, she's here."

Di looked up at him, fluttered her eyelashes.

"We're going through some notes. We're hosting a workshop together tomorrow."

Di gave him a thumbs-up.

"What's it about? The theatre of the absurd. Ionesco, Antonin Artaud."

"Well, you should read them one day."

Di wriggled on the armchair, trying to get more comfortable. Her skirt fell back, exposing her thighs. She smiled at Philip.

"I didn't mean that to sound unfriendly." His voice sounded thick.

"Well, it wasn't. I should get back to work now."

"Oh, well, how was your day?"

Di undid the top button of her blouse.

"I do care, look, I'm just a bit preoccupied right now. Let's talk about this tomorrow."

"Okay, goodnight." He sighed and turned his mobile off.

"Scary," said Di, "the ease with which you lie."

Philip didn't answer.

"Well," she said, "we'd better get stuck into the theatre of the absurd." She unbuttoned her blouse further.

"Before you go on," said Philip, "can we do this in your room?"

"Sure, but why?"

"My mini bar is empty."

"I like a man who gets his priorities straight," said Di. She looked wistful and he could see, in her face, where age would lash its moorings.

A WALK IN THE PARK

Libby had felt a flutter of happiness. She had found a boy she liked. They had been close, cuddling on the narrow bed in her room. It was the best. Afterwards she had written him a letter. Nothing much really, though she had never written like that, giving someone a glimpse of her world, not even to Dad.

And then: zilch. She hadn't heard from Gecko for six days now. Had he thought her letter was stupid? Shown it to his mates and laughed? Had he expected more that afternoon? Was she too high-maintenance, all talk and no action? Or was it her misshapen body? Had he gone off her? Was he even okay? She couldn't very well turn up in Silvan. Would just make her look pushy. So annoying he didn't have a mobile.

The doorbell rang. She heard footsteps downstairs, then her mother answered the door.

"Libby! It's for you. A boy," she added, rather incredulously.

Libby flew out of her room and raced down the stairs.

Gecko looked scruffy: hair bedraggled, the sleeve of his jacket torn. Libby's mum stared at him with a mixture of disapproval and resignation, as if this piece of flotsam was the only catch her scrawny daughter was ever likely to land. She muttered something under her breath and steamed back to the kitchen.

"Gecko, where have you been? I haven't heard from you in ages!"

"Yeah, I'm sorry," he mumbled. He hugged her. He smelled sour.

She pushed him back by the shoulders, gently, so she could look him in the face. He looked down.

"You look terrible… What happened?"

"I was in a fight, at school… Broke a guy's nose."

Libby frowned. Then she heard shuffling in the kitchen, glass bottles being pushed across tiles, right next to the door, where they kept their recycling.

"Let's go for a walk," she said, raising her voice for her mum's benefit, "then you can tell me everything, without people eavesdropping…"

There was a chill in the air and the streets were wet. It was overcast, and some cars had already turned on their headlights. They walked past the garden that always smelled of basil and rosemary, down to the nature reserve at the bottom of the street. Pink galahs were foraging for seeds in pairs on the oval.

Libby felt unsettled when Gecko told her of his fight with Matt. Her letter had caused this. She could see that Gecko had been provoked, but the episode diminished him in her eyes all the same. She didn't want a boyfriend who fought for her; she wanted one who would not be drawn into primitive payback games.

Then it got worse, as Gecko told her, in dribs and drabs, about this horrible bikie.

"Hang on," she said, "let me get this straight. This bikie, like, comes to the rescue of a sixteen-year-old schoolboy? Why would he bother?"

Gecko frowned and pursed his lips. Libby could tell he didn't like her question. She knew he felt uncomfortable about being younger than her; and this was the first time that she had referred to his age. Wrong move. Calling him a schoolboy made it worse.

"He didn't come to my rescue," said Gecko, sounding peeved. "I'd taken care of Matt myself."

"By breaking his nose. But why get on that motorbike? Like, obviously, this Shiv guy wasn't going to deliver a bunch of flowers."

"You sound like my foster dad," Gecko bit back.

Libby fell silent. She looked at the rubbish bin next to the picnic tables. A bulging plastic bag protruded from underneath the metal lid. A crow landed on the rim and began pulling the plastic to shreds.

"I'm sorry. I didn't mean to get narky..." Gecko said. "I suppose it was a stupid thing to do. I was still angry, and I liked that Shiv was on my side. We were a team, you know, and I liked that. I'm never in a team..."

Libby took his hand.

"We can be a team," she said.

"I know."

The crow had pulled a half-eaten pork chop out of the bin. Gross. From time to time he interrupted his feast to scan the parkland.

"So what happened after your raid on Matt's house?"

"It wasn't a raid." He sniffed.

"It wasn't exactly a friendly visit, though, with a motorbike ploughing the nature strip."

"You making fun of me now?"

"No, Gecko, I'm not. But this is such a weird story. I'm trying to understand why you do things like that."

"Like what?"

"Fighting and stuff. Hitting back. It seems so alien, like the stuff you watch on telly. You don't expect it in your own life."

"Well, you've been lucky then." He sniffed.

"I suppose."

A Labrador ran across the path, sniffing the wet gravel and wagging its tail. The crow flew up, cawing in disgust, and sought refuge in a stand of pine trees. The Labrador sniffed the pork chop and started chewing it.

"And then the cops came to Silvan—" Gecko continued.

"The police are involved?"

"They think I killed Matt's dog."

"Killed his dog?" Libby looked aghast.

The Labrador ran off with the chop in its mouth.

"I didn't do it, alright. The dog was fine. Someone killed it two days later, the cops reckon."

"What? That's awful!"

"They wanted to question me. And then I got expelled from school."

"Gecko!"

"The principal rang my foster dad. Said I was a disruptive influence, he called it, an unacceptable security risk. No one asked for my fucking side of the story. My foster dad gave me hell, so I ran away."

Libby was astounded. She didn't know what to say.

"So where have you been living?" she finally asked.

"In Heathmont. Tags has been away but Shiv's been dropping off food."

"Why does he do that?"

"I don't know. 'I look after my mates,' he says. At first I thought he was a real creep, with his tats and stuff, but I'm beginning to like him."

"Hmm."

"What?"

"He does sound creepy. What if he killed that dog?"

"Why would he do that?"

"Someone did. Someone sick enough to murder a dog."

"It could just be a coincidence."

"Yeah, sure. A bikie trashes your place and two days later your dog is killed. Just a bad run…"

"Don't get all sassy dissing my mates."

"Oh, he's your mate now, is he? You just said yourself you thought he was a creep at first."

"He stands by me. Everyone else is ready to drop me in it. Teachers, the cops, my foster dad. And I'm not so sure whose side you're on."

"But Gecko, this is freaking me out. This is all new for me… this violence."

"Oh, I get it," he sneered, "sor-ry for mucking up your neat shiny world, with your paintings and drawings and your hero dad."

A sharp intake of breath. "That's mean." A membrane tore and the well of pain inside her started bleeding again. That familiar feeling of happiness sliding away, irrevocably, a golden sunset sinking below the horizon. So this was not meant to be after all.

"We should get back," she said, "it's getting chilly."

"I think I'll walk to the bus stop."

"Oh... okay."

"See ya," he mumbled.

Libby could not reply. Tears welled up in her eyes. She watched Gecko walk up the track. He took a piece of paper out of his pocket, scrunched it up and threw it in the high grass at the edge of the oval. It was raining now and she heard a frog croak in the nearby pond. The crow flew down from the pine trees and landed on the bin. Its cold blue eyes examined the ground at its base, but to no avail. Its treasure had disappeared.

THE MORE IT CHANGES

The glass doors slid open and Kurt recognised the familiar smell of the office. A mix of adrenaline, stale sweat and carpet glue.

"Hey," said Debbie, "welcome back! How was your trip?"

"Oh, it went as well as could be expected."

Petra joined them. She was showing now.

"How's your mum?" she asked.

Kurt shrugged. "Varies from one day to the next. She still recognised me though. On most days anyway."

"That's a blessing," said Petra, "I'll pray for you and your family."

Kurt never knew what to make of Christian well-wishers. He would never inflict *Good Karma* or some such thing upon anyone, but the sentiment was well intentioned, so he settled on a simple "thanks, Petra".

"So," he continued, "what's the goss? What did I miss?"

"Well," whispered Debbie, "Fran's gone—"

"Fran gone!" exclaimed Kurt, "Hallelujah, the dragon's gone!"

Debbie and Petra looked embarrassed. Only then did Kurt notice the man in a taupe linen shirt fumbling with the photocopier tray. "Excuse me," he said, as he squeezed past the three of them, giving Kurt a hostile look.

It was Kurt whispering now. "Isn't that—" he began.

"Damian," nodded Debbie.

"From Wirralong Partnerships," added Petra.

Kurt remembered. "They gave that presentation on indigenous issues…"

"Yes," said Debbie, "and Fran's not gone for good…"

"She's on a secondment," said Petra, "in head office. For three months."

"Yeah," continued Debbie, "with Damian acting in her role."

Kurt's endorphins were evacuating his cortex. He pictured them as clever little leprechauns with rope ladders. They saw what was coming. They were taking to the lifeboats.

Petra delivered the punchline. "And, as you may remember," she said, "Damian is Fran's brother-in-law."

"Okay," he said, "and I just called her a dragon to his face." He puffed up his cheeks and blew out a stream of air. "Not a career-enhancing move."

When Kurt turned up at his workstation Eileen, Damian's partner at Wirralong, was sitting on his chair. She had placed picture frames all over his desk and his belongings appeared to have been dumped in an empty printer paper box. Eileen was engaged in a lively telephone conversation that involved waving arms and clattering bangles. Joe raised his eyebrows and looked through the upper part of his bifocals. "We need to talk," the look signalled, so Kurt turned around and walked to the kitchen.

"Where am I even meant to sit?" Kurt asked.

"I know, I know," said Joe, "there's so much to tell you. Better make yourself a strong coffee."

Joe walked him through all the changes that had occurred during his absence. Fran had announced her acting assignment and a fortnight later Damian had waltzed in and taken over her role. The vacancy had never been advertised. And when David had retired, Eileen had been brought in to backfill his position.

"Sounds like the mob," Kurt mused, "jobs for the boys."

"Shush." Joe looked alarmed. "Keep your voice down."

"Why? Do you think I might wake up tomorrow and find a horse's head in my bed?"

"What?"

"Never mind."

Joe continued his briefing. Kurt was to have David's workstation, next to the old fax machine. Damian was on a mission to instigate a new culture, Joe explained. Priority was to be given to following up notifications of child abuse involving Koori families. Indigenous status was to be a mandatory parameter for all statistical reporting. All staff were to enrol in cultural sensitivity training.

"Do you reckon he's genuine about focusing on Indigenous families?" asked Kurt.

"Don't get your hopes up," said Joe. "He's basically writing Wirralong Partnerships into our work plan for the next two years. By the time Fran returns there will be such a strong focus on Indigenous families, and so much work in the pipeline, that whoever manages us will have no choice but to contract out some of that work. And the only viable option in this region—"

"Is Wirralong Partnerships."

"Exactly."

⁓

Kurt glanced at the posters in what was now Damian's office. An elderly Indigenous man staring into the distance, Uluru in soft focus behind him. *The Dreaming*, it said. Giant photos of Katherine Gorge in the Northern Territory, the Blue Mountains and the Barmah Forest wetlands. Fabulous places all of them, and totally irrelevant to life in Melbourne's eastern suburbs.

"So I'm counting on you to keep providing me with timely statistical reports," Damian continued. "And in your protective case work I want you to focus more on investigating abuse notifications pertaining to Indigenous families."

"I get that," said Kurt, "but I also have current clients who need following up."

"Are you thinking about that Serbian boy?"

Kurt was surprised that Damian knew of his actual cases.

"Amongst others, yes," he answered.

"Fran mentioned him specifically in our handover meeting," Damian went on, "she said you were likely to bring up his case. She asked me to tell you that there was no need for you to engage any further with his case at this point in time."

"Has anyone seen Gecko or spoken to his foster dad?"

"I don't know the specifics but she led me to believe the boy was doing well and attending school."

"The boy is at a crossroads, Damian. He has strengths, but he's also vulnerable. He wavers between engaging and dropping out. An incident could tip him over the edge and we could lose him."

"And how is his case any different from thousands of others, Kurt? We can't let protective workers pursue their pet cases; that wouldn't be professional."

"I would have thought the hallmark of professionalism in our work was the capacity to bring about change, to keep children and young people safe. Not just clocking up investigations."

"That sounds noble. Keep in mind, though, that we provide an emergency service. We investigate families in crisis. When the immediate crisis has been addressed, we take a step back and let others move in. Schools, healthcare or counselling services, non-government organisations. And this boy's not in a crisis, Kurt. It's up to his foster parents now, his teachers, a counsellor maybe—"

"But if I could—"

"Look Kurt, I don't have time for this. I am directing you to stop work on this case until the next review scheduled in Childproof."

"Very well then." Kurt got up.

Damian tried being conciliatory: "How was your trip to Holland?"

"Belgium," Kurt said. He slammed the door.

FOG

Libby noticed her breathing. An endless rhythm, weaving in and out of her. No need to do anything. The cycle that kept her alive: wisps of oxygen. That, and her heart, though her heart seemed to miss a beat every so often. Hearts were overrated.

"Libby, please say something."

The voice came from the milky universe on the other side of the desk. She'd forgotten about her. Silly really, going to pieces at school, in front of a counsellor.

"Libby," the voice said, "you have to talk if you want me to help you."

Libby stared at her uniform skirt. She hadn't eaten since yesterday and it looked as if the chequered fabric was moving before her eyes. Maybe this was the start. Maybe things were actually falling apart all around her.

"What are you thinking, Libby?"

"Nothing," she whispered.

"Feeling down is very common," Emma said. "Maybe you should try to talk about it. Bottling it up never helps."

This is so boring, Libby thought. All these people wanting to help. Trying to understand you when you know perfectly well you just don't want to be here anymore. Not at this school, not at home, not on this miserable planet.

"Why do you think you fainted in class?"

"Dunno… I haven't eaten."

"How come?"

She didn't answer. Her hands and feet felt cold. What if you could stop thinking and you were just staring eyes? And then closed your eyes.

"Oh Libby, I know you're having a hard time but you need to let people help you. You can't let yourself go like this."

"Why not?"

"Because you're too young to give up. Because you should never make big decisions when you're feeling down."

"Who cares?"

"You should. You should care about future You."

Libby snorted.

"What if I don't want a future?"

"I got bullied too, at school," Emma said.

Libby did not react.

"They teased me because I was so thin. The boys asked me whether I had to run around in the shower to get wet."

Libby just stared.

"I've put on weight since then," Emma added, as an afterthought.

See, Libby thought, everyone knows, about my eating and stuff. I never told her anything about my weight.

"Teenagers can be cruel," Emma continued, "judgmental. When you get older, you understand that what you look like doesn't matter. It's what inside you that counts."

"What if there's nothing inside?"

"I think you're selling yourself short. You're clever and funny. You're a great writer—I read your piece in the school magazine last term."

"That was rubbish."

"Don't talk yourself down, now. It was a light-hearted piece, but witty. I think you're talented and I feel for you, that you're going through such a rough patch."

Libby thought of the girl who had written the story about the skink who fell in love with a butterfly. That was only a couple of months ago and she'd been a different person. Her life had gone downhill since, at an ever faster rate. And Gecko, who might have stopped her fall, had instead propelled her into the abyss. She started to cry.

Emma pushed the box of tissues towards her. She took one.

"I'd be happy to see you again, later this week maybe," Emma said after a while, "but you may also benefit from professional help."

She went on about having to check with her mum, which rattled Libby. She missed most of what Emma said next, about getting a GP referral and tests and stuff. And something about Outer Metro Health or whatever they were called, and how they had a good mental health service for young people.

"A mental health service?" Libby pictured herself in a straitjacket, being marched through a corridor by two orderlies.

"It's okay. Mental health services are part of any hospital these days. We sometimes need help with our moods and our thinking," Emma said, "just like we need help with our bodies."

Yeah, and I've copped the whole trifecta, Libby thought.

The librarian popped her head into the room. She looked pale.

"Sorry for interrupting," Nerissa said, "but have you heard?"

"Heard what?" said Emma, with irritation in her voice. "Can this wait? I'm with a student."

"It's the Head of English," said the librarian, "Raeleen Osmond. She's been in an accident. She may not live."

SIBLINGS

Philip arrived in Port Fairy earlier than expected. He had left Melbourne before lunchtime and taken the Great Ocean Road. It took longer but the scenery more than made up for that. And the way his Alpha Romeo hugged the road in those hairpin bends. Like a Bond movie.

He pulled up just before the inlet, where the road crosses the Moyne River. Yachts were lined up along the nearest bank, and across the river stately timber homes were backed by a wall of cypress trees. The homes all had a yacht moored where the front yard might have been. The late afternoon light cast a golden sheen over the low hanging purplish clouds. A neat white picket fence running along the river reminded Philip of Maine. Not a bad place to buy an investment property, he thought.

He looked at the map again. The local lake, Belfast Lough, looked like a giant sperm whale swimming eastwards, the Moyne River a stream of blue blood seeping out of its tail fin. The Western Districts had always survived off nature. Whaling, sheep farming. And these days wind farms.

He drove on to Griffiths Island and got out of the car. The lighthouse looked out of place, with its firetruck red top, like a child's toy or an oversized fire hydrant. Forlorn it stood, a white beacon on a rocky outcrop. As the light faded, the waters at its base turned a darker shade of grey than the gunmetal sky. The last sunlight lit up the crest of the waves and one side of the tower. Something about the scene made Philip feel melancholic. Was it the fleeting light, or the chill that had crept into the air? Was it the place itself, where nothing he knew was of any value? Was it the contrast between the accidental tourist and the eternal ocean breathing its waves onto the shore? Or was it standing here all alone, watching the shearwaters fly home in pairs? Chastened, he got back into the car and drove toward Southcombe Beach. His sister would be expecting him.

He had to look for her house. He remembered a photo of a yellow brick mansion and a pebbly drive, incongruous against the ocean backdrop. Edwina had lived here for three years now, but he had never visited her. Then he saw the house, on a low rise covered in heather and coarse grass. It looked smaller and shabbier than he remembered from the photos on the real estate website.

A slight Asian woman opened the door.

"Hi, you must be Sriti," he said, "I'm Philip."

"Hi, Philip, nice to meet you at last. Please come in." She spoke with a strong American accent.

There was an awkward silence as he stood in the hallway. Then he heard his sister's booming voice and Edwina appeared, talking on her mobile. She beckoned Philip to come into the kitchen. Sriti looked relieved.

"Well, that's all right," Edwina said, "I can ship him thirty crates next week. And that was shiraz and merlot, half and half. No probs. That should arrive in Sydney, let's see, by Tuesday… What?… Beautiful! No worries."

"Sorry about that," she said.

"Business booming?" said Philip.

"Can't complain." She explained how her vineyard had won an award for their 2007 cabernet sauvignon at the Adelaide Wine Show.

That had been their big breakthrough. She was now employing four staff and a driver, and a neighbour was doing the books.

"I'll show you the vineyard tomorrow. You've got to see the vats— Scandinavian oak. A grand each."

Philip whistled between his teeth. Sriti joined them in the kitchen and skinned a chicken while Edwina cut vegetables.

"Pick yourself a bottle from the wine rack," Edwina said.

"Thanks, Sis. Love your kitchen windows, by the way."

"Except you can't see a thing now. Wait until you wake up tomorrow morning!"

Over dinner they talked about wine, terroir and French cheeses. Philip told them about the new house he had bought. With Caitlin, he added. Edwina revealed how she and Sriti had met, in a lesbian bar in Fitzroy. Sriti looked down, abashed. Philip was interested when Edwina told him that Sriti was a dalang, or puppeteer, in Wayang Kulit, Javanese shadow theatre. Highly unusual, she said, as most dalangs were male. She was pretty good—she'd been asked to perform for Indonesian expats in Singapore in January. Flight and all expenses paid. Sriti blushed. Philip asked whether he could see her puppets. They followed her to the study. Sriti took four long, rectangular bundles off a shelf. She carefully opened the first and lifted a puppet from its bamboo cloth wrapping. It was a male character, intricately drawn, on a stiff, flat surface that looked like gilded parchment. The parchment, or whatever it was, was mounted on a thin black bamboo stick. Two other sticks enabled the dalang to control the puppet's arms. The figure looked sideways and its movable arms made it look both gracious and angular. Sriti seemed to enjoy Philip's obvious interest and took out some more puppets. They were all fascinating, Philip thought, the females with their extravagantly long, elegant limbs; the grotesque male deities with their bulbous noses. He wanted to ask her about narrative patterns in Wayang Kulit when, for no apparent reason, Sriti became agitated and looked at her watch. She exchanged a couple of sentences with Edwina in Indonesian.

"Let's go back to the lounge room," Edwina said, "it's time for her Skype call."

Philip looked at her inquisitively. Edwina topped up their glasses.

"She rings her parents once a week. They don't know she's gay. She pretends she's boarding here."

"And what, you have to hide in another room on those nights?"

"That's something we've agreed to do. Her family's very traditional. They'd find it difficult."

"And you're comfortable living a lie?"

"That's not how I would describe it at all, Philip."

Warning light, he thought, she's using my name. Back in their childhood, it had always been the harbinger of serious trouble. If you were lucky, she would dob you in with the oldies. If not, you were in for a beating.

"Well," he said, treading carefully, "it does mean you can't be recognised as her partner. What if you ever go to Indonesia?"

"Things may change. Right now, this is how it stands."

"Okay, okay... I thought you were braver... I suppose we all compromise in the end."

"Oh, Philip, you can be so infuriating. I haven't seen you in three years and give it three hours and I've already had a gutful."

Philip felt hurt. "Am I such a difficult person?"

"I wouldn't say 'difficult'. 'Self–righteous prick' would be more like it."

"Hey, don't hold back."

"Well, you're such a wanker. It's always all about you."

"What do you mean?"

"You stay away for three years but you start lording it over me as soon as you arrive. You criticise my relationship, yet you're the one who begged me to come here so you could have a break from Caitlin—"

"'Begged' may be overstating it—"

"Listen! You wanted a break because Caitlin was getting *increasingly tense*, as you put it. Now I've only spoken to Caitlin on the phone once or twice, but she sounds like a perfectly lovely woman. I suspect you take her for granted, as you did with Erica and Isabelle."

"That's dredging up old stuff. That was way back in Adelaide, those two."

"I know, but you haven't changed, have you?"

"Oh come on, I was a lad back then. Wild oats and all that."

"And what was in it for them?"

"They had a good time."

"For a while maybe, but they ended up pretty miserable, didn't they, both of them?"

"That's not my problem."

"It never is, is it? Love them and leave them."

"It's not like that with Caitlin."

"What's it like then?"

"I feel comfortable around her. I like her being there—she's like a comfy old jumper—"

"Lucky her."

"But she can also be prickly—"

"No, really—how awful for you!"

"Spare me the sarcasm, Sis."

"No way, buddy, you deserve it all."

"She can be so critical, judgmental even, that I feel torn at times. Is this the one, I think then. Is this forever?" He sipped his wine. "Will I never again experience the thrill of courtship, unhooking that bra for the first time?"

"Spare me the details."

"What if, I sometimes think—what if Caitlin and I had a more open relationship?"

"So you could play around…"

"Well, we could both be open to new encounters. It's just that I think she would not be receptive to the idea."

"Few women would be, Philip. It's such a classic ploy for men who want a bit on the side, a philandering licence."

"That's a big word."

"Is it though? Why, why be a collector, why not settle down with one good woman and get close to her? Works for me. Or do you really need that limelight on you, of someone's… infatuation, a new chick swooning over your brilliance every so often?"

"When did you get so wise, Sis? Last time we talked like this you had a freckly face and no tits. But seriously, are you saying I'm addicted to love or something?"

"Love, no. Addicted to yourself maybe, like one of those sad budgies that have the hots for their mirror."

"Ouch."

"My pleasure."

"Is this hereditary, you think? Does this have to do with Dad leaving his DNA all over Adelaide?"

"Oooh, clever boy!"

"What?"

"Can't you see? It's all about you, until blame comes into it; then you look further afield."

"Well, don't tell me our parents haven't left their mark on you."

"Hey, don't focus on what went wrong in the past. Look at my motorbike. It's got scratches all over. The night I got drunk. The day I scraped the concrete on the way to the airport. But it's still a great bike and it can take me to new places. Unless I decide to sulk around in my backyard, moping over those imperfections. Build a bridge, mate, and get over it!"

Philip winced. "I wish you wouldn't mix your metaphors," he said, "the motorbike parable was corny enough."

Edwina gave him the finger.

BODY MASS INDEX

Caitlin put down the receiver and sat there, doodling on a notepad from one of the pharmaceutical companies. *Philip*, she wrote, in fat three-dimensional capitals, and then, underneath, *dickhead*.

The irony did not escape her. She was about to assess someone's mental health and wellbeing when she was feeling low herself, and rather unsure whether she had the resilience and the interpersonal skills to make a success of her own life. What had happened to her, she wondered? She had it all: a partner, a house, a job. So why wasn't she happy anymore? At uni everyone had praised her quick wit, her zany sense of humour. These days, with Philip, she was the dour one, the one who imposed rules and regulations. And what had come first, her attempts to rein in his escapades or his urge to snatch bits of wild, unregulated living? Great, she thought, a psychologist without insight into her own private life. Makes me about as credible as a pilot with cataracts or a dermatologist with a rash.

Someone knocked at the door of her office and opened it without waiting for her response.

"I have Libby Rogers' test results," the nurse said in her matter-of-fact tone, "BP normal, urine clear but BMI 16.1." She handed a printout to Caitlin.

A body mass index of 16 meant that Libby was probably anorexic.

"Oh," said the nurse, "and I noticed lacerations on her upper left arm as she stood on the scales. Looked like typical self-harming wounds—recent, but healed. Fell on the beach, she says, on some shells." She rolled her eyes.

"One of the more original excuses. Thanks Andrea, send her in."

"Will do. And just so you know: her mum's in the waiting room but she doesn't want her to come in."

Caitlin was hardly ever entrusted with a full initial client assessment. The psychiatrists did those. The Rat had strong preferences and had instructed the triage team to direct to him all cases of clients presenting with psychosis or severe depression.

Young children presenting with autism or attention deficit disorders were allocated to Margot, the part-time psychiatrist, because she was a mum herself. Young persons who presented with a mental illness and an intellectual disability were shunted to Suresh: the Rat did not like organic disorders, for how could he weave his therapeutic magic when the brain to be examined was hamstrung by genetics?

And eating disorders, well, Dr Ratnawarpal considered those a self-inflicted condition, an attention-seeking strategy used by middle-class girls in their late teens. He liked to point out that no one in Africa or Latin America ever seemed to develop an eating disorder—was it a western fad? Caitlin had queried that once, saying the absence of reliable data should not be confused with low prevalence. The Rat had just glared at her. Either way, he deemed eating disorders not deserving of a medical specialist's time, and to be delegated to the team psychologist.

"Come in," said Caitlin, in response to the timid knock on the door. A slight girl slid in sideways, as if she didn't want to open the door any further than necessary. She had a pleasant face but looked worried.

"Hi, Libby. Sit down please. I'm Caitlin Murphy. I'm the psychologist here, in the CAMHS team."

"CAMHS?" The girl sat on the edge of her chair and held her daypack clasped tight.

"Child and Adolescent Mental Health Services. Sorry, after a while you forget that not everyone knows those acronyms! Are you cold?"

"Yeah, but it's fine. I got cold when the nurse weighed me."

"And what was your weight?"

"Forty-seven kilograms."

"That's very low for your height. Has it always been so low?"

"Pretty much… Sometimes a bit higher, maybe," she conceded.

"And what do you think about that?"

"I'm fine with that. I'd hate to be fatter."

"Why is that?"

"Dunno. That just wouldn't be me."

"So tell me about yourself."

"There's not much to say… I'm pretty boring."

"Tell me what you like, maybe."

Libby thought for a moment. "Drawing," she decided.

"What do you draw?"

"Things around the house. Animals… Flowers…"

"And what about school? You're in Year 12, aren't you?"

"Yes."

"And you're pretty bright, academically."

Libby shot her an inquisitive glance.

"Your counsellor, Emma Rubenis, told me a couple of things about you when she referred you."

"What else did she tell you?"

"That you fainted in class."

"Just the once. I hadn't eaten that morning."

"Do you often skip meals?"

"No. I was upset."

"Why was that?"

"Does that matter?"

"I respect your privacy, Libby, and you don't have to answer my question, but if I'm to help you I need to know more about you."

"Who says I need help?"

"Judging by what Ms Rubenis told me, Libby, if you're honest with yourself, you would probably agree that you do need help... You were a star student in Year 11. When you started Year 12, things went wrong. You were being bullied at school. Your mother announced you were going to move in the middle of your final year."

Libby cried. "I'm sorry," she said, "I don't want to snivel."

"That's okay," said Caitlin. She pointed at the box of tissues on her desk. Libby took one and blew her nose.

"Are there any health issues that I should be aware of?"

Libby hesitated. "I haven't had my period for some time." She blushed.

"When did you last have your period?"

"Three months ago. But I'm not pregnant."

"I know. Your urine tests were all clear."

Libby frowned. "That's a bit sneaky, isn't it? What else did you check for?"

"Drug use, and for any medical conditions that may affect your mood."

"I don't do drugs."

"That's great. And missing your period is quite common when you are underweight, as you are."

"Is that bad?"

"Have you had abdominal pains?"

"Yes, on and off."

"Listen Libby, I'm a psychologist, not a doctor, and you should discuss all medical issues with our team doctor or with your own general practitioner, does that make sense?"

Libby nodded.

"I can tell you, though, that missed periods, abdominal pains and increased sensitivity to cold can all be symptoms of starvation."

"Starvation?" Libby looked shocked.

"Yes. I'm not saying you've reached that point, but there can be serious health risks when your body weight is as low as yours."

Caitlin asked Libby more questions about her eating habits, her attitude to food, her body image. She liked this young woman. That shouldn't come in to it, of course—as a professional she had to provide the same level of care and attention to every client. But what appealed to her in Libby was her gentle nature. She was intelligent, articulate and polite—a welcome relief from sullen clients who would clam up and swear or even spit at her. I have to be careful, Caitlin thought, not to project my middle-class preferences onto my clients, or I will become a cherry-picker, like the Rat.

Libby seemed to sense that Caitlin liked her. They worked through a couple of mental health questionnaires. Libby appeared to enjoy that activity and wanted to know how she had scored. Several themes emerged, Caitlin thought: problems with peers, problems with family relationships, a strong likelihood that Libby was anorexic, a pronounced level of background depression. And there was more to canvass. Libby hadn't mentioned her father, for example, or a boyfriend, but this was only the first session. Caitlin decided that she had to address the self-harming behaviour though; the rest could wait.

"So when did you last cut yourself?" she asked.

Libby's eyes narrowed, but then she seemed to consider the question, and relaxed. She's decided to trust me, Caitlin thought.

"A couple of months ago. I'm sorry—you must think I'm really weird."

"No, Libby," Caitlin said gently, "we see so many young people who are upset." And some of them express their upset, their anger or their frustration by self-harming, she thought, but I'm not going to normalise your behaviour by telling you that...

"So you don't think I'm crazy?"

"Not at all. You're going through a rough patch; and I would like to help you."

Libby's eyes welled up again.

"Did this have to do with the bullying at school?"

Libby nodded.

"And did you ever consider doing worse things to yourself?"

Libby nodded again.

"So what was going through your mind at the time?"

"I wanted to end it all. Not be here anymore."

"Did you ever make any plans to act on that?"

"Plans? Not really. It was just a feeling. I hated existing. I loathed my body. I cut myself—it was like punishment."

"Punishment for what?"

"For being me."

"And when did you stop cutting yourself?"

Libby looked at the venetian blinds. They were shut. "I met this boy," she whispered.

CALLING IN A FAVOUR

Gecko woke up when Tags put his music on in the other room. He recognised the monumental intro to Bayou Jim's *Shiloh Heartbreak*. The keyboard in the opening chords sounded like church music and he wasn't too sure about the sugary slide guitar in the first half of the song, which made it sound like a ballad. But the three-guitar solo in the second half made him sit up, wide awake. It would be so cool to be able to play like that. He could see why Bayou Jim and the Catfish were one of Tags's favourite bands. With their bushy beards, tats, whisky and confederate flags they represented the America of the 1970s as Tags liked it. The tough, rebellious look that Tags went for but could never pull off with his wiry frame and his pale skin. Maybe that was why Tags had to draw demons on station walls. Maybe it was why he hung out with Shiv. If you wanted tough, Shiv was your man; he made Bayou Jim and the Catfish look like a bunch of choirboys.

Tags had been talking about going to the States. He seemed restless for some reason, and uncomfortable when Gecko mentioned Shiv, even though they used to be mates. Tags reckoned he was going to move to the US and become a tattoo artist. His eyes lit up when he showed Gecko tattoo magazines. But he was dreaming, Gecko thought, he didn't even have the money for an airfare. Where would he live? What would he eat? What about his mum and her diabetes? You had to be rich to do that sort of stuff. If you were a loser, you were stuck with where your parents had plonked you. You went to the shitty local school until you got kicked out. Then, if you were lucky, you picked up a trade somehow. Like Bob in the navy, or Shaun in the car yard. Wonder how Shaun was doing, whether he was still in hospital. He should maybe visit him again, but what was there to tell? I got expelled after a fight. I ditched a really nice girl. I became mates with Shiv. Like Shaun would want to hear any of that. He missed him though.

Gecko got dressed and stumbled into the kitchen.

"Look who's here," Tags sneered, "the creature from the black lagoon."

Gecko grunted.

"Kettle's just boiled if you want coffee."

"Okay." Gecko sat down on the creaky blue chair and yawned. He flicked through some junk mail, checked out the computer games. All crap though.

Tags plonked a thick mug in front of him. The coffee was still swirling. It smelled aromatic and sharp.

"Hey, have you heard anything about Shaun?"

"I was gonna ask you that," said Tags, "seeing he's become more your mate. I suppose you lost interest when you started seeing that girl."

"Well—" Gecko began.

"Hey, I don't care. Last thing I heard he was in some fancy rehab place near Warburton. Learning to use his muscles again. Dunno who pays for all that. That's what this bloke said, anyway, who worked with him at the mechanic's. Bumped into him at the bottle shop. Why you asking?"

"Just thought of him, that's all."

"Shaun's a cool dude. You'd be better off hanging out with him than with Shiv."

"I thought you liked Shiv."

"Used to. On and off. We had some wild times together, few years back. Somehow he always had money to help out a mate."

"Well," said Gecko, "I don't see the problem."

"You'll wise up," warned Tags, "but you won't like it when you do."

Jealous, thought Gecko, just because Shiv's gone cold on you. He often relived that afternoon in his fantasies, pushing aside the sour feeling at the end of it. Gliding through the suburbs on a Blunta G-40, showing morons like Matt who was top dog. Shiv had been like a warlord out of *Savage Glory*, a mythical demigod, an avenger on a steel steed, buckled up in boiled leather, his head covered in war paint. And Tags, puny Tags, who only ever wielded a can of spray paint, had missed out. No wonder he was pissed off. Guys were so much easier to figure out than girls. Girls said things to test you, it was like speaking in code. There was so much talking always; they seemed to say everything that came into their heads. It made him tired. But he also missed Libby, and sometimes he could picture her smile or bring back the sweet scent of her hair, like raisins left in the sun.

Gecko decided to change the subject.

"I love that solo in *Shiloh Heartbreak*."

Tags took the bait. "Oh man, it's so sick! Bayou Jim are awesome. Did you know the band was almost wiped out in a crash in 1979?"

Tags was on a roll. He told Gecko how the band's touring bus had crashed into a ravine, how the survivors had re-formed the band almost a decade later and how more than twenty musos had been part of the line-up at some stage or other. After Tags's exposé on southern rock they made some raisin toast, and the conversation drifted to graffiti and stencils in Melbourne laneways. Gecko liked the laid-back morning. Life was easy without teachers, girlfriends or social workers. He spent a couple of hours playing *Savage Glory* while Tags lay on the couch thumbing through his tattoo magazines. They smoked a couple of joints.

～

The unmistakable deep rumble of a Blunta grew louder, then stopped outside the door. Tags, who had dozed off, sat up with a jolt. Gecko swivelled his chair towards the door. It opened and Shiv's frame filled the opening, blocking most of the pale winter sunlight.

"Whisky," he said. Tags veered up and shambled towards the kitchen. Gecko heard him rummaging in a cupboard.

"How'd you feel about earning ten grand?" Shiv asked Gecko.

"Ten grand?"

Shiv did not respond. Tags came back from the kitchen holding a tumbler.

"Shit, yeah," said Gecko. "How?"

Tags put the tumbler down on the coffee table. He looked as if he wanted to say something, but he just sat back down on the couch.

"All you need to do is go on a trip and collect a parcel for me."

The afternoon just got complicated, Gecko thought. Drug running, what the hell!

"The kid's clean," Tags said—

"Did I ask you something?" Shiv snapped. He drank some whisky. "It's a simple thing. You go on a holiday to Thailand, all expenses paid. You bring me back some goods."

"But Thailand," Tags said, "the death penalty."

"The boy's clean," Shiv said, "you said so yourself. No one will suspect him. I did him a favour; he owes me one. It's that simple. Now, if you're gonna to be all fucking nervous just fill up my glass and get lost for the afternoon so I can discuss this with my associate here."

Associate, Gecko thought, partly flattered but mainly terrified at the sticky web that was being spun around him. Tags filled up Shiv's tumbler, left the bottle on the table, put on a jacket and headed off with a scowl.

"Now," said Shiv, "let's get organised." He took a square box out of his side pocket and tossed it at Gecko.

"A smartphone!"

"All set up. And let me make this clear: if you ever ring or text me using that phone, or have my name anywhere in it, I will split your skull."

Gecko grinned.

"I'm not joking," Shiv said. He threw a wad of hundred-dollar bills on the table. Gecko had never seen so much money.

"Expenses," Shiv explained. "Get yourself a passport, within the next week. Use the leftover to buy yourself some new clothes. Nothing grungy, nothing outrageous. You don't want to attract any attention."

"I'm not sure I'm ready to do this," Gecko tried.

"You're doing it already. It would be… unhealthy to pull out now. Hardly anyone knows you live here. Who's gonna miss you?"

Gecko swallowed. He wished he could run away, he wished Tags would come back. He'd been threatened before, but never like this.

"But the passport… I'm under eighteen… I'd need the signature of my foster dad. He'd never—"

"Don't worry about that. I've got a guy who can fix that for you. Now listen close and don't write any of this shit down. You're flying to Pattaya. Tags doesn't know yet, but he'll hand you your tickets in a week or so. You'll check in at the Conch of Paradise resort in Pattaya. Repeat that!"

"Conch of Paradise," echoed Gecko.

"You'll have prepaid accommodation for five nights. Ask for Kanda at the counter. She'll show you to your room and bring you the goods on your last night. Don't drink any alcohol or smoke any pot on your last day. I want you to look clean and alert for your flight back. Is that understood?"

Gecko felt hot and agitated. He couldn't believe he was getting instructed as a mule. Shiv put his hand in his other side pocket and threw a box of condoms on the table.

"What are those for?" asked Gecko. He felt indignant.

"You might as well practise."

"Practise what?"

"You'll need to swallow some of those on your last night. With the goods in them. Kanda will help you. Mash some banana and stuff it in one of those, then swallow it. You need to get used to swallowing them without throwing up. And figure out how long it takes to come out the other end."

"What? This is gross."

"It's ten grand," Shiv said, "worth a pain in the butt. And we got you the smallest size they had." His laughter boomed across the room, contorting his tattoos into a diabolical grin.

AUGUST 2009

BRIGHT SHINY WORLD

Gecko loved his new phone, with its colourful icons. The device was part of the bright, shiny world that was normally out of reach. But he had one now and he could sit under his doona, pretend the world did not exist and play games until his fingers went numb. But when the battery ran down he was reminded of the outside world with its rules and expectations. He felt nauseous every time he thought of Shiv's visit. He had finally freed himself, of Bob's whingeing, of that shitty school and what had he done? He had raced headlong into the employ of the creepiest thug he'd ever seen. How could he have been so stupid? There was no freedom there, no joy, only the oppressiveness of a new set of rules. No detention or time-out here, no well-meaning social workers who would gently chide you. Cross Shiv and your life was at stake, he had no doubts about that. So this was it. His life was over. He was a mule now, a disposable pawn in the empire of some drug lord. He could stick his head in the sand and play on his phone, he might have a good time in Thailand, but sooner or later he would get caught. If the Australian Feds nabbed him, he would cop a long jail term. If the Thai authorities caught him, he would spend two or three years in a mouldy prison, exhausting all appeals. Then, one morning, they would line him up with other drug runners in a clearing in a rainforest and shoot him through the heart. If he ran foul of Shiv, he would end up in a swamp somewhere, his maimed body weighed down with a rusty engine block. Fuck, he thought, how did I get in this mess? Just a couple of months ago I was standing on that bridge in Melbourne, holding Libby's hand, looking out over the Yarra, looking up at the night sky.

He flicked through the screens of his phone again. Somehow it had lost its lustre. He pressed the *Phone* icon. The app opened. *Import your contacts now*, it said. He had no contacts to import. Then he thought of Libby. He would like to hear her voice again. What could go wrong? He sat for a while, turning over his phone in his hands. He rummaged through his old backpack until he found a piece of paper. He unfolded it and keyed Libby's name and number into his phone.

He pressed her name on the glass surface and was startled when the phone immediately dialled her number.

"Hello," she said. Her voice sounded dull.

"Hi, it's me." It was silent on the other side for a while.

"… Gecko?"

"Yes." His heart was pounding.

"You have a phone."

"Yeah."

"Why did you ring me?"

"Dunno. Wanted to see how you were…"

"Well, I'm shithouse."

Gecko was taken aback. He'd never heard her angry before. He felt panicky—he hadn't thought this through.

"I'm sorry," he said.

"About what?"

"That you're feeling bad…"

She said nothing.

"Can I help?"

"Huh!" she sneered.

Here it came again, Gecko thought, the brain freeze. It happened when he got stressed. Just as he needed to think clearly, come up with something reasonable to say, his brain would set, harden like a clump of resin, and all he could see was his own paralysis. Not now, he thought, not with Libby. He realised now that walking away from Libby in that park had, for him at least, been like a move in chess, something that required a response. It dawned on him that the chasm he had created might never be bridged, that he might have lost Libby forever. A lance of ice pierced his stomach. He racked his brain for something to say, an olive branch, a crack of light, a hint of getting together again.

"This isn't much use," Libby said, "maybe we'd better hang up."

"Wait!" he said, "What have you been doing?"

Libby snorted. "Packing... Stuffing boxes. Packing everything away."

"So you're moving."

"Got it in one."

He wasn't good with sarcasm. This was like snakes and ladders. Everything you said made you tumble down further.

"I'm going to Thailand," he said.

"Who with?"

"Just by myself."

A long pause. "That's just weird," she said.

"I know."

"Why are you going there?"

He hesitated. He pictured the firing squad again. Then Shiv barging in, the tats on his forehead distorted with rage.

"Just a holiday," he said.

"Well, have fun," she said, with an air of finality that alarmed him.

"Wait, don't hang up."

"There's no point going on, is there?"

"I thought we could talk for a while."

"You're not being honest with me. About this trip to Thailand. You're all guarded. I don't know what you're up to. It's creepy. And I tell you we're moving, and you don't even ask for my new address. You're just not interested."

"What's your new address?"

"Oh, for god's sake!" She hung up.

He looked at his phone. There was an entry under *Recent calls* now. *Libby Rogers*, it said, *3:12*. He kept staring at it until the screen went dark. Then he clicked on the music app and played Convex Laughter's *Let Me Hold You*, on repeat. Tears streamed down his face. If only he could use words like that, he thought, words to talk about feelings. He thought of ringing Libby again and just playing the song for her, but that seemed stupid.

Gecko got up and blew his nose. He rummaged through his backpack; found what he was looking for. He unfolded the scrap of paper Shiv had given him and tapped out the number on his phone.

"Yeah, hi," he said, "I need a passport. What do I do?"

BACKLOG

Damian looked up as Kurt walked into his office.

"Take a seat," he said. "You've got something on your shirt." He pointed at Kurt's stomach.

Kurt looked down and winced.

"That would be olive oil," he said, "I was making a salad as Emma was working late and I guess I went a bit feral with the dressing. Couldn't find a fresh shirt this morning, sorry, things are in a shambles."

"Never mind. Does your wife work late often? She's a counsellor, isn't she?"

"That's the thing. The Head of English at her school had a serious car accident and will be in rehab for the rest of the year. And because Emma was Head of English at her old school the principal asked her to act in that position. She's been under the pump."

"Has anyone taken over her counselling role?"

"No. They've put that on hold until the end of the year, although I suspect they want Emma to deal with any major crisis as well."

"Isn't that always the way," said Damian, "counselling being seen as an add-on."

Why is he being so chummy, Kurt wondered. And he actually remembered what I told him about Em.

"Anyway," Damian said, "what I wanted to talk to you about is the Patterson case. Joe mentioned it the other day. Can you fill me in on the details again…"

"Sure. They're an Indigenous family living in Greensborough. Rod used to work near the railway station as a parking lot attendant. He lost his job about a year ago because of his drinking. Since then he's become violent, beating Sandy, his wife, and his kids too, on occasions. They have three children, Charlie—"

Damian waved his hand. "I don't need to know their names."

"Well, the kids are aged between three and seven. A teacher noti-fied us when the eldest turned up in class one morning with a black eye and bruises all over his legs. Fran allocated the case to me and I visited the family on a number of occasions."

"What did you do by way of intervention?"

"I eventually got through to Rod. He was ashamed of his behaviour, blamed the grog. I taught him some anger management strategies."

"Like what?"

"I started with time out, but we also developed a crisis card. I gave Sandy the phone number of the local crisis centre. They were okay for a while, but you know how it goes with domestic violence: it builds up, erupts, and after the initial remorse and good intentions the cycle starts all over again."

"Yeah yeah. So what did you do?"

"In July the family was re-referred. Cathy, the youngest, had been left in a locked car in a supermarket car park and Charlie had welts on his arms." Damian shook his head. "I decided to involve the broader community." Damian raised his eyebrows. "I contacted Aunty Rose, who's an Elder of the Wurundjeri—"

"I know who Aunty Rose is."

"—and I told her about the case."

Damian whistled between his teeth. "What about privacy issues?"

"What about safety issues?" Kurt retorted.

"A bit of a gamble, mate. I don't want you to become a loose cannon. But go on."

"With Aunty Rose's support I convened a family case conference. That was last week. More than twenty family members attended. I booked the local scout hall—you'll get the invoice for that." Damian frowned. "They talked for four hours and there was a lot of crying and hugging. The upshot was that when Rod gets drunk he is to sleep at his cousin's place, away from the kids. Sandy's cousins will take turns to visit her every week and to help her with the household. There will be another case conference in two months' time, to see whether these arrangements have worked."

"That sounds fantastic, Kurt. You might want to showcase your intervention with this family at next week's staff meeting. Just don't mention the privacy thing."

Wow, Kurt thought, a compliment at work. That hasn't happened since I was at Northern Outreach.

"There was something else I've been meaning to tell you," Damian said. "It's about that Serbian boy."

"Gecko?"

"Yes. That case has been re-referred to us."

Kurt edged forward on his seat. He felt his temperature rise. So the compliment about the Patterson case had merely been a sweetener. And he had fallen for it, allowed his ego to be stroked. He willed Damian to say what had happened to Gecko. His silence seemed to last an eternity.

"Apparently the boy's foster parent—"

"Mr Morrison."

"Yep. He rang us to let us know that the boy had been expelled from school after a fight."

"What? When was this?"

"Hmm, in early June."

"What? That's two months ago. Who took the call?"

"Petra, but that's immaterial. You were overseas. The foster father said that Gecko had broken a boy's nose. Later that day he turned up at the boy's home, accompanied by a bikie."

"A bikie?"

"Yes. They threatened the boy and trashed the nature strip. Even more disturbing, two days later the boy's dog was found dead in the front garden. Slaughtered. Mutilated."

"But that's impossible. That's not like Gecko at all! He hasn't got a cruel bone in his body."

"It's the facts, I'm afraid. The police are involved now."

"Why isn't any of this on Childproof? I checked the case notes last week."

"Even though I had told you to drop the case? Anyway, it's all on the database now. We had a bit of a backlog with our data entry. I explained that at our staff meeting…"

"A bit of a backlog!" Kurt was appalled. "I told you about this boy! 'We can't have pet cases,' you said. 'We take a step back,' you said, 'and let others move in.' Was this what you had in mind? Let bikies move in? Where's Gecko now?"

"Well, Mr Morrison rang again yesterday. He was in quite a state. It appears that Gecko's nowhere to be found. He's been checking for him in this place where he used to stay, in Heathmont. No trace of Gecko. His housemate told Morrison that Gecko has a girlfriend now, so it may all be innocuous, it may explain where he is. Shacked up somewhere."

"Damian, we're beyond the point where we can make assumptions," said Kurt.

"Well, yeah, and that's where you come in. I want you to find out where the boy is. Talk to his housemate, talk to Morrison. Gecko's still in foster care and as such he's our responsibility. We need to know where our kids are. We cannot risk the Minister being exposed on this issue."

"I think we have a different understanding of risk," said Kurt. He got up and walked out.

LEADS

As a Buddhist, Kurt thought, you should be immune to the four worldly winds of gain and loss, praise and blame. But he feared, as he dialled Bob Morrison's number, that a hefty dose of blame was coming his way. Served him right, for touting his commitment earlier in the year and not following through. Never mind that it was all unforeseen; it confirmed Bob's prophecy that workers move on, leaving their clients in the lurch. There was a knot in his stomach as he dialled the number.

"Here I go," he said to Joe, "my humble pie call."

Joe gave him a thumbs-up sign.

Kurt felt as if he was eleven again, standing in the headmaster's office for having thrown a firecracker into the playground. Bob tore strips off him, but that moment, too, passed. When Bob finally calmed down, they compared notes. Tags's mention of Gecko having a girl-friend was the first thing Bob had heard about it. Tags had been reti-cent and skittish and knew nothing about a bikie. Bob had also gone to the mechanic's place where Shaun worked. They told him Shaun had been transferred to some sort of rehab centre in Warburton. The police were looking for Gecko, Bob said. They wanted to question him in relation to vandalism and animal cruelty incidents. Maybe that was why Gecko was lying low somewhere.

As Kurt typed up his file note, he remembered the motorbike on Tags's nature strip, just after the fires. And the bikie—how could he have forgotten him? He had only glimpsed the hulking figure, but he had seemed sinister.

So Tags had lied to Bob Morrison. Kurt jumped up.

"Where are you off to?" asked Joe.

"Heathmont. Send a posse if I'm not back by four."

"Haha, you're so funny," Joe said drily, "you could do stand-up."

When Kurt pulled up in Inverloch Road, he spotted the ambulance parked in the middle of the road. The doors of numbers 12 and 14 both open. Two paramedics. A body on a stretcher. Oh god, surely not. His salmon sandwich came back to life in a lake of bile, threatened to swim upstream. There was Tags, standing in the front yard, looking all dishevelled. Kurt walked over to him. Tags turned around, recognised him, ran back to the door. Kurt jumped over the low fence. Caught the door before Tags could shut it. This might be trespassing, he thought, but I don't care.

"Fuck mate, what do you think you're doing?" asked Tags, out of breath.

"What happened here? Why the ambulance?"

"Shit, man, it's just the old guy next door. Fell over or something."

"Where's Gecko?"

"Dunno."

"I need to find him."

"Like I said: I don't know."

"What's the name of his girlfriend?"

"Dunno."

"Don't lie to me. You lied to Bob."

"Who's Bob?"

"Gecko's foster dad."

"How did I lie?"

"You said you knew nothing about a bikie."

"Well, I don't."

"There was a bikie here last time."

Tags did not reply. Kurt looked around. Two cheap carry bags and an old backpack stood next to the couch.

"Are you going somewhere?"

Tags remained silent.

"And who did that to your face?" He pointed at the burn mark on Tags's cheek.

"I fell," he said.

"Yeah, straight on someone's cigarette, by the looks of it," said Kurt. "Why don't you tell me what happened. Maybe I can help."

Tags snorted. "You can do fuck all," he spat, "you're just a limp dick getting everyone into trouble. You're a waste of space. Now piss off."

Back in the office Kurt looked up rehabilitation centres in Warburton. Shaun was his last lead. The Mystic Mountain Convalescence Clinic seemed a likely contender. The receptionist did not want to confirm or deny whether a Shaun Metcalfe was a patient. Sounded like the US Navy, Kurt thought, plausible deniability. She was right though; he should take privacy more seriously, as Damian had pointed out. The receptionist had agreed to take a message and two hours later Shaun rang him back. He sounded hoarse and spoke slowly. Gecko had only visited him once, Shaun said, and he didn't know about any of the facts Kurt, in his latest privacy breach, had doled out. Gecko's fight, his expulsion from school, Matt's dog being butchered. Nor did Shaun know that Gecko had a girlfriend. He'd never seen him with a girl. Finally Kurt asked him about the bikie at Tags's place.

"That'd be Shiv, he's bad news."

"In what way?"

"In just about every way."

Bad in every way. Kurt pictured a fearsome god of destruction, creating havoc with its four arms, evil incarnate, then called his flapping imagination to order.

"Does he do drugs?"

"Yep. Sells them. Uses them too. Heroin. Ice. Makes him even nastier than normal."

"Could Gecko be hanging out with him?"

"Hope not."

"Where do I find this Shiv?"

"Dunno. He lives somewhere in Collingwood, or used to, couple of years back. Also, he's in this bikie gang. The Mutineers. He's their enforcer."

Note to self, Kurt thought: update life insurance policy.

"Thanks Shaun, you've given me something to go on with. Best wishes for your recovery."

"Thanks. And Kurt..."

"Yes?"

"Be careful."

HEAD OF ENGLISH

The Year 7 spelling tests, the Year 8 compositions, the Year 10 debating point outlines. Emma tucked all yesterday's marking into her briefcase and gulped down her coffee. Kurt was still buried behind his paper at the breakfast table.

"Look at Lord Leisure," she said. "Has all the time in the world, by the looks of it."

"Hmm," he grunted, "I'm starting with a home visit just three blocks from here. Joe's picking me up."

"You're both going?"

"Yes, there's been a history of violence, drug-induced, so we're not taking any risks."

"Be careful."

"Sure. Hey, how did you go last night with Midnight?"

"Oh, we had a lovely dinner at the Golden Lotus—you know, that Vietnamese restaurant in Box Hill. The new shop in Armadale's going really well. She's as happy as a pig in mud. What did you get up to?"

"Nothing special. Did some channel hopping. Wrote a letter to Mum."

"Oh, great! Show me tonight; I've got to run." She kissed him.

Emma loved the letters Kurt wrote to his mum. Irene could no longer read, but Kurt had devised a format that worked. He started each letter with a brief request to the nursing home staff: could they please read out this letter to his mum. He then inserted a photo from Irene's youth, taken in the 1930s or 40s. Underneath the photo he wrote one or two paragraphs describing it: here's you in the backyard, helping to dig up potatoes. You were only three years old. Your face is all covered in dust, but look at that cheeky smile! And look at Uncle Gregoor's enormous white moustache! Kurt knew the people, the names, the memories. Axel, Irene's brother, on pilot training in Texas, leaning against a De Soto. Her father in the garden, with his cap and eternal stubble, pointing at his tobacco plants. Kurt remembered the Flemish dialect words that would strike a chord with Irene. His mother had told him countless stories in his youth, and now, in her old age, he acted as her antipodean backup. Every week he sent her one of these vignettes.

Emma felt so proud that he had figured out a way of keeping in touch with his mum and of stimulating her memory in spite of the distance, in spite of her dementia. And they knew, from the odd phone call to the nursing home, that Irene reacted to these letters. She—

A horn sounded and a cattle truck thundered past her. Emma had almost turned onto the main road without giving way. She thought of Raeleen and shuddered. That was all it would have taken, a few seconds' inattention. The difference between life and death or, in Raeleen's case, between life as you knew it and months of painful rehabilitation, with broken bones and bruised organs.

It made sense that Roslyn had asked her to act in Raeleen's position. Patrick was an inspiring teacher but had only two years' experience and his admin skills were untested. Mona was going through a messy divorce. None of the other English teachers had taught Year 12. So that left her. She at least knew the school, and she'd had years of experience in the role at St Genevieve's.

It had been hell, of course. Winding up all her counselling work while taking over Raeleen's teaching load. Five classes, including Year 12 English. Planning meetings with Patrick and Mona. Listening to

Mona's tales of marital woe. Curriculum design for next year. Over-seeing excursions for the junior levels. Parent–teacher nights. All the stuff she had baulked at—it had caught up with her again.

Moreover, she was not particularly enjoying teaching Year 12. She had been a popular teacher at St Genevieve's, but here something seemed to have shifted. Patrick, with his youth and good looks, was the rising star. He played footy with the senior boys and made the girls swoon. The Year 12s, ever mindful of their marks, seemed to regard Emma as a jumped-up casual teacher at first and challenged her in class until it became obvious that she knew her stuff. But those early skirmishes had soured the mood. They had taken the gloss off her return to glory and shed an unflattering light on what the students really thought of the careers-teacher-cum-counsellor role that she was destined to return to when Raeleen got better. If Raeleen got better.

"Okay, class, settle down." She didn't have Raeleen's booming voice. Stewart was showing a computer magazine to his mates. "Stewart, put that away please. Ingrid, settle down please. And put that lipstick away. You know you're not meant to have that."

"Naughty girl," said Mark, "we'll have to spank you." Monique giggled.

"Come on, folks, we have a lot to get through today." From the corner of her eye Emma noticed Libby in the back row, ashen-faced and looking sullen.

"Okay, let's continue our discussion of *The Young and the Fallible*. Samantha, yesterday you drew our attention to the passage where Ewen shoots the tramp in the underpass. Why does he do that, do you think?"

"Because he's a terrorist," Gavin yelled out.

"Come on, Gavin, you're not being helpful."

"He might be," said Gavin, "how do you know he's not?"

"Does anyone want to answer that?" asked Emma.

Helena raised her hand. "We shouldn't impose our frame of reference upon a text," she said, "because then we can read all sorts of things into a book."

"But that makes it relevant to a modern reader," objected Gavin.

"No," said Helena, "that just makes the text irrelevant. You're then focusing on yourself—"

"Classic Gavin!" interjected Steve.

"Shut up dickhead," retorted Gavin.

"What I want to say," Helena continued, "is that our interpretation needs to be based on the text."

"That's well put," Emma said, "and very concisely."

"Ugh, teacher's pet," Gavin hissed.

"Grow up," said Helena.

"Bear in mind," Emma continued, "that the examiners will want to see evidence that you have read and understood the text. In addition to that they expect evidence of original thinking."

"Gavin's certainly original," Steve observed.

Gavin gave him the finger.

"Come on, guys, let's get serious," said Emma. "Your final school-assessed task is due next month and while your essays about *The Great Gatsby* were of a reasonable standard, most of you can still improve."

"Did you read the essays we submitted to Mrs Osmond?" Helena asked.

"I did," said Emma. "I wanted to know where you were at." Helena looked pleased at that. It was hard work, winning over a class. "There was some excellent work in there." She looked at the back row. Libby just turned her head.

The class finally settled down and Emma led a more or less focused discussion on what she called Ewen's emotional atrophy, his inability to show emotion. They talked about how he always walked past the beggars, how he had yawned while watching footage of the tsunami. The author was making a point about social expectations, Samantha offered. People judged you if you did not behave like they expected you to. Things should make sense, Monique thought. Shooting a guy just because you felt bored was weird and scary. Why was literature always about weirdoes, she wanted to know. Emma wanted to engage Libby in the discussion but she avoided all eye contact.

The bell rang and they all shuffled out. Emma called Libby back.

"So how are you going?"

"Fine."

"How are your sessions at Outer Metro?"

"Fine."

"Libby, you can still talk to me."

"I know. Thank you."

There was no life in her eyes, Emma thought, as she watched the waif-like figure shuffle away down the corridor. It saddened her and she resolved to ring Caitlin Murphy at Outer Metro Health. She stashed her notes into her briefcase and headed for the sensory over-load known as Year 7 English.

REMOTE CONTROL

Philip put down his cutlery. "That ratatouille was divine," he said, "thank you." He wiped his lips. "So this patient with the anorexia, is she just seeking attention? I mean, why would you starve yourself?"

"It's more complex than that," Caitlin started, "consumers—"

"I wish you'd stop calling them consumers. What do they consume?"

Caitlin smiled. "It's what they want to be called, Philip. *Patient* is too clinical; *client* too business-like. They're consumers of mental health services and so they're entitled to standards and protection and to having a say in their treatment."

"Okay, okay, I get the point."

"What I wanted to say is that consumers with an eating disorder often have a distorted body image. They may think of themselves as fat when in fact they are severely underweight."

"Can't you put them on a set of scales and show them?"

"Those perceptions are internalised, deep-rooted. It's what they believe."

"Why don't you just tell them to get over it? I mean, don't they take attention and resources away from people with a serious mental illness, like psychosis or schizophrenia or whatever?"

"Hmm. That would be like telling Hamlet to lighten up about his father's death. Eating disorders are serious, Philip. Anorexia has one of the highest death rates of all mental illnesses."

"Really?"

"Yes. People can die from the side-effects of severe malnutrition, like cardiac arrest or kidney failure. But also, the suicide rate of young people with an eating disorder is thirty-two times higher than expected for the age group."

"Wow. I love how you have all those stats whirling in that pretty little head of yours. It kind of turns me on."

"Philip! This is serious!"

"I know. Just kidding. Please continue the lecture." He slid back on his chair, looked sideways at the television.

"It's not meant to be a lecture. It rips me up to see this kid I'm treating. She's so gifted—a really nice girl—and she's imploding."

"And what can you do then, when they're like that?"

"Well, we normally start with CBT, that's Cognitive Behavioural Therapy."

"I know what it stands for."

"The aim is to help the person realise that their behaviour is ultimately self-destructive. That can be hard work because, at some level, the behaviour has worked for them. Losing weight or refusing to eat may have been a way of asserting control, managing anxiety or warding off negative emotions, you name it."

Philip picked a sliver of eggplant skin from between his front teeth.

"So you have to uncover this hidden motivation," Caitlin went on, "and replace it by an alternative set of behaviours. That can take a long time. We often use family therapy too. That can be a big help in reinstating good eating habits. In this case though, the girl I'm treating has fallen out with her mum, so family therapy is not an option."

"And if CBT doesn't work?"

"It can get to a point where the client gets so weak that they need to be force fed."

Philip frowned. "Force fed?"

"Yes, with a nasogastric tube. That's done in hospital and the patient is restrained."

"I thought that's what the French did to their geese!"

"I know it sounds awful. The thing is, dying is worse."

Philip topped up his wine glass. "You know what," he said, "I think you're pretty clever, doing all that stuff. I'm proud of you."

"Thank you for saying that," she said. She leaned over and kissed him on the lips.

"But mind you," he said, "I think those wafer-thin waifs can look really hot."

"Oh, Philip," she said, "it's an illness. Why do you have to sexualise everything?"

She lifted the dish with the leftover ratatouille and took it to the kitchen. That was so like him; every time she thought they had a special moment he would go and ruin it. The Midas touch in reverse: all the gold he touched turned to lead. Or was she overthinking it again? Was she disappointed because he had trotted out a line that clashed with how she'd wanted the conversation to go? Did it all have to be so politically correct? At least he had listened, taken an interest, paid her a compliment. He also seemed to have gone off Di. Not a word about her this past fortnight. Maybe she should relax more, lighten up, be more playful.

The doorbell rang. Caitlin checked her watch. Ten o'clock. Philip answered the door and she could hear Kevin's frantic giggle. Not Kevin, she thought.

"Do you want to hear the latest?" Kevin asked, all big-eyed and excited. "Anaïs and Bas have split up!"

"Oh really," said Caitlin, "that's a shame." Anaïs is getting on a bit, she reflected, where will she find someone new? The thought made her inner censor jump into action: there I go again, she berated herself, canvassing the long-term implications instead of focusing on the here and now.

"We'll be able to take down that garish painting," said Philip, "I suppose she won't want to be staring at the butt of her ex every time she visits."

Kevin grinned.

"Was it a mutual decision?" asked Caitlin.

"Well, that's a whole story in itself!" Kevin launched into romantic forensic mode and dissected the whole breakup. Bas had cheated on Anaïs with a crime reporter from Channel Eight, whom he had met in a coffee shop in Brunswick. Anaïs had found out. There had been yelling and recriminations. Anaïs had called Bas an untalented house-painter. He had called her a suffocating cougar with no eye for colour or composition. She had called him an arse without class. Caitlin wondered how Kevin invariably came to know all these intimate details. Then things had turned nasty, Kevin said, with Bas, as a de facto, laying claim to half of Anaïs's possessions. Solicitors had pored over the couple's papers and Bas had flown back to Suriname, signifi-cantly wealthier after an out-of-court settlement.

"So," concluded Philip, "Paramaribo paramour no more."

"Ah, that's witty," said Kevin, "quite superb. I must tell Ramon—he likes that sort of stuff. You know, verbal brilliance. Have I ever told you the story of Alan Pinkerton? He was Abraham Lincoln's head of security. And do you know how he died? He bit his tongue stepping off a pavement, and it turned gangrenous and—"

"You know, Kevin," said Caitlin, "it's getting rather late and we have work tomorrow…"

"Ah yes," said Kevin, "work. I remember it well."

They finally wrangled him out the door.

"I thought he'd never leave," Caitlin sighed. "And what do you make of Bas and Anaïs breaking up?"

"Oh well, it's sad of course, but I never thought they'd last. She'd let herself go. You know, packed on a few kilos. And he's so much younger, what do you expect?"

Oh, of course, Caitlin thought, the firmness of the flesh is para-mount. Never mind loyalty, intimacy, shared memories, common purpose. But she didn't have the stomach for another fight. She went to the bedroom and had a quick shower. As she dried herself, she examined her body in the mirror. Her breasts were still firm, but she had put on weight around her hips. What would she look like in ten years, in fifteen? And why did that seem so important to men? What were our bodies but lumpy contraptions that stored energy and all sorts of chemicals? Lumbering shapes that enabled us to stumble through life on this planet. Self-contained little factories that converted fat and protein and produced sugars and endorphins, sweat, blood, egg cells and piss, all with molecules on loan from the universe. Miraculous really, though mediaeval scholars in their sour rants held that the body was but a bag of blood and bones. The outline of the female form, though, seemed hard-wired in the male brain, guaranteed to trigger a response. As she considered Philip in these Pavlovian terms, she unaccountably felt desire herself. She dimmed the ceiling lights and slid into bed. She picked up her phone from the bedside table, photographed her breasts and sent the grainy image to Philip. The ultimate remote control, she thought. Caitlin slid over to his side of the bed and waited for the door to open.

THE ORIGIN OF THE MOON

Libby sat on her bed, flicking through the pamphlets that Ms Rubenis had given her. *Guidelines for Applying for Interrupted Studies Status. Compassionate Late Withdrawal: Your Rights Explained.* They all looked similar, the high-gloss flyers produced by the education department. Cool colours, blue and green. Illustrated with pictures of pleasant people sitting around a table. Helpful teachers and grateful students. Finely balanced for gender and ethnicity. Whatever the students were applying for seemed a worthwhile thing to pursue. It was all false, Libby decided, just for show. The pamphlets were confusing rather than helpful. She felt bewildered. She didn't really want to interrupt her studies. That meant giving Mum way too much power over her life. Nor did she want to sit the final exams and scrape through with a mediocre result. That would be so unfair after all her hard work over the past years. She might not get into the uni course of her choice. But repeating Year 12 to secure a better result did not appeal either. She should have rung that course coordinator lady at Parkville High already but somehow she could not be bothered with any of this. And lacking the energy to rescue herself, she had allowed things to slide.

She stared at the collapsed cardboard boxes that her mum had placed against her bedroom wall. Libby hadn't even started packing.

She felt like contracting inwards, divesting herself of her body and her belongings. She ate even less than usual: a sprinkling of muesli in the morning, an apricot bar for lunch. Dinner was the worst, with Mum and Nathan badgering her. But she could not face mashed potato anymore, it looked like maggot paste; she could not force it down her throat. So she picked a bit at broccoli or squash. Clean, watery stuff.

She had deleted her Facebook account. It had felt like a momentous step at first. Dialogue boxes had warned of impending doom, but Libby had persisted. She felt liberated now that she was no longer being notified of everyone's status updates. Next she stopped using her web browser. It was just pumping filth into her room. Wars, suicide bombers, murders, tales of betrayal and unspeakable cruelty. She did not want any part of that world. She was better off looking at dusk smudging over the banksia trees in the garden. Listening to the plaintive, wintry calls of the currawongs in the tall gum tree. She kept using her iPod though. Music was her last solace.

"Libby! Dinner!"

She felt so weak these days as soon as she got off her chair. She inched down the stairs, probing each step like a stick insect. Dad's sundrenched seascapes had always held the shadows at bay but Mum had taken down his paintings a couple of days ago. The stairwell looked eerie now, a funnel drained of colour, a grey descent into Hades.

"Macaroni cheese today," Melanie announced cheerfully.

Nathan flopped three place mats on the table.

"Hey, Mum, I came first in the 200-metre sprint today," said Nathan as they sat down.

"That's great! You beat Rowan McMillan?"

"Yep. I get to run in divisional now," he said, chewing a mouthful of macaroni, "in Glen Waverley, next month." A lump of cheese stuck to the corner of his mouth.

"Fantastic!" said Melanie. She pointed to the corner of her mouth and Nathan wiped his lips.

"Is there bacon in this?" asked Libby, raking her plate with her fork.

"Only tiny bits," said Melanie, "it'll make you strong."

"I don't want to eat pig's bottom."

"Whoa, gross," said Nathan.

"Take out the bits you don't want to eat," said Melanie, "but don't put everyone else off their meal."

"I can't eat this, it smells of meat."

"It's natural to eat meat," proclaimed Nathan, "humans are carnivores."

"Suit yourself," said Melanie, "if you want to waste away completely. I don't know what to do to feed you anymore."

Libby sipped her glass of water.

"You're way too thin," said Nathan, "that's probably why your boyfriend dumped you."

"Mind your own business, you moron."

"Language, Libby!"

"He started it."

"I don't know why we always end up fighting," said Melanie. "I think we should make a fresh start in the new house. The previous owners are moving out next Thursday, so we'll be able to go and have a look. Maybe take a few things over."

"Can I have the bedroom next to the garage please, Mum? Please? Then I can set up a network and my mates can come and play *Savage Glory*."

How irritating that Nathan would have an interest in common with Gecko. What did it matter though? Gecko was gone, somewhere in Thailand. Doing what? Melanie's voice brought her back.

"I said, when are you going to start packing?"

"Soon,"

"Well, it'd better be soon or you'll be carrying all your stuff to the city."

Libby shrugged.

"It goes fast," said Melanie, "once you get the hang of it. I packed all of Murray's paintings in the stairwell in just forty minutes."

"Where are they now?"

Melanie looked annoyed. "I gave them to charity. It was time to make a clean break."

"You did what?"

"They wouldn't have suited the ambience of the new house…"

"I can't believe you gave away Dad's paintings!"

"Calm down, Libby."

"I won't calm down! Did you ever consider asking me whether I wanted to keep any of them?"

"You never said you were interested."

"Oh, I can't believe you," sobbed Libby, "you're the worst mum ever!"

Melanie stared at her daughter, taken aback.

"I can drive back to the op shop," she said, "see whether they've all sold. If it means that much to you."

"Don't bother," sneered Libby. She ran out of the kitchen.

She flung herself on her bed and sobbed. After an hour or so of absolute misery and self-pity she fell asleep on top of her doona, exhausted. When she woke, she was chilled to the bone. The house was quiet. It was after midnight. Libby turned off her bedroom light, wrapped her fluffy quilt around her and pulled the curtains aside. She looked at the full moon. She'd read somewhere that the moon was the result of a gigantic meteor impact on Earth. Tonnes of debris had been flung into space and had coalesced into this milky planet. What would the earth think, she mused, having to face this part of itself every night? This estranged, disembodied part, carved off, forever lost. Bits had been spinning off her too, all this year. She had lost her confidence, her friendship with Monique, her joy and inquisitiveness. Her sense of direction. She'd lost Gecko. Her school. She hadn't made a drawing in months. Now her dad's paintings were swirling through space and soon this house, with its nooks and crannies and memories, would follow. It felt as if there was more of her out there, in irreversible oblivion, than here on Earth. What was she left with? A thin bag of gristly bone and muscle, dull hair that fell out... Her tears spent, anger rolled in like a toxic tide. She grabbed her toiletries bag and opened the plastic zip. The shower razor looked brand new in the suffused light of the moon. She pulled up her sleeve and set to work.

SEPTEMBER 2009

WHAT COMES FIRST?

His online search for *Shiv* and *Collingwood* didn't get Kurt anywhere. He had more luck locating the headquarters of the Mutineers. They were based in Bayswater, that hybrid blot on the eastern outskirts of Melbourne, part suburb and part industrial badlands. It somehow always seemed to rain in Bayswater, an incessant drizzle that leached the soul. The roads were busy, congested with trucks and delivery vans. The streets all looked the same: single storey factories, no more than large steel sheds really, separated by concrete driveways, cyclone fences, garlands of electrical wire and bisected by the railway line.

The Mutineers headquarters was in a dead-end street. That would make it hard to stake out, Kurt thought. You couldn't drive past to check the place out, or have a coffee in a local cafe. You would stick out like the proverbial dog's balls. Still, he had to give it a go; this Shiv character was his only lead if he was to find Gecko. The assignment also held some appeal. He had already indulged his undercover agent fantasies.

He pulled up in the cul-de-sac, in front of the SteelExpo factory. *Gates Fencing Screens,* said the sign on the cyclone fence. That's how the macho guys do it, Kurt thought. Simple syntax sells steel. To the right of SteelExpo, on the next lot, crouched a squat concrete building painted black. It looked like a bunker rather than a factory. The only indication of its purpose was a painted banner underneath the roofline. *Mutineers Motorcycle Club*. Grey letters, spray painted to look like rivets. *Don't mess with us*, the font seemed to say, *we mean business*.

Next to the Mutineers headquarters stood another factory. *Pinnacle*, announced the sign over the open double garage doors, *Abselling Equipment*. An irksome spelling mistake. How could you work in an industry and not even get its name right? Not that it mattered much; he hadn't seen another car since he had pulled up here. And locating an abseiling company in flat, featureless Bayswater was no more perverse than the naming of the suburb, which was more than thirty kilometres away from the nearest bay.

He looked again at the steel factory and the abseiling place. They had regular fences and the gear you would expect to see in any factory yard: wooden pallets, a forklift, delivery trucks and dumpsters. The bikie headquarters had none of that, but its fences were higher and of thicker mesh steel, with two strands of barbed wire along the top. Immediately behind the fence two shipping containers had been lined up, parallel to the street. Cameras on every corner of the building. This was no club, he thought, this was a bulwark. The shipping containers would stop gunfire and even deflect the blast of a car bomb. He'd heard about gang rivalries, and he remembered reading about the Milperra bikie shoot-out in New South Wales in the eighties, but it was still confronting to see this barely camouflaged fortress in a suburb of Melbourne.

The black metal doors of the club swung open and two bikies walked out. They came straight for him. Kurt swallowed. The taller one signalled him to wind down the window. Kurt obeyed.

"Bit of rubbernecking, hey?" the man said.

Kurt decided to play it straight. Excuses would just rile these guys.

"I'm looking for Shiv."

"Why didn't you say so," the bikie said, with mock geniality, "you must be his long-lost cousin."

"No—"

"Get out!" the man snapped.

They marched him into their clubhouse, a dank place that stank of stale beer and tobacco. Three bikies looked up from their poker game. Two others were playing pinball machines in the far corner. The place was fitted out like a British pub, with plush dark velvet benches. There was even a darts board. But no sign of the bikie he had seen at Tags's place.

The tall guy pushed Kurt onto a chair, sat down opposite him. The fat guy stood right next to Kurt.

"Now tell me why you're here," the tall one said.

Kurt told him about his attempts to track down Gecko. How Shiv was his last lead. The tall guy listened. His mate stood staring at Kurt with his malicious beady eyes and a mocking smile. He fished a brass knuckleduster out of the pocket of his jeans and slid it over his fingers. Kurt thought, hoped, he was bluffing.

"Okay, Wolf," said the tall one when Kurt had told his tale, "you keep an eye on smartypants here. I'll go see Shiv." He disappeared up a set of stairs to the left of the bar.

Wolf was not into small talk, Kurt thought. At least he'd found Shiv. He looked around. The place looked as if it had been decorated by twelve-year-old boys. A Confederate flag, posters of racing cars and buxom nudes. It all seemed a bit infantile.

"Stop looking round. You done enough snooping."

"I just—"

Wolf hit him in the face.

Hot pain ripped through his jaw.

"Keep your eyes down until Rocco comes back."

The fucking idiot! Kurt's cheek felt like a pouch holding a bony puzzle. He wanted to rub, check the damage. Decided against it. No way of knowing what would antagonise this maniac.

Rocco came down the stairs. "Okay," he said, "Shiv will see you now." He nodded at Wolf, who pulled Kurt off his chair.

Kurt moved toward the stairs.

"No," said Rocco, "other way." He pushed him past the bar towards an opening in the far wall. As Kurt stepped into the darkened room, someone kicked him in the groin. He doubled over, in agony. Something hit him on the back of the head and he passed out.

Kurt had no idea how long he had been unconscious.

"Think he's a cop?"

The voice sounded faintly familiar but unpleasant.

"Nah, he's too dumb for a copper. A copper wouldn't be this old, or poke his nose in here without backup."

Kurt remembered. The bikies. Wolf.

"What's he doing then?"

"An arsehole from welfare, like he says."

"We'll look after his welfare," Wolf said, kicking Kurt in the kidneys. Kurt groaned.

"Go easy, mate. Make sure he doesn't cark it on our doorstep."

"Let's get rid of him then."

One of them went away. The other one lit a cigarette. Kurt's eyes felt swollen. When he opened them, the light hurt. Wet concrete, empty beer crates, a pair of steel-capped boots. He shut his eyes again. All he wanted was to sink back into deep sleep. In his mouth the taste of stale blood, rich and sickening. They're going to get rid of me, he thought. Was this it then? An unceremonious exit from life, topped by two heavies with bad BO? He thought of the Buddhist saying: *What comes first, tomorrow or death?* The question we can never answer. And what could he do about it? In his present state, precious little. He resolved to stay awake though.

Wolf said something. Rocco answered. So they were both back. Rocco knelt down next to Kurt.

"Hey, buddy, you can hear me, can't you?"

Kurt smelled the beer on Rocco's breath. A faint whiff of garlic too. He felt stupidly pleased that Rocco had called him *buddy*. An echo from a kinder world.

"Say something." Rocco punched him in the ribs. A coil of pain reached right up into his ear.

"Can hear you," mumbled Kurt. He felt nauseous.

"Okay, listen. We know where you live. So if you care about your family you'll steer clear of the law. Get it?"

Kurt nodded.

They lifted him up. A car door opened. He recognised the back seat of his own car. One of the bikies started the engine. To the right he heard a heavy bike start up. A sharp pain jolted through his back as the car took off. He passed out.

～

It was dark when he came to. His car smelled of blood and urine. The bikies were gone. He slowly sat up. He could see the outline of gum trees. They had dropped him off in some sort of parkland. He didn't recognise the place. He closed his eyes for a couple of minutes. Focused on remaining upright. He started to feel chilly, forced himself to wake up.

The keys were in the ignition but they had left the lights on. The battery was dead. His phone was gone. His wallet too. I am alive, he thought. Emma, I will see you again. He felt grateful for the mercy of the universe that allowed him to go on a bit longer. Then he vomited all over his shoes.

LOST IN THOUGHT

It was not what she had expected a psychiatric ward to look like. Libby had imagined screaming patients in straitjackets, creepy matrons and locked cells with spy holes. Instead, the adolescent inpatient unit looked more like an upmarket holiday camp. Two bedroom wings led to a large living area comprising a kitchen and a lounge area overseen by a glass-walled nurses' station. The ward wasn't even locked and you could abscond from the unit if you had the nerve to walk out past the psych nurses. The only area that was locked was the core of the building, what they called the HDU. That stood for high-dependency unit, Sasha had explained. That's where they took you for shock treatment, she said, or to lock you up if you were out of control.

"Shock treatment?" Libby asked.

"Yes," said Sasha, "they zap your brain."

Libby was aghast. "Do they still do that these days?" It sounded barbaric.

"Yep, my dad's had it a few times."

"Your dad's been admitted too?"

"Yeah, several times. Not here of course, in the adult unit. He's bipolar. Would work for weeks on end, all on a high. He's an architect, you know, a pretty good one. Would be all wrapped up in a project and then something would snap and he'd sink into one of his moods. As if someone dropped a block of concrete right in front of a train—all action one moment and then a pulverising stop."

Pulverising, Libby thought, that's a word you only read in books. It made her like Sasha. She also liked people who said *conversely* or *obfuscate*.

"And how's your dad now?"

"Yeah, he's been good for more than a year. Lost his firm, though. The big players steer clear of you once you drop your bundle. No second chances when you're in business."

There was no second chance in parenting either, Libby thought—sorry about that, Mum.

"Hey, you still with me?"

"Sorry, lost in my thoughts."

"Yes," said Sasha, "that's what we're all here for." A cloud slid over her face and she fell silent.

~

Libby counted herself lucky to have Sasha on those first days on the ward. She was her guide and did a better job than the information pamphlet Libby had been given on admission. She had not been in a state to read it, anyway. When Libby finally glanced at it, she scoffed when she recognised the same guy with the brown hair from the education department flyer. So now he was pretending to be a mental health patient. What a fraud. And fancy making a career as a problem-hopping young person, she thought. The likeable face of troubled adolescence. Nothing too scary or visibly distressed. No pills, no scratches or slashes.

Sasha had been awesome, explaining all the stuff that didn't make any sense to Libby. Like why they had taken away her mobile, her charger, her belt and shoelaces.

"They don't want you to hang yourself while you're in here," she said, "they want you to do that in the comfort of your own home."

"I thought they want to make us better?"

Sasha snorted. "And how do you think that's going to happen?

They hardly talk to us; they don't listen. How often have you seen your psychiatrist? The nurses control us, like a herd of freaks. Once they've figured out the exact dosage of whatever pills you'll be popping, they discharge you. Check it out—no one's in here for more than nine or ten days, fourteen max."

"Really?" Libby sounded hopeful.

"Yeah, but that's not such a great thing. 'We don't want to stigmatise the young person,' they say, 'we want to minimise intervention.' Shit like that. What they really mean is 'we want to keep costs down. We can't help you change in under a fortnight but we'll figure out what mix of drugs will keep you numb and reasonably safe on the outside.'"

"You make it sound so bleak."

"It's what my dad always said; and now I see it with my own eyes every time I'm admitted."

"Have you been here that often then?"

"Six, seven times a year."

Sasha quickly asked why Libby had been admitted, as if to divert attention from herself. Libby told her about her depression and about how everyone thought she had an eating disorder. How her mum had found her collapsed in the hallway, blood seeping from her shoulder, after she'd cut herself.

"See," said Sasha, "that's it—blood. Always does the trick!"

Libby looked at her, confused.

"You can be depressed and suicidal all you like," said Sasha, "but they'll keep you out until you act on it. But bleed and you're golden. Blood is your entry ticket to mental health services. That and violence, for guys."

"That sounds so cynical. Some of the staff seem pretty cool. Like that Ms Murphy, she really listens—"

"The psychologist, yeah, she's okay I suppose. I've had her too, but really, how often do you see her? She comes to the unit maybe once a week... You have a pleasant chat. Does that help you eat? Does it solve your depression? Does it make you stop cutting yourself?"

Libby looked down. Her jade green shoes looked stupid without laces.

"And what about your psychiatrist, that Rat–something guy?" Sasha asked.

"He barely said anything. He just asked some questions. Didn't seem interested in me. It was like I had this illness and he wanted to stick the right label on it. He just went on about depression. Did I have suicidal ideation, he kept asking."

"That's what they're scared of, that you'll do it here. Have you noticed the door knobs in your room?"

"Yeah, what's with them? Why are there no handles?"

"It's so you can't hang yourself on them. That's why the knobs are all weird, like cones."

"But stuff slides off them, even towels, which is really annoying."

"It is. And check out the curtains in your bedroom. They're attached with Velcro. Try to hang yourself from them and the whole place hears the Velcro rip as you come tumbling down. A dead giveaway."

They both laughed.

"Seriously though, a girl our age managed to kill herself here last year," said Sasha. "Her sister had given her a scarf when she visited. A birthday present. That's all she needed. Happy birthday."

Libby felt overwhelmed by the enormity of it all. A girl like her had taken her life in one of these poky rooms. Maybe even in her bedroom. So sad.

The following day Sasha was discharged and Libby sank into a new level of loneliness. She asked for pencils and paper so she could draw but Janice told her she was not allowed to have any sharp objects. She attended a fitness session in the gym room but that was cut short when one of the boys had a meltdown, swearing and banging on the walls. He put his fist right through the plaster. One of the psych nurses tried to talk him down while Janice escorted the others back to the lounge area. Libby spent the rest of the morning watching *The Today Show* on Channel Nine. Floods in Turkey. Four teenagers killed in a car crash in the Hunter Valley. A long saga about frustrated homeowners and unfinished plastering jobs in Reservoir. Then Oliver, the new guy, started hitting on her. He had hard, penetrating eyes. She got off the couch and went to her room. She locked the door.

~

On Wednesday afternoon she had just returned, quite deflated, from a session on life skills and goal setting when Janice knocked at her door.

"You have a visitor," she said.

She followed the nurse down the corridor. Some of the other patients were in the common area, ensconced in beanbags, watching *The Bold and the Beautiful*. Janice showed Libby into a cramped little meeting room.

"Oh, it's you," she said to Melanie.

Her mother stood up and gave her a quick hug, as if she was contagious.

"How are you, darling?"

Melanie smelled of face cream and cigarettes. Libby had never noticed the vertical lines on her mother's upper lip before. They made her look older, more severe.

"Get me out of here," said Libby. "There's creeps on the unit. Yesterday a guy walked into my room when I was in the shower. They say last week the same guy got into a girl's bed as she was sleeping and felt her up."

"What! That's not on!" said Melanie. "Can't the staff do anything about that?"

"Like what," sneered Libby, "lock him up?"

"Well, yes, put him in prison!"

"I don't know, Mum. I don't know why we have to be locked up with guys, it's not fair. I'm dealing with enough stuff already."

"But you can lock your door, can't you?" said Melanie.

"Yes, there's a latch, and the staff have an override key, but sometimes you forget."

"Maybe you should pay more attention—"

"It's the medication, Mum," she snapped. "It makes you dopey. You forget stuff." It sounded harsher than she had intended.

And just as Libby expected to be admonished to try harder, she saw that rarest of sights: tears welling up in the corners of Melanie's eyes, smudging her mascara, gathering speed over the greasy expanse of foundation and blusher and plunging in reckless abandon onto her mother's baroque jacket.

Melanie pulled her chair closer to Libby's. "Come here," she rasped, hooking her daughter closer to her in an unfamiliar gesture of affection.

Libby felt startled. Her mother clutched her near her chest in an awkward pose, like holding a garden rake on an overcrowded tram. Her face cream smelt warm and salty, almost reassuring. Now what, Libby wondered, though she could not help feeling moved by this bewildering and clumsy expression of love. After submitting stiffly to her mother's embrace for a while, Libby tried to extract herself, and Melanie, taking the hint, sat up again and slid her chair back. She pulled a tissue out of the box on the table and dabbed her eyes.

"Well..." Melanie said.

Yes, Libby thought, let's be strangers again.

Melanie looked at her watch. Then she too reverted to form, with an upbeat announcement: "Guess what, we moved to Carlton yesterday! That's our big news! It all went well. I love the new place, so clean and modern! Nathan does too. He said to say hi."

"Say hi back," Libby responded mechanically.

"It'll be so good when we're all together in the new home. Any news about when you're allowed to come home?"

"Friday maybe. A girl who was here says they often discharge patients on a Friday. Keeps their weekend overtime costs down. If not, probably Monday or Tuesday. That's what the psychologist thought."

"Well, I can't wait darling! Then we can start over and leave all this silliness behind us. It'll be great!"

Libby stared at a poster from a pharmaceutical company on the wall. A young woman was running through a field of daffodils. Somehow it made her think of her dad and Karla. Dad doesn't even know I'm here, she thought. Mum gets points for turning up, she conceded, grudgingly.

BANDAGES

"What have you done now?" Fran had said on her first morning back in the office. Kurt felt sheepish. His lips were swollen, the socket of his right eye looked like a cross between a peat bog and a localised outbreak of bubonic plague. His head was bandaged like something from an Egyptian sarcophagus. It felt too large and his brain was still spinning. He kept involuntarily bowing his head, as if nodding off or paying emphatic tribute to his returned manager.

"How wash your shecondment?" he had managed.

Fran had sidestepped his diversionary tactics and homed in on his condition. There was no way Kurt was going to do casework if the doctor had said that he had suffered mild concussion. How could he drive? How could you work with children when you looked like the abominable snowman? She had sent Kurt home for the rest of the week. "Rest and keep up your fluids," was her parting comment. Fran was even scarier when she attempted to joke, Kurt decided.

He spent the rest of the day on the couch, reading computer magazines and watching daytime television. His mind went round in circles thinking of Gecko's trail, which had gone stone cold. When Emma came home, he could not muster the energy to ask her about her day.

Emma started talking about Libby again. Could she find out what had happened to her? Why she'd missed her last day at Banksia High? Was there anything protective services could do?

Kurt bristled under the barrage of questions, looked down at his leftover fettucine. He spoke slowly, pedantically, lining up his arguments: "The girl's eighteen now. She's not been previously notified. You've already referred her to Outer Metro Health. What more could you do? She's going to a different school, for god's sake. It's out of your hands." He threw his fork down. Emma, startled, withdrew to the study.

Kurt felt bad about the exchange. The desperation of his fatigue only partially explained his reaction, and it did not justify his cantankerousness. Emma was only trying to do what he had wanted to achieve for Gecko: make sure the young person in your care is okay. And he had snarled, like Fran might have. Self-loathing washed over him. He knew he should go into the study and apologise. But the dullness behind his forehead kept his eyes glued on the television screen, where contestants were making their way through an infernal obstacle course. Ouch, that would have hurt. Being pummelled for no reason at all—he could relate to that. After a while he dozed off.

That night he slept fitfully. Wolf figured prominently in his dreams. The next day he fired up *Savage Glory*. He went on what seemed an endless quest. Every completed task revealed a new objective. It was too much like work. The orcs reminded him of Rocco and Wolf. Great, he thought, now the Mutineers have ruined *Savage Glory* for me.

He decided to empty his backpack and give it a good clean. Tucked into an inner pocket, he found an enrolment confirmation for a seminar. *Engaging Troubled Adolescents. Models for Interdisciplinary Casework.* He had totally forgotten about that. He blew a little dust ball off the crumpled sheet, looked at the date. Tomorrow. Fran had said nothing about attending seminars, he figured, so he might as well learn something new.

∼

I hate parking at Southern Corridor Health, Kurt thought. It's always the same. Takes you ages to find a spot and then you have to race through this warren of walkways trying to figure out where you need to be. And these hospital buildings have such ludicrous names. The Margaret Johns Building. The John Meadows Building. They all sounded alike: bland, eminently forgettable. What if you could name them after their function, throw in a tad of fantasy maybe? *The Hall of Healing*? *The School of Sharp Scalpels*? He couldn't think of anything good.

He was late and out of breath as he stumbled into the Yarra Theatre. He burst in through a side door at the front of the auditorium, attracting everyone's attention. The presenter paused as he took in the spectacle of a middle-aged male flapping into the lecture hall, his head swathed in bandages.

"Are you here for the seminar or were you looking for the emergency department?" he asked, scoring laughter from the audience.

Kurt mumbled something about late and no parking and plonked himself down on one of the few empty chairs, right in the front row. The woman on the chair next to him gave him a polite smile and stood up. Surely I can't smell that bad, Kurt thought, but the woman took up position at the lectern and smiled confidently into the room. The presenter introduced her as Caitlin Murphy, Clinical Psychologist at Outer Metro's Mental Health Service. The name sounded vaguely familiar but Kurt felt sure he had never met her. He would have remembered.

His attention started to drift, his battered mind replaying the search for a car park and the scramble through hospital corridors.

"It is crucial for tertiary services, such as specialist mental health services, to develop strong linkages with primary services, such as education," said Caitlin. "Let me give you an example from a recent case, where a young person with depression and an eating disorder, I shall call her Anna, was referred from a local high school."

The case Caitlin described sounded familiar. A high achiever who went into a meltdown, started self-harming. Just like Libby, the Year 12 girl Emma had told him about. This had to be more than a coincidence. Caitlin outlined her interactions with the school's counsellor and explained the importance of communication being clear and specific within the context of a well-defined case plan. She praised the professionalism of the school counsellor, whose work had ticked all those boxes. Must tell Emma, Kurt thought. But first make sure. No more assumptions.

During the break Kurt moved in Caitlin's direction. She was still holding her papers and answering questions. When she got a chance to extract herself from the throng she moved towards the urn. Kurt approached her cautiously, not wanting to come across as a mummified stalker.

Caitlin stirred her tea and had a sip.

"Hi," she said, "where are you from?"

"I'm a protective worker," he said.

Caitlin sniggered. "Sorry," she said, "but you look as if you need protection yourself."

"I know," moaned Kurt, "that's fast becoming the joke of the week."

"I'll try to be more original," said Caitlin. "Do you work for Southern Outreach?"

"No, Eastern."

"Esposito's team. I know quite a few of her protective workers. What's your name?"

"Kurt Edelman."

"Oh yes," she said, "I know your name." She looked sideways, seemed annoyed.

"Where from? I don't think we've met before."

"Maybe not," said Caitlin. She appeared no longer interested in the conversation.

"I just wanted to say," said Kurt, "the case scenario that you described, the girl's name is Libby, isn't it?"

"Look, I cannot disclose any identifying details about my patients. You would understand that." She sounded tetchy.

"Sorry, I don't want to put you on the spot. It's just that my wife used to be the counsellor at Banksia High. Emma Rubenis."

"Used to?"

"Yes, she's the Head of the English Department now."

"Well, that's a shame. Sorry, I've just spotted someone I need to catch."

What did I say? Kurt thought.

~

Kurt still felt bewildered, and slightly miffed, as the second speaker began her talk about the consequences of childhood sexual abuse. She knew her stuff and presented it well. A riveting presentation. Kurt forgot all about his awkward moment with Caitlin. Then Bernie Hickworth of the Salvation Army spoke about managing risk with young men and coordinating service provision across child protection services and juvenile justice. Kurt felt like his brain was starting to reboot after its clobbering. He felt so pleased he hadn't just stayed at home, on the couch. Hickworth made a quip about promptly returning phone calls; and Kurt thought he saw Caitlin tilt her head in his direction. It was nothing really, a minuscule movement, but the penny dropped.

Caitlin Murphy. Of course. The yellow sticky note Debbie had handed him, way back in January, just before he flew out to Belgium. By the time he remembered the urgent message he was flying over Asia. Caitlin's aloofness made sense now. To her, he was the noise in the system. A blocker rather than a facilitator. The person you ring in an emergency who never gets back to you. He would have to say something to her. Or could he let it go? What did it matter what others thought of him? In Zen they called this the worldly winds of praise and blame. But it did matter, he decided. He was a performer, an achiever. He couldn't stand being thought of as a slacker, as unreliable. Kurt spent the rest of Hickworth's presentation planning his opening lines.

In the break he tracked down Caitlin and offered his rehearsed apology. She still seemed sceptical, so he told her about his trip to Belgium. She seemed to relax more. Finally he told her about how concerned Emma had been when Libby had not turned up at school.

"Hang on," Caitlin said, "maybe we can just grab a bite to eat while you're telling me all this."

They got themselves sandwiches in the hospital canteen—miserable refrigerated slices of anaemic bread with limp fillings. Kurt asked

Caitlin about her presentation and her work at Outer Metro and she became more forthcoming. Then a curious smile came over her face.

"Okay," she said, "I just have to ask. Who did this to you?"

He told her.

"Bayswater bikies," she mused. "Rocco and Wolf. They sound like characters from a Raymond Chandler novel. Have you read Chandler?"

Kurt's mobile rang. "Sorry," he said, "I have to take this… Fran, what can I do for you?"

Caitlin concentrated on her egg and lettuce sandwich.

"No, not a word from Gecko. Don't know where he is. Tell Morrison I'll drop in next week, in Silvan, when I'm back on deck. Yes… Yes… Sure… Bye." He put his mobile in his shirt pocket.

"I didn't mean to eavesdrop," said Caitlin, "but did you say 'Gecko?'"

"Yeah, he's one of the kids I work with. Except he's gone missing."

"This may be a coincidence," said Caitlin, "but Libby keeps mentioning a Gecko. It was her nickname for the boyfriend who broke up with her."

"You're kidding," Kurt stammered.

Kurt told Caitlin more about Gecko and she said it all tallied with what Libby had told her.

"That's unbelievable," Kurt said, "do you know where I might find him?"

"Try Thailand," she said.

DISCHARGE

Caitlin kept thinking about Kurt. What a funny little man, laid back and tense at the same time. Laid back in that he seemed impervious to her gentle taunts. Tense, or maybe just persistent, when it came to his questions about Gecko. She had told him what little she knew and vetoed his requests to speak to Libby. He had insisted. There was a lot at stake, he said. Why did he think Libby was in an inpatient unit, she had countered, there was even more at stake for her. He had conceded that maybe this wasn't the best time.

Anyhow, Libby had settled down and Suresh was satisfied that her drug regimen was working. Discharge was scheduled for 4:00 p.m. The office staff had notified Melanie.

Caitlin had wanted to pop in at the unit before then to give Libby a few pointers for her ongoing recovery in the community, but she had been called away to conduct an urgent risk assessment of a twelve-year-old boy who had swallowed his father's anti-depressants. By the time she had completed all the paperwork and briefed the Rat it was almost six, so she packed up and headed for the station.

As she walked down the hill towards the highway, she noticed a band of pale yellow sky above the strip of little Asian grocery stores. It looked tentative, unstable, an anaemic watercolour. She shivered. Not long now until the start of the warmer weather, she thought. She smiled. If there was going to be a baby, he or she would be born around late April.

She crossed the highway and followed the red brick promenade to the shopping centre above the station. The Vietnamese checkout girl in the pharmacy, a pimply thing of maybe fifteen who was probably putting in a couple of hours after school, gave her a warm smile as she paid for the test kit. Fancy if Mum had still been alive, Caitlin thought, that would have been so much fun. And Philip, how would he react? Anyway, let's do the test first, no good getting carried away.

Opposite the station entrance, she was jolted out of her reverie when she spotted Libby sitting on a concrete planter box, smoking, and talking to two boys in baggy pants and hoodies. She headed over to the trio straightaway.

"Libby, what are you doing here?"

"Oh, hi, Ms Murphy. Mum didn't turn up, so I discharged myself."

The boys looked at each other. "Let's go," the older one said. They sauntered off towards the food court.

Libby smiled sheepishly. "I don't know those guys," she said apologetically, "I just wanted a smoke." She stubbed out her cigarette in the gravel of the planter box.

"I didn't know you smoked."

"I don't really. Just tried a couple this week on the unit, in the courtyard. Something to do, you know, with my phone confiscated and all that."

Great, Caitlin thought, we taught her to smoke.

"Why didn't your mum come?"

"It's okay, I'm an adult now, I don't need her to be discharged." She put on her backpack, a small triangular nylon thing.

"You're right, but it would've been nice to have some support."

"I'm okay. Except... I don't have any money for a train ticket..."

"I'll buy you one."

"Oh really? Thanks so much. I'll pay you back."

The train to the city was not crowded. Too early for the Friday night revellers. Still, Caitlin was mindful that she couldn't talk freely. She tried to be discreet.

"So whereabouts in Carlton do you live now?"

Libby looked alarmed.

"Oh my god, I don't even know. I've forgotten what Mum said. It's those stupid pills messing with my brain. I had the address on my phone but my battery's dead."

"What about your discharge papers?"

Libby checked. "They still have the old address."

"So where will you go now?"

"I don't know."

"I'll ring your mum."

She tried twice but kept getting voicemail. Libby was getting agitated. Caitlin looked up Melanie's company and rang the office. Voicemail again. Everyone had gone home for the weekend.

"Never mind," said Caitlin, trying to sound cheerful, "we'll keep trying, she'll answer sooner or later. We can go to my place and charge your phone. I'm in Carlton too."

"You shouldn't have to do that, Ms Murphy."

"I'm happy to, Libby, I can't just leave you alone in the city. And by the way, you can call me Caitlin."

Her thoughts were racing. It wasn't on, taking a client home, even with the best of intentions. But what other option was there? She could hardly ring the mental health crisis team, because there was no crisis—just a young patient who had been discharged. The cops would laugh in her face if she said she had an unaccompanied eighteen-year-old. But she couldn't let Libby wander off into the night, after everything she had been through, with no money, a flat phone and no idea where her new home was. Anything might happen. She would take Libby home, contact Suresh first, brief him on the situation, then start ringing anyone who might know where the hell Melanie Rogers was.

As they walked up LaTrobe Street, Libby chatted about the books she had read for English. It was as if she realised she was putting Caitlin out and wanted to be amiable, make polite conversation. Caitlin felt distracted. It had been a tough week, and she had been looking forward to a night in with Philip. It was cold enough to have a cosy wood fire. She could have taken the pregnancy test. Anyway, none of that was going to happen tonight. Instead she had redefined the notion of bringing work home.

"Wow, nice house," said Libby, as Caitlin opened the cast iron gate.

Caitlin looked up at the stately two-storey terrace house, as if seeing it for the first time. "It is, isn't it," she said, "I suppose we're lucky."

SANCTUARY

"Hey, Philip," Caitlin called, "we have a visitor."

"Just sit on the couch for a minute," she said to Libby when there was no reply, "I'll be right back."

Libby smiled politely and put her backpack on her lap. Caitlin ran up the stairs and opened the bedroom door. Philip lay naked on the bed, snoring. He reeked of wine and garlic.

"Philip," she said, prodding the shape, "are you all right?"

He moaned.

"Are you drunk?"

He opened his eyes.

"Oh, it's you. I'm not drunk," he slurred. "Had lunch with colleagues... Jessica's farewell."

"The secretary?"

He grunted.

"Listen, Philip. I have a client here. The girl I've told you about, Libby. She's downstairs. I've had to bring her here. I'll explain later. So just stay here. I'll get us dinner later. Okay?"

He grunted again and his eyes fell shut. She left him there and ran down the stairs.

"Let's try your mum again," she said to Libby. The call went through to voicemail.

"I'm sorry I don't know my own address," said Libby. "How stupid am I."

"Never mind. I'm happy to have you here. Hey, you know what, I'll pop a few mini pizzas in the oven. You'll feel better when you've had a bite to eat."

Talk about being stupid, Caitlin thought as she shut the oven door. I'm offering food to comfort a young woman with anorexia. So easy to slip back into mainstream expectations. What we consider normal. I should know better, but there you go.

Caitlin finished her pizza and watched Libby cut up the dough with knife and fork into tiny squares. She had scraped off all the bacon and onion, and some of the cheese. She put a tiny square of pizza base in her mouth and chewed it for an inordinate amount of time.

Caitlin turned on the television. A lazy option, but she'd just had it. She flicked through the channels: a car chase, a distressed woman running through the woods at night, a man in a balaclava firing a shotgun, a body on a mortuary slab. Libby covered her eyes.

"Sorry. Hopefully this is less violent." They watched old music videos for a while. What does it say about our culture, Caitlin wondered, that we watch others suffer and die for entertainment? And Libby's still not okay. She's going through the motions, all proper and polite, but she seems deflated underneath. Flat affect. Like she's not watching telly right now, just staring at the box, all in a world of her own.

"Here we go," said Caitlin, as her mobile rang and vibrated on the coffee table, "your mum, finally."

Libby looked weary rather than relieved.

"Melanie, at last we connect!"

"I'm sorry, Caitlin, I'm in Lorne. I've been at a seminar all afternoon and there was no mobile reception. When I got back to my hotel, I checked voicemail. Someone from Outer Metro left a message saying Libby was to be discharged at 4:00 p.m. Then I found all your messages."

"Yes, Libby discharged herself just after five. I've got her here with me."

"I'm really sorry about the mix-up. Can I speak to her?"

"Sure, but can I just confirm that the inpatient unit staff left you a message without making sure that you had received it?"

"That's right."

"So they never actually spoke to you?"

"Correct. I first heard of this five minutes ago. Libby had mentioned she might be discharged on Monday or Tuesday. And now I'm in Lorne—that's a three-hour drive to Melbourne, maybe more, in the dark. And I've had a few drinks with dinner…"

"Libby's at my place here, in Carlton. We're in Creswick Street. I guess she could stay here."

"Are you sure?"

"Absolutely."

"That's awfully kind of you. Much appreciated! I'll pick her up before lunchtime tomorrow."

"I'll put you on to her now."

Libby talked to her mum for a couple of minutes. It seemed to go haltingly, but Caitlin wasn't really paying attention. One of her clients was going to sleep over at her place. At least she had the mother's verbal consent now, for what that was worth. She would have to ring Suresh next, and ruin his Friday night, to cover herself. Not that anything much could go wrong now that Libby was here. But the fact that she had ended up acting unprofessionally filled Caitlin with a sense of foreboding.

"What's the address here?" whispered Libby.

Caitlin told her, and Libby passed it on to her mum.

Libby looked pale after she had hung up. Caitlin thought she saw her shivering.

"I'll show you the guest room. And why don't you have a shower, that'll make you feel nice and warm. When you come out we can have a chat or watch a bit more telly, or you can just go to bed—whatever you prefer."

"Thanks, Ms Murphy, you're so nice!"

"Caitlin."

"Thanks, Caitlin."

"Let's get you some towels."

～

Caitlin rang Suresh. He wasn't happy.

"Why did you have to take her home?" he asked. "That's most irregular."

He conceded that there was little else Caitlin could have done, other than abandoning Libby on the streets. A crisis service wouldn't have taken her on; and the inpatient unit wouldn't have taken her back without a referral. "Ring me tomorrow," he said, "once the mother has picked her up, and then we'll discuss the situation first thing on Monday. Kindly send me your written report by Sunday night. I'll have to brief Dr Ratnawarpal."

This is getting bigger and bigger, thought Caitlin.

Upstairs the water was still running. Good, she thought, I'm getting ten minutes to myself. She took an old plastic container from the kitchen cupboard, picked up her handbag and went into the small downstairs bathroom. She caught her urine in the container. Note to self, must never again use this container for vinaigrette. She opened the box and took the soft purple cap off the test stick. No need to read the instructions, she had explained this to so many of her clients. She inserted the white stick into her urine and waited. She felt on the cusp of something momentous. And when would she tell Philip? This was not what she had imagined, with him in a drunken stupor and an unexpected guest in the house. She closed her eyes to savour this last moment where everything hung in the balance. Then she opened her eyes and looked down. Two parallel pink stripes told her that a new life had started. She smiled. Deep happiness bloomed up inside her. She would have to hide it from Libby, just in case her periods hadn't come back yet.

Then she heard commotion upstairs and shouting. Someone running down the stairs, Philip calling out, the front door slamming.

Caitlin put the container down, with the test stick in it, washed her hands and rushed out.

"What's happening?" she said.

Philip looked flushed and dishevelled.

"This girl," he said with a thick voice, "she ran away."

"Why? What happened?"

"I don't know. I came out of the bedroom and she was there. I must have given her a fright. She screamed and ran off."

"That doesn't make any sense. Get your car keys. We have to look for her."

"What, now?"

"Yes. Now."

"But—"

"No 'buts', Philip. If we don't find her it'll cost me my job."

Philip slid into his leather coat. As he squatted down to tie his shoelaces, he spotted the open bathroom door and the test stick protruding from the plastic container next to the toilet.

"What's that?" he gestured.

"We need to talk," said Caitlin.

DEBRIEFING

When Caitlin entered the meeting room, the others were already there. Bronwyn Guilfoyle, Director of Nursing across all of Outer Metro Health, Veronica Tyler, Head of Legal Services, Ivan Kwiatek, Inpatient Unit Manager. And Suresh, of course, who attended both in his role as psychiatrist and as her supervisor. Quite a line-up. The only heavy missing was the Rat, who was chairing a hearing of the Mental Health Review Board. Suresh would be meeting with him at lunchtime.

Caitlin's throat felt constricted. This was just a debriefing about the events of the weekend, Suresh had said in his brief phone call, but at the same time he had also cautioned her to be very careful about any statements she made.

She sat down and smiled across the room. Veronica smiled back, Ivan just nodded and Bronwyn stared intently at her blank notepad.

"Thank you all for coming at such short notice," Suresh said. "You have read Caitlin's preliminary report about the Rogers case. And though it is incomplete in some important ways, it provides us with a good starting point for this meeting."

Incomplete in some important ways, thought Caitlin, what is he on about? She decided to let it go. No good seeming defensive right from the start.

Suresh summarised the events of Friday night. Communication with the patient's mother had been less than ideal and had resulted in the patient discharging herself at 5:07 p.m. without a pickup arrangement in place. He related how Caitlin had spotted Libby at the station and accompanied her to Carlton. When it became clear that Libby did not know her new address and was unable to contact her mother, Caitlin had invited her to her home in Creswick Street. By the time Melanie Rogers responded to Caitlin's calls and messages it was too late to arrange a handover on that day and Melanie had agreed to collect Libby from Caitlin's house on Saturday morning.

"Let us put aside for a moment the events that ensued at Creswick Street between approximately 9:00 and 9:30 p.m. that evening," he continued.

Why, thought Caitlin. Why treat that separately rather than as part of the chronology of events he was outlining? This was not going well.

The room was slowly getting stuffier and the fluorescent lights seemed to be buzzing louder by the minute.

"All parties agree that Libby Rogers fled the house at Creswick Street around 9:30 p.m. on Friday. Caitlin and her partner, Philip Wheelwright—"

"How do you spell that?" asked Veronica.

Suresh spelled out the name.

Caitlin shifted in her chair. "Do we have to bring Philip into this?" she objected. "I don't see how this is relevant."

"This is not a hearing," said Veronica, "not yet. But we need to establish all salient facts."

Suresh continued. "Caitlin and her partner went searching for the patient in Carlton. After about an hour, not being able to find her, they contacted the police. Caitlin also rang Melanie Rogers and myself. Around 4:00 a.m. I received a phone call from Carlton police. The officer advised me that a young female matching Libby's description had jumped into the Yarra off Princes Bridge at 1:15 a.m. in an apparent suicide attempt. Two football players who'd been out celebrating jumped in and brought her ashore. She was taken by ambulance to the Inner Melbourne Medical Hub. I immediately notified Melanie and Caitlin."

"How's the girl now?" asked Bronwyn.

"She has a severe chest infection. She talked to her mother and to hospital staff on Saturday and made a number of allegations. Since then her mood has deteriorated sharply. She's not communicating now, appears almost catatonic."

"What allegations did she make?" asked Caitlin.

"We'll come to that," said Suresh. "But first let me make clear that Melanie Rogers has initiated legal proceedings against Outer Metro Health."

"What's the name of her solicitor?" asked Veronica.

"Let's just complete this overview first," said Suresh, "so we're all on the same page." Veronica frowned.

"The Inner Melbourne Medical Hub undertook a risk assessment," Suresh went on, "and the psychiatrist determined that Libby Rogers needs to be admitted to an inpatient unit for treatment and for review of her medication. However, they are 'bursting at the seams', as their registrar put it, and are unable to admit Libby at present. They recommend that we readmit her, for the sake of continuity, even though that makes it an out-of-area referral, since Libby now resides in Carlton. They, of course, have helped us out in the past, when we were full."

"We have a patient due to be discharged this morning," said Ivan.

"Great," said Suresh, "I've spoken to Dr Ratnawarpal and he supports Libby's readmission in principle. He anticipates that, given her presentation, she may require a course of electro-convulsive therapy. Maybe not straightaway but—"

"Not ECT!" Caitlin blurted out. "Suresh, you know damn well Libby freaks out at the thought of ECT! She specifically asked never to be given shock treatment, as she calls it. She thinks it will scramble her brain, destroy her memories, wipe out who she is. We should review her medication first, give it time to work."

Everyone looked up at the ferocity of Caitlin's outburst.

"This is not the time or the place to have a discussion about clinical treatment options," said Suresh, "but I would like to pause this meeting for five minutes as I need to ask Caitlin something in private. I'm sorry I haven't had a chance to do so earlier."

"In private?" said Caitlin, bewildered. She followed Suresh out of the conference room. They went into the small meeting room across the hallway.

"Sorry for being so dramatic, Suresh," she said, "that wasn't a personal attack. It's just that administering ECT will destroy whatever remains of the therapeutic relationship. Libby will feel betrayed. She'll just walk out and never come back. And you know what Dr Ratnawarpal is like—always quick to prescribe ECT."

"Dr Ratnawarpal," said Suresh, "believes ECT may be indicated given the patient's suicide attempt and the severity of her depression, including further suicidal ideation, according to the Medical Hub psychiatrist. He will, of course, need to examine her in person."

Why does he sound so officious, thought Caitlin?

"I understand your objections," Suresh continued, "but you must realise that, after what happened…"

Here it comes, she thought.

"… the Director of Clinical Services is in no mind to take your advice on this patient's treatment."

Case closed. She took a deep breath, pursed her lips, looked at the noticeboard over his shoulder. A printout of staff phone numbers. The hospital emergency codes. Last season's footy tipping score sheet.

"Sure," she heard herself say, "I understand." She was going to be on the outer even more from now on.

"But there is something else," said Suresh. "Libby alleges your partner behaved inappropriately towards her. She says he walked into the bathroom naked at your place while she was having a shower. He urinated in her presence."

Caitlin was stunned. She covered her mouth. Her temples were throbbing.

"She claims he ogled her as she scrambled to get out of the shower and quickly dress herself. He reportedly made comments about her body, saying he found her attractive—"

"What? Enough!" Her voice quavered, her legs were shaking.

"I am so sorry, Caitlin. This must be so difficult for you to hear."

Philip harassing Libby? Two worlds colliding in the worst possible way? She closed her eyes, pursed her lips against the nauseating despair that welled up in her chest.

"Libby was distraught. Understandably." Suresh paused for a moment. "Do you think she would ever make up things like that?"

Caitlin licked her lips. They felt like dry husks. "Libby's always been honest with me," she said at last.

Suresh nodded. "And did you witness anything unusual when Libby had her shower?"

"No," she said. She spoke slowly, playing back the reel of Friday's events in her mind. "I was doing something else though." She thought of the two pink stripes on the paper strip. Her short-lived happiness. After that: the shouting, the confusion of Libby's flight.

"What did your partner say about Libby running away?"

"He came out of the bedroom, she got a fright and started yelling. It made no sense to him." Then she remembered Philip's thick voice, his nervousness, his reluctance to involve the police. How could she have been so blind? Had she pushed them aside, all those signs, to the furthest recesses of her mind, because there had been this other thing so much in the foreground, clamouring to be heard?

"This is a delicate question," said Suresh, "but I have to ask whether, in your opinion, your partner would be capable of the alleged behaviour?"

Caitlin just stared at the wall. Philip had betrayed her once again. This was worse than Di or his compulsive flirting. Alcohol or not, he had harassed a vulnerable young woman, violated her privacy in an outrageous manner. This time there was no glossing over, no going back. It dawned on Caitlin that she had gained a child and lost a partner on that fateful Friday night. And driven Libby to attempt suicide while trying to keep her safe.

Suresh was looking at her with his gentle eyes, giving her time, but expecting an answer all the same. But her silence, Suresh would understand, was the most definite answer she could give.

OCTOBER 2009

CONSENT

When Brenda collected her from her bedroom, Libby just trailed along. What did it matter? It wouldn't be long now. Sooner or later they would have to let her go. And then she could try again. She shivered as she recalled the moment her body pierced the surface of the water like a sly arrow. The icy chill, the panic as the water burst into her lungs, her frantic struggle to foil her own plot. She felt grateful towards her rescuers for what they had done, but in an impersonal way—the world needed heroes. Above all, she felt deflated: she would have to go through the whole thing again. Find another way—not the river.

So what did Brenda want her for? She'd said something about a chat with the psychiatrist. She hoped it was the younger one, not the old gasbag. But what difference did it make? They were all the same. All in cahoots. What a strange word: cahoots. Caitlin had seemed nice and supportive at first but had set the monster upon her. She hadn't seen her since. Libby shuddered, pushed the memories aside and reverted to autopilot. If you kept your eyes still long enough, she had discovered, it would quieten your brain too. You could stare without seeing. Hear sounds without listening. People could touch your skin and it would not matter. Like a tree doesn't care if you brush past its bark.

Far below her, two feet in pink scuffs shuffled across the floor tiles in Brenda's wake. The nurse's close-cropped curly hair made her look like a poodle. An overweight poodle, Libby thought, as she watched her lumbering along the corridor. Brenda was okay, though, she had let her keep her iPod this time. What would it be like to be fat, to take up so much space in the universe? It seemed arrogant and powerful at the same time. The assertiveness of a huge body, proclaiming *these are my molecules and I plonk them down wherever I want; what are you going to do about it*?

I have to stop eating or I'll end up just the same. And also, if I stop eating they'll realise I'm unhappy. An animal in captivity, pining away. They'll just have to send me home. Wow, my mind is, like, weird and floating, but I'm still coming up with all these ideas.

Someone told her to sit down. Two other people in the room? She squinted against the glare, made out the bulk of the old psychiatrist opposite her. Someone asked her whether she had a headache. What a stupid question, she thought, all she needed was for someone to lower that blind.

The man pushed a booklet towards her. It clipped the corner of a yellow sticky note on his desk, made it come unstuck. This sets out your rights, he said, or something like that. Press down that yellow sticky note again, she wanted to tell him, or it will blow off your desk when someone opens the door. He went on about electro mumbo jumbo, that horrible thing, and she didn't want to listen to any of that. Wonder what it said on that yellow sticky. Maybe an important telephone number or the name of a new drug. Or maybe it just said *Feed the cat*. She sniggered.

The man looked displeased, said this was important. He was talking about consent, he said. There was a purplish sheen over his lips, the same colour as in the wrinkles under his eyelids. His mouth was a nice shape but there was a thick black hair coming out of his nose that moved as he spoke. He mentioned consent again, and her rights.

All she wanted was the right to go home. But home was gone, of course, she kept forgetting. Mum and Nathan were in the new place she hadn't seen yet. Dad was in Byron Bay with Karla and she'd never been there either. But the house where they'd all been together, and the glorious garden with the orchids and the skinks and the mottled light under the gums, that was all gone.

They asked her more questions, and she nodded. She just wanted to be back in her room, where she could sleep. And forget.

MURPHY'S LAW

The smell of strong coffee greeted Kurt as he walked into the Mean Bean Cafe. He felt disoriented as he peered into the room, bewildered by the chatter of patrons, the scraping of chairs on the wooden floor and the hissing of the espresso machine. A woman sitting at the back wall waved at him and he recognised Caitlin.

"I wasn't sure it was you," she said, "I didn't recognise you without the bandages."

"So glad they're gone. I can have a normal shower now."

She examined his face. "You're older than I thought."

"Now I want those bandages back," Kurt joked.

She smiled. "It's just... protective workers are generally younger, fresh out of uni..."

"I know. I've used up a few lives already. I started out as a history teacher in Belgium—"

"Is that where you're from; I couldn't place the accent."

"Yeah, I'm from the north of Belgium, which is Dutch-speaking. Or Flemish, as they call the local variant. I migrated here after a messy divorce. Retrained as a social worker. Spent almost a decade as a researcher for the Institute of Health and Welfare before I realised I wasn't cut out for an office job. Call me a slow learner. I wanted to help vulnerable kids instead of just describing their plight. So I became a case worker. Worked for Western Outreach and in Carlton. Been with Fran's team for less than a year. There you have it."

"I'm sorry. I didn't mean to pry."

"That's okay. I have no secrets."

"What a blessed existence!"

"Hm, I'm intrigued. Tell me about the skeletons in your cupboard."

"Some other time maybe. I called you because I've found something that may interest you." She put a scrap of paper in front of Kurt.

He looked at the phone number, then at Caitlin.

"Gecko's mobile."

"What? How did you get hold of that?"

Caitlin looked around her. "Please don't tell anyone where this came from. I'm in enough trouble as it is."

"Now I'm hooked," said Kurt. "Tell me."

Caitlin told him how she had taken Libby home with her. She seemed to hesitate for a moment, then told him about Philip's outrage.

"What a mess," said Kurt. "You went the extra mile to protect Libby and then things go wrong in a way you could not have foreseen. Murphy's Law…"

"You realise that's my actual surname, don't you?" She looked at him sharply.

"Sorry, I'd forgotten. I didn't mean to be flippant."

"I'm suspended pending an investigation. That feels so weird. One day you're part of a team, the next day a pariah. And all your cases, all those priorities… everything becomes irrelevant."

"That must be hard to take. I found it difficult already just to hand over my cases earlier this year when I had to go to Belgium. Your priorities become someone else's optional extras, and opportunities vanish. That's how Gecko's case went off the rails… So tell me, how did you get hold of his phone number?"

"After Libby had run away and we couldn't find her I checked her mobile, which she'd left behind in a charger at our, at my place. It came up in the call register."

"Wasn't the phone locked?"

"It was—until I keyed in four zeroes."

Kurt groaned.

"When I saw Gecko's name come up, I thought it might help me find her, so I jotted down the number. Later I also thought of you…"

"Thank you!"

"Major privacy infringement and all that, but I thought something good might come from all the confusion on that dreadful night. So I'm a hacker now, as well as pimping my patients." There was bitterness in her voice.

"Well, I won't let on where this came from." Kurt folded the piece of paper and put it in his wallet. "I can swallow it," he suggested, "like they do in spy movies."

"That won't be necessary. Maybe we can have a Danish pastry instead?"

"Good idea. I'm feeling peckish." Kurt called over a waitress and ordered.

"How did you go at the Children's Court?"

"Oh," said Kurt, "the lawyer raised a technical objection and the judge deferred the case until next month. My trip into the city would have been wasted if it hadn't been for this."

"Thanks," said Caitlin, as the waitress put the pastries down.

"How's Libby doing? Emma was keen to find out."

"Not great. I don't know the latest, but I hear she's refusing to eat, and they're considering giving her ECT. Against her will. I shouldn't be telling you this…"

"Can they do that?"

"Definitely. More than one third of ECT treatments are involuntary, authorised by the psychiatrist on the patient's behalf. That's where duty of care enters into a grey zone. Personally, I believe there's a bit of over-prescribing of ECT going on in our service. Interesting too, that ECT is prescribed more frequently for women, but don't start me on that… On the other hand, if the person's not eating, things can deteriorate pretty quickly… Makes it hard to challenge the decision when you're no longer close to the case."

"When to intervene, and how… Sounds familiar. We can get clobbered in the press for removing one child from their family and for leaving another one at home, all within the one week. How horrible for

Libby, though." Kurt thought for a moment. "And as I said to Emma: it was bizarre, her counselling Libby and me trying to help Gecko. And all along we had no idea what the other was doing, or that the two were an item."

"An allegory of service provision in this state," said Caitlin.

"That sounds bitter."

"It's not bitterness, just quiet despair."

THE PROCEDURE

"Why am I here?" Libby asked. She pointed at the seclusion room. A grey plastic mattress lay in the left corner. Next to it a paper cup with water, a plastic bedpan and a roll of toilet paper.

"Because you hit a nurse," said Brenda. "You scratched Margaret, knocked her glasses off."

She must have sent a duress signal, Libby thought. The pleasant female voice on the public address system had calmly announced *Code Grey in Ward One. Code Grey in Ward One.* Libby had always liked this warm voice and, as they were holding her down, part of her had felt inappropriately pleased to be the subject of one of her announcements.

"And we're not locking you up," Brenda continued, "we just need to prepare you for ECT. You need to put on that gown."

"Well I told that nurse I don't want ECT. I also told Ms Murphy—check my file."

"You have to have ECT for your depression. The psychiatrist prescribed it. This has nothing to do with Ms Murphy."

"I want to see Ms Murphy!"

"She's not here. She's… on special leave."

"I want to see my mum."

"You're eighteen, sweetie, you're an adult. Your mum has no say in this. The Act says only you can consent to ECT—"

"Well I'm not!"

"Or the psychiatrist can consent on your behalf if you're too sick to make that call."

"I'm not too sick."

"Well, the psychiatrist thinks you are, sweetie. You've not been well, have you? And now you've stopped eating too. How do you think that's going to end? Anyway, the paperwork's all done up for ECT."

"But how can that be?"

"Dr Ratnawarpal is authorised, they call it, an authorised psychiatrist. That's a special thing in the Act. Every mental health service has one and they can call the shots."

"That's so unfair." Libby had never felt so alone. "I don't want fucking ECT."

"It's for your own good, sweetie, and swearing won't help you. Now better put on this gown."

"What if I refuse?"

Brenda looked her in the eyes. "Then I'll have to call for backup. I'd rather not do that."

Backup. She knew what that meant. They'd called in backup when Oliver went off his head in the lounge area. A five-person takedown, Janice had called it afterwards. The leader had mumbled something and the four others had each grabbed a limb and before you knew it Oliver was on the floor, helpless.

"It doesn't have to be like that," said Brenda. "You can fight us and we'll have to undress you. Or you can put this gown on yourself and keep your dignity. Either way you're getting ECT."

Get undressed with nurses watching, Libby thought. Maybe even one of the male nurses. Yuck yuck yuck.

Libby sobbed. She felt defeated.

Brenda sat down and put her arm around Libby's shoulders.

"You're scared—I get that. But I've seen lots of kids go through it and come out okay. Saved their life, ECT, for some of them that had stopped eating, like you. You're going to feel a bit groggy and fuzzy after, but that passes."

Libby cried against Brenda's massive shoulder. She wished she could stay here and let her tears flood the seclusion room, the secure unit, the entire ward, the hospital, washing away every trace of her puny life. But the machine would do that for her. What if it erased all her thoughts and memories? Nathan as a cute chubby baby. Feeding the swans with Dad. Building sand castles on Rye front beach. Riding a camel at the school fete. Drawing. Gecko.

"Well," said Brenda, "maybe you can put on that gown then."

They got up and Brenda handed her the square parcel of starched white linen. She looked away as Libby unfolded it and began to undress, still sobbing.

"So you are Dr Cortez," said Dr Ratnawarpal as he entered the ECT treatment room and stepped towards the new anaesthetist. "I am Dr Ratnawarpal, Edward Ratnawarpal, Director of Clinical Services, but please call me Ed. No need to be formal." They shook hands.

"Cortez is what, a Spanish name?" said Ratnawarpal. "Imagine if it had been Cortex, that would have been so funny, an anaesthetist called cortex." The anaesthetist grimaced.

"I once knew a Doctor Panic," continued the psychiatrist, before his colleague had a chance to respond, "and he specialised in anxiety disorders, isn't that hilarious! As for me, I like dabbling in ECT. And that brings me to our young patient."

Libby looked tiny on the trolley and rather wan under the pale blue light.

"I'm your anaesthetist," said Dr Cortez. "I'm going to give you an injection and then you'll be unconscious for the next ten minutes or so. Do you understand that?"

Libby nodded almost imperceptibly.

"Just count to ten in your head." He injected the fluid into Libby's left arm. Her eyes turned upwards within seconds.

He placed an electrode pad on either side of Libby's head, an oxygen mask over her nose, inserted a mouth guard to prevent her from biting her tongue, and hooked her up to the EEG reader to monitor her brain activity during treatment. He strapped Libby firmly down on the trolley and gave her a muscle relaxant to minimise muscle injuries caused by convulsions.

"I see you're going for bilateral ECT," he said. Bilateral ECT involved placing electrodes on both sides of the brain, with the current passing through both hemispheres.

"Always do," said Dr Ratnawarpal, unsure whether he was being challenged; and now eyeing his new colleague with something akin to suspicion. "All these proponents of unilateral ECT, and especially low dosage ECT, are just pussy-footing around. It's the worst of both worlds: the patient is upset anyway at being prescribed ECT, yet the dosage is too low to be of therapeutic value."

Cortez grinned but remained noncommittal, fully aware that even a minor disagreement with a Director of Clinical Services might be a career-limiting move.

Ratnawarpal went on: "These kids come to us with bleak pictures in their heads, a sinister puzzle that they cannot make sense of. ECT rattles that puzzle so hard that it falls apart; the bleak picture dissolves. It gives them a chance at a new beginning. A much underrated treatment. Anyhow, let's get this show on the road."

He turned on the Corticotron 1200, a silver-fronted machine that looked like a 1970s amplifier. The EEG machine next to it whirred and made furious red scribbles on graph paper.

"Okay," he said, "this should get us some response," as he pressed the button on the ECT machine, sending an electric current through Libby's brain. After a few seconds he released the button.

Libby's toes curled up. She was convulsing. She was having a seizure and the spidery red EEG graph charted new peaks. Then, gradually, the seizure ebbed away, like the memory of a tsunami. Her body came to rest.

"That should do for today," he said.

He pressed a button on the intercom. "Pamela, Miss Rogers is ready for the recovery room."

"It's been a pleasure working with you, Dr Cortez," he said, as he swanned out of the treatment room.

THE HEARING

"The first allegation," said Dr Ratnawarpal, "is that you have breached professional ethics by taking a client home. By doing so, you have also breached your duty of care to the client, as your actions placed her at risk. That this risk was material was subsequently borne out by events. The client felt violated and attempted suicide."

Caitlin stared at the wall behind the Rat. A black-and-white picture of the Queen hung to his right. To his left a sepia portrait of Dr Hobson, founder of the Mental Health Hygiene Board and Victoria's first Master-in-Lunacy, as the Chief Psychiatrist was called at the time.

The Rat continued. "The client's mother has since initiated legal proceedings against your employer, Outer Metro Health, and this panel will determine, among other things, whether your actions are covered by the terms of your employment agreement or whether they were so reckless in nature as to effectively constitute a revocation of said agreement."

Did they just want to throw her under a bus? Like it or not, Caitlin was still an employee. She was about to protest when Veronica Tyler looked at her and shook her head. Caitlin decided to hear the Rat out.

"Furthermore," he went on, "it is apparent from your own statement to police that you have shared client information pertaining to

Ms Rogers with your partner, Mr Wheelwright. This constitutes a breach of the confidentiality provisions of the *Mental Health Act.*"

Jeremy Ambrose nodded sagaciously. That old lecher, thought Caitlin, my conference stalker. Why did *he* have to be the independent member of the Board of Inquiry?

"Then there are a number of attitudinal issues," Ratnawarpal said. "You foster unrealistic expectations in your clinical practice, you foment patient resistance against proven therapeutic interventions, such as ECT, you challenge clinical leaders in open forums—"

"Hang on," Caitlin burst out, "this is so unfair—"

"See," said Dr Ratnawarpal, "I cannot even finish my introductory remarks!" He gave Jeremy Ambrose a wan smile.

"Exactly how is my clinical practice unrealistic?" Caitlin fired back, leaning forward. Her cheeks felt flushed.

"If I may interrupt for a moment," said Veronica.

The Rat looked at her with annoyance.

"I would like to remind the panel of the terms of reference for this inquiry," the legal expert said. "With the utmost respect, Dr Ratnawarpal, the attitudinal issues you just raised may well be pertinent to clinical practice within your team. However, they fall outside the scope of this hearing. They would need to be explored within a more appropriate context, such as, for example, Ms Murphy's performance review."

"Very well," the Rat grumbled, "we have enough here to... review the case."

To sack me, thought Caitlin, why don't you come out and say it.

They grilled her next on the details of Libby's treatment. Caitlin had to walk them through the referral from Banksia High and provide a rationale for some of the statements in her intake assessment of Libby and in the treatment plan.

"What does this mean?" asked the Rat, pointing at a treatment goal in Libby's Individual Service Plan, "*Strengthen client's self-esteem.* How do you do that? How could you measure such a thing?"

The Rat made much of the fact that Caitlin had listed *Atypical Anorexia Nervosa* as the primary diagnosis and *Depressive Episode* as the secondary diagnosis. In his view, those should have been reversed.

Veronica needed to intervene again to steer the discussion away from the contentious area of clinical decision-making.

"And why did you feel a need to step in, to take Ms Rogers under your wing, when you spotted her at the train station?" asked Jeremy Ambrose.

"Libby was talking to two young men. She seemed vulnerable. Her mother had not turned up to collect her when she was discharged from the inpatient unit. She had no money on her, did not know her new address and had no means of contacting anyone."

"Yet you knew none of that the moment you decided to accost her at the station," Jeremy pointed out. "You could have walked past, caught your train home, had an easy Friday night."

"Walk past? I cared about her, she was my client."

"Did you care more than other staff?" barked the Rat. "Were you wiser than the people who discharged her? You intervened when you no longer had a mandate to do so. It was, frankly, none of your business. And look where it got you!"

Caitlin's eyes felt prickly, but she steeled herself. I have to be strong, she thought, for myself, for this child growing inside me. I'll have to face worse things as a single mum. I can handle the Rat. She considered bringing up the error in the discharge process but decided against it. She wasn't going to clutch at straws, fight a desperate rearguard action. She'd rather go out with dignity.

"I did what I did," she said calmly, "and nothing can change that. I accept full responsibility for my actions. I acted to protect a young woman. It led to consequences that I regret, but which I could not have foreseen. At no time did I think that my actions would place Libby at risk. And I will have to live with those consequences, both personally and professionally. That's all I have to say."

"Very well," said Ratnawarpal, "you may go then. The panel shall review all the material pertaining to this case and compile its report. Your supervisor, Dr Kapoor, will inform you of the panel's findings and determination in due course. In the meantime, you will remain suspended and are instructed not to enter the premises and not to engage in any clinical or other activities related to your role at Outer Metro Health. Is that clear?"

It was, said Caitlin. She collected her notes and got up.

"She's a firebrand, that one," said Ratnawarpal after Caitlin had left the room. He turned to Jeremy Ambrose and shook his head. "Those do-gooders always get themselves into trouble. They don't understand how the system works."

"I last saw her a couple of months ago at a seminar," said Ambrose. "She fobbed me off, told me she was going to the Sorbonne!"

"Typical!" said Ratnawarpal. "Grandiose thinking!"

Veronica Tyler held the door open for her colleagues and looked at her shoes.

KURT'S BRILLIANT IDEA

Kurt left his desk and strode to the small meeting room. He needed to play his cards right for this call. He opened his notebook, had his pen ready and punched in the number.

A sleepy voice answered.

"Gecko, Kurt here, your social worker, don't hang up on me."

A pause. "How did you get this number?"

"I can explain but I need to see you."

"Nah, I don't want to do that shit anymore."

"I really need to see you, Gecko, and check that you're okay."

"I'm okay."

"I need to talk to you."

"So talk."

"In person."

"What, so you can put the cops onto me? No way."

"Gecko, it's nothing like that."

"You know the cops are after me, right?"

"Yeah, I know. But that's nothing to do with me. I'm concerned with your welfare."

"As I said, I'm fine."

"I do need to see you in person, Gecko. You're still in foster care and Bob's worried about you. And I have news about Libby."

"How do you know about Libby?"

"Did you know she's in hospital?"

"Why? What's wrong with her?"

Kurt felt bad about using Libby but he needed to find a way to re-engage with Gecko, to nudge him back to safety, to prevent him from slipping into a life of petty crime or worse. This was his last chance.

"I can't tell you over the phone."

"Bullshit. You just want to trick me into telling you where I live so you can come and stick your nose in again."

"Don't tell me where you live, then. We can meet in a public place. Just say where and I'll be there."

Kurt looked at the dense traffic rolling down Victoria Parade. The burger place at the corner of Smith Street, Gecko had said. Did it mean that Gecko was living in this area or had he picked a random suburb to cover his tracks? Kurt stirred his flat white and had a sip. Tepid. He looked with a vague sense of longing at the hipster cafe across the road. Wonder whether he will show up, he thought, or whether I am wasting my time.

Then he saw a young man walking along the other side of Victoria Parade. He had Gecko's height and walk but looked quite different. Kurt strained his eyes. The boy was well dressed, a dark charcoal shirt and black jeans. He stopped at the traffic lights but did not cross when the light turned green. Instead he looked up and down Victoria Parade and into Smith Street. When the lights changed for the second time he crossed and walked into Smith Street, past the eatery. Kurt saw Gecko's face clearly. He looked older, and better groomed. He's checking the area for cops, Kurt thought.

Finally he came in and sat down opposite Kurt. He still had his ear stud.

"So," he said, "tell me about Libby."

Then Kurt had a brilliant idea. "Why don't we pay her a visit?" he suggested. Maybe the boy would open up more in her presence.

They talked in the car on the way to the hospital. Kurt told Gecko Libby had been admitted for depression and later transferred to an eating disorders ward. He made no mention of the incident, or her suicide attempt. Gecko seemed reluctant to talk about Libby with him, so Kurt changed the subject. Had he considered going back to school? Gecko sneered. He'd been looking into career options, he said. Thinking about becoming an entrepreneur. Gecko deflected all Kurt's attempts to find out more. But how was he managing to get by, Kurt wanted to know. He had friends, Gecko said. Like Tags? No, Tags had moved to Sydney and no one had heard from him since.

"Tags is a loser," said Gecko, with a harshness that surprised Kurt.

He appeared more interested when Kurt mentioned that he had rung Shaun.

"That's great that he's on the mend." It sounded distracted rather than friendly. There was an aloofness to Gecko's responses that was more than just lack of cooperation. Kurt felt as if he was still shuffling old pieces around while Gecko had moved on to a different puzzle altogether.

Kurt decided not to mention Shiv yet, or the Mutineers, even though they might well be central to the new puzzle. He needed to establish rapport first.

Gecko rushed towards the hospital bed, then held back when he saw Libby's eyes were closed. She sat propped up against a bunch of pillows. A pale waif, Kurt thought. Beautiful, but unnaturally thin. Fragile as a butterfly. A plastic tube was inserted into her right nostril and taped to her cheek. The other end of the tube led to a bag hanging from a metal pole next to the bed.

She opened her eyes and stared at her visitors.

"Hi, Libby," said Gecko. He pulled up a chair and reached for her hand.

"I hadn't expected to see you," she whispered.

"Yeah," he said, "a lot's happened." He paused. "And look at you, all hooked up." She did not respond. Gecko looked at Kurt. "Shaun had a feeding tube, too, after the fires."

Kurt nodded and moved to the foot end of the bed. He looked at the charts that kept track of Libby's BMI, potassium and electrolytes. So weird, he thought, these eating disorders. Some street kids are fighting just to stay alive and this girl is prepared to throw it all away. He realised he was being unfair. This was a mental illness like any other, not a lifestyle choice. So easy for prejudice to creep into your thinking. All the same, he felt a sadness in the room. It settled over him like a cloak. He thought of that teacher's question, at the principal's party at the start of the year. How did he cope with such depressing work, day after day? Right now he was lost for an answer.

"I was thinking about the market the other day," said Gecko. "You never bought me that shirt."

Libby nodded in Kurt's direction. "Who's that man? Is he a psychiatrist?"

"Nah, he's just a social worker... Why are you here, Libby?"

She scoffed. "I was going to ask you that."

"Dunno... Thought maybe, we could still be friends, you know..."

Libby pursed her lips, looked down, adjusted her sheets. Kurt looked at his watch.

"Do you remember the river?" Gecko asked.

Libby's face clouded over.

Gecko seemed anxious, as if he thought he'd said something wrong. He glanced sideways at Kurt.

"You know, the Yarra," he prompted, "at the bridge in the city, after Monique's birthday party?"

"There's a lot I don't remember," said Libby. Sweat was pearling on her forehead. "I'm a bit tired... I need to rest I think."

"Okay." Gecko got off his chair. "Oh, I nearly forgot! Bought you something..." He fumbled with his backpack in the narrow space between the bed and the wall and produced the orchid from the hospital gift shop. He took it out of its plastic cylinder and scanned the bedside table. No vase, so he placed the flower in Libby's glass of water. It slid sideways along the rim of the glass and ended up with its heart facing Libby.

"I'd better go," he mumbled.

"Thanks," murmured Libby.

He was already striding down the corridor. Kurt had to run to catch up.

~

"Why is she like that?" Gecko said as soon as they were in the car.

Kurt started the engine. "She's had ECT," he said.

"What's that?"

"Shock treatment."

"Fuck! Why?"

"She's been severely depressed. Stopped eating altogether. They feared for her life."

"Shit."

Kurt swiped his credit card in the machine at the gate and the boom lifted.

"Did I do this to her?"

Heavens no, Kurt thought, this is taking a wrong turn. I didn't want to guilt trip him! That's not why I brought him here.

"No, no, not at all. She's had a lot of other stuff happening in her life too. You know, like having to move, and then the guy in Creswick Street…"

"What guy?"

Kurt weaved across two lanes, working towards the freeway entrance. The truck behind him blasted its horn and in the rear-view mirror Kurt saw the driver giving him the finger.

"Well, she ended up at this lecturer's place and the guy harassed her—"

"What, he raped her?"

"No, but he barged in on her in the bathroom. She was very upset. Enough to run away and try to commit suicide."

"What?" Kurt felt Gecko stare at him.

"She jumped in the Yarra."

"What the fuck!"

"Two guys jumped in and rescued her. She was pretty shaken, as you can imagine. Afterwards she went into a tailspin. Deep depression. And when she stopped eating, a psychiatrist decided she needed ECT."

"How do you know all this?"

"From a colleague, a psychologist. She was there when it all happened."

"What, she just stood there and took neat little notes, like you?"

Touché, thought Kurt.

"No," he said, "she was the guy's partner. She was in the house when it happened."

Gecko slammed his fist against the dashboard.

"This is so fucking wrong. What happened to the guy? Is he in jail?"

"The police are still investigating," said Kurt. He realised how lame that sounded.

"That'd be right," said Gecko, before withdrawing into a sullen gloom.

That night Kurt told Emma about his visit. She was furious.

"So you took Gecko for a guided tour of the eating disorders ward? What were you thinking? What do you think that would have been like for Libby?"

"I thought she would have liked seeing him," he said sheepishly.

"What on earth made you think that? They've broken up, she's all vulnerable, at her lowest ebb and in walks this stranger, this… clown, with her ex-boyfriend."

He'd never seen her this angry. Her words hurt, but the idiocy of what he'd done also dawned on him. Belatedly. How could he have been so stupid, so driven that he had been oblivious to Libby's needs?

"You've totally lost it," Emma continued, "you had no right to confront Libby like that, to use her like bait, to expose her."

"But I thought—"

"And what about her safety, or Caitlin's for that matter? You know Gecko's in with those bikies and you've seen first-hand what they can do. I don't know what it is with this boy—he's your white whale."

"Huh?"

"*Moby Dick*. Captain Ahab. How he scours the oceans for this elusive whale."

"Heard of it. Haven't read it."

"Maybe you should. It's a tale of obsession. It doesn't end well."

IRRECONCILABLE DIFFERENCES

In his dream Philip was the twelve-year-old boy at the athletics carnival again. A bright pure sun shone over the red track and he looked down at his new runners. When the shot rang out, he pushed off against the starting block and willed himself to the finish. His lungs pumped like bellows, his legs thumped like pistons. At first he could hear someone's breathing over his right shoulder, then that fell away. He had to come first, and he did. They gave him a blue ribbon, but the best part was his mother's golden smile when he joined her on the spectator benches, still drenched in sweat.

He woke with the sheet twisted around his ankles. One day I must change the sheets, he thought, it's getting fetid. The lair of an old boar. Caitlin was blending something in the kitchen. So she was up already. Her fruit and yoghurt smoothie, maybe. She had been sleeping in the spare room since what she called *the incident*. Oh, that infernal noise. Why did his head feel like a lump of concrete? The bottle on the bedside table. Single malt whisky. Japanese. Empty. That explained things. Up to a point. Philip decided to savour a few more minutes of respite in the master bedroom before fronting up for another morning of conflict and tension.

He had been so unbelievably stupid, coming on to that girl with

Caitlin in the house. He thought with his dick, Caitlin had said. It meant nothing, he had countered, and that was true, but it had just infuriated her. "It meant nothing?" she had repeated, her eyebrows raised to just below the ceiling. Never a good sign when they quote your words back to you. That was a woman's way of placing something on *Hansard*—the indelible record of your misdemeanours.

"You have traumatised Libby. You have jeopardised her recovery. You have wrecked my career—and you say it meant nothing?" she had said. That was a nice rhetorical flourish he had thought, even then— anaphora—but he had wisely refrained from pointing out the elegance of her speech. And, truth be told, he did feel a bit of a bastard. Caitlin was a good woman. She deserved better.

And fancy the whole episode coinciding with Caitlin finding out she was pregnant, and her about to tell him. So poignant from her perspective, doubly embarrassing from his.

But do you want to keep it, he had asked. That was a reasonable thing to ask, wasn't it, given the circumstances? But you should have heard her. She went right off the deep end. Wasn't going to terminate a life just to make things easy for him.

All right then, he had responded, we can keep it. That was pretty flexible on his behalf, he had thought. Doing the right thing. Stepping up to the plate, to use that dreadful cliché. But that was no good either. "I don't want the father of my child to be a primate who goes around flashing young girls," she had said. Turns out she wanted to have the kid, but not with him. He felt hurt at that, her wanting to part ways over something so trite. Okay, it had all become really heavy, with the girl jumping in the Yarra and all that, but that was caused by a pre-existing illness, wasn't it? She had just been discharged and yes, he had made the wrong call. But a normal girl would have shrugged it off. Might have felt flattered even, like some of his students. If Caitlin could see past Di, how could everything fall in a heap because of a bit of drunken bravado?

He pulled on a windcheater and slouched into the lounge room.

"Hi," he said, "good morning."

"Hi."

Here we go, he thought, the icy politeness. It was worse than a row, more insidious. You expended less energy, but it lasted longer. All day to be precise. A precarious existence. Like turning your back to a sniper. You knew you were in his sights and that any wrong move would be your last.

"Did you sleep well?"

"So-so."

Don't ask her about the pregnancy, he thought. Don't ask her about work.

"Any plans for today?" he tried.

"Yes. Looking at flats I can afford."

"You know you can stay here."

"I don't want to stay here."

"Until the baby's born?"

"I'm moving out, Philip. The sooner the better."

"But how will you afford a place? What if you…"

"Lose my job? Bit late to think about that, isn't it? I have some money in my account. Enough to see me through until this place sells."

"You want to sell the house?"

"Get real, Philip, what did you think? That I would just conveniently clear out and leave the house to you and your floozies?"

"But we've only been here for, what, ten months? We're going to lose on that, big time."

"Well, you should have thought of that earlier!"

It has come to this, thought Philip. Here we are, trotting out spiteful platitudes, the sort of snide remark you hear in any soapie. What had happened to the cautious exploration, the *pas de deux* poetry of their early days? Like that balmy night in Siena when they watched a theatre troupe on the Piazza del Campo? He knew the answer well enough. It was all in the script. He knew chapter one by heart. How to conquer a woman. He had browsed through chapter two but never made it to chapter three—how to make it last. He was like those writers who keep retelling the same story. A fetishist in the house of love.

"Yes, I should have," he said.

Caitlin looked up, confused. She had moved on.

NOVEMBER 2009

KOI

It had been the first hot day of spring, a brief foray into the mid-thirties. And now evening brought its own melancholy joy. A wistful dusk on the cusp between past and future, redolent with memory and budding with anticipation. There was a slight breeze and Emma felt caressed by the balmy, scented evening air as she stepped through the Formosa Gardens car park. She halted in front of the narrow concrete bridge leading to the restaurant entrance and looked at the Koi pond. She could still make out the colours of the fish in the fading light. One was all white, but most were brocaded white and red. One pair was white with black patches—an aquatic version of Frisian cows.

"Aren't they beautiful!" A voice behind her.

Emma turned around. "Oh Midnight, great to see you!"

They hugged.

~

Emma smoothed the paper serviette next to her plate. That's a Kurt mannerism, she thought—we are becoming more and more alike.

"I'll have the vegetarian spring roll for entrée," said Midnight, looking up at the waiter, "and then the mixed vegetables with Chinese mushrooms."

The waiter looked at Emma.

"Sesame prawn please, West Lake duck, and a pot of black tea."

"Where's Formosa?" asked Emma after the waiter had gone.

"It's the old name for Taiwan."

"So we're in a den of nationalistic expats, are we? Bypassed by the Cultural Revolution?" That's a Kurt thing to say, she thought. But Midnight wasn't in the mood for banter. She seemed preoccupied. Emma changed the subject: "So, what have you been up to?"

"Well," Midnight said emphatically, "guess what!"

"I don't know…"

"I'm getting married!"

Emma shrieked. Midnight joined in. The other diners looked at their table, so they toned it down. Emma grabbed Midnight's hands. "That's fantastic news! Oh, and look at this ring, how could I have missed that! It's beautiful! Show me!"

"And there's something I'd like to ask you: will you be my maid of honour?"

"Oh, Midnight, yes, of course! Thank you!"

She quizzed Midnight. When had Gordon proposed and how had he done it? Did he go down on his knee? And had her mum come round now? What date was the wedding and where would it be held?

"On that," said Midnight, "can I ask you a favour?" She explained she was interested in a wedding venue in Carlton. Looked fabulous online but would Emma mind checking it out with her?

Of course not, Emma said. She had a curriculum day later in the week and would probably finish early, could drive into the city after that. Then she continued with her questions: what had Gordon's parents said? Had she bought a dress yet?

The entrée was served and eaten. Emma was so absorbed by the wedding talk that she wouldn't have noticed if they had served her cardboard.

"And what about you guys?" asked Midnight.

The smile disappeared off Emma's face. "Us… Turbulent times. Kurt got bashed up by some bikies."

"What?"

Emma sighed, told Midnight the story. "You should've seen him, he was bandaged up like a mummy."

"Oh my god, what a story! How disturbing!"

"Yeah, he could've been killed. I was furious with him for taking such a risk. Who did he think he was? My armchair philosopher trying to be a hard man. And the work it entailed! The hospital, the bank, Medicare. We had to have his car seats cleaned, his credit cards blocked and replaced."

"How awful!"

"Yeah, and he hasn't quite been himself since... But what about you, did they ever catch the guy who broke into your old shop in Warrandyte?"

Midnight's face clouded over. "Got a call from the cops last week. They wanted to check on some details. I was surprised. Thought they'd have given up on the case long ago. Normally I try to block that entire episode. But, yeah, the guy's still on the loose."

"Scary thought."

"Yeah, nightmare stuff. I don't want to talk about it, I just get upset. I wish it would go away."

Emma made another feeble assault on her duck's ribcage with her chopsticks. "How do you eat duck?" she asked in frustration.

"With knife and fork."

"That's not authentic."

"But much easier." Midnight smiled. "How's your work going?"

"I told you I'm acting Head of English, didn't I?"

"That's right! How's that going?"

"Much happier in that role. Here's the thing: I felt like such an impostor when I moved into that careers and counselling role. Having to be so clear and decisive in my advice. And you know me, always hesitant, thinking through every step, looking at every option from every possible perspective before making a decision. And then, as soon as I have decided, I wonder: where did I find this resolve? Can I trust myself on this? And the whole process starts all over again."

"That's my gal."

"But literature isn't about black and white, it's about exploring uncertainty. Irony, ambivalence, paradox. That feels like more natural territory to me."

"That all sounds very learned but I'm pleased you're happy!"

"Yeah, and we have big news too: Kurt wants to have kids after all."

"Wow! But you're not pregnant yet, are you?"

"No." Emma blushed. "I guess it's too early to announce—"

"What? That there's an ulterior motive to you guys doing it?"

Emma looked at her plate.

"Sorry," said Midnight, "I didn't mean to trivialise this. It is big news and I'm happy you're sharing it with me. What made him change his mind?"

"I think his run-in with those bikies gave him a more acute sense of his own mortality. He's been waffling about the transience of things for years, with his Buddhist thing; but this drove it home in a tangible way. And his work, all the misery he sees, used to leave him wondering about the wisdom of bringing another child into this world. But now his views have mellowed. Having a child together is one of the best things a couple can do, he said the other day; and he trusts that between the two of us, we'd be able to do a decent job raising a kid."

"And you, of course, have been ready for this for years."

Emma nodded. "I'd almost resigned myself to not having kids. The biological clock, you know… I felt I didn't have a lot of time left…"

"Oh Emma, that's wonderful! I'm so happy for you. I always thought you'd make a super mum!"

"Thanks," said Emma. "I don't know about being a super mum, but being a mum, that's something I've always wanted."

"No doubts there?"

"Not a shred."

BROODING

If he had stayed with her this thing wouldn't have happened. Gecko thought of Libby, so frail, so kind, and imagined this stranger taking advantage of her. Harassing her, Kurt had said, but what did he know? Who knows what really happened? Maybe Libby was holding back. What if the dude had raped her?

Gecko's anger kept rising. He felt pent up in his flat. Lie low when you're in Melbourne, Shiv had said. But sometimes a man had to stand up. He would not get Libby back, that much was clear. He had seen it in her eyes. There was a distance now, he only had himself to blame. But he still cared about her. She had cared about him.

Gecko fired up *Savage Glory* on his new computer and logged into the Delta of Doom battleground. He sent his avatar up into one of the dune lookout platforms and manned the gun turret. He fired furiously at the shoreline, trying to keep the enemy landing party at bay before they could demolish the bonus bunkers. It was no good. The noobs on his team had all rushed to defend the wrong bunker and one idiot seemed bolted onto the beach, immobile. I mean, why bother if you're not even going to try. He typed an angry comment in the team chat box about newbies camping. *Cool it, dude*, came the reply, *it's only a game*. He logged off and cracked open another rum and coke.

Only a game. As if the real world was any better. The real world, where going to school got you into trouble and running drugs made you rich. Where guys pawed you because they could get away with it. Unless someone stopped them.

Gecko lay down on his bed and dozed off. Maybe it was the harsh light slanting through the venetian blinds. Maybe it was the over-heated room. Memories seeped into his dream of the room under the house in Morwell, with its grey concrete bricks. It was the shape of an egg carton and not much larger. Its aluminium framed window looked out over the smoke stacks of Hazelwood power station. They towered over Morwell, belching fumes. The brown coal the remnant of life that had been crushed, trampled into the earth. Now, millions of years later, it could still burn, with a dark angry fire. It was what you saw every day; it was the hills in the distance that looked out of place. City folk thought the giant chimneys ugly, terrifying even. But that was not where true terror lurked. True terror welled up in those nights after a heavy dinner. It began with the sound of the television dying upstairs, the silent dread, the click of the bedroom door opening. Uncle Milosh with his shifty eyes and sleazy grin. "I've brought a present for you, Srecko," he would say. Or later just: "This won't take long, Srecko."

Gecko woke up with a start. His heart was pounding and his lips were dry. This will haunt me forever, he thought. I can run to Thailand and eat spicy curry from a street stall but some Aussie sauntering through the Pattaya night market will have a paunch like uncle Milosh or the sour smell of stale sweat and I'm back in that room. Always pressing on my heart, those memories, a slimy toad that won't budge. And now they've started on Libby. This has to stop. He got up and had another shower.

He opened his browser. The guy was a lecturer, Kurt had said, and lived in Creswick Street, which was right near the university. Chances were that's where he worked. He looked up the university website. *What does the future hold for you?* the homepage asked. Don't care, Gecko thought. *Find out more about us*, a hyperlink said, Gecko followed that link. There were pages about notable staff and Gecko looked at each profile with suspicion. Was one of these confident, smiling faces the mug of a molester? How would he ever know? Other pages helped you search for a supervisor or a subject expert. He didn't know this site was so huge. What had he expected, a simple alphabetical list of staff, with known creeps marked with a red asterisk for his convenience? He didn't even know what faculty this guy was in, just that he lived in Creswick Street. Who would know more? Who could help him? He smiled. That's it! Worth a try. He'd pulled off more daring stunts getting through customs…

"Carlton Police," said the voice on the other end, "how may I help you?"

"Yes, good afternoon," said Gecko, "I'm ringing about the Rogers case, in Creswick Street… I'm the partner of the psychologist and I'd like to speak to the detective in charge."

"Certainly, one moment please."

Gecko listened intently.

"Brendan, I have Philip Wheelwright on the line for you… Okay…"

"Brendan Conroy," a male voice said.

Gecko hung up. That was too easy. Didn't think that would work.

He went back to the website and searched for Philip Wheelwright. Three entries came up. The first one brought up a list of staff members of the English department. There he was. *Lecturer, Modern English Literature and Literary Theory.* Some weird letters for his degrees. Nothing else. The second hit led to course descriptions for 2010 honours courses, whatever that meant. The third entry linked to a newsletter announcing a special lecture the bastard was going to give. He looked at the date. More than six months ago, but the article also had a photo of the guy. He looked thirty-something, with designer stubble and an arrogant mug. Gecko whipped out his phone and took a photo.

From there on it was easy as. He looked up *Wheelwright, P* in the telephone directory and found the house number in Creswick Street. I might just go for a stroll through Carlton, Gecko thought.

THE BEAST

The curriculum day had given Emma a much-needed breather. No students, and the team meetings had concluded earlier than she had dared to hope. And when all the teachers started packing up to make the most of what remained of the afternoon, the principal had pulled Emma aside. Raeleen Osmond wouldn't be coming back, Roslyn had said, because of health reasons. In other words: the job was hers if she wanted it. Emma had driven home in high spirits. She wanted to ring Kurt but remembered that he was chairing a case conference with that family where there had been domestic violence a couple of months ago. A big day for him.

Emma felt happy, in tune with the universe. She wanted to share her good luck, pay it forward. Her thoughts turned to Caitlin, who had been so helpful and whose job was now on the line. Kurt had told her about the extraordinary sequence of events. Poor Libby, after all she'd gone through already. Emma resolved to visit her over the weekend if she was still in hospital. But today she could maybe do something to help Caitlin. The outcome of the hearing still hung in the balance, Kurt had said—so a glowing testimonial from a school counsellor might do some good.

Emma had drafted four paragraphs when she realised that she

didn't have Caitlin's contact details. She had her work number and email address on her school computer, but they wouldn't be of any use now that Caitlin was suspended. She went to Kurt's desk. So convenient he's a neat freak, she thought. A yellow sticky note was precisely aligned with the edge of the desk. *Caitlin Murphy*, the spidery scribbles said, with a mobile number and an address in Creswick Street underneath. Emma keyed in the first three digits on her mobile. Then she changed her mind. She would have to explain to Caitlin. Endless complications arose at this thought. What if Caitlin declined her offer of assistance out of politeness? What if Caitlin thought she was interfering? What if she was in the middle of an argument with that lecherous partner of hers? And above all, what if Caitlin had found out that Kurt had visited Libby, with Gecko in tow? Emma knew she'd feel mortified on his behalf. How could she possibly justify his behaviour? Here I am again, Emma thought, weaving a web of hesitation and indecision. It would be simpler to drive to Carlton—I'm meeting up with Midnight there anyway. I might as well park in Creswick Street, drop off my testimonial in Caitlin's letterbox and walk to the wedding venue from there.

~

"Are you sure?" Gecko asked as they walked up to the abandoned warehouse.

Shiv gave him the death stare. His eyes looked red.

"I mean," mumbled Gecko, "it's a big deal. I mean, I feel grateful and all that..."

"You talk too much. Do the right thing by me, I help you out. That's how it goes."

"Thanks," Gecko said, but he felt an impending sense of doom. He hated it when Shiv was on ice. It made him erratic, unpredictable. Best to go along with him though. The only option really... Gecko was almost looking forward to next week's flight. He'd be clean on the way there, so getting through customs would be a breeze. And he knew his way around Pattaya now and would be able to relax more.

Shiv unlocked a padlock and pulled open the massive sliding door.

Philip looked out of the window. Normally working from home helped his writing, but today his paper wasn't coming together. That article in the *New York Review of Books* had taken the wind out of his sails. He would need to find a different angle now or be accused of plagiarism. But all he could think of was Caitlin moving out tomorrow. It wasn't thinking so much as an undifferentiated bluntness in his head. Very literary actually, this ruefulness, though quite unpleasant in this instance. That funny black bird was back, foraging for grubs on the median strip. Philip sighed and looked back at the blinking blue cursor on his screen.

Gecko laughed incredulously when Shiv pointed at the colossal four-wheel-drive.

"The Beast? Me?"

Shiv did not respond.

"I've only ever driven off-road, in the bush. This is such a monster."

"Driving is driving." Shiv threw him the keys and got in on the passenger's side. He placed the sawn-off shotgun between his legs.

Emma came off the freeway at Alexandra Parade and slowed to a crawl in peak hour traffic. At least she wasn't in a hurry. Nice too that the days were lengthening. Spring was her favourite season. Not so long now until the end of the school year. She needed to pin Kurt down for a serious chat about the holidays. He had mentioned the Grampians, but who wants to go clambering over rocks with temperatures in the mid-thirties or hotter? She had suggested flying to Belgium to visit Irene while they still could. Kurt was not so keen on that idea, having flown over twice this year already. He'd also used up his leave, so he would need to take leave without pay…

"This is it," said Gecko, turning into Creswick Street, "the double storey house there, on the left, the one with the big bush in the front yard."

"Got it. Take her round again." Shiv lay the shotgun across his knees.

Gecko swallowed. "You sure about this? What if we get caught? How many of these cars are there in Melbourne?" He shook his head. "It's like a military vehicle. We stand out like dogs' balls."

"Just drive. It's a warning shot. Teach the guy a lesson."

"But a shooting in the middle of Carlton? Someone will ring the cops."

"Will you shut the fuck up!" Shiv yelled. "You're a pain in the arse with all your yapping!"

Gecko made two right turns and steered the Beast down Rathdowne Street, heading back towards the top end of Creswick Street.

Emma locked her car. The last sunlight cast a glow over the police headquarters in the distance. The yellow brick Bauhaus building was dwarfed by the high-rises behind it. The red and white transmission mast on the roof of the complex, like a giant vuvuzela left behind by a prankster, made it look particularly silly. She crossed the road to the median strip and looked at the terrace houses across the street. Fantastic properties. And there it was, Caitlin's house. She waited for a lone cyclist to pass and headed for the letterbox, an ornate brass slot in the imposing wooden front door.

Shiv lowered the passenger window. He slid the shotgun over his left arm and aimed at the door.

"Wait," called Gecko, but a shot rang out. It sounded deafening and Gecko swerved. He clipped the median strip, then oversteered towards the left. The Beast swiped a small Mazda parked alongside the kerb.

"What the fuck!" said Shiv. He threw the gun on the floor of the cabin.

"You fuckwit! You shot someone!" yelled Gecko.

"That'll teach him!"

"It was a woman!"

"Just fuckin' drive!"

Gecko panicked and accelerated. Let's get out of here, he thought, and then I quit. That's the end of Shiv. I don't care what he does. The man's a maniac. Gecko took the roundabout at full speed. He never noticed the truck coming from the right. The impact propelled the four-wheel-drive over a traffic island and into the side street, where it crashed into a lamppost.

Gecko had never been aware of his rib cage before. Now it felt crushed. He felt like a rag doll discarded in a pile of metal sheets. He forced open his eyes. Smoke was coming from under the bonnet but his mind felt curiously at ease. There was evening sky where his door had been. Shiv, he thought, where is Shiv? He looked at the signpost of the little business on the corner. *Pain Management Clinic*, it said. What are the chances, Gecko wondered—and blacked out.

That was nearby, Philip thought when he heard the gunshot. He ran and opened the front door. A woman stood on the doormat, holding an envelope in her raised left hand. Her white blouse was all red, a violent bloom spreading from her chest. Her eyes did not seem to notice him. After seconds that seemed like an eternity he was about to address her when the woman opened her mouth. A thick gush of dark blood spurted out, and he recoiled in horror. Then she fell forward, right into the hallway. Her letter shot across the tiles.

DUST TO DUST

Kurt had spent the past days on autopilot, suffocating under multiple layers of disbelief: Emma, his soulmate, was gone. Murdered—something that only happened to strangers. Shot by the boy he'd vowed to protect. Killed because of his own carelessness. He had tried to keep at bay, at least until after the service, the fathomless grief and guilt that were in store for him. Had sought refuge in a myriad of tasks. It hadn't worked, of course, and the nights had been hell. Midnight had come over every day, making arrangements for Emma's service, notifying her colleagues, forcing him to eat a little. When she offered to say a few words on the day, he had accepted immediately. It had been hard enough to deliver a eulogy at his dad's funeral—he knew he'd break down if he tried to speak at Emma's.

And finally, the dreaded day had come. A small, non-denominational chapel. A brief service conducted by a civil celebrant. Bunches of red roses from the Latvian community. Emma would have approved, Kurt thought.

Roslyn, the Banksia High principal, spoke first. "Conscientious," she called Emma. "Dedicated, loved by students and staff alike." It was all well meant but ultimately nothing more than platitudes cobbled together by an outsider. Clichés that ricocheted off the essence of who Emma was.

'Was'—it ached every time anyone used the past tense to refer to Emma. Yet this was the last moment she was present in any physical sense. That was her, over there, in that pine coffin. So what comes first, he thought? Tomorrow or death? This was no longer a *koan*, an intriguing philosophical conundrum. Emma hadn't seen it coming. A trip to the city to check out a wedding venue with Midnight. And then… Don't go there, not now. Keep it together, for her sake.

Midnight came to the end of her eulogy: "And despite those many talents you were low-key, humble, not one to blow your own trumpet. You often doubted yourself, but we never doubted you. In you we had a friend who was loyal and reliable. A good listener and a kind heart. A loving partner to Kurt. And it rips me up that we're telling you this only now." Her voice broke and when Kurt looked up, he saw tears running down her face. "We love you, Em, and you'll live on in our hearts forever…"

The music swelled to a crescendo and a hidden mechanism made the coffin glide towards the wall. The inevitability now, of the mechanics of death. Kurt knew what was coming, but it still gave him a sickening jolt. He wanted to run out there, jump on that little platform, conjure Emma back to life. But her coffin disappeared behind the black curtain undisturbed, on its final journey to the business end of the crematorium. The pain and grief contracted behind his eyes into a bitter knot. He bent forward on the rickety plastic chair, felt like screaming out in anguish.

Kurt had agreed to lay on a meal after the service. The venue, a social club for Italian migrants, was way too large for the modest gathering but the staff had done their best to create a sense of intimacy by partitioning off a corner of the hall that looked out over a manicured garden with a water feature.

"This is a nice place," Midnight said, "you should check out those photos on the back wall. They're all about the Snowy Project."

"Huh?" said Kurt, who had just seen Fran Esposito walk in with Petra, Debbie and Joe.

"The Snowy Mountains, you know, in the fifties, the hydro-electricity scheme. Lots of migrants came out to work on that. Italians, Greeks, some Dutchies. Latvians, of course."

"I see. How's Gordon?"

Midnight gave him a strange look. "He couldn't make it, Kurt. Said to give you his love. He'll say a prayer for you."

We already had this conversation in the chapel, Kurt realised, my brain is just shutting down.

Fran walked up to him. "I'm sorry about your loss," she said, "I know what you're going through."

He realised she meant it; she had lost her sister on Black Saturday.

"Thanks Fran," he said, and felt tears well up.

He wandered off into the garden and looked at the water feature. A concrete cherub aimed his arrow at a heart held aloft in Neptune's left hand. In his right hand, the king of the sea held his trident. A carp came up for air on each side of his massive thighs, as if to escape a foul underwater fart. What did it signify, this jumbled symbolism, other than that its maker had been adept at handling concrete while devoid of any artistic sensibility?

He turned around when he heard the glass doors slide open. Caitlin Murphy. He had noticed her in the chapel. And just now he'd also spotted Libby on the other side of the glass panels, talking to two Banksia High girls. He was surprised to see her. She must have found out via the school or Facebook. Emma would have been pleased to hear Libby was out of hospital. But this was the new, post-Emma world, in which he was alone with his thoughts.

"Kurt, what can I say?" Caitlin began.

He just grimaced.

"I hope you don't mind me being here."

"No, that's alright."

"I'm so sorry for your loss. And I feel I set off this whole chain of events. By taking Libby home. By giving you Gecko's number."

"Yeah, and I took Gecko to visit Libby and then blabbed to him about your partner."

Caitlin raised her eyebrows.

"I didn't know that," she said.

"Gecko thought he was to blame for Libby's depression and ECT. For her suicide attempt, maybe. So, to reassure him…"

"You told him about Philip."

"Yes. Emma gave me a hard time about it. How unprofessional I'd been. How I'd placed Libby at risk, as well as you."

And she'd always respected my work, he thought with deep regret. Until, to his enduring shame, he had blundered so spectacularly. With no way to make up for it. It was a tired cliché, but the best of intentions had propelled him on this road to hell. It was devastating.

"In the end it was Emma who paid for my mistakes," he went on. He felt his chin tremble. "If I'd kept my mouth shut, she'd still be alive."

"I'm so sorry, Kurt… That things turned out the way they did. You couldn't have known."

They stared at Neptune's mossy beard.

"The police tell me Emma wanted to hand-deliver you a letter," said Kurt. "Were you expecting her at all?"

"I had no idea. It was to have been a reference for me, the police said, a testimonial. Emma must have thought it would have helped my review."

"And did it?"

"I haven't seen the letter, Kurt. The police are keeping it as evidence. The panel have completed their investigation, so…"

She doesn't want to spell it out, Kurt thought, that it was all to no avail.

"I'll find out tomorrow whether I have a job."

"Good luck."

"Thanks. And, Kurt…"

"Yes?"

"When all of this… settles down, could we have a coffee or something? There are so many loose ends I'd like to discuss with you, about Libby, about Gecko… I mean, only if you want to… When you're ready…"

"Sure, why not."

"I'm sorry, I shouldn't have brought this up—this is hardly the occasion…" Caitlin looked flustered.

Kurt shrugged. "Never mind…"

"Thanks, Kurt. Take care."

Dazed, he watched her walk back to the hall and out the front door. So Emma's last act had been one of altruism, reaching out to a colleague in need.

It started raining and he went inside. Some people had left already. Libby was talking to a young man now, on the other side of the room. He was bald and his head was raked with thick white scars. A large patch of terracotta-coloured skin enclosed his neck like a brace. It looked like a burn mark. Shaun? How could he be here? And why was he talking to Libby? How did he know her? Kurt felt confused, as if he'd missed an episode of his own life. He was about to walk over when the Banksia High librarian collared him. Kurt listened to her words of appreciation for Emma, her interminable words of comfort for him, and his eyes glazed over. He felt exhausted. He mumbled something apologetic at the librarian, extracted his hand from her clasp and turned around. Libby and Shaun had gone. He accepted a lift home from Joe and collapsed on the couch.

When he woke it was already dark. He changed out of his suit and poured himself a glass of wine. A dramatic swirl of burgundy liquid contained by the curve of the glass. A tiny bubble of oxygen rose to the surface and popped. It reminded him of a well-known image from the Buddhist teachings. At birth we are like a single drop of water separating from the river we come from, going over the cliff, tumbling down the waterfall. And all along, as we tumble down the fall, we start believing in this new, separated state. This is who we truly are. No other drop is like me. We construct life stories and fiercely guard our identity. We may join up with other drops and separate again. We believe this ride will go on forever. But before we know it, we land in the pond at the foot of the fall, indistinguishable from the matter around us, once again part of the universal flow.

Kurt looked at his wine glass again. Emma deserves better than cheap plonk, he thought. He poured the wine down the sink and went looking for his meditation cushion.

He lit the candle in the miniature stone temple in the garden and sat down in front of it. Emma, he thought, Emma. No monkey mind tonight, there was just a single thought that filled his mind. My dearest Emma, my friend, my lover. You were my wife, warm, vibrant, funny. Now you are just a thought, a memory, a name, an urnful of ash. Tears streamed down his face, but he kept sitting. A chopper went over nearby and he could hear the neighbours' television. His fingers went cold, his toes went stiff, but he kept sitting. The night grew darker around him. Silence fell over the suburban gardens. An owl hooted. A possum jumped on the corrugated iron roof of the neighbour's carport. The moon kept its steady course overhead and Kurt just sat. He sat with the pain. He wanted to feel it in every nerve of his being. Memories reeled through his head. The night he first noticed Emma. Her shiny eyes, the silvery bubbles of her laughter. Unable to decide whether she was clumsy or graceful. The afternoon they first had sex. He remembered the scent of the coarse linen in her flat. But alongside the pain there was also a sweetness to those memories. They were more merciful than the dull ache of futures foregone, the loss of a child that would never be conceived. A soft drizzle was coming down now but Kurt did not move. He could smell the rain on his shoulder, little scented pearls on the wool of his jumper. A small dark shape emerged from underneath the grevillea shrubs. Tinkerbell, the Bennetts' cat. She stole around Kurt's back, then rubbed up against his thigh. Kurt stroked her wet fur. He could feel hairs stick to his palm. He folded his hands into a furry *mudra* and thought of the *Heart Sutra*. Understand emptiness, it said, and the mind will be without hindrance. No hindrance and therefore no fear. No knowledge and nothing to attain. Well, Kurt thought, he understood fucking emptiness now, he could see it around him in four dimensions, it held Emma in its icy grip, it embraced him more firmly than her red mittens had ever done, it slashed through his chilled bones like the reaper's scythe. He knew there was no healing, no solution, no resolution. There were only two options: to end it all here, or to go on.

DECISIVE ACTION

"Come in," said Suresh, "how have you been?"

"Things have been better," said Caitlin. She shut the door of his office behind her. Another wave of nausea lurched through her stomach. This is Suresh, she kept reminding herself, we're friends.

"I can imagine. I read about the shooting. How are things with your partner?"

"We split up."

"Oh. I see… I'm sorry to hear that. Yet more stress and upheaval for you, Caitlin. How are you coping with it all?"

She just raised her eyebrows.

"I gathered from the paper that you were not there at the time of the shooting?"

"No, I wasn't. I'd popped over to my new flat, to take a few measurements in the kitchen…" Now why did she tell him that? Totally irrelevant. She felt knocked off-centre by the horrific chain of events, struggling to regain a foothold in her own life, to function at her normal level.

Suresh gave her a strange look. "But you knew the victim?"

"Yes. A school counsellor I used to work with. She referred Libby to us." It sounded clinical. She thought of that soft voice on the other side of the phone, advocating, gently but irresistibly, for Libby to be seen soon.

"Why would anyone shoot a school counsellor? Shocking."

"The police say she wasn't the target."

"Oh?"

"They were after Philip. Because of what he did to Libby."

Suresh looked startled. "What are you saying, that Libby Rogers had a hand in this?"

"No, but her ex-boyfriend did. He drove the car."

"Who fired the shot then?"

"A bikie, apparently."

"And the getaway car crashed, I read in the paper?"

"It did. Libby's ex-boyfriend's in hospital, under police guard I heard. A witness saw the bikie limp away. She ran over to help but he swore at her. He hasn't been seen since... Maybe I shouldn't be saying any of this, Suresh. The police might want me to testify when the case goes to court."

"Of course. I'm sorry, I shouldn't have probed. I wanted to understand what happened. I will treat everything you told me as confidential."

"Thanks, Suresh."

"Maybe it is better then to move on to the matter at hand—the panel's report." He glanced at a slim report with a laminated cover on his desk.

"I'm finding this very difficult," he said.

She started trembling. She hadn't expected this. A severe reprimand, yes, but she thought they'd give her a second chance...

"As you know," Suresh began, "I've always held your commitment and your professionalism in high esteem and that hasn't changed. So it is with some... discomfort that I will convey to you the findings of the review panel and their ultimate determination."

"I'm out, aren't I?"

Suresh nodded.

Caitlin looked at her lap, fought back the tears. Okay, she thought, unemployed, as well as single and pregnant.

"I can walk you through the panel's reasoning. They have dropped the charges relating to privacy but upheld the ones alleging a breach of professional ethics and duty of care." He pushed the report away from him. "I want you to know I stood up for you. I told Dr Ratnawarpal about your skills and dedication but found him, shall we say, unresponsive. The legal representative also advocated on your behalf and highlighted the errors made in our discharge process. Dr Ratnawarpal's focus, however, remained firmly on what he called the assault on Libby Rogers and on her subsequent suicide attempt. I think he wants to be seen as taking decisive action in response to those critical incidents. Personally, I think that's not fair on you, but—"

"He wants a scapegoat..."

Suresh shrugged with the detachment of one who had learned to accept an imperfect world.

"I know this is a lot to take in," he said after a while, "and it's none of my business, but as a friend I was just wondering. What will you do now, Caitlin, and is there any way I can help?"

"What can I do? When it comes to scandals like these Melbourne is like a village. Everyone in the sector will know. That makes me damaged goods. My career is over, Suresh."

"Dr Ratnawarpal has signalled his intent to retire in two to three years. I could always help bring you back into Outer Metro Health at that time... In the interim I could refer to you some clients from my private practice..."

"Thanks for your support, Suresh, but I need to make a clean break. I think I'll just focus on my pregnancy—"

"You're pregnant?"

"I am."

"Oh, Caitlin! We are terminating your contract just as you need more support!"

"I'll be right, Suresh. It happens all the time. Pregnant, single and unemployed. It doesn't stop us from turfing consumers out of inpatient units or residential care, does it? Why should things be different for me? At least I have a share in a house, I have a degree, I have experience." She snorted. "Slightly tainted experience, but anyway, I don't want to be a wimp."

"You're brave, Caitlin, and I wish you all the best. Let me know if I can help in any way."

"Thanks, Suresh. It's been great working with you."

"I'll let you pack your belongings then."

Caitlin got up and frowned as she backed out of the door. She walked to the photocopy room, picked up an empty cardboard box.

Rosa, the Rat's executive assistant, looked up from her photocopying. "Oh, you're back," she said cheerily as she took a letter off the glass plate.

You bitch, you know damn well I'm not back, thought Caitlin. "Just popping in," she said airily. "Gee, you look well. Have you put on weight?"

Rosa's face clouded over. She grabbed her copies out of the side tray and stomped off.

I may be beaten, thought Caitlin, but I don't have to play nice anymore. She walked into her office and surveyed her lost empire. What was the point of collecting any of this stuff? She grabbed the notebook with her meeting notes. Just in case she needed to check something for the trial. They could fight over her gel pens and enjoy the December picture on her *France 2009* calendar, a dappled market scene in Saint-Rémy de Provence. Philip had given her the calendar, but she suspected it was a cast-off from Di. She binned the photo frame on her desk and looked for a moment at Philip staring back at her from the bottom of her wastepaper basket.

The front doors slid open and Caitlin stepped out into the spring sunshine. She put her crocheted purple hat on, for comfort rather than warmth. The maintenance guy was mowing the nature strip and a whiff of petrol mingled with the midmorning breeze. And that battered silver Honda, that was Mrs Eckhart driving off with Robbie. Wonder whom they had seen in her absence. That was all over now, she thought, the intake meetings, the case planning, the team reviews. A world of poverty and nappies beckoned. But she would find a way. She knew.

And there, would you believe it, was the Rat pulling into the director's spot in his black Statesman. He got out of his car before he noticed her standing there, right in front of the entrance. She gave him a sour smile. He looked away from her, opened his briefcase and started burrowing for a crucial yet strangely irretrievable document. What a glorious morning, Caitlin thought, as she stood there like a giant milk thistle. I have all the time in the world.

SURVIVORS

The doorbell rang and on the first floor the small monitor flickered to life. The image was grey and streaked but Libby recognised Shaun.

"Hi," she said, "press hard. The door's jammed." She heard a click and then footsteps coming up the concrete steps.

"Sorry," she said as she let Shaun in, "that wasn't much of a welcome. Good to see you again."

He took in the interior. "Nice place."

"I hate it. How come you're in Carlton?"

"I've been to see me counsellor."

"You're seeing a counsellor?" Shaun had seemed so matter-of-fact when she met him at Ms Rubenis' funeral. She couldn't quite picture him talking about feelings or emotions. They sat down on the leather couches.

"Yep. It's part of the treatment. First, they do all the medical stuff, the operations and skin transplants. Then they start planning your psychological recovery, as they call it." He laughed and the thick white seam running from the corner of his mouth looked slightly sinister. "Sorry for the big words! They reckon a lot of guys get depressed after they leave rehab and try to pick up where they left off. You know, people look at you funny, or you can't do your job anymore. A lot of folks get nightmares."

"Will you be able to go back to work?"

"Think so. Me boss has been great. He says he'll let me ease back into work in the new year. Me right hand's come good, but the left is still weak and a bit stiff. No strength there. Still, can't complain."

"And you haven't had nightmares?"

"Not so far. Fingers crossed. I'm a laid-back sort of bloke, anyway."

"That's lucky." She often woke up drenched in sweat, fighting off river demons cloaked in algae who were trying to pull her down a slimy hole. Part of her felt like telling Shaun. Where did that urge come from? She barely knew him. She also knew she could not tell him, out of sheer shame. He had fought to cling to life in a bushfire; she had sought to douse hers.

"I saw Gecko," said Shaun.

Libby's face clouded over.

"Did he ask you to come here?"

"No. I just thought you might be interested to know how he is."

"I'm not. He's a murderer."

"He's an idiot, but he's not a murderer."

"He killed my teacher." She was surprised to hear herself sound so shrill.

"Hang on, hold your horses. Gecko cares about you, as a friend. He knows he's lost you, he gets that. The kid's not trying to win you back. He wants to know you're okay. That's why he asked me to look for you at that funeral."

He paused, looked down, seemed to think of what to say next. He looked her straight in the eyes again.

"And today I'm not here as his messenger or something. I'm here for meself. It didn't sit right that I couldn't explain about Gecko the other day, not properly, with the funeral and all... I still care about him even though he's been an arsehole, pardon me French. Also, you were so upset, when I gave you that lift home, and fair enough, I know you've had a hard time of it. I just wanted to check you were all right."

His words calmed her down a notch.

"Anyway, they've patched him up and he'll be discharged from hospital soon. They'll take him to the MAP."

"What's the MAP?"

"Melbourne Assessment Prison. Fancy name for what used to be the remand centre. You know, far end of Spencer Street?"

"No idea."

"They've thrown the book at him: accessory to murder, drug trafficking, possession of marijuana. What else? Oh yes: culpable driving, driving without a licence, cruelty to animals—"

"Cruelty to animals?"

"That's the one he'll contest. He reckons Shiv did that behind his back."

"Not Shiv again. That name keeps coming up."

"Shiv shot your teacher. Gecko said he just wanted to scare that uni bloke who... you know... He needed help and stupidly asked Shiv. Whole thing spun out of control from there. Can't make a pact with the devil and expect to call the shots. Shiv was on meth, Gecko says, went full psycho."

Libby covered her mouth. It was too much. That night in Creswick Street, the river... Her inpatient admissions, the ECT... The shock of reading her teacher had been murdered. The photo in the paper showing the house in Creswick Street that already had so many bad memories. Not some random crime then. The description of the young driver matching Gecko down to the silver stud. The realisation that Gecko's botched revenge was somehow inspired by her, that she, Libby, had indirectly contributed to her teacher's death. And here was Shaun, saying it out loud. It was out in the open then, everybody would know. She remembered the strange looks people had given her at the funeral, and she hadn't realised. It was too much. She was reeling.

"Are you okay? You look pale."

"So this Shiv," she forced herself to say, "has he been caught?"

"Nope. He crawled out of the wreck and vanished into thin air. Hard to do with a head like that." He grinned. "Take me word for it."

"You don't look so bad," she heard herself say. Her thoughts were still racing. She had no idea why her teacher would have gone to the house in Creswick Street. Poor Ms Rubenis. She felt relief that at least Gecko wasn't the one who'd shot her. But really, how did that help?

"I wasn't fishing for compliments. I'm not gonna win any beauty contests. Unless the jury's blind!" He laughed hard at his own joke. Libby noticed that white seam again. It made him look harder, as if he was sneering.

"I don't care about appearances. It's personality that counts." That was a gross simplification, she realised, something to keep the conversation going. As if this year hadn't happened…

"I'm with you there."

"How long do you think Gecko will get?"

"Hard to say. He won't be able to wriggle out of the murder accessory charge. Premeditated too. He'd tracked that bastard down online and checked out the neighbourhood… The drug running won't help. All he's got going for him is that he's so young. Also his clean record until a couple of months ago. They'll probably toss him into Turana. That's a juvenile detention centre, in Parkville. Then, when he turns eighteen, they'll transfer him to an adult prison."

"How come you know all these things?"

"I've had two mates go through Turana. Good guys who made some bad choices. They're fine now."

"I don't know anyone who's gone to prison." This makes me sound so uppity, she thought.

"You do now."

"I suppose…" conceded Libby.

"And how are you going?"

"Better, thanks. The anti-depressants are helping. I've had no side effects so far."

"You're lucky there."

"I know. I'm also seeing another counsellor…" Her voice trailed off.

"Sounds like you're doing okay." He seemed genuinely happy for her.

She was getting used to his weird smile. She felt grateful that he hadn't asked about her weight or her eating.

"Can I ask you something?" he said.

"Sure…" she said warily.

"Could I have a cuppa? I'm parched."

She laughed. It felt like a strange thing to do, laughing. Reckless and irresponsible.

"Sure. Except…"

"What?"

"I don't know how to do that."

"You're kidding."

She smiled sheepishly.

"What, you're in Year 12, studying all this fancy stuff, and you can't brew a cup of tea?"

"I'm sorry. Hopeless, isn't it?"

"Can I show you?"

"Sure."

"Okay, where's your kettle?"

Making tea. It was the best fun Libby had had in months. Shaun was so different. Terribly disfigured but kind at heart. So self-assured that it made him reassuring. He had lived through a crisis but come out stronger. He seemed so present. When he made tea, he gave it his full attention, and that made it seem a worthwhile skill to have. When she talked he really listened. He caught a bogong moth, cradled it in his big scarred hands and let it escape through the kitchen window. I wish I could be more like him, she thought. He has suffered so much but he refuses to be a victim. She felt useless by comparison, a prima donna, anxious and spoiled.

"What's wrong? Tea no good?"

"No, no," she said, "the tea's fine. It's just that sometimes…" She hesitated.

Shaun waited. At least he didn't finish her sentences, like the new counsellor did.

"Sometimes I feel so sad. The mood just comes over me."

He nodded.

"And then it feels as if I could lose it all again," she said. "All the progress I've made. It's like rolling a boulder up a dune and you run out of puff before you make it to the top."

"I know."

"Do you? Do you ever feel like that too?"

"I think everyone does."

"Really?"

"Life can be tough," he said, "and we grow weary. You need to protect yourself, be kind to yourself. And sometimes that's not enough and you need a bit of help."

"What do you do, when you feel like that?"

"I meet up with some friends, have a good old chat. Or start doing things. Like chopping wood or washing the car, anything to get away from what's worrying me."

"I can't see myself chopping wood." Libby smiled.

"Me neither—no offence. When I lived at Kinglake I had all these animals: goats and chooks, even a horse at one time, and they always used to make me feel better. Caring for another living creature, you know. I even named them. Bessie and Leah… They're all gone now, of course…" He swallowed. "That was really hard, in hospital and later in rehab, everything around you being so sterile and lifeless. I really liked it when Gecko visited and just held me hand. He was a good mate then. I can't just drop him, know what I mean?"

Libby's eyes welled up.

"Sorry," Shaun said, "I didn't mean to make you cry. I think you'd make a top lumberjack!"

She laughed through her tears.

"Hey," he said, "wanna hop on a tram with me? There's a great park I know. We could feed the swans."

"I'd like that," she said.

"I haven't been to the Botanic Gardens in years," said Shaun as they walked away from the ornamental lake.

"We used to come a lot, when Dad still lived with us. Mum had this wicker picnic basket with fancy plates and cutlery. We'd sit on a car rug and there were always ants. We were allowed to drink lemonade, from brown plastic mugs." She stared at the little clusters of people dotted across the sloping lawns—instant tableaus of her past.

"Sounds like fun."

"It was, except Nathan—that's my little brother—would always spill his lemonade on the rug. And Dad would quaff too much wine, which made him boisterous on the drive home. He'd always end up fighting with Mum."

"Where's your dad now?"

Libby told him. About the divorce. About Karla and Byron Bay. "I should call him, really," she said. "Haven't heard from him for ages."

They reached the southern part of the gardens.

"This is my favourite part," said Libby, "the Oak Lawn."

Shaun looked at the majestic oak trees planted twenty or thirty metres apart, rooted in an inkwell of black shadow.

"How did they know how far to plant them apart?"

"I know, right, it's like a canopy."

They sat down at the base of a tree.

"Yeah, it's so different. The shade of gum trees isn't solid like this. It's way more... patchy."

"Dappled," Libby offered.

"Yeah, dappled. That's a good word."

Shaun told her her how he loved the bush, the misty winter mornings up on the mountain in Kinglake, the violent summer heat that presses the oil out of gum leaves into a shimmering blue haze. He told about wombat holes and the soft white egg sacs of the brown snake. He explained how echidnas are egg-laying mammals and how the platypus has a poisonous spur.

Libby knew most of this, but she loved listening to Shaun's voice. It was like a mantra of healing, the affirmation of a world more natural and less fraught than the horrifying mindscapes she had inhabited. Her breathing became slower, less shallow. It was weird, she thought, how Shaun worked with cars and engines—stuff guys liked. How he knew that monstrous Shiv and people who had gone to jail. But he loved animals and the bush, and understood it better than Libby did.

"Am I boring you?" asked Shaun.

"Not at all," she answered, "please go on."

He rewarded her smile with a broad grin. She was getting used to that scar.

DECEMBER 2009

BLEAK HOUSE

It was the first time Philip sat at his desk again. Wasn't it ironic, he reflected, how his research into narrative structures had ground to a halt just as his private life had exploded into fireworks? He had seen enough action to fill a lurid novel. His drunken satyr episode, the prospect of fatherhood, his break-up with Caitlin, a drive-by shooting, with that woman collapsing on his doormat. A car crash in otherwise quiet and genteel Creswick Street. The realisation that those shotgun pellets had been meant for him. It was like *The Picture of Dorian Gray* in reverse: his magnum opus resided in a mesh of megabytes somewhere under all that brushed aluminium of his laptop, stultified, unchanging, while his life was ripped to shreds by the winds of change.

He thought of the poster in Caitlin's study, the snowy outcrop with fraying Tibetan prayer flags flapping in a blizzard. So quaint, how she was drawn to shamanistic paraphernalia. Prayer wheels, singing bowls, those beaded armbands—what were they called again? Malas? He never understood how a highly trained professional could be enticed to wear that quasi-religious junk. Well, he wouldn't have to feel embarrassed anymore if she went to a party decked out as a hippy.

Not that he had been invited to many parties lately. There had been gossip. He could tell, from the whispered conversations, the averted eyes, the phoney geniality. And the avoidance of certain topics, of course. He had enough elephants in the room by now to set up his own circus.

Seriously, he thought, a life change may well be what I need. Do something totally different. Leave academia behind. He could sell the house and travel. Go sailing on the Aegean. Travel down the Mekong on a barge. Explore a souk in Marrakech.

But something in his brain reminded him of a couple of impediments. He needed to put the house on the market. He had to give some thought to Caitlin's pregnancy and how that would affect him. And then there was the police investigation into the shooting. He would be called as a witness at that boy's trial. That was likely to be a drawn-out affair, with the usual false starts and delays as lawyers quibbled over procedural issues. Finally, there was the matter of whether that Libby girl would press charges. He wished she would make up her mind so he knew where he stood. He realised, of course, that even if she let him off the hook, the story would still come out, in the murder trial. The judge would want to know why a seventeen-year-old boy would go to the trouble of recruiting a bikie as a hitman.

So Melbourne it had to be, for at least the next year, maybe longer. Philip plopped down on the couch and grabbed one of the photo albums Caitlin had left behind. Their weekend in Kevin's tiny tent in the Grampians National Park. Caitlin in that dyed T-shirt. And here the day they had slogged to that lookout over a winding, stony track. Their reward a glorious view over the lake and the valley, all shimmering blue and green, with the clouds casting their shadows on the forest below. They had feasted on bread, a nice camembert and the only bottle of merlot in the Halls Gap store. The bread had gone limp and the cheese sweaty inside Caitlin's backpack, but it was one of the best meals he'd ever had.

He turned the page and smiled again. The surprise party at Kevin's before his trek through Peru. He was still with Stuart then, Stu had organised it. They had given Kevin the largest first aid kit ever. It included false eyelashes, nail polish remover and a tea cosy. Kevin never made it out of Cuzco. He spent ten days in his hotel, racked by waves of intestinal trouble. "Show us your photos of Machu Picchu,

Kev," they would say in the months following his return, and this would invariably trigger a convoluted explanation of his various ailments. They all had a go, and he never caught on.

The next page took the smirk off his face: a photo of Caitlin in her garden, crouched over some potted violets, looking up at him. The look in her brown eyes struck him. He saw deep love, trust and amused acceptance. She knew him and liked him, those pixels said. A shiver ran down his spine. What had possessed him to drive her away? Why was it never enough for him, the love of one woman? He thought of what Edwina had said. A collector, his sister had called him. Was that who he was? Maybe women played the game of love with a multi-sided die, the sort geeks use in role-playing games. The sides would be emotion and talking and friendship and whatever else. Fantasy maybe, loyalty. Humour, yes. He had no such die. He was playing with a two-sided coin. It had conquest on one side and boredom on the other. Who was the simpleton in this scenario? He looked at the picture again. Would there ever be another woman who would look at him this way? He took the photo out of its sleeve and laid it on the coffee table.

The doorbell rang, and he reluctantly went to answer it. He hated the hallway, which figured so prominently in his dreams these days.

"Hi," Di said, "I thought I'd pop in to return these." She held up a string bag full of books.

"Fletchie. Come in."

Di stepped gingerly over the threshold.

"This was where…" she said, almost reverently.

"Yes." Philip hastened back to the lounge. "They have specialised clean-up teams," he said, "they sanitise the floors, the walls. All very efficient."

"It's so awful." She shuddered. "How are you doing? We haven't seen you much at the uni."

"The nightmares are the worst. Wake up feeling exhausted. Haven't achieved much at all lately…"

"And what about Caitlin? You're still thinking about her," Di said. She pointed at the photo on the coffee table.

"Oh," he said, "that's beyond repair. I was drunk and stupid and this time I got caught. I betrayed her under her nose, that's how she sees it, and that ended up ruining her career."

"And there's her pregnancy too..."

"I know. I've been a moron." He picked at a piece of dirt under his thumbnail. "So what's in your bag?"

Di pulled the string bag open, lifted the novels out one by one and stacked them into a literary cairn on the coffee table.

"What's this for?"

"They're all the books you lent me."

"I can see that. Why are you returning them? All at once?"

"I've resigned. I'm going to be doing some travelling."

Philip was baffled. The university had offered to renew her contract for one year only, Di explained. The Department of French was going stale, she felt—the whole faculty for that matter. Instead, she wanted to do something new, adventurous, inspiring. She had enough money to travel for a year, two perhaps. She would focus on her writing. After that, she would have to start teaching again. She would find something.

"I could come with you," Philip said, "I need a break too."

"That would not be a good idea."

"I'm sorry if I've taken you for granted. I'd be prepared to make things... more regular."

"No, Philip, that's out of the question." She sat bolt upright on the couch.

"But why?"

"Oh, come on Philip, don't you get it? You're an intelligent man. The way you treat Caitlin. The way you terrorised a schoolgirl. You've changed this year, Philip. You've grown harder, more self-centred. Maybe it's the alcohol... Anyway, it's not up to me to lecture you. I just know that, for me, you've become a toxic presence."

"Toxic?"

"You flirt with me, sleep with me, then put me back on the shelf. For a while I thought that was okay, that I could handle it... Thing is, I can't go on like this." She looked him in the eyes. "It's not good for me, for my self-esteem. It holds me back... The last thing I want to do is to travel with you."

He was speechless.

"This is the end for us, Philip. If there ever was an 'us'."

"I see."

She shrugged and stood up.

"I'd better go. Take care. I'll let myself out."

He heard the door fall shut and her steps on the pavers. Then there was silence. He took the Márquez book off the top of the pile and placed it next to the photo of Caitlin. The title had lost its melancholy resonance and sounded menacing instead. A curse tailor-made for him: *One Hundred Years of Solitude*.

LIFE ON THE INSIDE

Shaun knew the drill by now. He had remembered to leave his pocketknife at home. It had caused him no end of trouble on his first visit. An oversight, he explained. The guards had heard better excuses… As if he would try to spring Gecko from prison, or slip him a blade. Anyhow, it had all been sorted in the end and Shaun was on the list of approved visitors now.

He had just sat down in the booth when the door in the back wall opened. A guard walked Gecko in and took up position against the wall.

"G'day mate, how are you?"

"Yeah, all right."

He looked down in the dumps. His acne was back, too.

"Had any other visitors lately?"

"Nah, just Bob… Last week."

"How'd that go?"

"He'd been before. He told me something new, though."

"What was that?"

"That guy, you know, that social worker pest?"

"Kurt."

"Yeah, him. The woman Shiv shot, you know, I found out from the papers she was a teacher at Banksia High, Libby's school. Now Bob tells me she was my social worker's wife."

"I know. Libby told me, at the funeral. I saw him there."

"You saw him?" Gecko stared at the pockmarked laminated counter in front of him.

"Obviously mate. It was his wife's funeral."

"What was he like?"

"Well what do you reckon, Gecko?" Shaun shook his head. "What do you think he was like?"

Gecko remained silent.

Shaun picked two fluff balls off his sleeve. "A right mess you're in, mate," he said.

"I was trying to make a point," said Gecko, "I wanted to show that bastard you can't treat girls like shit. And all I've done is fucked everything up. Libby's teacher's dead and she's upset. I let Bob down. He tried to protect me and all I did was can him and wag school. And now this shit…"

Shaun said nothing, so Gecko went on.

"And that social work dude was a pain, with his little notebook and lining up his pens, but now his wife's dead and that's my fault too. It's like I'm cursed, everyone who tries to help me comes a cropper. The only one who got off is that rich bastard in his big house." He looked up at Shaun. "Libby better get a lawyer that goes to town on him."

"Libby's not pressing charges."

"What! Why not?" Gecko kicked the partition. The guard moved forward.

"Keep it together, mate, or they'll take you back to your cell… Libby says what happened was so upsetting she doesn't want to go through it again. You know, testify in court, being interrogated. Traumatic, was the word she used. Too traumatic. She doesn't want to go to court."

"But then the bastard gets off free!"

"She's pretty much made up her mind. She's doing a bit better. Trying to eat, working on her mood. I think she's brave… But it's one step at a time and she doesn't want to risk a relapse. Nothing toxic in her life, she says."

"Sounds like you two get on well…"

"Well, about that…"

Gecko looked him in the eyes.

"You're kidding."

"Well, you said—"

"Yeah, but, I mean… This is soon."

"I know… Sorry man, hope it's okay."

"Yeah, I mean like, me and her, that's over. I blew it and now she hates me…"

"She doesn't hate you, Gecko."

"Oh, fucking hell, I dunno. I've just stuffed everything up. Wish I'd fully smashed that car and that would've been the end of it." He slumped back on his chair.

"Don't say that."

"But seriously, there's nothing to look forward to. I'll get old in here."

"No, you won't, you drongo. Listen to me, Gecko, listen! Get this into your head. The drug trafficking might get you three years max, because of your age. The accessory charge is the big one but they'll let you serve all your sentences at the same time. They have a word for that, con something…"

"Concurrent?"

"That's it. So, say you get fifteen years for the murder—"

"Wouldn't they give me life?"

"You're under eighteen, mate. Until a couple of months ago you had a clean record. Say they give you fifteen years. Take off a third for good behaviour and you'd be out after ten. You wouldn't even be thirty when you get out…"

"Thirty's old…"

"Anyway, you can use the time inside. Learn a trade so you can make some coin when you get out."

"You can study in prison?"

"Sure. Some inmates do uni courses. All by computer. They'll let you study if you don't cause trouble."

"Didn't know that."

"Okay, time's up. Round it off," announced the guard.

"I'd better get going," said Shaun, "I have to see another bloody skin specialist. Wonder when it will ever end."

"They've patched you up pretty well."

"Dunno. Mum reckons the back of me head still looks like a quilt."

"You still get the girl, though."

"I suppose."

"Thanks for coming. You're doing better than I did. I only came to see you once after the fires."

"That's okay."

"Please keep coming, yeah? After the sentence and stuff. Even if you're with Libby…"

"Sure. I will." Shaun got up. The plastic chair scraped across the concrete floor. "See you next time."

"And Shaun…"

"Yeah?"

"Do you think I'll end up in a cell by myself? In adult prison?"

"Dunno. Why?"

"I wouldn't wanna share…"

Shaun thought he saw fear in Gecko's eyes.

"Come on, break it up," said the guard. He grabbed Gecko by the shoulder and pushed him towards the door at the rear.

LIFE IN THE MOUNTAINS

Libby noticed the furtive glances as Shaun walked into the petrol station. The kids were less discreet.

"Ew, Mummy, look at that man," she heard the toddler in the station wagon say.

"That's a monster," explained her older brother, "it looks just like you."

"Mum," the girl whimpered, "Jack's mean to me."

It affected her more than when she overheard people whisper about her own appearance. She felt protective of Shaun. Not that he needed it —he seemed to shrug it all off.

She saw how he joked with the cashier as he put his wallet away.

"So," Shaun said as he got back into the car, "that should get us up the mountain."

They drove on, with the windows down. The main street of Eltham was busy, with Saturday morning shoppers in a tizz about Christmas being only a week away. Libby relaxed once they hit the open road at Kangaroo Ground.

"What a great day for the party," she said. "Can't wait to meet your mum."

Shaun nodded. He seemed tense.

"Are you okay?"

"Yeah, sorry. Still feels weird, driving up the mountain."

"Oh, of course…"

"Sort of brings it all back, you know."

Libby nodded. She knew exactly what he meant. It was why he was still couch-surfing at his mate's place in Mitcham. The safety of the suburbs.

In St Andrews she noticed the first evidence of the fires. Stands of gum trees that had burnt. Most of them had sprouted new growth, dense clusters of leaves that surrounded every stem and branch like a bottlebrush. It looked unnatural. Gum leaves were meant to look like a silvan veil, drooping grace. These green stubs looked like fumbling fat fingers raised to heaven. A second chance came at a cost—that was something they both understood. All the fences and road signs were either burnt, missing or brand new. They fell silent as they drove past the first burnt houses. Some were still surrounded by police tape.

As they drove up the mountain, the devastation became worse. Hardly any regrowth here. The ferocity of the fires had incinerated the forests of mountain ash. The mountain looked like a pincushion, burnt umber soil, black sticks as far as the eye could see.

Shaun seemed disoriented. He overshot Smithy's Track and had to reverse. He kept looking for his mum's driveway but the tall gums marking the entrance had gone. Then they spotted the cardboard sign —*Metcalfe Lot 14*. Shaun swung the car up the rutted driveway.

She saw it straightaway. The timber frame for the new house. It was clad in blue plastic sheeting and surrounded by builders' rubbish on all sides but Libby felt moved all the same.

A woman with thick grey hair walked over from two trestle tables that stood next to a battered truck. She smiled at Libby.

"Mum," said Shaun, "this is Libby."

"Hi, Mrs Metcalfe, pleased to meet you."

"Call me Martha, darling, and good to meet you too." She hugged Libby. "And this is my partner. Dougie, come over here."

A wiry old man came up to the car.

"Hi, Libby, good to meet ya! Checking out Shaun's old stomping ground?"

"What's left of it," said Shaun. He looked at the ruins of the old house. Only its core had survived: the chimney, the fireplace and the bread oven built into the other side of the stone wall. The tractor shed had collapsed into a corrugated iron lasagne. Bracken was coming up where the animal enclosures had been. The metal feeding trays had molten into flat discs.

"It was even worse at first," Dougie said to Libby. "We've already taken trailer loads to the tip."

"I wanna walk down to the dam," Shaun said. He sighed.

"I'll come with you," said Libby.

They walked down the hill to the dark rectangular pond that had been the dam. It was contaminated now, Shaun explained, with ash and residue of burnt plastic and chemicals that had washed into the water. Dougie's mate was going to come with his bobcat and dig a new dam on the other side of the hill.

"There it is." They stared at the scorched bathtub near the water's edge.

"Oh, Shaun." Libby took his arm and pulled him closer. She felt a chill, in spite of the heat.

Shaun stared at the tub with grim determination. I can imagine the things going through his mind, Libby mused, those thoughts in the portal of death, the ones you think will be your last. She gently led him away, back up the slope, towards the noise of the festivities.

Martha and Dougie had decorated a burnt banksia trunk as a makeshift Christmas tree. The silver tinsel stood out against the jet black branches. A few old rattlers trundled up the driveway and more neighbours spilled out, carrying eskies and wine coolers, baskets of food and picnic blankets. It was becoming quite a party. Shaun had told his mum he didn't want a barbecue. Didn't like the idea of smelling smoke up here. Martha had thought it was a fair call.

"I hope your dad finds the place," said Shaun, "seeing as I almost missed it again meself…"

"I'm sure he will," said Libby, "your little map was pretty clear. And he won't be looking for trees that aren't there anymore…"

"Speak of the devil," said Shaun. He pointed at the blue combi that laboured up the drive. "That little van'd be worth a lot of money."

"It's so old," Libby scoffed, "rust on wheels."

"It's a collector's item."

Murray got out of the combi with his winning grin. Libby flung herself into his arms and started sobbing. Murray just held her and stroked her hair.

"It's all right darling," he said.

"Sorry," said Libby as she let go of him, all flustered, "I didn't want to make a scene."

"It's all right," said Dougie, "we've all had a rough year up these parts. People understand."

"Karla, sorry," said Libby, "how are you?" She embraced her. "And guys, this is Shaun."

It wasn't long before Shaun was talking about gaskets and car resale values with Murray and Dougie. Karla was already teaching Martha some exercises for loosening up neck muscles.

Her boyfriend talking to her dad, who would have thought? Sometimes life also surprised you in a good way. Libby smiled and looked at Shaun's old neighbours. Their community was wiped out just months ago. They'd almost all lost their homes; some had lost a partner, a parent or a child. But they hadn't given up. Scarred, but not defeated, as Shaun says. If only she had some of that strength… And they were all making the most of today, on this bald hill. This scorched hill where Shaun almost perished.

After some time Murray took her aside.

"I've got something for you in the van," he said.

He opened the sliding door and carefully pulled out a large rectangular object wrapped in paper.

"A painting!" Libby gasped.

She tore the paper off and saw the best watercolour her dad had ever painted. It was a seascape of two sailing ships at anchor in a small, curved bay. The shallow water in the foreground looked translucent. The sky looked cleansed, as if a storm had just moved through, unleashing pent-up energy and heralding a new beginning. Libby felt a wave of happiness surge through her.

"Oh, Dad," she said, "this is fantastic."

"Yeah, it's not bad. I'm glad you like it. I heard what happened to my other paintings... Nathan texted me. He said you were really upset."

"Nathan told you that?"

"Yeah."

"I didn't know he ever texted you."

"He's just started to, over the last year or so. He's a good little bloke."

Libby was dumbfounded. She had been hard on herself. Now it transpired she'd also been hard on others.

Shaun came sauntering over. He whistled in appreciation.

"Wow. Now I see where Libby's got that from."

Murray smiled at him.

"Hoi, attention everyone," boomed Dougie.

"He's got a strong voice," said Murray.

"An ex-teacher," said Shaun.

"If you could all gather here," Dougie continued, "we shall now proceed to carve up the Christmas pudding. Or puddings, actually, for we have two. One which the lovely Karla brought all the way from Byron Bay—"

People cheered.

"All the way from Byron Bay," he repeated, "and one made by the inimitable Martha Metcalfe, the love of my life."

"Oh, shush," said Martha, "how many beers have you had, you old fool?"

Dougie carefully sliced the first pudding and deposited a generous slice on each plate.

Martha took a plate and offered it to Libby.

"Will you have a slice of pudding too?" she asked.

"Sure," said Libby, "why not?"

MARCH 2010

METUNG

There had been good days and bad days. He missed Emma like hell and blamed himself for blabbing to Gecko about Philip. He had wanted to keep the boy safe and it had cost Emma her life. Every day he thought of his ghosts: Emma, Leo, Kylee and Jade. And then, just before Christmas, Irene had passed away. Kurt had talked to her on Skype the week before, when Joris had set up his laptop in the nursing home. Irene had been dressed up extra nicely for the occasion and she looked well groomed, dignified, happy to see him. She spoke softly, and sometimes he couldn't understand a thing for sentences on end, but she did recognise him, and he felt immensely grateful for that. And then, two days later, the nursing home manager had rung him in the middle of the night to say that his mum had suddenly passed away.

Kurt knew that frontal lobe dementia was one of the more aggressive varieties of the illness. He also knew that the medication itself ultimately posed a significant risk. He tried to tell himself that Irene's death meant the end of the merciless decline and the thousand little indignities she'd had to face. But try as he might, such rationalisations welled up against the granite needle of pain in his heart. His mum was gone, for good, and he hadn't been there to hold her hand in those bewildering, terrifying moments of the great parting.

He had flown over to Belgium, for the third time in just over a year, to do what he had become so good at over the past twelve months: mopping up after the event. He had arranged the funeral, delivered a eulogy and hosted a meal with the remaining family members. On the Saturday he had stood in the snow, watching his mother's coffin being lowered into the frozen ground. A few days later he had pulled into a burger place with Caitlin to escape the forty-degree heat. It did things to your brain, these sudden transitions.

He had stopped playing computer games. There had been so much death around him that he was unable to tolerate any more violence, even in pixellated form. Instead, he had resumed his meditation practice, haltingly at first, and coming up against waves of stubborn resistance. But he had exhausted the self-pity and let the pain in, bit by bit, and cradled it near his torn heart, understanding that's where it would settle forever.

～

So, Caitlin. That was part of the good days. To start with, they had just met up a couple of times, talking about Gecko and Libby. Then the conversations had become more personal as they talked about losing their partners. Kurt thought Caitlin was pretty gutsy, remaining cheerful despite being pregnant, single and unemployed. Caitlin thought Kurt had been through hell and back and had an uncanny ability to land on his feet.

He thought of Emma every day. Her death had slashed a gaping hole in his soul. The empty pillow spoke of her absence. Her favourite chocolate in the pantry, untouched. Finding a final strand of hair in the shower. How could there also be room for a living, breathing woman?

He remained alone with his confusion, Emma frozen in time, receding behind the thick glass panes of time. He felt drained, a mere husk, his stores of empathy and resilience too depleted to cope with the pain and anguish of child protection work. He had taken time off work, was seeing a counsellor.

One day he had accidentally brushed Caitlin's fingers when passing her some cutlery in a cafe and something had stirred when he felt the warmth of a human touch. He felt guilty afterwards, as if he'd cheated on Emma. Worse, he had told Caitlin an anecdote from his childhood that he'd only shared with Emma. It felt like a betrayal.

It had all gone faster than either had expected or thought reasonable.

He had mentioned his feelings for Caitlin to Midnight, and she'd been scathing. It was way too soon, she said, how could he get over Emma so easily? And with the woman who had, indirectly, contributed to her death? And was he going to care for Caitlin's child now, having resisted for years Emma's desire to have a family?

Kurt didn't know where to begin. He had contributed to Emma's death as much as Caitlin, if not more. And he wasn't over Emma in the slightest, it was just that he wasn't done with life, either. He felt surprised by how much Midnight knew, shaken by her hostility. Telling her had been a blunder. Another one. It had soured the relationship, maybe for good.

To get away from it all they had treated themselves to a week in Gippsland. Caitlin had booked a cottage in Metung, a small village on a narrow spit of land insinuating itself between Bancroft Bay and Lake King, its probing headland ending in a teardrop shape. There was not much to do in Metung without a boat, they discovered. But that did not matter. They enjoyed ambling down the boardwalk along the lake to get groceries in the village. Caitlin was very big now, so it took ages.

She had slept in her room most of the afternoon to make up for a disturbed night. Kurt had meditated in the shade of a massive oak tree.

At dusk they walked back to the village. *Lest we forget*, said the inscription at the base of the grey concrete war memorial. No one's forgetting anything, thought Kurt. They waded through some young kids playing footy.

"Be careful, Jason," a mum called from a bench, "let the lady pass."

"You're just a bumhead," a little boy yelled to his sister.

"I'm gonna tell on you!" she replied. Her nose needed a good wipe.

"That's what's in store for us," Caitlin said.

"Bring it on," said Kurt. He liked it when Caitlin talked about *us*.

"There's a table free there." He pointed at an elderly couple getting up in the outdoor area of the pub, where tables had been placed on the wharf.

They sat down under the wide blue umbrella and ordered two lattes. Pelicans were flying in from the lakes, skimming the surface of the water. They reminded Kurt of those flying boats from the Second World War, Catalinas and Sunderlands. It was pandemonium every time a fishing boat berthed. In between, the massive birds bobbed on the water or sat on a ramp, preening their feathers or drying their outstretched wings, like cormorants. Metung is growing on me, thought Kurt, as he looked from the marina to the gum trees bordering the village green and coming right up to the water's edge.

A worried look had come over Caitlin's face.

"Penny for your thoughts?" asked Kurt.

"I'm just thinking… there's been so much pain… What makes you keep going on? Like at work, I mean. Do you think you'll ever go back?"

"I'd like to, yes. Once I get my act together again… As for what keeps me going: I've often wondered about that, too. I guess, for me, it's bits I pick up here and there, stuff that opens a window on the suffering of others, shards of insight that jolt me wide awake."

"I'm not sure I get that, Kurt. What do you mean?"

He paused, looked out over the moored yachts.

"You remember the girl I told you about, from the housing commission flats?"

"Jade, yes. What about her?"

"I read her diary."

"Wasn't she only six?"

"Yeah, it wasn't much of a diary. Drawings of fairies with feet that were way too big, some notes."

"What did she write?"

Kurt took a deep breath, got the words out without his voice breaking: "'Every night I pray for someone to look after me.' That's what she wrote. Clumsy uneven letters in purple pencil, but the most powerful thing I've ever read. That's what keeps me going."

Caitlin looked down at the stained wooden slats of the table, swallowed, then took his hand. Tears rolled down her face too.

"Look at us," Kurt said, "crying our eyes out. If anyone asks we'll tell them our eyes are sweating."

Caitlin smiled wryly.

"We've been through the wringer, haven't we," said Kurt.

"We sure have."

The waitress walked towards them and picked up their coffee cups. "Will that be all for youse?" she asked.

"Will that be all?" Kurt echoed, "we haven't even started yet!"

Caitlin smiled. Kurt helped her up and paid for the coffees. The bewildered waitress stared at the odd couple as they walked towards the pier. A crimson rosella flitted past with a shriek of joy and disappeared in the darkening foliage.

～

ACKNOWLEDGMENTS

There is a point in the writing process where you decide to share your draft with another person. It is a harrowing moment, as you wonder whether the reader will delight in the world you invented, or stumble over clumsy phrases and innovative punctuation. It is exciting to see the characters you've dreamed up acquire a measure of reality in the minds of others. It also cranks up a gruelling, humbling but crucial quality assurance process, as these first readers spot continuity errors, implausibilities and assumptions. They help you burnish the stone until it (hopefully) shines.

My deepest thanks therefore go to the following people: to Miriam, my wife and soulmate, for sharing this journey with me. She reviewed successive drafts of the manuscript and her high standards, underpinned by her wide reading, made me lift my game, again and again. I am also deeply indebted to Estelle, my youngest daughter, for her extensive and perceptive commentaries on my manuscript and for helping me tweak the dialogue of younger characters.

I am grateful to Kate Ryan from *Writers Victoria* for her detailed manuscript assessment, which boosted my confidence at an important time in my writing process and provided useful pointers for refining and balancing some characters. I thank Bee Mitchell-Dawson, Claudia

Mulder, Helen Pausacker and Veronica Spillane for reviewing an advanced draft in depth and commenting on a range of plot, stylistic, cultural and clinical issues. I thank my editor, Lu Sexton, for commenting on issues ranging from word choice to character development, bringing a new perspective and fresh energy to my manuscript when I had exhausted my own editing process. I also thank Jane Bennett for her thorough proofreading of the final text.

Finally, it was a delight to write a novel using the incredibly versatile *Scrivener* app developed by the people at *Literature and Latte*.

Gilbert Van Hoeydonck
    Melbourne, October 2018

ALSO BY GILBERT VAN HOEYDONCK

SHORT STORIES

Fate and Asparagus

First Snow

Spitfire

Bait

Visit Gilbert Van Hoeydonck's website
to receive updates about new projects:
https://gilbertvanhoeydonck.com

www.ingramcontent.com/pod-product-compliance
Lightning Source LLC
Chambersburg PA
CBHW020650110726
47901CB00001B/131